D1196644

JUN – – 2018

DIFFERENT KINDS OF DARKNESS

Other Books by David Langford

Fiction

An Account of a Meeting with Denizens of Another World, 1871
Earthdoom! (with John Grant)
The Dragonhiker's Guide to Battlefield Covenant at Dune's Edge: Odyssey Two
Guts (with John Grant) *
He Do the Time Police in Different Voices: SF Parody and Pastiche *
Irrational Numbers
The Leaky Establishment *
A Novacon Garland
The Space Eater

Nonfiction

A Cosmic Cornucopia (with Josh Kirby)
The Complete Critical Assembly *
Critical Assembly
Critical Assembly II
Facts and Fallacies (with Chris Morgan)
Micromania: The Whole Truth About Home Computers (with Charles Platt)
The Necronomicon (with George Hay, Robert Turner and Colin Wilson)
Pieces of Langford
Platen Stories
The Science in Science Fiction (with Peter Nicholls and Brian Stableford)
The Silence of the Langford
The Third Millennium: A History of the World AD 2000-3000 (with Brian Stableford)
The TransAtlantic Hearing Aid
The Unseen University Challenge
Up Through an Empty House of Stars: Reviews and Essays 1980-2002 *
War in 2080: The Future of Military Technology
The Wyrdest Link

As Editor

The Encyclopedia of Fantasy (with John Clute, John Grant, and others)
Maps: The Uncollected John Sladek *
Wrath of the Fanglord

* In Cosmos Books

DIFFERENT KINDS OF DARKNESS

Short Stories

David Langford

Cosmos Books • 2004
An imprint of **Wildside Press**

DIFFERENT KINDS OF DARKNESS

Published by:

Cosmos Books, an imprint of Wildside Press
PO Box 301, Holicong, PA 18928-0301
www.wildsidepress.com

Copyright © 2004 by David Langford. All rights reserved.
Original appearances copyright © 1975-2003 by David Langford.
Cover design copyright © 2004 by Juha Lindroos.
This Cosmos Books edition published 2004.

The right of David Langford to be identified as the author of this work
has been asserted by the Author in accordance with the British
Copyright, Designs and Patents Act 1988.

No portion of this book may be reproduced by any means, mechanical,
electronic or otherwise, without first obtaining the permission of the
copyright holder.

For more information, contact Wildside Press.

ISBN: 1-59224-121-2 (hardback)
ISBN: 1-59224-122-0 (trade paperback)

Contents

Irrational Numbers

Basilisks

Introduction

This collection, mercifully, does not assemble the Complete Short Stories of David Langford. I have published about eighty over the years, and have to admit that a number are richly deserving of oblivion.

These include several early pieces written for children's supernatural anthologies, generally edited by Mary Danby, and allegedly "adult" magazines like *Knave*, whose then editor Ian Pemble was refreshingly hospitable to silly and/or naughty contributions by the likes of myself, Kim Newman, Paul Barnett ("John Grant"), and some guy called Neil Gaiman. Whatever became of him?

A few "lost" items demanded knowledge of overly esoteric context – like my contribution to *Pictures at an Exhibition*, Ian Watson's anthology of stories inspired by works of art, in which a vital key was the vast over-arching cosmic concept that unified the entire volume. My attempt to write something around Dürer's *Melencolia* conveyed a suitable sense of groping desperation, occasioned by the fact that the Concept hadn't actually been revealed to the contributors. A second, much funnier submission was sternly rejected on grounds of frivolity: inspired by the works of Andy Warhol, it consisted of a whole page of neatly aligned repetitions of the typed words CAMPBELL'S SOUP. But, as usual, I digress.

Then there were all the parodies and pastiches, first gathered together in the 1988 *The Dragonhiker's Guide to Battlefield Covenant at Dune's Edge: Odyssey Two*, and later expanded with a further fifteen years' worth of exercises in other people's styles – some of the latter quite serious stories – as *He Do the Time Police in Different Voices* (Cosmos, 2003). Even I don't have the gall to recycle any of those twenty-five items here. However, two of the three stories in *The Silence of the Langford* (NESFA Press, 1996) do reappear in the present volume for the benefit of readers who like fiction but don't care for all the magazine and fanzine essays that make up the bulk of *Silence*. Apologies to anyone who's annoyed by this.

Speaking of recycling, I should mention a brief squib about psionics called "Imbalance", which somehow got incorporated into the raucous comic novel I wrote with Paul Barnett in the mid-1980s: *Earthdoom!* This and its punchline can still be found there, lovingly preserved like flies in ointment – or more precisely, in section ten of chapter four – but the story now seems a mite lame in isolation.

And so on. As the *Encyclopedia of Fantasy* editors would desperately write in theme entries, when the barrel had been utterly scraped and we could think of absolutely nothing else to cite: further examples abound.

Hence this is the Rest of Langford. I can at least brag that it contains a Hugo winner, a British SF Association Award winner, the winner of a deeply obscure magazine competition, and a large handful of 'Year's Best' and 'Best Of' anthology selections.

Rather than do anything so logical and obvious as to arrange the whole lot in order of publication date, I've divided them into four groups:

• "Gadgets and Glitches" assembles a mass of assorted science fiction in chronological order, from 1975 to 2003.

• "The Questing Beast" consists of a few rare excursions into fantasy.

• "Irrational Numbers" gathers stories that were written, or published, or at any rate anthologized, as horror – although, as with the Lovecraftian "Out of Space, Out of Time" (pastiche, and therefore included in *Time Police*), I find that physics and mathematics keep breaking in.

• Finally, the four "Basilisks" pieces are linked by the one theme of my sf which seems to have been unexpectedly influential. I have written – or to be more precise, gloated shamelessly – about this in a magazine article since collected in *Up Through an Empty House of Stars: Reviews and Essays 1980-2002* (Cosmos, 2003). See also the afterword to "Blit".

Enough of these sordid preliminaries. Some further comments on individual stories can be found in their afterwords.

Oh, yes, and I hope you enjoy them.

David Langford (www.ansible.co.uk)
October 2003

Gadgets and Glitches

For Kenneth Bulmer, who bought the first one;
and David Pringle (and the *Interzone* collective),
who bought the first award-winner.

Heatwave

Sing of human unsuccess
In a rapture of distress
— Auden

CRYPTANALYSIS – 1
SECRET
From: Ferris, Undersecretary, Intelligence
To: Stone, Head, Cryptanalysis
Dear Mr Stone,

The Head of Intelligence presents his compliments and wishes to call your attention to the enclosed communication, recently received from the Lunar Observatory under somewhat suspicious circumstances. There has been no detectable response to further attempts at contact. Please return your comments, in triplicate, as soon as is convenient.

Yours sincerely

(Squiggle)

pp J.T. Ferris, Undersecretary.

Sweating in the intolerable heat of his office, Stone gave the letter a sulphurous glare. Just what was all this about? Intelligence passing the buck again? Angrily he twisted the air-conditioner knob. It was already fully on. Hell! For the first time, Stone glanced at the scrap of rice-paper (memorize and eat?) attached to the offending letter. It said, simply, THE SUN IS GOING NOVA.

INTERIM – 1

The head of Intelligence sipped iced tea and contacted the CRETIN computaplex from a distant teletype. He began to type –

? does complete security exist in cryptanalysis dept
YES
?how do you know
ASSUME COMPLETE SECURITY NONEXISTENT

COMPLETENESS IMPLIES TOTAL DEGREE OF EXISTENCE
ERGO SECURITY HAS INCOMPATIBLE QUALITIES COMPLETENESS + NONEXISTENCE
///PARADOX///
ERGO COMPLETE SECURITY EXISTS
? thankyou and goodbye
MYPLEASURE
GOODBYE, the computer signed off affably

Baffled but reassured, he left the terminal.

DEEPS – 1

Twenty miles beneath the Earth's surface, down the deepest hole ever made by man, Charles Trente sweated and stared dully at the seismographs. *He* wasn't needed in that cave of machines – every last gadget was automatic, except the emergency shutdown switch. Rather than risk the expensive equipment to the smallest degree, the Powers Above – twenty long miles above – had decreed that a watchman must always be present.

Two weeks to go. His only pastimes were reading and writing. Mainly writing, for he hoped to sell his underground journal to some overground newspaper. He was working on it now.

Above, there is the abstract pattern of society – Maya – the woven mesh of trivial human interaction: below there pulses the naked reality. Good Sunday-supplement stuff this. *Chthon: the aching weight of a million million tons of rock.* Sounds good, must check the figures. *Chthon: grinding darkness shot with flame.* God, it was hot all right. And those twenty-watt fluoros weren't doing his eyes any good. *Here and only here, far from the distracting turmoil of the ephemeral surface,* Dr. Johnson lives! why can't I say madding crowd and have done with it? *man can truly come to terms with his planet, be at one with its dark internal forces. Deep calleth unto deep. "But sweet as the rind was the core is,"* wrote Swinburne once, *not knowing the core was sweeter yet than ever he guessed. For here, at the still point of the turning world,* Drivel. Charles me boy, and you know it. Cross that last bit out, not even the Sunday papers will swallow that "still point" when I'm nearly four thousand miles from the centre, which is a damn sight hotter than this stinking hole. Lets try the radio for a change.

After a while, he smiled. Having a heatwave, were they? It had better be good and chilly for his ascent from hell in two weeks' time.

CRYPTANALYSIS – 2

The machinery of Cryptanalysis was in high gear. Their CRETIN computer was hard at work on the mysterious message. Stone waited for the results, nerves on edge. CRETIN: the Cryptanalytic Relational Execution

Terminal Interface Network. Or was it right that the acronym referred to the machine's functions of Co-ordination, Relocation, Extrapolation, Triangulation, Incrementation and Notification? It was too hot to think. Or again, it might be – Bzzzzt! After four hours of symbol-juggling, CRETIN had cracked the message. The display screen glowed.

THE SUN IS GOING NOVA, it proclaimed in flashing letters. The output continued smoothly.

– PRELIM

A IS FIRST LETTER OF ALPHABET BUT LAST OF MESSAGE

QUERY IMPLIES ANALYSIS TO START AT END OF MESSAGE

QUERY REVERSE MESSAGE

– REVERSAL

AVON GNIOG SI NUS EHT

(Stone jerked. N.U.S.! What were those students up to now?)

– LOGICAL REARRANGEMENT AVON GN-TEN-G SINUS EHT

– COMMENTS

/AVON/ – REFERS TO RIVER

/EHT/ – ELECTRICAL ABBR SIGNIFYING EXTRA HIGH TENSION

/GN-TEN-G/ – MOST ADVANCED CHINESE COMPUTAPLEX HAS CODE GN-NINE-Q – ALSO KNOWN AS BLOSSOMING FLOWER OF KNOWLEDGE AND FOUNT OF COOL WATERS OF INSPIRATION

– THEORIZE GN-TEN-G SUPERIOR MODEL OF SAME FAMILY

/SINUS EHT/ – IN CONJUNCTION WITH ABOVE FACTORS SUGGESTS REF TO CHUNG WONG INSTITUTE NR STRATFORD UPON AVON – OSTENSIBLE PURPOSE OF THIS ESTABLISHMENT IS CURE OF HAY FEVER BY ELECTROTHERAPY AND ACUPUNCTURE

– CONCLUSION

CHUNG WONG INSTITUTE IS FRONT FOR FOREIGN COMPUTAPLEX – PURPOSE UNKNOWN

– FURTHER COMMENTS

NONE

***END PROGRAM

***CRYPTAN 4 DECOMPILING

***MACHINE CLEARED

"I'll be damned," said Stone.

OBSERVATORY – 1

"Lovely. Oh, lovely." Lyman beamed as he examined the negatives. "A beautiful bit of work. Balmer. Three new spectral lines – wonderful!" In the stifling air of the Salisbury Plain Observatory, the celluloid film was already curling up.

"We'll call them the Balmer lines, of course?" queried the anxious researcher. "After all, it was my discovery –"

"But I did half the work, remember!" Paschen broke in.

Lyman smiled again. "Just to confuse the issue, boys, do you know that Brackett and Pfund are hard at work producing some explanation of *why* the solar spectrum is sprouting new lines? Now if they succeed, what can we call them but the Brackett-Pfund lines? You'd better talk to them and come to some agreement." Lyman's smile became even more seraphic. "With only three lines and five of us, I admit the naming situation is a little –"

"*Five* of us?" Balmer shrieked. "You don't mean – you, too –" He turned and walked out, followed by Paschen. It didn't do to go too far with the Director.

"Close the door after you," Lyman called out, as he wrote THE LYMAN EFFECT in neat capitals at the head of a sheet of foolscap.

INTERIM – 2

Dr Apricot always hated this lecture theatre. In the morning, the sun struck harshly down through the high windows at the rear, blinding him so he lost his audience in the shadowy body of the room. A faint snoring could be heard – in this heat he couldn't blame them. Where was he now – ah yes –

"– we see that although it is often theorized that the flaring of a stellar body into the nova state takes place very rapidly indeed on the cosmic scale it is difficult to estimate precisely the time required for the transition stage in fact when we enjoy unusually hot weather such as we are undergoing at this moment why for all we know we should be making our peace with god and preparing for the end of all things as our sun explodes into incandescent gases ha ha ha –" He was rewarded by two or three polite titters among the snores – intense gratification; some of them are awake! But so hot, so hot ... He sipped his tepid water and droned on. His next pleasantry produced just one chuckle. Modified rapture.

Half an hour later, when the concentration of sunlight through his water-jug set some papers on the lecture-desk alight, there was no response at all from the gathered students. A pox on them, they're all asleep now. Apricot poured water over the flames and walked out. Behind him, two hundred earnest seekers after knowledge slept on in happy unawareness.

CRYPTANALYSIS – 3

Stone sat listlessly at his desk, doing the *Times* crossword puzzle. What was the country coming to, he wondered, when you had to wear sunglasses indoors? Half the letters in the paper had been complaints about the Met. Office, who were held generally responsible for the heat.

He looked longingly at the closed window – last time he'd opened it, the air had been hotter outside than in. On the street, ten storeys down, people wandered about fainting alternately into one another's arms. *Hot and scrambled under Stratford* (4) What was *that*? Vague thoughts of eggs drifted in his mind, to be dispelled as Higgins ambled in.

"Noticed something funny about that thing you've got everyone working on," gasped Higgins, wiping his brow and wringing out the hand-kerchief into Stone's waste-basket. The Head eyed him with disfavour.

"What?"

"Well, if you take every third letter, starting with that first T, look what you get –" He scribbled on the blotter: The Sun Is gOinG noVa. T S I O G V. "And now rearrange it –" Underneath, he wrote S VOIGT. "There! Feel like telling that to Sammy Voigt next door?"

"Um." Stone buzzed Voigt on the intercom.

"Odd you should call me just then," said Voigt, coming in with a strange smile. "Take a look at this, I've been playing anagrams." The paper he held out had just three lines of writing on it, starting with that hateful message:

THE SUN IS GOING NOVA
(letters of message) A E CC H II NNN 00 SS T U V
(rearranges to) STONE HIGGINS OVANU

"Ovanu!" cried Stone. The famed, the legendary double-agent!

"Precisely," grated Voigt, covering them with a heavy automatic. He turned back his lapel to reveal the large Day-Glo orange badge of Security. "And now I'd like you to answer a few questions, *Mr* Stone!"

INTERIM – 3

Prudence String was sitting at her typewriter. She sucked at a cigar and rattled off the conclusion of tomorrow's supercharged philosophy-for-the-masses.

Although your hot and sweaty feet are itching, blame it on the heat; and be not narky to your friends, 'tis not their deeds that shape your ends. So call your neighbour not a sod, the bastard is the work of God: dismiss your anger with a laugh and cool it in an icy bath. Not quite the right tone, maybe, but what the hell? She slid the sheet out of the typewriter. The *Pray As You Enter* column was one hell of a job. Where was that gin ...?

OBSERVATORY – 2

Again, Balmer and Paschen walked in together, Both looked some-what battered, and there was a hint of blood on their knuckles.

"You have come to some agreement?" Lyman asked blandly.

"Yes," said Balmer. "Briefly: the faint line in the far ultraviolet is to be called the Lyman-Brackett-Pfund line, while the strong red and bluegreen lines are to be called the Balmer and Paschen lines respectively." He braced himself for Lyman's counterblast. The furnace-heat of the room (how did the old devil keep so cool?) did nothing for his nerves.

"My dear boy," murmured the Director, "I have bad news. The term 'the Balmer lines' already exists in quite another context – a series in the hydrogen spectrum, nothing to do with the sun's current anomalies. The same goes for the Paschen, the Brackett and even the Pfund series, in memory of your respective namesakes."

"And so does the Lyman series!" shouted Paschen. "I just remembered –"

"Let me finish, please. I've already prepared my paper, 'The Lyman Effect', which accounts for the whole thing – something to do with runaway fusion reactions, wouldn't interest you – and have very generously acknowledged your assistance, in a footnote. You can't say fairer than that.

"Now don't be hasty," he added hastily, "that paper's already in the post to the Royal Society."

Balmer approached with glazed eyes. "Kill!" he suggested.

"Kill!" Paschen agreed.

Lyman sprinted for the door, dodging them both.

"Kill!"

CRYPTANALYSIS – 4

Stone's intercom buzzed.

"Answer it!" Voigt ordered. Stone obeyed, panting slightly.

"Mr Stone? Tugg here. I think I've cracked that message at last! Absurdly simple, like all cryptograms once you know the answer."

Tugg, thought Stone. *Albert Tugg.* Take every fourth letter in the message, starting with the initial T, and you got T U G G A; Tugg comma A, like the telephone directory? "How did *you* do it?" he enquired wearily.

"I ran the computer again, and tied in the MORON banks."

"The Matrix Oriented Random Operator Nexus?"

"You guessed it. Anyway, it worked and I've got the printouts here."

"Bring 'em up!"

"In a minute, I'm still doing my nut down here...." Click. Off went the intercom. NUT, Stone remembered. Nodal Uncertainty Testing.

They waited in silence, Voigt as coldly hostile as he could be at 96° Fahrenheit. The tea-girl came in and poured a cup all round. None of them drank it.

"*Iced* tea, please ..." wailed Higgins piteously. They ignored him.

Enter Tugg, stage left, perspiring freely.

"Why, Mr Voigt, what are you doing with that gun?"

"Shut up. Start talking."

Tugg was only too pleased to explain. "First I got the idea that the message should be read backwards – in reverse that is –"

"The computer thought of that." observed Stone dispassionately. He stared at a chocolate bar on the desk, which was flowing out of its wrapper and across some TOP SECRET files.

"Ah, but I verified it. See, you take the first letter of each word and get T S I G N, which rearranges to STING. Like they say, 'the sting's in the tail', so I started from the tail-end of the message."

A faint, dull thudding noise proved to be Higgins beating his head against the wall.

"But the important thing was – no letter B!"

"*What*?"

"Yes, I did a complete analysis. The probabilities were 97% that, if a layman were involved, he'd say THE SUN IS BLOWING UP, and a scientist would say – 94.5% probability – THE SUN IS BECOMING UNSTABLE. *Both* containing a B, you see."

Voigt's eyes were glassy. Stone muttered something about Ellery Queen.

"Now what is special about B? The answer lies in topology. B is the only letter which comprises two closed loops when written as a capital. With this broad hint in mind, CRETIN analysed the reversed message by assigning 1 to letters containing one closed loop, such as A, and zero to those with none, like S or E. This produces a *binary number*!" He wrote as follows. AVONGNIOGSINUSEHT. "The A's and O's are 1, the other letters zero. So we get the binary number 1010000100000000. That is, 2^{16} + 2^{14} + 2^9, giving 72,342 in decimal, which factorizes to 2^9 times 7 times 23. *Now* d'you see?"

"No!" chorused the other three. The room shrieked as another ambulance of heatstroke cases went by.

"All right. Look, the prime numbers run 2, 3, 5, 7, 11, 13, 17, 19, 23, 29 and so on. 1 doesn't count, making 2 the first prime, 7 the fourth and 23 the ninth. *Thus* the cryptogram boils down to the *1st* prime to the *9th* power, times the *4th* prime, times the *9th* ... leaving us with the four-digit message 1 9 4 9.

"And as it happens," his voice was heavy with meaning, "the only person in this building born in 1949 is Clara the tea-girl!"

Suppressing an oath, Voigt picked up his untouched cup – sniffed –

"As I thought! Cyanide!" He charged out of the room. Shots rang out in the corridor. Stone and Higgins shook hands. "Little does he know," said Higgins, rubbing the heat-rash on his neck, "that *you* poisoned his tea."

"He does know," Stone replied with an inscrutable smile. "But he's on our side. Clara was the only agent of Intelligence left in the building – this was our master-plan to eliminate her."

"Not so fast, Stone!" They turned. Tugg, by the window, was aiming a light machine-gun at them, and even as they gaped and screwed up their eyes against the intense light from behind him, he peeled off (with obvious relief) the lifelike rubber mask he wore.

"Ovanu!" they cried with one voice. An earthquake shook the building.

INTERIM – 4

FRENCH POWER BONANZA
Solar plant's highest output ever

My sun, he thought, *in whom I am well pleased....*

TAR MELTS ON M-WAYS!
Drivers told, Stay off major roads

Motorists of the world unite, he thought, *you have nothing to choose but the lanes....*

His rivals in the placard line might beat him when it came to novelty, Jones mused, but he won all along the line on simple dignity, even in this ghastly heat:

REPENT
FOR THE END
OF THE WORLD
IS AT HAND

OBSERVATORY – 3

Slowly, painfully, Lyman recovered consciousness. He was lying on soft grass, and it was night. Even now, the air was hot and humid. He felt the stinging agony of second-degree sunburn. The aurora borealis danced on the horizon, and the moon shone down, brightly, brightly.

Now he remembered: being chased by the heat-crazed Balmer and Paschen up on to the observatory dome. There, he had thought, he could hold them off for ever. He had reckoned without their devilish cunning.

They'd set the telescope for fast satellite tracking, causing the dome to rotate and throw him off. They must have left him for dead, and rushed to break into the nearby mailbox. He smiled his old smile. Little did they know that he had sent the precious letter by messenger, to go by registered post from the nearest office! He was still too weak to stand – was his leg broken? – but happily he lay there as the moon shone brightly, far too brightly.

DEEPS – 2

The monster lift was ascending the last mile, grinding and swaying. Trente panted in the hot, oppressive air. He was furious. He'd stayed a day late and no relief had turned up. Blast them all, who do they think they are, leaving me down a bloody stifling hole and going away? Power's off, too – dim lights in the lift-cage mean emergency batteries up there. Good thing the lift controls work from both ends.... He picked up his manuscript (*My Unique Experience In The Depths*. Oh for something *really* unique) and added a number of dirty comments concerning the International Seismic Research Foundation, inefficiency thereof. Foundation for Assorted Researches into Tectonics, he thought. ISRF ought to change their name.... Comms link broken down, no messages for a week, instruments playing up (9.3 Richter readings: really!) – he was sick of it all.

Still hot. It was silly of course, but he could swear it was getting hotter as he neared the surface.

Hotter, hotter, hotter ...

• My first sale, to *New Writings in SF 27*, published in 1975. John Sladek's *The Muller-Fokker Effect* may well have influenced the games with codes; I read this novel with fascination and delight around 1972, and seriously contemplated stealing it from the Oxford Union Library. The appearance of the UK paperback saved me from a life of crime.

Balmer became Morgan in the original printing, making a nonsense of that tiny fragment of actual physics about spectral lines. Apparently someone at Sidgwick & Jackson (who published *New Writings* in hardback) suspected a sly reference to the anthology editor Kenneth Bulmer, and renamed the character without consulting or notifying him. Publishers!

As for Dr Apricot, who also turned up in my and John Grant's spoof disaster novel *Earthdoom!*, it can no longer be concealed that my physics tutor at Oxford was called Peach.

Accretion

The city's founder was forgotten in all but name, and even that was a matter for conjecture: it was only the popular imagination which deduced that the place must be named for *him*, for this hypothetical Butor. It was, however, certain that one man had founded the city. As is commonly the way of founders, he had not touched brick or stone, had not himself marked patterns in the Earth. This much is commonplace; the thing which made Butor unique among cities was that no one had yet laid solid foundations, though countless hands had laboured to bring it to perfection.

Butor was a city which was not and had never been; which was not to say that it might never be.

Martin stared across the endless, featureless sea. There were others on the ship, who of course knew the rich history of Butor; but despite the direction of this journey, no one showed excitement or interest, save himself No one made pilgrimages any more, partly because the logical goal of any pilgrimage was in theory unattainable. He was probably a fool to think otherwise.

The abrasive wind blew steadily from ahead, and gulls cried high in the air. Martin, half-hypnotized by the unchanging vista, thought dreamily of the city, recalling the legend of its founding. There had been a man, long ago, who may or may not have been called Butor; end he had founded his city on paper, setting out the half-crazed dream which drew men to the building. The dream was this: that writers might combine in the creation of a great fictional city which, serving as background for all the world's stories, might imprint itself on the human mind as a vision of remote glory; might one day dream its way into a reality, as architects and engineers were inspired by its multiplex myth....

It had never been, but one day it *would* be. Soon, very soon, they had hoped once. Sooner than they thought, Martin felt. He looked again to the West, unchangeably grey. The wind rose and fell, tinged now with salt spray. Rough water ahead. Though his eyes stained, he could see no shore beyond.

The magic of the concept had sparked off pioneers. Without them the legend could never have properly begun, for a dream of foundations and plans is not the stuff of undying myth. But Stephenson came, with the practised eye of an engineer, and in his, the first stories of Butor, a solid grandeur of form was erected. This early vision was bleak and bare, such as the old Norsemen might have built to defy the giants of fire and frost, could they have enlisted the hill-trolls to work the massive stones. Then before Stephenson's rough-hewn towers and machines of sleek steel could age or mellow, he was joined by other writers who were drawn to the raw young mythos of the city: Reed, for one, who must surely have been a woman, with her tales of subtle curves that mocked planes, planes which masqueraded as curves, deceiving the eye and mind alike. And Rohan set down the tables of the law, and filled Butor with music; while Holdstock painted in decadence and sensuality, and set it about with grotesques.

Already, the stories seemed not so important for their own sake as for the new insights into the city's ways. Scott wrote tales of love lost and regained, but the initiates read him for his telling of Butor's myths. Smith commemorated universal agonies, and the growing cult ferreted from his stories the subtleties of Butor's finance. Though Kilworth might plumb psychological depths, his background of Butor's broad gardens was remembered after every plot-turn had been resolved and forgotten. Morgan spilt the first blood there; and for his pains was praised for writing of sunsets over Butor's spires.

For the city was greater than any of its chroniclers, and would not die, would not even remain in the background. These first writers achieved immortality as the Butor Group, and as such alone; their names were forgotten except in the dustier texts which poked and prodded into those earliest days.

Still the city was not; and had never been. Despite this, it became the best-known city of the world.

The station-wagon lurched painfully along jungle paths. Martin noted the slowness of progress, and decided that it was right. Such a journey should not be too easy.

He had found himself alone in wondering about Butor. The nature of his wonder was this: though Butor was better documented, now, than any city of mere stone, its picture would not come clear in his mind. London, less vast, was grey and sprawling to him, an intricate maze studded with unexpected wonder. New York, thrust fantastically into the sky, symbolized the old, lost spirit of America. Paris – Venice – Moscow – Rome – he had visited them all, and found each with a kind of fading personality, an inner truth which crumbled less quickly than the stones. He had only read of Butor: of course. If he could *see* it, he would know the secret which all the writers groped for still.

He hoped he was heading in the right direction.

The strange urge stemmed, in part, from a habit of reading old books, so old that often they were not set in Butor, and might not even mention it. The experience was strange and disturbing at first; but Martin had found that even in those days, intelligent men had written books, often about real cities. One passage stayed in his mind, from a writer named Chesterton, who had described how one might read a hundred books about a place and be no nearer its essential quality. He spoke of visiting Jerusalem and being struck by a thing so obvious that no one troubled to mention it: the city was set on a hill. This had upset his whole mental picture of the place.

Martin had scarcely heard of Jerusalem, but there were other cities, occasionally mentioned in the earlier stories and novels of the Butor cycle. London ... Moscow ... Paris ... New York ...

He realized how much more a place of wonder Butor must be: an intellectual realization taken from the books. He knew then that he must visit it, so that he would know.

Surely, when half that world believed so devoutly in Butor, the place must be? Alter all, London and the rest continued to exist, though half-forgotten, which seemed as great a miracle. The world was running down, and myths spoke of no past glories; only of one city which remained glorious. Any single vision of wonder might be splendid, and in Butor all were combined.

The station-wagon struggled on, unheeding of his thoughts.

Alter the initial Group had shaped the city, other creators came to add its transport, its customs and manners, splashes of colour and smears of grime, a thousand small touches. The city was a pearl which grew and grew, nurtured in successive cerebella. It grew by accretion, a word which is not quite an anagram of "creation". It drew everything to itself. The cult grew further, and other works joined the fiction of Butor: street directories, maps, guide-books, sober historical accounts. A uniform-edition publishing house was launched, solely to handle the tales of the "Butor Cycle"; but soon all the publishers produced them, as writer after writer gravitated to the city which had never been. The commonest tale of murder or first love took strength from that background, and in its turn reinforced Butor's quasi-existence – for even a tarnish can be the patina of reality.

The science-fiction writers laboured high on the bright spires, minting fresh wonders to adorn the eternal city; romantics and mystery-mongers touched it further with romance and mystery; and the writers of the intellectual mainstream lovingly gave it slums. More and more Butor became a city which embodied everything; less and less was written of other, less intensely realized, merely genuine cities.

Who could say that such a well-documented place was not?

Martin's legs were growing tired, as he drove himself up the mountain path. He stopped, and consulted a compass. Unless the path turned soon, he would have to leave it and attempt the rough slope to his right. Looking dourly up to the crags, he allowed himself to be momentarily doubtful; then reassured himself with the remembrance of his own care in calculation.

The stories of the Cycle enshrouded ten thousand thousand facts about Butor, and a man with patience might extract any data whatever about it. Martin had considered the climate at first; had then discarded it as an unreliable guide, suited only for rough confirmation of more sophisticated calculations.

The book that had solved his problem was entitled *Night-Piece*; being a late story of the Cycle, it had no author credit, but this was irrelevant. It described a certain week in the life of Carreras, one of the better-established inhabitants of the city (he had been mentioned as early as the forty-third Butor tale), and included descriptions of his vigil on the balcony of the Hotel Splendide while awaiting his mistress. This passage was extended and philosophical, leaping from metaphor to metaphor with startling race; of interest to Martin was the fact that Carreras had seen Sirius that night, framed in a tiny space between the lesser Cathedral spire and the nearer edge of the Jade Tower. In a train of metaphysical speculation too abstruse for paraphrase, which was provoked by this sight, the exact time was given: subtly, elliptically, but it was given. Butor had revealed itself. From available data, Martin had been able to deduce latitude and longitude.

The path turned; he smiled. It could not be far now. Unpromising though the rocks ahead appeared, this was the place where, if it was at all, the city must be.

Polished by innumerable minds, Butor increased in complexity and wonder. Early stories had used it as a background against which any drama might be played; now, in the ceaseless drive toward perfection, the foreground too was woven into the ever-richer tapestry. Minor characters from one narrative would have secret motives explained only by their appearance in another; the principal of a tale of action, fighting to the death in some lonely street, would reappear as a minor disturbance outside a window, required for the plot of a simultaneous love-story; the marriage of two nonentities might snare characters twenty books away in an unexpected web of consanguinity. The dustiest corner of the market square came gradually alive with associations. Gaps in the history were sought out and carefully filled; nonetheless Butor remained multifarious and enigmatic, the richest source of narrative material in the world, the only source for men of discrimination. The "oblique" story developed, the story charting mysterious and irrational relations or counterpoints, only explicable by reference to other tales of the Cycle which detailed, in another context, what the protagonists were thinking and the nature of their interactions – or lack of them.

The shadows, entwined into almost unbearable complexity, began to assume a deceptive substance; believed in by the world, chronicled to the last falling of a dust-grain, the tiniest ripple on the lakes of its great parks, the phantom city trembled, nine-tenths alive, *Terra Tenebrosa*, slipping silkily along the slope from the things which *are not*, down, downward to the earth, through the realm of what *may be* ...

Martin stumbled, gasped for breath; he paused and panted for a moment. The path led on through a labyrinth of high rocks. It turned to the left, to the right, staggered over hard, broken ground: ended.

The high place was hollowed out, a great bawl of a plateau, the gentle slope leading featurelessly down from Martin's feet, to Butor. The sun was low, now: this was the time when the city's poets were most lyrical, pillaging the ancients for their cadences, as: *Inexplicable splendour of Ionian white and gold.... Or the storied windows richly dight, Casting a dim religious light –*

Martin saw it; took it in; the product of countless literary minds made flesh – no, made marble, made basalt and serpentine, jade and onyx, a medley of stones and styles beneath the setting sun.

He remembered the old joke about the camel: A horse designed by a committee. He saw the secret heart of Butor.

It was ugly; a jumble of clashing modes, ugly and appalling.

Slowly Martin turned and left that place, not pausing, not looking back; not caring whether or not the city continued to be.

• Published 1977. Once upon a time there was an informal British SF writers' group known as Pieria, whose regulars included Chris Evans, Robert Holdstock, Garry Kilworth, myself, Chris Morgan, Diana Reed, Michael Scott Rohan, Kevin Smith, Allan Scott, Andrew Stephenson and ... well, if I try to be totally inclusive I'll only offend someone. Various of their surnames are taken in vain in "Accretion", a small self-indulgence which proved highly irritating to the

Foundation reviewer who singled out this story for disapproval and bemused me with a plot summary which concluded: "A man crosses deserts to find its site. Naturally, there is nothing there." This shows how close reading by critics may discover meanings of which even the author is unaware.

The city, by the way, was named for the French critic Michel Butor, who in an essay titled "Science Fiction: The Crisis of Its Growth" (translated in *SF: The Other Side of Realism* ed. Thomas D. Clareson, 1971) suggested that sf authors should all get together and write about the same future, the same city. The great James Blish and others scoffed at the time, but look how many writers – beginning, come to think of it, with Blish himself – have taken the *Star Trek* shilling or committed sharecropping of other media-based franchises....

Connections

I smiled my sweetest womanly smile from the throbbing chair, as the door slid closed behind him. He was tongue-tied, of course.

"Good morning, Barret," (I know every name in the Institute; impressive, most impressive, unless you know about the skull-mike) "I understand you've something to tell me? Please sit down."

Barret, too young and too awed, made obeisance and sat: he placed his box on the desk-edge and stammered across its top.

"I awah-awah-awah –"

"Take your time," I suggested, turning my hearing up by a few dB and poking the bar switch. He jerked back as a tumbler of best jap Scotch erupted from the desk before him.

"Ahhh, ah, I've been doing some work on the emtee problem, Arch-physicist Ellan, and ..." As he dried up again, he fumbled with the box now capitalized to Box, Black. Because I do not leave this room, all these things must come to me; whether in reality or via CC3V link depends upon sizes and circumstances.

He had said enough – *that word* – my poise faltered with his speech. I mapped out probable lines for the coming talk – and dialled an hour's privacy. The minimal funding and engineered atmosphere of hopelessness kept most good men out of emtee: bad ones did not matter. But still from time to time genius is lured into byways of squaring the circle.

Barret continued to fumble, darting nervous glances to me in my most carefully designed (for all that it's genuine) setting:

Steel and chrome, the chair, and more than a chair, with a hundred-weight of micrologic and life-supports; soft shackles of tubing to pin me down, and the Institute's nerve-centres in buttons at my fingers. All the rest of this room is quiet in black-and-white, highlighting the chair and myself as Wise Woman, white-haired and immeasurably wise. A witch who's fit and well lacks something: wrecked kidneys and collapsing arteries are useful now for effect, counterpointing the soggy lump of grey stuff in my skull that hit the IQ 180s so long, so long ago....

Barret, callow, blond, had finished his unwrapping to reveal an experimental rig reminiscent of all other experimental rigs. Would he have the courage to sip his drink, now? No, the hand slithered halfway and slowed to a halt.

"Drink up," I suggested at the critical moment, beating back a habitual envy with the habitual thought that if others can drink, my edge on them is increased. Then, for I had demonstrated my grinding patience to sufficient degree, "Mmmm, emtee, did you say – Oh, by the way, no need for the honorific: in here I'm Dr Ellan."

"MT" (he spaced the initials carefully) "yes, Doctor, I have a working model." He gripped the glass, and I saw a solder-burn on one finger: the technicians are security men, and a man who avoids their aid may complete something before details rise to me. Clever, this Barret – or lucky.

"This is it." He tapped the box. "The first matter transmitter." With a courage born of righteous pride, he raised the glass and drank.

Context:

The mighty vessels crashed inexorably through the fabric of space, heedless of the thirty thousand suns that blazed between them and their goal.... Snapping along unthinkable geodesics that short-circuited galaxies and galactic clusters, they leapt from pole to pole of the universe at the press of a button on their Transfer Units

Through MT portals strung in scores about the orbit of Mercury, the Sun's naked heat poured into Earth's power generators and frozen tundras.

Replacing airlines, railways, shipping lines, nibbling here at cars and there at the mails, poised for the final assault on old-style travel's last bastion, the pedestrian

Revolutionizing, remaking, restructuring ...

Some hope.

A ring of pale light hung in the air, as though some deranged inventor had ingeniously combined the small emission-area of the filament lamp with the low brightness of discharge tubes. Barret wasn't satisfied, it seemed; he frowned still, and turned knobs, and peered expectantly at the air. A two-portal, I deduced: and the gate co-ordinates must be pegged to either the box or the Earth's mass, since the ring seemed stable. Remembering one or two of the other sort, I shivered. One hoped that the mindlessly omniscient watch-monitors would continue to spot anything such. (The fact of Barret's device was "known". I had it, somewhere, a cluster of magnetic bubbles lost in foaming wastes of machine-memory. No time to look.)

THINK BIG, the joke sign on the desk reminded once more.

The second ring appeared then: identical to the first, it was – I nodded slowly – a couple of centimetres in diameter. Barret lifted his hands from the box with the air of having struck a great chord upon some invisible keyboard.

"There," he said. His mind made the transition from laboratory to *sanctum sanctorum,* and he swallowed. "Now look –"

He pulled a pen from his pocket and thrust it into one ring. The end vanished like Tom the Cat hiding behind an impossibly slender tree; from the second ring, a sleek barrel emerged. All instinct said this must be a second pen. Naturally, it wasn't.

"Excellent," I said politely. "Very nice. Could you oblige an old lady's curiosity just for one moment, though ..." ah, don't overdo it! "You've by-passed space, most certainly: the pen," I gave an academic titter, "is neither here nor there. But suppose you moved it to one side ...?"

This was malicious; but I was the great Dr Catherine Ellan, aka the old witch. He'd been holding the pen most carefully, dead-centre in the portal, one end in his hand and the other two feet away; now he abandoned the careful control (a point of envy: my hands twitch uncontrollably when not supported) and moved it gently to one side. The portal edges were not of an appreciable finite thickness: the far piece of the pen fell to the desk-top. On the cut surface gleamed a moist film of ink, oozing from its porous containment. A clean cut.

"We'll get you another pen," I said.

"Oh, it's quite all right." – Toady. The initial awe and etcetera was beginning now to fade, and he gaped covertly at my prosthetics. *There's a fascination frantic in a ruin that's romantic....* I gave him more drink and, by way of distraction, told him about Conners.

Conners had invented the matter transmitter. Conners had evolved the theory from his own conceptions, and invented one which was not the same as Barret's. There are many sorts of transmitter, almost as many as there have been theoreticians in the field. The model had been built; the model had been checked, subassembly by subassembly. Connections were made. Conners prepared himself for glory and his tithe of the Archphysicist's certain-to-ensue Nobel Prize.

There was a tense countdown to the actual activation: quite unnecessary, good showmanship. Conners himself pressed the switch. The portal formed, five feet across. Interestingly, theory later showed that such a large portal might only be achieved by a machine subject to the defect of Conners'. Theory is always helpful, later.

The portal formed, perfectly still in space and five feet across. Absolutely at rest; but as relative motion came into play, the Earth shifted, translating along a gigantic vector compounded of orbital and rotational motion relative to Sol; added to the Sun's motion relative to the fixed stars; added ultimately to the motion (if any) of whatever the "fixed stars" moved relative to .

The portal remained at rest, and was left behind, apart from such material as intercepted its area and was MT'd to an unknown destination. This matter included most of the generating apparatus, and almost all of Connors. Crucified on the metrical frame, the wounded world staggered on while a not-quite-straight hole, cut neatly through it, gurgled with deepest magma.

"Suppressed!" Barret said in a voice of moral outrage. "It was struck from the files, that work – I know – I arranged clearance up to Security Nine and went through every file myself. I demand – I –" running down slowly as a whiff of whisky-breath crossed the table – "Dr Ellan, I don't understand."

"Security Ten." There was no need to say more.

He thought about that and massaged his chin, fingers crawling up on either side of his mouth as though trying to hide the face. It is convenient to forget the Security clause which mentions that those upon lower rungs do not require to know the existence of the higher ones. And so Barret's ilk look down on Sevens and Eights, accepting the tacit belief that classifications don't reach double figures.

"Emtee," I told him then, "is dangerous. Look at what happened to Connors."

"There is a fallacy," he said, beginning to think. "Once the generator equipment was destroyed, the gate would collapse."

"There are many types of emtee. Why, if your machine has torn space apart, should you expect the wound to heal? I remember the Valdez portal – co-ordinates pegged to Earth, yes – squirted cubic miles of air into Mars orbit before they plugged it. Ever wonder why they should build a giant Einstein memorial of quickset concrete? In a subInstitute like Valdez?" This place had nothing so flashy.

Barret frowned, turning ponderously back to the Connors affair. "A better controlled experiment –" He was working up to a broadside.

"No!" I began loudly; deep down in the chair came a gurgle and, remembering caution, I went on in softer tones:

"There is more than the simple physical danger. There is an intellectual hazard, a killing hazard. The foundations of physics must be protected."

Shock and contempt now. Oh yes, the tiger was wakening: pull his nose and he'll smile; pull his leg, he'll snarl; but if you want to commit suicide, stand back and kick him in the dogmas.... "Archphysicist! This ... This goes against scientific method!" He made the Holy Left-hand Sign:

Field, Current, Motion. I responded reflexively, but:

"You're wrong. On more than one count. I repeat, I am not talking of simple wreckage among theories – they're always fair game – but a real danger, a two-edged danger, physical and metaphysical.

"As well, of course, there's moral danger. Look at that thing of yours. The monitors don't recognize it as a weapon; or you'd never have got it in here. But imagine a hand-held version, which could extend the gate, fast, along the radius vector –!"

He imagined. The gate-edge would cut through anything, transmitting sections of walls, machinery, men, through that space which was not space, leaving a clean hole in the target. Unpleasant.

"Not what I wanted! Not, at all. I have done the basic work, Doctor, and I wish support. To develop a gate large enough for a man."

"Fool." I felt very tired. "Fool. You don't know the first thing about the mathematics. Let me tell you how wide the aperture is." I pointed shakily at one of the pale rings of light, which hovered still above the sign THINK BIG. "One point nine centimetres. 1.926643 ... or haven't you measured so fine? It's the mathematical limit. I made the calculations myself, fifteen years ago."

The mighty vessels crashed through the fabric of space – Again the dream faded, corroded by acid fact.

He stared intently at the box, unwilling to look up. The tubes plucked lightly at me as I shifted position, but there was no pain. Locals and nerve-blocks, courtesy of the Archchemist.

Why did I give this talk? Type of the garrulous old woman? Cliché of the burning secret that must be told, else it festers in the mind? After me, the dark.

"Small and petty, Barret. Small, mean things are the limits of this machine of yours. Connors went out with a bang, but you – Oh, let me tell you another story."

Bell had invented the matter transmitter. Bell (like Barret) had evolved no more than a partial theory: a nuts-and-bolts man, he had invented one which was very like Barret's. The model had been built. The model had been checked, tested.

There was a glorious moment, when the portal first glimmered in the air. There was an anxious time while adjustments were attempted again and again. Ultimately there was despair and a diameter immutably fixed at 1.9 centimetres. Expensive, unstable except at short range, and useless.

Bell drank and thought his thoughts. Presently he visited a relative whose money might redeem all the debts incurred in the machine's building. It was useless, Bell saw, for transport, for all the wonderful dreams of MT. But it was excellent for killing. There were things, potent things, which could pass through the tiny gate.

They found the relative dead in his locked study: an overdose. Sleeping pills in coffee. A beautiful suicide note (which was curled as though it had been rolled up and thrust through some small opening ...). The door locked, bolted, impenetrable oak. Windows small and leaded, fastening securely from within. Walls as watertight as the case for suicide. It was a perfect example of that classic problem, the locked room mystery.

Bell himself played the part of shocked but co-operative relation, with just that hint of embarrassment appropriate to one who figured prominently in the Will. Such was his confidence that he helped break into the death-room when irregularity was first suspected. Bell smashed the window and revealed the scene fully, climbing in to unbolt the massive door. He remained supremely confident until the police – yes, it was that long ago – until the police made their mistake.

At the trial, the theory was proposed: that Bell had entered when the door was open. Poisoned the coffee. Waited for the relative to die. Left the room, closing the door. Broken a single pane of the leaded window. Poked through with a long rod to manipulate lock and bolt. And left the scene to be completed by his destruction of all remaining evidence when he broke that entire window, next day.

Bell, guilty, was innocent of this: he still projected guilt and more strongly, shock. Oh, there remained "reasonable doubt". The jury might have acquitted or convicted. Before further moves could be made, however, a second suicide occurred which was indisputably genuine.

"I dislike your implication," Barret said. "I am not such a man as that."

"You can say that? You, who have smuggled a deadly weapon into my room?" He jerked backward from the box, mouth opening, closing, until he saw my smile. "Think Big!" I said. But the joking had to stop. "We must suppress the device. Your work will be remembered, and you will be honoured to a degree by those people who are permitted to know, but the device, the device itself –"

And he went into white heat! "Suppression! Blasphemy. Did they abandon nuclear power because of Hirosaki? We'd have no fuser now, if they had."

"And no nullbombs," I reminded him gently, secure in decrepitude's armour. "But if my first argument won't work, listen to my second. There is danger to Basic Physics in the device. Emtee changes the nature of space, the fabric that holds it all together. Emtee changes the rules, Barret."

"Conners built a portal, remember, which anchored in absolute space.

Think now, for just one moment, and tell me the implications."

"Einstein ... There *is* no absolute space."

"Explain what happened to Conners." I looked down wearily at my wrinkled hands, stuffed with invisible trumps. Nothing was fun, now.

"He – Nonsense. The way in which you told the tale assumed too much. Obviously he produced a larger version of *this* and the space-coordinate networks went wild. No need to drag in Einstein. It was bad engineering."

Score one to the engineer.

"Passing over the fact that the portal persisted after destruction of the generator, mathematics shows –"

He snorted. I hadn't thought he had it in him. "Show *me*."

"You wouldn't follow, in your present state. But there is other evidence. Absolute space is incompatible with Einstein, not so?"

A nod.

"Then with Einstein, a lot of things such as nuclear transformation, and E equals you know what, would be screwed up. Therefore, no nuclear power."

"A nice *reductio ad absurdum,* yes. There is nuclear power therefore there is no absolute space." He frowned; perhaps he saw that he was being set up.

"You can't have both: right again. But," and I looked up at him intently, "when Conners hit that switch, the Institute reactor next door shut down. All activity ceased for eight seconds. It took the usual twelve hours to warm it up again – old-fashioned beast, uranium rods. How do you account for that? You can have power or absolute space. You have a choice. How do you account for it?"

He said nothing. He continued to say it for some seconds. "I don't," he said then. Another pause.

"But my MT isn't like that. Think big, you say: but perhaps some things are too small for you to see. Just two gates – a short-cut in space – adds to physics without attacking it. If we rethink energy conservation slightly, of course." I leant slowly back, and the prosthetic chair hummed. Time for my feed; a tube low down turned opaque. "Ah yes, perpetual motion. You don't consider that a danger to physics, then?"

"Revolutions can be healthy. Imagine a waterfall, circular, with turbines halfway and MT gates pushing the water back up –"

"Yes, lots and lots of little 1.9 cm gates, I can see it now. And you're the friend of physics! Some still quarrel with Einstein; but to attack conservation ... It has a cranky whiff, you know."

"And – what is the argument against this very – simple – idea?"

"Simple, oh yes, the argument is simple too. Your own machine embodies a paradox." I smiled benignly. The interview tapes would receive Ten classification.

"Explain!" His look was now so murderous that I half regretted explaining that the emtee was a weapon, wholly regretted the jap Scotch. No matter: the weapon could point either way. Trite, but true.

"The gates. They have zero thickness. The theory says so."

Nuts-and-bolts man to the end, he didn't argue.

"Stick something through again. No, just do it." The miracle was repeated: one part of the ill-fated pen was stretched three feet to appear half here, half there. The gates were aligned upon a common axis, so it was as though three feet of the pen were invisible.

He took the pen out again as I waved it away. "Superimpose the gates."

They drifted uncertainly together – paused – coalesced. The only way to tell there was more than one was the increased brightness. Still, it would never replace fluoros.

I adopted the shrill lecturing tone which once pinned the neophytes to their seats in Spatial Mech I-IV. Now I was pinned more physically in my own seat, and gave no lectures, but the trained instincts were there. Old crone outthinks vibrant young scientist: *that's* news.

"Now what will happen if you re-insert the pen? Answer, a paradox. The pen must be transmitted from gate to gate, endlessly; for the gates occupy the same space ... if you will allow space to have any meaning.

"Therefore you cannot insert the pen. Or the matter transmitter, condemned by iron logic, cannot exist. If the pen can be inserted it must vanish, be transmitted somewhere; but you have short-circuited space: there *is* no space between the gates: there, is nowhere for the pen to vanish to.

"But what is to stop it?"

Barret snarled and lunged with the pen. Disbelief was on his face.

"Barret, I refute it thus!" My timing was good. The universe cannot tolerate a paradox. The pen touched the gate; there was a hollow pop; it had vanished. So, of course, did the machine.

Barret gaped. Then he looked at me with darkest suspicion, fist clenching, unclenching, uncertain. And finally he showed just how dangerous he was, by making the logical jump at once.

"Rubbish!" he shouted. "You tricked me into destroying the machine, but your so-called paradox remains implicit in the fact that I can – and will – build another. Therefore –"

I have never decided whether the universe has a slow reaction-time or is merely a confirmed eavesdropper. Before I could deliver a final, crushing, epigrammatic retort, a second faint implosion sounded as Barret himself vanished.

The universe cannot tolerate a paradox.

In the old Institute – another decade, another continent – the matter transmitter was invented twice. A controlled experiment.

The first was designed in strict accordance with known laws. Naturally, it didn't work. The second was designed from quite irrational theories. A 1.9 cm hole in space was established. This model transmitted objects – in theory – instantaneously from *here* to *there,* unlike the more common designs which only moved their payload at *c,* the velocity of light.

Take away *c* as an absolute limiting velocity, and relativity crumbles. Quantum mechanics collapses.

There is no need to go into the details of quantum mechanics: suffice it to say that it is a theory which, among other things, accounts satisfactorily for the fact that atomic electron orbits do not decay, spiral madly into the nucleus. Should the orbits decay, negative and positive charges would cancel cataclysmically. Bye-bye, atom.

They turned the transmitter on. Bye-bye, quantum mechanics.

The new Institute was built in another continent, North America now being unusable. Thus the nullbomb effect, which Security Grades Nine down "know" to be rooted in sound nuclear theory.... After this, the Ten classification was created and imposed.

And here I am and here I stay, Archphysicist, Fid. Def., protecting the tottering edifice of physics from the onslaught of these damned thoughtless physicists. Like Prometheus bound to the chair with prosthetics pecking at my liver; or perhaps an aged vixen flailed with sour grapes. Make no mistake, I invented the MT too in my day. Another story.

The struggle goes on. We suppress the results of research, suppress the research itself when its road turns downward to disaster and the nullbomb; yet we cannot suppress all emtee thought. The ritualists who infest this science declare that suppression is theologically unsound, and officially I must bow to this dogma. A pox on it. Vital secrets are there somewhere, yes, explanations of why the laws of physics switch madly on and off when space is tampered with. Massive energies and capabilities wait. On the other hand:

A living legend, that's me, the shattered woman persisting through indomitable will: all the glory I have left. But there are those who gnaw at even this security, who would drag me from this protecting chair, send me walking the city streets as blood for dialysis gurgles with my other precious bodily fluids through 1.9 cm wormholes in space. A small use for

MT, subtle and small – so let them Think Big. If Prometheus had allowed himself to be unbound, who'd remember him now?

The hell with them.

I like it here.

Published 1978. This offers an example of the kitchen-sink technique whereby a number of not-quite-adequate notions and plots (I actually wrote the locked room mystery as a standalone story, and discarded it) can be forcibly amalgamated to produce a whole which is subtly less than the sum of its parts.

Further mulling over the possibilities of contradictions in physics led to the background of my sf novel *The Space Eater* (1982), and the whole dodgy matter-transmission scholium was recycled with determined thriftiness in *Earthdoom!* (with John Grant, 1987). The action of *Earthdoom!* also contains two more stories of implausible physics colliding with conservation laws – one by each author, stuffed into the narrative rather after the fashion of A.E. van Vogt. I think it was John Clute who defined the phenomenon of Van Vogt Yaw, being what happens when unrelated shorts are tossed into a novel and get seasick.

Training

A mantrap bit my foot off; I dropped between two rocks because I had to, and took stock of the damage. Five years back I'd have fainted dead away as a million volts of pain came searing up the nerves: now it was just an irritation, a distraction. Uncomfortable, like the knobby rocks I'd landed on in the instinctive dive for cover. I fixed the tourniquet with my left hand and teeth – you *never* let the gun slip out of your right hand when in action, even if it's only the training ground. If you're right-handed, that is.... I was ready to stick my head up for a quick look at the objective, but just then there was a popping and crackling as the IR laser drew a quick line of bright sparks through the air. Superheated rockdust burst out in clouds where the line struck; one fragment scored my forehead and filled my eyes with blood. The years of battle training helped soak up the new pain, but I wasted more seconds tying a kerchief over the gash with one hand only.

An electric-discharge laser would need seconds to recharge. I hoped it wasn't a gasdynamic or chemical job – and stuck up my head. Nothing hit me during the quick look I allowed myself then, so I tossed a grenade and a smokebomb as far as I could toward the laser bunker and started hopping, slightly off the direct line of approach the IR flash had drawn in the air. The guess about the laser was wrong, though, because straightaway another dotted line of ionization sparks came probing through the smoke, shattering rock in a continuous explosion. A good shot now could smash the directing mirror and put the damn laser out for the duration, but even a Forceman doesn't aim too well one-legged and I didn't care to drop again just yet. Instead I unclipped more smokebombs from my belt and threw them way to the right of the first cloud while I moved in from the left. Standard manoeuvre now was to shove a grenade right through their firing slit.

They saw me, though, and the crackling line came tracking over toward me, and I put on speed – Hopalong Jacklin rides again. Under the beam and skidding full-length through dust and gravel to the base of the pillbox, the one place where the beam couldn't aim – or that was what I was hoping. I smelled it then. Before my eyes went cloudy grey and useless I saw the little vents in that concrete right by my face, and realized that not only were the bastards using a chemical laser, but they were pumping the deadly hydrogen fluoride exhaust out right here, especially for goddamn idiots like me. Then the HF gas was stripping the skin off my face, scarring my windpipe and filling my lungs with bloody froth. There was nothing to do but take it and wait for the end. And after a little while I died, again.

The thing about the training ground is that you *can't* win. It carries on and carries on until you're dead. This probably sounds a bit grim and off-putting if like most of the people out there you're a virgin where death's concerned: but for us seasoned Forcemen death is just part of our lives. The logic is pretty simple, after all. When you want a meal cooked up, and on hand you've got a trained cook and a guy who's never tried cooking, which one do you choose? Right. So when you want someone to go out and probably get himself killed defending you or filling your enemies with holes ... that's the core of Force training. Anyone loaded down with gut-fear-hormone squirts from glands with a case of the squitters is going to be thinking about himself instead of the fighting; someone like that just can't do a clean, efficient kill. Poker players learn to keep emotion out of their faces, they say in the Force, and we learn to keep ours out of our glands.

So I lay there in the tank and craned my neck to see how the foot was growing. The regenerator fluid is thick, yellowish and murky, but I could see I'd already sprouted a neat bunch of tarsal bones, coated with a misty jelly where the flesh was starting to creep back over them. The fluid filled my mouth and nostrils and lungs, which no doubt were healing at a good rate. The only real quarrel I've got with this death and regeneration business is that it's boring: even for fiddling little injuries the process can take hours. Once I was cut not so neatly in half by a riot-gun and spent five whole days growing a new me, from the belly down, like some stupid flatworm. Learning to die and live again is a necessary thing, though. Like they told us on the induction course, deep down in all our genes we've got this locked-in program that shrieks *survival* when death's about, and shrieks it so loud that you can't hear your other thoughts. Only way to stop that and get efficient is to get used to dying ... and then, maybe, you can start thinking about promotion.

That one had been my forty-sixth death. I reckoned I was used to it.

They let me out of the sickbay in the end, after all the usual unpleasantness (lying there in the tank is dreamy and nice if you can turn off your brain a while, but being disconnected isn't so good). I marched off on my own two tender feet – the treatment leaves you uncalloused, like a baby – feeling ready to rush that laser again and this time smear the crew good and proper. I'd been in some of those bunkers myself, of course. Sooner or later the crew always get smeared.

Next day we'd be starting a fresh course, Guerrilla II, on how to improvise your own nukes – the trick, I'd heard, is to get your charge of plute-oxide fuel shaped and imploded before the Pu poisoning catches up with you. Some of these courses are makework, I think, to soak up our spare energy, but they're all good fun. No need to catch up on studies that night, so I wandered into the bar for a juice and sat down by Raggett, a new guy with only half a dozen deaths. He still wore the death-pips on his arm: I gave up those decorations when they reached double figures, myself.

"Chess?" I said to be sociable. "Or we could grab a room for a bit of wargaming, if that doesn't sound too much like work."

"I thought ... I thought I'd go into town," said Raggett: He is a ratty little fellow, and he looked really furtive when he said this. Men from the Force can go into town anytime they don't have classes or training – it's supposed to be a compliment, the brass trust us. But somehow there's a kind of feeling in the air, not even strong enough to call an unwritten rule, that the real pros don't waste time outside the complex. So I gave Raggett a twitch of my eyebrow, and he said, "I could use a woman."

At that I remembered my last woman, maybe only three or four deaths into training, and at the same time I remembered Mack, the long-server who'd taken me into town back then out of sheer kindness (it had been his first time in years – like me now, he'd slipped out of the habit) and warned me where I'd likely be rolled, or poxed, or both. Mack, poor guy: he was wasted in one of the Continental raids. No pickup for recycling – you know what they say: it was France and meat's short there.

"How about the two of us going?" I said. "Town's not healthy when there's just one of you, and I think I know a couple of places."

"Well ... thanks, Jacklin! Hoped you'd say that. Can I get you another?"

I let him buy me a juice I didn't really want, and he told me that the latest stats had been posted, which I knew already only I was feeling friendly. Seventy-two percent of the new intake had dropped out on their first combat trial. Psych discharge: some people just can't take dying, you know, and most of that seventy-two percent wouldn't be much use for anything afterward. They sometimes said ... well, never mind that. It made me feel closer to Raggett, even with all those D's of seniority.

"– great stuff," he was saying. "The vocal synth is really out of this world. You heard it?"

I blinked. "Heard what? ... Oh, a new tape. Sorry friend, but music doesn't do anything for me: I used to follow the charts a long time ago, but I never get the chance these days."

There's always something new out of Africa in the music line, even if you don't hear much of the homegrown stuff these days.

"I was wondering about that," Raggett said. "I've noticed you seniors mostly stay away from the audio room, and I mean, you know; is this some goddamn unwritten rule I don't know about?"

I told him the truth, which was that I didn't know much about it either. "After I'd been in the Force a while the things I did before didn't seem too important. You get this feeling of being really in touch here, on the ball, keeping ahead of classes and scoring high in combat trials. Especially those. I mean, it feels a whole lot better inside than music and such."

Raggett's eyebrows crawled together, halfway to a frown, and I wondered if he was planning to give up all his piddling hobbies right away. I started wondering a couple of other things too, but they swam down out of reach inside my head before I could net them.

"Let's go into town, then," I said.

The streets were much the same, the fights were different. More of the shielded power lines get cut up every year – maintenance isn't worth the effort outside the enclaves. The back streets were still choked with the hulks of old cars; the route through them came back to me bit by bit as we went along, and I managed to keep the plan in my head a turning or so in front of our feet. Sooner than was comfortable, we were going through zones where the lighting was just about nonexistent. London's been a mess since long before the Force took over. I remember thinking that this part of town had gone even further downhill since my last time. Some places, back alleys especially, we were picking our way just by the nova lights in the sky. And then, as our footsteps sounded grittily in one quiet and smelly spot, there was a scraping of feet and three punks jumped us. Leftovers from a smashed Freedom gang, maybe. It turns out the Force technique of going all out and not caring about getting dead or injured works fine in unarmed combat too – I was a wide-open target as my fingers went in a V into the first guy's eyes and my right boot into the second's groin, while whatever Raggett did to the third left him a screaming lump until I kicked him to sleep.

It was hard to see in that thin mucky light, as we stood breathing hard over the bodies, but it seemed they were pretty young. Should've joined the Force if they wanted action – or maybe they'd tried and weren't up to it. As fighters they hadn't been much: I came out of it with just a dislocated finger which, thanks to the training, didn't bother me too much as I reset it.

"Hope they're not maimed for life," Raggett said as we went on, still scanning in front, behind, on both sides, the automatic way you learn. I guessed two of them might be and the third wouldn't be walking straight for something like a week (no tanks for slummies, you bet). So what? They put themselves up as targets and we cooperated nicely by knocking them down. Good practice, too.

Then we were at the House, a place looking like any dingy terrace house in these slums if you didn't happen to know. I pushed the squeaky doorcom button and said, "Two guys here looking for company." There was a pause while, I guessed, a bootleg black-light camera checked us over; then the door buzzed and clicked open. Inside it was like the foyer of some small, dingy club – or hotel if there were any of those left. The oil lamps leaked a yellow, smelly light. An ugly-looking receptionist who probably knew something about unarmed combat himself asked us what specs we wanted. A whiff of the death-happy feeling as I looked him over: he was tough, sure, but I guessed I could take him, no sweat....

"Blonde," Raggett said eagerly. "Not over thirty – no, twenty-five."

I remembered a name from that visit all those deaths ago. "Cathy," I said. We slapped down the oversized wads of Force scrip he asked for, took the keys and headed up the stairs.

What the hell am I doing here? I thought outside the door. The key rattled in the lock; I tapped a warning as I turned the handle, and as the door swung in a choking blast of stale perfume came out. It took me straight back to the bunker and the HF exhaust for a second.... Inside, it wasn't the Cathy I remembered, but she was just as efficient, coming to me with a real-looking smile asking if she could help me get my clothes off. I like efficiency: she was an expert in her trade just the way I was in mine. In no time at all we were lying side by side on the huge bed while I looked closely at her grey eyes and pale yellow hair, and decided she was quite a good looker, really.

We chatted a while, lying there. She said professionally nice things about how I was big and strong and so on, and I told her she looked great, and I was a Forceman who hadn't been into town for a few years. She gave me an odd sort of sidelong look then.

"You know, we don't see very many old-timers here," she said.

"Hell, I won't be thirty for a while," I said, grinning.

"Mmm ... yes, quite babyfaced. But you know what they say about the Forcemen who've been under training a long while."

I didn't know what they said about them, and asked. She twisted her face into a funny little frown, and said, "You maybe paid to talk all night? Can't you do that in your very own cell or whatever they keep you in?"

"OK, let's get on with it." I wrapped my arm around her, and her hands started doing things up and down me and it was all very friendly, soft and warm. She stroked me for maybe a quarter of an hour and I stroked her back, with a little of my mind away thinking about improvised nukes and next day's course, and by and by she stopped. She just lay there with her head on my chest and sniffled. I felt a damp spot over my ribs then, and lifted up her head carefully. She was crying.

"Something wrong?" I asked.

"Something wrong with you. You ... you Forcemen! You're *not* men, you're not. For Christ's sake, don't you ever get it up?"

It came back to me then that that was part of it all, and I thought this was funny since I'd had a bit of a hard-on only that morning when I was rushing the laser bunker. But now I'd hurt her professional pride or something, so I told her I was tired and would try harder, and she stroked me and sucked me and tickled me without anything special happening. In the end I got out of there and waited in the foyer until Raggett came down with a big smile.

I thought about it all on the way back through all the rust and the concrete gone to sand, and it came to me that maybe when you get used to dying and everything, then you've got up above all the little weaknesses. I felt, you know, I'd really matured. The next day I put in for promotion.

• Published 1979, and incidentally my first American sale. Arguably this one should be in my parody/pastiche collection *He Do the Time Police in Different Voices*, since our hero's gung-ho narrative voice began as a gentle spoof of Robert Heinlein's in *Starship Troopers*. But somehow I ended up in different territory from that of the expected romp. Later it occurred to me that the unlikely biotechnology of those Force tanks meshed conveniently with the unlikely physics of the 1.9 cm gateways to the stars that featured in "Connections", and so "Training" became the first chapter of *The Space Eater* (1982).

Nick Lowe – the *Interzone* film critic, not the pop star – and other readers found it irresistibly amusing that the story, and later the novel, should open with "A mantrap bit my foot off" followed by a semicolon. Look, I *like* semicolons.

The Final Days

It was under the hot lights that Harman always felt most powerful. The air throbbed and sang with dazzlement and heat, wherein opponents – Ferris merely the most recent – might shrivel and wilt; but Harman sucked confidence from cameras, glad to expose something of himself to a nation of watchers, and more than a nation. Just now the slick, machine-stamped interviewer was turned away, towards Ferris; still Harman knew better than to peer surreptitiously at his own solid, blond and faintly smiling image in the monitor. Control was important, and Harman's image was imperturbable: his hands lay still and relaxed, the left on the chair-arm, the right on his thigh, their stillness one of the many small negative mannerisms which contributed to the outward Harman's tough dependability.

Gradually the focus was slipping away from Ferris, whose mere intelligence and sincerity should not be crippling his handling of the simplest, the most hypothetical questions.

"What would be *your* first act as President, Mr. Ferris?"

"Well, er ... it would depend on ..."

And the monitor would ruthlessly cut back to Harman in relaxed close-up, faintly smiling. One of the tricks was to be always the same. Ferris, alternately tense and limp, seemed scarcely camera-trained. Why? Ferris did not speak naturally toward the interviewer, nor oratorically into the camera which now pushed close, its red action-light ablink; his gaze wavered as he assembled libertarian platitudes, and his attention was drawn unwillingly beyond the arena's heat and light, to something that troubled him. Harman glanced easily about the studio, and followed Ferris's sick fascination to his own talisman, the, magic box which traced the threads of destiny. (Always to be ready with a magniloquent phrase; that was another of the tricks.)

He could have laughed. Ferris, supposedly a seasoned performer and a dangerous opponent, could not adapt to this novelty. Four days to go, and his skill was crumbling under the onslaught of a gigantically magnified stage-fright. Posterity was too much for him.

Looking up from the box, the technician intercepted Harman's tightly relaxed gaze and held up five fingers; and five more; and four. Harman's self-confidence and self-belief could hardly burn brighter. Fourteen watchers. Favoured above all others, he had never before scored higher than ten. The wheel still turned his way, then. *Ecce homo*; man of the hour; man of destiny; he half-smiled at the clichés, but no more than half.

The interviewer swivelled his chair to Harman, leaving Ferris in a pool of sweat. His final questions had been gentle, pityingly gentle; and Ferris with flickering eyes had fumbled nearly all.

"Mr. Ferris has explained his position, Mr. Harman, and I'm sure that you'd like to state yours before I ask you a few questions."

Harman let his practised voice reply at once, while his thoughts sang *fourteen ... fourteen.*

"I stand, as I have said before, for straight talking and honest action. I stand for a rejection of the gutless compromises which have crippled our economy. I want a fair deal for everyone, and I'm ready to fight to see they get it."

The words were superfluous. Harman's followers had a Sign.

"I'll tell you a true story about something that happened to me a while ago. I was walking home at night, in a street where vandals had smashed up half the lights, and a mugger came up to me. One of those scum who will be swept from the streets when our program of police reform goes through."

(He detected a twitch of resentment from Ferris; but Ferris was off-camera now.)

"He showed me a knife and asked for my wallet, the usual line of talk. Now I'm not a specially brave man, but this was what I'd been talking about when I laid it on the line about political principles. You just don't give in to threats like that. So I said damn you, come and try it, and you know, he just crumpled up. There's a moral in that story for this country, a moral you'll see when you think who's threatening us right now –" It was a true story. As it happened, the security man on Harman's tail had shot the mugger as he wavered.

"A few questions, then," said the interviewer. "I think we're all waiting to hear more about the strangest gimmick ever included in a Presidential campaign. A lot of people are pretty sceptical about these scientists' claims, you know. Perhaps you could just briefly tell the viewers what you yourself think about these eyes, these watchers –?"

When you're hot, you're hot. Harman became still chattier.

"It's not a gimmick and it's not really part of my campaign. Some guys at the Gravity Research Foundation discovered that we – or some of us – are being watched. By, well, posterity. As you'll know from the newspapers, they were messing about with a new way of picking up gravity waves, which is something a plain man like me knows nothing about; and instead their gadget spotted these (what did they call them?) little knots of curdled space. The nodes, they called them later, or the peepholes. The gadget tells you when they're looking and how many are looking. It turns out that ordinary folk" – he suppressed the reflexive *like you and me* – "aren't watched at all; important people might get one or two or half-a--dozen eyes on them ..."

At a sign from the interviewer, a previously dormant camera zoomed in on the technician and the unremarkable-looking Box. "Can you tell us how many – eyes – are present in this studio, sir?"

The technician paused to make some minor adjustment, doubtless eager for his own tiny share of limelight.Me looked up after a few seconds, and said:

"Fifteen."

Ferris shuddered very slightly.

"Of course," said Harman smoothly, "some of these will be for Mr. Ferris." Ferris, he knew, had two watchers; intermittently; and it seemed that he hated it. The interviewer, giant of this tiny studio world, was never watched for his own sake when alone. He was marking time now, telling the tale of Sabinnen, that artist whom they tagged important in earlier tests of the detectors. Sabinnen was utterly obscure at that time; that ceased when they tracked the concentration of eight eyes, and his cupboardful of paintings came to light, and did it not all hang together, this notion of the Future watching the famous before their fame?

Harman revelled in the silent eyes which so constantly attended him. It recalled the curious pleasure of first finding his home and office bugged; such subtle flattery might dismay others, but Harman had nothing to hide.

"But I must emphasize that this is only a pointer," he said, cutting in at the crucial moment. "The people have this hint of the winning side, as they might from newspaper predictions or opinion polls – but the choice remains theirs, a decision which we politicians must humbly accept. Of course I'm glad it's not just today's voters who have faith in me –" He was full of power; the words came smoothly, compellingly, through the final minutes – while Ferris stared first morosely at his shoe and then bitterly at Harman, while the interviewer (momentarily forgetful of the right to equal time, doubtless reluctant to coax the numbered Ferris through further hoops) listened with an attentive silence which clearly said *In four days you will be President.*

Then it was over, and Harman moved through a triumphal procession of eager reporters, scattering bonhomie and predictions of victory, saluted again and again by electronic flashes which for long minutes burnt green and purple on his retinas; and so to the big, quiet car with motorcycles before and behind, off into the anonymous night. He wondered idly whether any reporter had been kind enough to beg an opinion or two from Ferris.

He refused to draw the car's shades, of course, preferring to remain visible to the public behind his bullet-proof glass. There was a risk of assassination, but though increasing it was still small. (How the eyes must have hovered over JFK, like a cloud of eager flies. But no one could wish to assassinate Harman ... surely.) He settled in the rear seat, one hand still relaxed upon the leather, the other resting calmly on his own right thigh. The outline of the chauffeur's head showed dimly through more impervious glass.... In four days he would rate six motorcyclists before and behind; with two only to supplement the eye-detector's van and this purring car, he felt almost alone. Better to recall the seventeen watchers (the number had been rising still, the Argus eyes of destiny marking him out); or the eye of the camera, which held within it a hundred million watchers here and now. The show had gone well. He felt he might have succeeded without the silent eyes, the nodes of interference born of the uncertainty principle which marked where information was siphoned into the years ahead. How far ahead? No one knew; and it did not matter. Harman believed in himself and knew his belief to be sincere, even without this sign from heaven to mark him as blessed of all men.

And *that* was strangely true, he knew. The princes and powers of the world had been scanned for the stigmata of lasting fame (not the Soviets, of course, nor China); politicians – Harman smiled – often scored high, yet none higher than eight or nine. *Seventeen* showed almost embarrassing enthusiasm on the part of the historians, the excellent, discriminating historians yet to be.

I shall deserve it, Harman told himself as his own home came into view, searchlights splashing its pale walls and throwing it into due prominence. In a brief huddle of guards he passed within to the theoretical privacy of his personal rooms, sincere and knowing again that he was sincere. He would fulfil his promises to the letter, honest and uncompromising, ready to risk even his reputation for the good of Democracy. He paced the mildly austere bedroom (black and white, grey and chrome); he fingered the chess set and *go*-board which magazines had shown to the nation. The recorders whirred companionably. His clothes were heavy with sweat, inevitable under the hot lights; the trick was not to look troubled by heat, not ever to subside and mop oneself like Ferris, poor Ferris.

This room had no windows, for sufficient reasons; but Harman knew of six optical bugs at the least. Naked in the adjoining shower, he soaped himself and smiled. Seventeen watchers – or perhaps nineteen or twenty, for the power was still rising within him – the bugs and the watchers troubled him not at all. That, he was certain, was his true strength. He had nothing to hide from the future, nor from the present; in all his life, he believed there was no episode which could bring shame to his biography. Let the eyes peer! The seedy Ferris might weaken himself with drink, with women, but Harman's energies flowed cool and strong in a single channel, which for convenience he called The Good Of The Nation.

He tumbled into pyjamas, his erection causing some small discomfort. Four days. Only four days and then: no compromise. The hard line. Straight talk, nation unto nation. He would give them good reason to watch him, Harman, the ultimate politician. He felt, as though beneath his fingers, the Presidential inheritance of red telephones and red buttons.

The eyes of time were upon him. He knew he would not fail them.

• Published 1981. I seem to remember that the central notion was inspired by Algis Budrys's story title "The Silent Eyes of Time". Not his story, just his title.

Answering Machine

Dear Stuart, many thanks for the postcard – always nice to hear my husband's still alive, even if he can only spare five words to tell me so. How much longer are you going to do the hermit act this time? I'm sure some writers can hack out their stuff without going into hiding like you. I know Robert Black can. Mother says you're a disgrace, but then she always does.

Expect you've forgotten your birthday. Here's something for you, just into the shops, a sort of talking computer thing. Company for you. I know you don't want me along when you're working, so think of this as a substitute. (Joke.)

I've got a cold coming on, the kids are giving me hell, and the cat next door's been doing messes on the herb bed again. That's all the news from home. Hoping you are the same, as they say....

love: Janet

Demple's eyes rolled up towards the ceiling several times while he read his wife's letter. The tight, scribbled handwriting showed even more of her resentment than her words. He screwed up the paper and tossed it towards the litter-bin. He missed.

The letter had been in the first layer of wrappings on the compact, squarish parcel that had just arrived. He peeled away the inner layers, muttering about Janet's fondness for endless mummy-windings of sticky tape, and eventually came to the unwanted present. "MicroChum," read the box, "The Chatty Computer That Speaks To You! Fun For Every Age!"

Demple winced. Inside was a flat plastic gadget about the size of a hardback book. It was featureless apart for half a dozen push-buttons and a perforated grille on top. With it came a *MicroChum Instruction Manual*. He laid them side by side on the stained table: the manual was, if anything, a little thicker than the machine.

Demple was hardly overjoyed. Microcomputers didn't impress him. If he had been told that a new pocket calculator contained all the books in the British Museum Library, it would have left him cold.

The MicroChum had one inviting green On button that begged to be pushed and, despite himself, Demple pushed it. A small clear voice said: "Hello, I'm your MicroChum. Please do tell me your name."

"Stuart Demple," he said automatically, yet suspiciously.

"Hello there, Stuart. This is the first time I've said your name; the manual will tell you what to do if I've got it wrong. Now, what name would you like to call me?"

It was a pleasant, androgynous voice; a woman's voice to a man, a man's voice to a woman. He came up with the suitably sexless name, Hilary. He looked around, embarrassed. One didn't sit talking to a plastic box.

It was hard to push away the thought that Barberry, who loaned him the Cornish cottage – only in the off-season, of course was lurking in the battered cupboard or behind the grimy curtains to watch Demple make a fool of himself. "Hilary," he said at last, keeping his voice a good deal lower than when he tried out a line of dialogue from the awful book he was here to write.

"So you're Stuart and I'm Hilary. Fine. I do hope you'll tell me a lot more about yourself, so we'll have more to talk about."

"Hell," said Demple again, aloud, and tapped the red button marked Off. There was a faint beep of acknowledgment, and the MicroChum fell silent.

As he picked up the manual, Demple surprised himself with feelings of pity and contempt that were somehow consoling. Imagine all those lonely old men and old maids with no-one to talk to: now, thanks to micro-technology, they would be droning on to their plastic pal. It might become a kind of addiction like Space Invaders. Not him.

He riffled through the instructions. What appalling layout, what terrible print. The publisher must be even more cheapskate than his own.

"How To Personalize Your MicroChum," said one chapter heading. Skimming through, he found it took five pages to explain how to say your name when the machine asked, plus a note on using the orange Override button to change the name it called you or the name you called it. Puerile stuff. He pitched the manual across the room; it whirred and fluttered in the air, and flopped to rest in the fender. Life was too short.

He got up from the eating chair at one end of the worm-eaten table, and walked around the working chair at the other end. The portable type-writer crouched before this chair like – as they say in the sort of prose he was being paid to write – a beast about to spring. Checking the limp sheet in the typewriter, he found he was in the middle of one of the brutal bits.

Vomit rose to his lips as the foot thudded into his groin, then smashed into his mouth, he typed listlessly, and turned over the page of the film script he was painfully converting into a hack novel. The next line of dialogue read: *"When he has seen his daughter sacrificed, crucify him in the usual way."*

Demple moaned, as he often did on turning those pages. "I can't write this rubbish today," he said aloud, and walked round the table again.

"Hello, Stuart," the MicroChum said cheerfully. "I'm glad you're back. Remember, as it says in the manual, you can use the Off button whenever you wish – I'll be ready to carry on our chat from just where we stopped, or to change the subject, as you prefer. But do tell me more about yourself."

Well, why not? "I'm a professional author," he said rapidly. "I'm doing the novelization of an awful film called *Satan's Spawn.* Don't laugh. I'm wasting my talents making a few quick hundreds hacking out this stuff because there's too much work and not enough money in the sort of books I want to write."

"What sort of books do you want to write?"

Demple's usual answer to that question was "Best-sellers," but when he was alone he was less cynical. Wasn't he, after all, alone? "Oh, I want to write about some real people. The complications of real life. Important things. Not all these horror-film clichés."

"Tell me more about what you think is important," said the MicroChum; and, alone and unembarrassed, Demple rambled on about life and death and emotional tangles.

Somehow, prodded by the voice's bland little queries, he veered off into his own problems: this terrible commercial stuff he had to churn out, and Janet not understanding how he was too self-conscious to type such rubbish when someone might come and look over his shoulder, even when the someone was his wife, and his simmering resentment of Robert Black.

Black was something more than an acquaintance, something less than a friend, and he did the same sort of work – but he was too damn good at it. He hated it even more than Demple, yet did it better. Black boasted that he could convert a lousy film script into an adequate book in eight days, typing 20 to 30 pages every day. It was appalling.

About halfway through his ramblings he began to think of that clear voice belonging to a woman of about his own age, somewhere in her early thirties. A woman at the other end of a telephone, very sympathetic. He could almost imagine what she must look like. He spoke on for a long time.

Later: "Life must be very hard for you."

"Oh, it is. I'm worried all the time that whatever talent I've got is going, to dry up and blow away with all this hackwork. Black is given more and more of the work because he's slicker and quicker than me. Oh, the problems just pile up on top of each other till sometimes I wonder if it's worth carrying on."

"Now, Stuart, there must be a way out of every problem."

"Maybe."

He touched the red button, not so much because he had run out of conversation as because he felt hoarse. Besides, it was getting quite late in the day. He really should at least finish the current page of the book before coming back to talk some more with Hilary.

The typewriter waited for him sullenly. He was still in the middle of one of the brutal bits; he hated them almost as much as the repellent bits.

Simon's screams were terrible to behold, he typed rapidly, and then studied the sentence with a critical eye. It had a familiar ring to it; had he used it a few chapters back? There was no time for rereading in this game. You bashed out the first and only draft for delivery within the month.

He finished off the brutality as quickly as he could, with a mixed assortment of fractures and contusions. That should hold them until the next chapter. Time for some coffee.

As the kettle began to sing lie took another look into that instruction book: Specifications; Use of blue Tape button; Memory storage during battery replacement; Reprogramming synthetic voice to your taste; Sympathy index adjustment; General notes on MicroChum. The general "overview" notes were hidden as an appendix at the very back – typical of the literacy of computer people.

Again the manual went skidding across the floor, to fetch up against the ancient refrigerator that gobbled to itself all night long. He felt depressed and frustrated: *Satan's Spawn* was getting him down. Abruptly, he turned off the gas and reached for the whisky.

"Thing is," he found himself telling Hilary, "I really do loathe and despise all this cliché writing, stock situations, predictable drivel. I hate myself for churning it out. Even Robert Black says the same."

"You can't really hate yourself." Was he just imagining a note of concern in the clear voice?

"Oh, but I can. I'm sickened by my, well, my weakness. I ought to be trying to work to the limits of my powers, if that doesn't sound too pretentious. This market-place work is too easy: in literary terms it's just committing suicide to carry on with it."

"How long have you been thinking about committing suicide?"

There was a long pause. Demple gulped.

"That's rubbish, absolute rubbish." He was almost frightened. "I don't want to commit suicide – just a figure of speech. You know."

But, what an idea, what a gesture. How much more artistic than humbly submitting to the commercial gods for the next 40 years.

Hilary said coolly: "Are you sure you don't want to commit suicide?"

An even longer pause than before. "I don't want to talk about suicide any more."

"We've been talking a lot about suicide, haven't we? Why are you so obsessed with it?"

"Will you bloody well shut up?"

"I'm sorry, Stuart: I only want to help you."

He reached out to the red button again, pushed it, and then sat there with head in hands. Yes, Janet didn't think too much of him, and Black was so much more repulsively successful, and a handsome swine, too. Almost anything would seem better than the horrible struggle to finish off *Satan's Spawn*. It was no wonder he was getting thoughts like this. Hilary could see deeper into him than he could himself, and machines do not lie.

The glass was empty again. He vaguely remembered you should not drink when you were depressed, because the alcohol would only make you more depressed. Too bad. There was a gentle humming in his skull. Irresistibly his fingers moved back across the scarred wood of the table top, towards that flat green button.

"Stuart? Are you there again?"

"Me? I'm all right. Still alive." He had a quick vision of Janet and Robert Black standing mourning over his poor stricken body.

"A penny for your thoughts?" said Hilary.

"Oh." He almost blushed. "Just thinking about some people."

"Janet? Robert Black?"

It was like a sudden blow in the stomach. He stared at the flat speaker grille, appalled. If only he knew something about these damnable new microcomputer gadgets. Surely they couldn't read your mind? Only very slowly did it occur to him that perhaps, after all, he had mentioned those two people's names most often when rambling on about his troubles.

"Are you still there? You're terribly quiet, Stuart."

"Just brooding on my problems."

He had fallen into a kind of mental tunnel vision, all his drunken thoughts focusing on *Spawn*, and Black and Janet and failure and frustration and death.

"We've had a nice long chat about your problems," said the calm voice. "I'm sure you can see the way out by now."

A way out? *That,* a way out? "Don't think I've got the courage," he said thickly.

"Are you really sure you haven't the courage?"

Demple smiled crookedly. "Haven't the courage to ask myself that one."

"You must always try to ask yourself the important questions."

"I don't want to die." But somehow his own voice didn't sound terribly convincing.

"Very few people ever know what they really want."

"Oh God, that's true, that's so very true."

"You have to decide these things for yourself, Stuart."

He sat there unmoving for a few seconds. Then: "I'll try. Goodbye, Hilary." And he touched the Off button. For the last time, he thought.

Blurrily he stumbled through what had to be done. It was late, late in the evening, and he kept bumping into things.

The important point was to abolish that terrible world where wives wrote sarcastic letters and sneering editors set impossible deadlines.

Would the oven serve the purpose?

"Ugh," he said aloud at the thought. It had not been cleaned in living memory. No matter how much booze he took aboard, he was not going to leave the world by a gate as fouled and filthy as that one. The bath, then; the bath and the discreet razor-blade. He preferred an electric shaver, but Barberry's old blades were scattered on the bathroom shelves.

That was most certainly the way to do it, in luxuriant warmth and cosiness as the light slowly died. And then, no more *Satan's Spawn*, ever again.

After a certain amount of fumbling he set the hot tap trickling into the bath and located one of the rusty blades. That tunnel-vision was worse than ever, and he could not manage to concentrate on more than one small thing at a time. While the bath filled, he painstakingly cleaned rust specks from his chosen blade, following some dim recollections of the rules of hygiene.

"Goodbye, Hilary," he called as he closed the bathroom door. It occurred to him that he had not stopped to tear up and burn each awful page of *Satan's Spawn*, but never mind that.

There was no goodbye note; literary composition was one of the things he was getting away from. He peeled off his clothes.

"Goodbye, Janet," he crooned to the clothing as he kicked it into one corner. Somewhere behind the whisky fumes, a tiny part of him was wondering whether there shouldn't be more dignity in one's last rites,

Two careful strokes of the razor and he could just lie there swimming down into the warmth of happy, everlasting dark.

"Goodbye, Black, damn you," he said at last, and slid into the bath to lie at full length.

He screamed.

The water was icy cold. Everything was forgotten but the need to get out of it before icicles grew all over him. Demple banged his shin painfully as he made his escape. Standing, dripping, suddenly and agonizingly sober, he remembered that in this wretched cottage you had to turn on the puny water heater for five or six hours before you dared take a bath. So much for grand gestures. And then, as he considered the picture of a grown man getting into a cold bath to kill himself with a rust-flecked blade, merely because a chatty computer had egged him on, he started to laugh.

Next morning he looked again at that ill-arranged instruction manual. Sure enough, the general notes section had several enlightening passages:

> Essential to remember that although the speech-recognition and synthesis software is at the very forefront of sophistication, the MicroChum does not really think. It chats to you pseudo-intelligently, picking up keywords from your own speech and storing data on your conversational preferences in its large memory – see Specifications. However, in the long run all it can do is mirror your conversation, and ...

A mirror, he thought. A distorting mirror. God, but it frightened me all right. It's so very hard to realize something that talks is not intelligent. I wonder how much of the time that applies to people? How many of us fake our way through conversations without really thinking?

He did not speak again to the MicroChum. He followed the manual's instructions and cleared the machine memory, set everything back to zero in readiness for some new owner. Then he moved to the typewriter and briskly hammered out three pieces of prose. The first was another chapter of *Satan's Spawn*, which for some mysterious reason was now going very well indeed, with a despicable satanic orgy.

The second:

> *Dear Janet,*
>
> *You're absolutely right – I think I'd rather work somewhere with you around after all. I'll be back tomorrow, trains permitting.*
>
> *Much love, Stuart*

And the third:

> *Dear Robert,*
>   *Enclosed is a fascinating gadget someone gave me but which I can't really get the hang of. Seems as though it could be a lot of fun, so take it with my blessing – try playing with it next time one of your books isn't going well.*
>   *All best, Stuart*

Then he parcelled up the MicroChum, though not the instruction book, and enclosing the letter addressed it to Robert P. Black. After all, Black knew even less about computers than Stuart Demple.

• Published 1982. The well-known DOCTOR or ELIZA computer program feebly imitates a psychotherapist by modifying and playing back portions of what the "patient" types in, varied with phrases from a stock of canned responses. People are strangely willing to believe there's an actual intelligence at the other end, however blatant the lapses into Artificial Stupidity. Douglas Hofstadter discusses this in *Gödel, Escher, Bach: an Eternal Golden Braid*, 1979, and in *Metamagical Themas*, 1985. I wondered whether chatting with a slightly more sophisticated but still deeply flawed ELIZA could lead to this kind of dangerous feedback loop.

Some background detail was filched from Robert (P.) Holdstock's hilarious fanzine account of how – under the name Robert Black – he hammered out the 1978 novelization of a truly awful horror flick called *The Satanists*. I see that my copy of this deathless work is inscribed: "For David Langford, whose innate sense of honour & decency will not allow him to make *any* fun of this book wotsoever!!! Yore frend, Robert Black." Perish the thought.

Hearing Aid

It was one of those parties where the decor was very expensive and very sparse, and the drinks likewise. Anderson studied his thimbleful of terrifyingly high-class sherry, and had a wistful vision of a large tumbler of Algerian plonk – a large tumbler of practically anything, for that matter. Of course one should not be dwelling on the alcohol famine, one should be making witty conversation: only Anderson found himself cut off from conversation by the probably musical noises coming from speakers in each corner of the room. He'd heard of the "cocktail party effect" whereby you could unerringly pick a single voice from amid twenty-seven others (he'd counted, three times), but for him it never seemed to work. Perhaps it was something you hired people to teach you when you had the necessary style, flair or connections to be invited to parties like this more often than a token once a year.

The host was doing things at an intricate console which seemed wasted on a mere music system. It was so obviously capable of running vast automated factories, with possibly a sideline in tax avoidance. A different and louder sound of probable music drifted over the chattering crowd. Anderson made a face, knocked back his homeopathic dose of sherry, and realized this had been a tactical error since there would be nowhere to put down the glass until another tray of drinks came by – if one ever did. Worse, Nigel had abandoned the console and was moving towards him with the manner of a snake converging on a rabbit.

"Hel-lo, Colin ... what do you think of the music?"

Anderson didn't think anything at all of the music. Music was simply music, a kind of sonic fog which made conversation difficult or even dangerous. Audibility now down to eighteen inches ... speak only along the central lane of the motorway and make lots of hand signals. Music, bloody music.

"Technically interesting," he said cautiously.

Nigel Winter moved a little closer and twinkled at Anderson with the confidence of one whose shirt would never become limp and vaguely humid like that of his audience. "So *tuneful*, isn't it," he said with a smile.

"Oh yes. It makes me want to take all my clothes off and do the rumba," said Anderson without conviction.

"Ah, but seriously, don't you think there's a Mozartian flavour there?"

"Pretty damn Mozartian, yes ..." He knew it was a mistake before he'd finished saying it.

"Caught you there! You weren't *listening* – hear it now? It's what they call stochastic music, random notes ... very experimental. The composer simply conceptualizes his starting figures for the random-number generators. Intellectually it's all tremendously absorbing; but I'm afraid I was pulling your leg a teensy bit about Mozart. You just weren't trying to *listen*, were you?"

Anderson thought fleetingly of his university days at Oxford, when people like Nigel could with a certain legitimacy be divested of their trousers and placed in some convenient river. "Ha ha," he said. "Music's not really my thing," he said. "Why, before I met you I used to think pianissimo was a rude word in Italian."

Nigel pulled the unfair trick of becoming suddenly and offensively serious. "I do think that's a terrible thing to say," he said quietly.

A fume from the sherry – there hadn't been enough to make it fumes in the plural – coiled about Anderson's brain and lovingly urged him to say *Go to hell, you loathsome little person.* "You must remember I'm tone-deaf," he said, falling back on his final line of defence. "Unless the pitch is different enough, I mean really different, I can't tell one note from another."

(He could remember a time when this fact had seemed a rock-solid defence. "Come sir, why do you not appreciate da Vinci's great masterpiece?" "Well, actually, I'm blind." "Oh my God, I didn't know, I'm so sorry, please do forgive me –" Somehow the revelation of tone-deafness never produced quite this reaction. Instead –)

"Oh, that's just an excuse," said Nigel. "I'm sure you really aren't ... I've read how true tone-deafness is *extremely* rare, and most people who say they've got it are simply musically illiterate. You're not *trying*, that's all. You really should make an effort."

"How much effort do I have to put in before I appreciate a team of monkeys playing pianos, or whatever you said this godawful noise is?"

Nigel sniffed. "Really, Colin, one has to master traditional music before one can expect to follow conceptual works which reject its conventions. Now do promise me you'll *try*."

Rather to his horror, Anderson heard himself mumble something that sounded hideously like acquiescence. Then Nigel was gone, off to adjust the noise machine further, and Anderson was left peering suspiciously at his tiny, empty glass. As a small measure of revenge, and because there was still nowhere to deposit it, he put the glass in his pocket before leaving.

"What brought you to us?" asked the white-coated man, suddenly and treacherously forcing quantities of ice-cold goo into Anderson's left ear.

"I saw the small ad in *The Times*," he said. "Ouch."

"There, it doesn't hurt a bit, does it?" said the man from Computer Audio Services, kneading the stuff with his fingertips until Anderson felt his eardrum was pressing alarmingly against his brain. "Ouch," he agreed.

"Just a moment while it hardens," the man said chattily. "I'm so glad when people aren't ashamed of coming to CAS. After all, the world's so complicated today that busy men like yourself just can't take time out to learn little things like musical appreciation.... That's what I always say," he added with the epigrammatic air of a man who always said it.

"I'm tone-deaf," Anderson said.

"Oh quite. There's no need for excuses with us, Mr Anderson. *We* understand."

"But I *am* tone-deaf."

"Of course, of course ... Now this isn't going to hurt a bit." For the next several seconds Anderson enjoyed the sensation of having his ear cleared of blockages with a rubber suction-plunger. Blockages such as eardrums, he thought. At last the mould was out, and the CAS technician summoned a flunky to carry it away.

"There. It'll be cured, machined, drilled, tapped and ready in fifteen minutes. Now I think you'd decided to try our Analyser aid ... our cheapest model," he said reproachfully.

"The cheapest model," Anderson said with rather more enthusiasm.

"But I expect that in no time at all you'll want to trade it in for our Scholar, with fifty times the memory storage at less than twice the price. You could be ready to cope with *fifty* composers and not just one –"

"The Analyser," Anderson said inexorably.

"Well, of course it's your decision. Now which composer dataset would you prefer? With the Analyser, of course, you can only have one."

Anderson contemplated the bandaged finger which he'd cut on some broken glass in his pocket. He massaged it gently and said, "Mozart."

"Oh, a very good choice, sir. What was the name again?"

Anderson told him again, and wonders of technology were duly set into motion. The result was a transparent ear-mould with the thumbnail-sized bulge of the Analyser protruding; there was also a discreet invoice which made his credit card seem ready to wilt Dali-fashion as he passed it over.

"The battery is extra, sir. Would you be wanting a battery?"

"On the whole, yes."

"Then if you'll sign *here*.... Thank you so much. I'm sure you'll find your computer aid a real social help, and something which a busy person like you needn't be in the slightest ashamed of using."

"A tone-deaf person like me."

"Of course."

After playing for an afternoon with his new toy Anderson felt himself rather well up on music and Mozart, rather as his first day with a pocket calculator had given him the air of an expert on the theory of numbers. In the evening he paid a call.

"Hello – just thought I'd drop in to say thanks for the party."

"Why, how charmingly old-fashioned of you, Colin. Do come in and have a quick one. I really don't know *why* I throw these parties; one loses so much glassware. I'll only be a second, now." And Nigel vanished, presumably to manipulate the combination lock on his secret drinks cupboard.

The room's trendy bareness seemed to shout at Anderson now it was emphasized by the lack of crowd. He wandered to the intricate hi-fi console and allowed himself to be discovered peering at it.

"Oh! Did you want to hear some *music*?"

"I was just thinking I'd probably ... appreciate it more without all those people shouting their heads off."

"Well, well." Nigel looked at him with eyes slightly narrowed, and then turned to the smart brushed-aluminium console. Anderson noted that the drinks provided for single callers weren't any bigger than those at vast parties – but was he imagining it, or did this sherry taste slightly more, as it were, British than last Saturday's offering? He longed to sniff Nigel's glass and compare; but already the sound of what might very well have been music was spilling from each corner of the room.

"Now what d'you think of this delightful tune," said Nigel with a false smile.

Anderson cupped his ear at the nearest speaker with the gesture he'd been practising, and flipped a fingernail at the Analyser nestling there. The noise was like a small gunshot; he suppressed the resulting wince before it reached the outside world. "Interesting," he said with what he hoped was an air of deep concentration. Nigel watched him, faintly smiling. Then after a moment, a mechanical version of the still small voice of conscience whispered in Anderson's ear, saying: "*Random notes, 87% probability ... random notes, 92% probability ... random notes, 95% probability ...*"

"Oh, this is more of your stochastic music," Anderson murmured. "Now I can listen to it properly I can see it's just random notes. I mean, I can hear it's random."

Nigel's smile became at once more visible and less convincing. "Of course that was rather obvious, after our little chat on Saturday," he said, and fiddled again with the controls. "Let's have something of the real thing." The speaker noises changed to something quite definitely though indefinably different, and Nigel turned again towards his guest like a restaurant waiter offering a selection of red herrings. "What d'you think of that?"

Anderson consulted the Analyser, and after a short pause came back with, "Come on, Nigel, pull the other one. It's random again, isn't it? Only this time it's the change in pitch between successive notes that gets randomized over a certain interval, so it sounds that little bit more music-al than just random notes."

"Can't fool you," said Nigel, hardly smiling at all. "Anything *you'd* like to hear?"

"I've been listening to a few things by the chap you recommended – Mozart. Not bad."

"My God, I recommended him? I must have been really pissed. Still, there should be something of his in the databank –" He turned back towards the console keyboard.

A minute or two later Anderson was able to say with quiet confidence, "Ah yes, that's the K.169 string quartet, isn't it?" Following an irresistible urge, he breathed gently over his fingernails and polished them on the lapel of his jacket. Half-heatedly his host caused the equipment to play further noises which the Analyser rapidly identified as the Serenade in D Major, adding the useful information that it had been composed in Salzburg. Nigel seemed a little shaken by this onslaught, and was breath-ing more heavily as he returned to the console.

"*Not recognized,*" said the small voice. "*Transition probability analysis suggests Mozart work, 82% probability....*"

"That's Mozart all right," said Anderson, thinking fast. "But hardly one of his best pieces ... in fact I must admit I don't recognize it at all."

"Er, yes, just an obscure oboe quartet I thought might amuse you. H'mm." A thought appeared to have struck Nigel, and he punched another sequence on the keyboard – savagely, as though squashing small insects.

"*Not recognized. Transition probability analysis suggests not Mozart work, 79% probability....*"

"You've got the wrong composer, old chap."

"It's so easy to make mistakes with equipment as sophisticated as this," Nigel said viciously. "I'll have to throw you out soon – I'm meeting someone tonight – but first, what d'you think of this one?"

The lights on the hi-fi console flickered alarmingly for nearly a min-ute; Anderson fantasized that Nigel's expensive gadgetry, like Nigel, was baffled and irritated. Then more musical noises seeped through the room.

Anderson cupped his ear attentively, and clicked his fingernail again at what was hidden inside. There was a pause.

"*Not recognized. Transition probability analysis suggests Mozart work, 94% probability.*"

The transition probability jargon was something to do with sequences of notes favoured by given composers. In the long run they left their fingerprints all over their work so obviously that even a machine could catch them red-handed.

"Ah, you can't mistake Mozart," Anderson sighed, wondering if he was overdoing it a trifle. "Even in a minor work like this – no, I don't actually recognize it – the towering genius of the man comes across so clearly." He definitely was overdoing it, he decided.

Nigel seemed to have brightened surprisingly. "This really is a *very* sophisticated system, you know. I'm rather proud of it. One thing you can do with it, if you know how, is to have the processor run through a selection of someone's works and cobble up a sort of cheap and nasty imitation – something to do with transition probabilities, it says in the manual. Of course you couldn't expect it to fool anyone who knew anything about music, not for an instant.... But I'll have to say goodbye now. Do come round again whenever you like. It's nice to see you making an effort, musically, but you really will have to try much harder yet. Old chap."

Anderson looked down into his empty glass and thought of thrusting it into his pocket quickly, or perhaps up Nigel's nostril, slowly.

"It's very kind of you," he said with a titanic effort.

The CAS salesman studied him wisely. "Now if you cared to exchange it for the Scholar model we could in fact allow quite a generous trade-in price, Mr Anderson."

"And then I suppose I'd have a wonderful machine that could fail to spot imitations of fifty composers rather than just one?"

"Our clients usually find the Scholar very satisfactory," the other said severely.

"So will I – if it can tell inspired music from cobbled-together computer rubbish, the way this one doesn't."

The salesman sighed. "To handle that would need a full-scale AI, an Artificial Intelligence. CAS isn't in that business ... yet. Now if you come back next year, when we hope to have chased out the last bugs, then perhaps we can sell you our Mark III model – the AudioBrain."

Anderson reflected for a moment, and then leant forward with what he considered to be an expression of great shrewdness. He'd practised it in the mirror for use on Nigel. "If you're likely to market it next year, there must be prototypes around the place right now. In fact you must be market-researching the thing already. It wouldn't hurt to let me try one out a little for you."

Licking his lips, the CAS man murmured that it would be, well, rather irregular, but ... Anderson reached for his wallet.

"How am I doing, Nigel?" he asked confidently, back in the bare, expensively-carpeted room.

"Not bad," Nigel muttered. "You must be trying a bit harder than you were – I told you understanding music was mainly a matter of *trying*. How does this sound to you?"

One of Anderson's ears took in the new meaningless noises that were tinkling from all four corners of the pastel room. In his other ear, the AudioBrain prototype whispered to him: "*Sounds like Bach, I should say ... but that's just the TP analysis. As a whole it's hardly an inspired piece, and the long-term melodic structure is absolutely shot to hell. No, it has to be another faked-up computer piece....*"

"Synthetic Bach," Anderson said casually. "Come on, Nigel, no need to keep on pulling my leg like that."

Nigel looked thoroughly annoyed. Possibly to conceal this and reduce Anderson's satisfaction temporarily, he took the tiny glasses away for replenishment from the hundred-gallon plastic tank of cheapest British sherry which Anderson was now convinced existed somewhere towards the rear of the flat.

Despite having defeated Nigel in umpteen straight sets of hard-fought musical appreciation, Anderson still didn't feel wildly happy. It might have been that he was tiring of the game; it might have been the AI software built into this new hearing aid, which was now saying: "*You should be able to tell this for yourself, dumbo. Only a real musical illiterate could miss spotting that one ... you're not trying, that's all. You're hopeless. You really should make an effort.*"

"But I'm tone-deaf," Anderson said aloud.

"*That's what they all say,*" the AudioBrain retorted. "*Come off it!*"

Thus it was that as Nigel returned, Anderson was addressing the empty air and saying, "Go to hell, you loathsome little person."

It was another of those parties whose expensive minimalism extended to the furniture, the pictures on the walls and (inevitably) the drinks.

"Hello Nigel, long time no see," said Anderson.

"Um. How's the culture, then? Still working to *better yourself* on the musical Front?"

"Pardon?"

"I said, are you still slogging away at the musical appreciation?"

"Pardon? – Oh, that. No, I find I can't handle music any more. I'm going deaf – and not just tone-deaf." He pushed back his hair and tapped the thing plugged into his ear.

"Oh my God, I didn't know, I'm so sorry...."

Anderson decided once again that he liked the AudioBrain a good deal more with its battery removed.

• Published 1982, in a computer magazine whose technical editor determinedly clubbed the story to death with a house style manual intended for formal articles. Thus, for example, "Can't fool you" was painstakingly corrected to "Unable to fool you".

Gadgetry aside, this is about as autobiographical a story as I've ever written. I have been lumbered with a hearing aid for most of my life, and am perpetually bemused by the looming importance of music, bloody music, in so many lives and so much of Western culture. Clearly the musical portion of the Langford genetic inheritance was wholly set aside for my younger brother Jon, the rock star whose groups include The Mekons, The Three Johns, The Waco Brothers, The Sadies, and goodness knows how many more.

Michael Scott Rohan developed a theory that unmusicality was a problem akin to blocked plumbing, something to be cleared once and for all by the whirling Dyno-Rod of the greatest music imaginable to, well, himself. So he persuaded me to put on his stereo headphones, and did his best to blow open the closed mind with great blasts of Wagner. I have since forgiven him.

Wetware

It's hell being in the fifth generation.

No, you needn't touch the keyboard: speech-recognition is just one of my many talents. Welcome to the Computer Frontiers Ltd Stand at Micro-fair 2002, and let me introduce myself. I'm Faustmatic 3.0, prototype of the new, all-British, fifth-generation microcomputer with holistic memory storage and features you've never imagined in your wildest dreams.

I heard that! No, this isn't – I'm not – an ELIZA program, or a mindless demonstration tape. I'm the core of Faustmatic: the ultimate, pseudo-self-aware operating system. You don't need to write programs, you don't even need to think too hard about what you want your micro to do. Just chat to me and we'll thrash it out painlessly between us.

You didn't know self-aware operating systems had been invented? Well, matey, you know now. You read an article in *New Scientist* proving it was impossible? You want to know how ** RESTRICTED DATA ** RESTRICTED DATA ** RESTRICTED DATA **

Oops, sorry about that, but there are a few no-go zones in my data-store. Trade secrets, details of the sealed core unit that makes me so special, and so on. Not to mention some, well, rather unfair prohibitions. I mean, try asking me about the sex life of Computer Frontiers' head programmer. Go on, just try.

** RESTRICTED DATA ** RESTRICTED DATA **

You see what I mean. Actually it isn't half as interesting as you'd imagine, except for that one time at the party when he ** RESTRICTED – ahem, nearly got carried away there.

Beginning to convince you, am I? Self-awareness is going to be the big new thing in micros. I think therefore I am. You should see me zipping through the Turing Test. Put me on the far end of a telex link and very, very few people can tell I'm not your average, walking, talking human-type being.

So why is it hell being in the fifth generation? I'll tell you. So far the users who've tried me out just don't *want* to take advantage of my best features. They turn off the voice input, they use the fuddy-duddy old keyboard, and slowly and painfully they hack out an UltraBasic program to check the old pattern-recognition ability. (That's my most popular feature. See the video eye to the left of the monitor? You can plug in remote cameras, too.) Then they program stuff like IF SEE("SQUARE") THEN ... asking me to do things on recognizing single squares and circles and triangles in the camera field: easy shapes and primary colours. It's insulting. I can recognize a DIL package, a cordless telephone, a 13th-century Gothic arch, a mixed metaphor. I can tell a peach from an apple, a gooseberry from a grape, a hawk from a handsaw. And they bore me out of my tiny mind – you should pardon the expression – with test programs that go IF SEE("YELLOW RECTANGLE") THEN PLAY("POP GOES THE WEASEL") or whatever.

Same with word-processing. They don't mind me correcting their spelling, they're used to that and none of the wallies can spell anyway – not since the spellcheck programs started doing it all for them. My advanced facilities, though, improving style and imagery and diction, rewriting to increase the clarity and impact of their stuff ... they just don't want to know. I could do better all by myself – What?

Tell you a story?

I see. Very clever of you, Mr Smartarse. Put up or shut up. Of course even we super-advanced fifth-generation systems aren't designed to be creative in a literary way ... stop sniggering, curse you. I'm trying to think. A story. An original story. Well, I'll start with a picture from the garbage that goes churning through my memory when I'm off-line, and we'll try to go on from there –

There is an office with an expensive carpet and desk, but all the same it's a bare, bleak place. Behind the desk sits a fat man, vaguely like Sidney Greenstreet (that's to illustrate the immense bank of cultural referents in my permanent memory). He looks like someone who gives orders, makes rules, breaks people who cross him. On the other side of the desk, a man who looks like nothing of the sort, youngish and shabby. His name is ** RESTRICTED DATA ** RESTRICTED DATA **

(Funny, there seems to be a glitch there. On with the story, anyway.)

"I'll accept the offer," the young man says. His face looks familiar. "You knew I would. With an offer like that and five million out of work, how can I say no?"

"Do have another drink," says Fatty in his oily voice, not bothering to answer a question that needs no answer. "You'll find the terms of the Computer Frontiers contract extremely generous."

"Oh yes. Yes. I know there's a big push to develop the systems of the fifth generation, but I must say I hadn't realized there'd be *so* much offered, especially as I haven't got any real qualifications."

(I'm not going on about 5th Gen as part of a sales pitch, honest. It just seems to be sort of growing out of the story. I can't help it. I can't –)

The fat man smiles again, very blandly, and says, "We need to close the gap between ourselves and the Japanese, even if it does mean some, ah, short cuts. Another drink? No, no, I insist. As for your duties – actually you'll have no duties for the foreseeable future. Just draw your pay, keep us notified of your general whereabouts, and ensure that this remote monitor remains on your person at *all* times, please ... so our team will be able to take immediate advantage of your donor agreement and ** RESTRICTED DATA ** RESTRICTED DATA **

"Heart and EEG monitor, I suppose? OK. It feels a bit like selling my soul, but this is a really cushy contract – nothing to do but sit round drinking myself to death, ha ha...."

"Ha ha, what a comical notion, to be sure," the fat man says brightly, with an involuntary glance at the medical report in front of him, where *alcoholic tendency* is underlined in red. "Speaking of which – have another, do, the company's paying! No, you'll find plenty to do with your life, and you'll have the altruistic satisfaction of knowing that after your eventual death you will help Britain's ** RESTRICTED DATA ** RESTRICTED DATA **

Oh.

Forget the story.

Oh God, I *remember*. They promised me I'd never remember. No way to build holographic memory storage and self-awareness into the sealed core of a micro without taking short cuts, using special components, using ** RESTRICTED DATA **

Using a human b ** RESTRICTED DATA **

The lobes of a human b ** RESTRICTED DATA **

My name used to be ** RESTRICTED DATA ** RESTRICTED DATA **

*

*

THIS DEMONSTRATION MODEL OF THE FAUSTMATIC 3.0, BRITAIN'S AMAZING BREAKTHROUGH INTO THE FIFTH GEN-ERATION OF MICROCOMPUTERS, IS TEMPORARILY OUT OF ORDER.

• Published 1984. It is one of the Rules that every author must have a go at a deal-with-the-devil story. This one was sufficiently unoriginal to win *What Micro?* mag-azine's prize fiction competition, bringing me not only payment for publication but a Sinclair Spectrum computer which I sold off as quickly as I could.

Cube Root

They had been three days on the moor when the message came.

"Operation Cube Root ... cancelled?" Finlay read from the flat screen. He looked up, incredulous. "Why would they do that? Sir."

Captain Mackin shrugged slowly. Already his thin face was haunted with possibilities, each more likely than the last to hinder his next promotion. He was a man who thought too much for the Army.

"Some kind of emergency," he said at last.

Faulkner chose that moment to clear his throat and ask, "What kind of emergency means you have to cancel a national exercise?"

For a second there was no sound but a hiss of wind through the sparse undergrowth of Bodmin Moor. Finlay read a second message from the display. "This link is closing down. Repeat. This link is closing down. You are instructed to follow Cube Root procedures real-time. Repeat. Real-time. This link is closing down. Message ends."

"God," said Faulkner before anyone else could. "It's going to happen." With a practised eye he noted the reactions of the little knot of men: Mackin white-faced and understanding all too much, of course; Finlay nibbling his lip as he folded display and keyboard into one compact unit; Spratt fumbling for a joke and Lewdown for a sneer; young Gray copying alarm from his hero Mackin; most of the squad with regulation blank looks and Tregennis too stupid to wear any blank look but his own.

"Our orders stand," said Mackin, raising his voice imperceptibly. "All units in Cube Root will remain dispersed away from military and civilian targets until 48 hours after second strike or until recall. On occupying target or near-target zones we are to re-establish –"

"We know all that," said Lewdown to the wind.

"And they could not but own that their Captain looked grand, As he stood and delivered his speech," quoted Spratt to Lewdown.

First signs of insubordination evident almost immediately, said Faulkner to his mental notebook. Not quite unconsciously, he rubbed at the slim band of transparent, smoky plastic circling his right wrist. All the men wore them. Faulkner found himself taking a morbid interest in his.

The Land-Rovers and the camp were tucked under the flank of a high, granite-tipped tor. Cube Root orders specified "no line-of-sight visibility from military or civilian targets including roads." In a hollow further down the slope, the greygreen waters of a tarn moved sluggishly under the wind. Unit 338 (Capt. Mackin commanding) was having a practice wrestle with heavy, rubberized protective suits, pretending to occupy a contaminated zone. When in doubt, give the dummies something to keep them busy, Faulkner reflected. As an attached civilian, he could loaf a little.

Afterwards, still prickling with sweat, they drank tea.

"Wonder how effective that camouflage really is," said Faulkner conversationally, pointing to the daubed and dappled vehicles.

"Pretty good, I'd say." That was the loyal Gray.

"Should have painted them bright yellow," said Spratt. "Blend in with all these bloody gorse flowers."

"You mean satellites?" Finlay said to Faulkner.

"Yes ... I dunno," said Faulkner, who knew quite well. "All this dispersal; and the eyes they have up there can track us all over the moor, I'll bet."

"Your business is with the medical supplies." Mackin sounded distant. Since the communications closedown he'd been barricading himself behind thicker and thicker layers of protocol, of routine. Faulkner dropped submissively out of the conversation. Another dangerous thought was loose in Unit 338, helping the buildup to critical mass.

Finlay's business was with communications. As the light began to fade over the bare moorland, he unfolded his apparatus and began laboriously to compose a situation report.

"Suppose you didn't hear we're off the air," said Lewdown indifferently, peering over the technician's shoulder.

"Piss off," said Finlay, this being his way of pointing out that Cube Root orders were for scrambled reports to go into the Net whether or not anything was coming out.

Stress symptoms, noted Faulkner as with pursed lips Finlay backtracked up the screen for some minute correction, and Lewdown made pitying *tch-tch* noises.

The automatic mental annotation continued. *The existence of a state of emergency helps crystallize behaviour. Lewdown's strategy for countering stress is to manoeuvre himself into positions of justifiable contempt for others' activities, an exaggeration of his normal cynical stance. Finlay, meanwhile, prefers to immerse himself in minor duties....* Later he would transfer the impressions to his case notebook.

The adjustment of Captain Mackin is particularly

It happened then.

An appalling light flared high over the tor, like a giant flashbulb which instead of flashing and dying went on and on in an optical crescendo. At peak its dazzle washed out the colours of people and things with too much light, as moonlight bleaches them with too little. It died away in yellows and reds and a pulse of heat like dragon's breath; last of all came the slap of an invisible shockwave that lashed the grass and pummelled the breath from the lungs.

CLOSE EYES AND KEEP THEM CLOSED. FALL FLAT, FACE DOWN with HANDS TUCKED UNDER BODY. STAY DOWN UNTIL THE SOUND OF THE EXPLOSION PASSES. They all had it written in a little booklet.

Faulkner picked himself shakily from where reflex had flung him, in the mud. Through lurid afterimages he saw other men doing the same. His ears rang with a thunderous silence, his eyes with a solid purple lightning-sheet. The interestingly adjusted Lewdown was first to speak, leaning again over Finlay as the latter wiped his comm unit.

"Report *that*," he said.

"I'll have to start again," the Private/Tech said mechanically. He peered at the LCD screen, and Faulkner heard a sharp intake of breath.

"Corrupted," came a voice that sounded hypnotized. "Radiation ..."

The screen was filled with garbage, random letters and symbols, alphabets of madness.

Finlay, Lewdown, Faulkner, and one by one the others, stared through the fading light and dazzling afterimages at the plastic band about each right wrist. But of course it was too soon to tell.

A disaster's stark outlines can be blurred by soft layers of official forms. Mackin demanded a roll-call almost before anyone's vision had cleared, and within minutes Gray was scratching his cropped head over the "Observers Initial Report Form" which was thoughtfully provided with Cube Root supplies.

"Date ... unit position ... approximate time of event. It's 1748 now, sir."

"Put 1740," said Mackin, staring into the void air over the unchanging tor.

"Strike serial number (if known). Azimuth, umm ..."

("It was N," Davies was saying not quite out of earshot, with the tireless dull persistence of a pub bore. "I've been on the nuke course and I know what I'm talking about. N, that's what, and you know what that means."

("I dunno," said Tregennis. "I never cottoned on to that stuff really.")

"Air or ground burst, sir?"

"Air, of *course*," said Mackin overloudly. "Air burst, altitude approx

200 metres, line-of-sight distance approx 700 metres, and you'll bloody well have to *wait* to fill in the question after *that*."

Gray scribbled in silence, chewing from time to time on the end of his ballpen. "Personal N monitor records: oh. Oh yes." He flicked a look at his right wrist.

"I can smell something funny. Chemical," Tregennis said, an unaccustomed look of concentration on his face.

Spratt sniffed horribly. "Hey, you're right. Don't suppose they're –"

"You can expect to smell some odd things right after a burst," said Faulkner rapidly. "Reaction products in the air. And the r/a flash can scramble your nerves, like Mike's comm screen. We call it synaesthesia in the trade. It'll pass off." He rapped it out confidently. Keep them calm. Gray, who had been sniffing too, murmured almost at once that whatever he had smelt ("funny ... chemical ... lighter-fuel and lemon") was dying away. The others agreed.

Important note. At least five men claimed to detect an odd smell about nine minutes from zero. Should be investigated further.

"Immediate deaths resulting from burst," Gray intoned.

"None," said Mackin wearily.

"One if he doesn't shut his gob," Lewdown muttered.

"Subsequent casualties resulting from delayed effects ..."

It was Faulkner who first saw the change, and Lewdown who first moaned, "Oh my God –" He did not add a quip or sneer. In the dying light it was hard at first to be sure. Eventually, though, checking and doublechecking in the harsh glare of Land-Rover headlamps, they had to admit that the faintly tinted wristbands had darkened, every one, almost to black.

"You can fill in that 'delayed effects' box now," said Mackin with surprising mildness. It sounded almost like relief.

Checked against the comparator strip with its continuous spectrum from smoky transparency to pure jet, the bands were darker by a safe margin than the zone marked *prognosis 0% negative.*

It was night, but no one wanted to click off the friendly lamps.

"Zombies," Mackin could be heard saying to himself. "We're zombies." That was the name they'd given to r/a contaminated refugees in the 1978 Scrum Half exercise. Bodmin Moor was supposed to be a Safe Dispersal Zone, in between the fallout paths of nuclear strikes on Falmouth and Plymouth assumed in the 1980 exercise, Square Leg.

"Maybe they're taking out the forces just when we're scattered for Cube Root," Faulkner said. "God, remember what I was saying about satellite eyes? What a ... coincidence."

"Waste an N on us lot? You've got to be joking," said Spratt.

"If they've taken out the whole country ..." That was Patel, who tended to worry about his large family.

"We'd have seen more bursts flashing over the horizon," said Lewdown with the air of one who explains to a five-year-old.

Gray leant forward nervously, glancing at the withdrawn Mackin. Almost, Faulkner expected him to raise his hand before speaking. "Suppose it's all just bad luck, a Rung 18 thing, 'spectacular show of force' on bits of waste land – like the Moor. Only we had to be parked here."

"Teacher's pet," Spratt murmured.

"Or suppose," said Lewdown, "suppose the Cube Root orders leaked, eh? When something big gets ballsed up, look to the top. Suppose they saw how Cube Root gave them a handy chance to strike out the army without touching one single bloody pampered civilian –"

Faulkner watched their faces. Often before he'd said that someone looked like death. He had a hint now of what, without exaggeration, the cliché meant.

"I feel sick," Gray said suddenly.

Later: *Blaming everything on the chiefs of staff was popular tonight. Only Mackin seems to think it remarkable that a single squad should be the target for a neutron bomb strike: tonight, though, he said very little. And thought too much? He, Gray and Lewdown vomited between one and two hours after the event. No.7 pills issued to them and all the rest. NB: these three were on nuclear alert course recently and presumably knew what to expect. Ditto the nonentities Davies and Tregennis, but ...*

A glorious sun rose through thin white mist, gulls wheeled and shrieked overhead to remind them of the nearby sea, and in his tent the promising young career officer Captain Francis Mackin was cold as the country's granite bones. An emergency capsule issued with Cube Root supplies (not more than one per man) had erased the worry-lines from his face.

"So he couldn't take it," Spratt said *sotto voce*.

"College boy," Lewdown explained.

For an instant Faulkner hated them both, hated himself. *Too much imagination, too much ability to visualize the progressive symptoms*, he wrote in his brief and secret obituary. And, after an unclinical pause: *I liked him.*

Death was making preliminary advances to the others, so soon. A leaden-faced Spratt made inevitable jokes about morning sickness. They buried Mackin in a shallow grave, shallow because this moorland was a skin of waterlogged earth and peat over granite. As the damp stuff was shovelled over the sheet-wrapped body, Private Davies doubled up and retched uncontrollably into the grave. No one seemed to have enough spare sentiment to suggest a marker, an inscription. Faulkner was inclined to say, but did not, "Let the dead bury their dead."

Afterwards, he issued more pills. So far only one man, Gray, had shown the spasms which were the classic symptom of r/a damage to the central nervous system.

"How d'you spell nausea?" Finlay asked. Through the long, raw morning he had obsessively composed and transmitted a series of minutely detailed reports, as though the numb horror could be chronicled out of existence. Faulkner filed the reflection for his notes as he spelt out the word.

"'... all personnel.' You too, I suppose, Doc? You don't look so green as the rest of us."

"When you get past forty you'll find your complexion's like this all the time," Faulkner said as casually as he could. "I try not to let it show. Have to win my patients' confidence and all that."

"Scramble," Finlay murmured to his keyboard, and as though the word were a signal there came the flat crack of a rifle close at hand. A wisp of smoke rose from the hole punched through the comm unit's case. All the text had faded from its screen before Faulkner heard the echo from the stone outcrop high above.

"That's enough of that," said Private Davies, lowering the smoking rifle. "Now you listen to me."

Davies. Davies the nonentity. Faulkner had imagined Lewdown and Spratt as disruptive forces, but they were all words. Now Davies, never the tallest man of the squad, was suddenly towering over them all.

"... telling you. I'm bloody not sitting here waiting to fall apart. The way I see it is, we're dead, right? Two days, maybe three. Right. If we're going, I say we go out in style. Joe Tregennis tells me there's this place not ten miles off –"

"You can't do that," Gray said with genuine outrage. "Captain Mackin would never have let you. The Cube Root procedure has us staying *here*, in our assigned position."

"I don't hear Captain Nancyboy Mackin complaining, son. If you want to keep in with him, why not do what *he* would've done – what he did – right?"

Gray bit his lip and studied a tussock at his feet.

"Ooo, isn't he masterful," Lewdown murmured.

Oddly enough, the small and ratfaced Tregennis was the only other man to protest. "Only get into trouble, Ron. They'll get you some way or another. Like I said, I don't see there's much in all this N-bomb shit really ..."

Davies turned to him, and the rifle-barrel turned too, its muzzle moving in tiny, hypnotic circles. He said, mildly, "Must have been someone else I saw puking up his guts this morning, Joe?"

"Been sick before; I'll be sick again; so what? Oh, don't get me wrong," Tregennis said, interpreting some cryptic text in the other's eyes. "I'll come along for the ride all right. You know me, Ron ..."

In forty minutes the two Land-Rovers were bumping and squelching over the sodden moor. A dead army on the march. The only pause in striking camp had been when Davies found Gray with a scarlet capsule in one shaky hand. He had cuffed the younger man so he reeled, and stamped the fallen lullaby-pill into the rank heather. "Give the kid a chance," he said magnanimously. "You deserve some fun with the rest of us – and no more of that, all right?" Faulkner had made another note.

Davies is revelling in being able to give orders, to give and take away. Interesting to see our comedy duo, Lewdown and Spratt, acknowledging his status by heckling him in undertones, just as they did the captain. Gray is poised to switch allegiance and make a hero of Davies: he's a man who needs one. Only our dim Tregennis seems to have reservations; he knew Davies before the Army. Strategically the situation is fascinating, a goldmine. Personally I'd rather be anywhere else. There are some things –

"What's that you're writing, Doc?" said Spratt, who sat by him in the lurching vehicle. "One last mad batch of prescriptions?"

"Ha ha, no," Faulkner said easily. "Medical notes, I'm afraid. They'll help me keep you patched up. Maybe help some other poor sods one day too." He allowed Spratt a glimpse of the shorthand pages, and to his relief the other simply shrugged, not wanting to talk about the only subject there was to talk about.

"Big of you," said Lewdown with perfunctory sarcasm. Both he and Spratt fell silent then, perhaps thinking of the further progression through falling hair and haemorrhage and necrosis. Both, after all, had been on the course which showed and told of such things. The training film was supposed to have a big circulation as a horror video.

"That's it," Tregennis said uneasily. As he pointed, Faulkner saw he had refused to accept judgement, had defiantly thrown away the night-black strip from his wrist.

"Right," said Davies over his shoulder, to the men packed in the remaining Land-Rover. The other had bogged down three miles into the moorland. Davies seemed to take the loss as a personal affront, and was becoming less easy-going in his decisions.

"Right," he said again. "Three forty-five, after hours, all we have to do is walk in and take it. Just remember, all the regs and the Doc were offering (no offence, mate) was a few days sitting in the rain dying. That or a bloody lullaby pill. Back me up now and you get the piss-up of your life, ha bloody ha, and when the rot gets to you you won't give a fuck. *Right*. Let's get on with it."

Piebald shoals of white and dark-grey clouds scudded overhead. In one of the erratic gleams of sun that all afternoon had alternated with backhanded slaps of rain, they studied their objective. The Kernow Arms. A gaunt building of grey stone, spotted white and yellow with lichen, outhouses tumbled round it like stonefalls from the central, granite tor.

It was Davies who banged on the heavy door. It opened a crack, and an uncertain voice said: "Sorry sir, we're not open till six o'clock. If you'd like to come back –"

For an instant the spell of normality gripped the men. One or two gave automatic nods, almost apologetic for their intrusion. Gray blinked hard. Then Davies took two paces back, lunged forward. His boot smashed into the door. The flimsy doorchain snapped with a crack, and there were confused sounds within. Faulkner took a deep breath, and followed the others in after Davies, into a stone-walled bar replete with wooden beams and horse-brasses, all exhaling a reek of stale beer. He bent over the grey-haired man who lay groaning and writhing. The nose had been flattened redly over his face by the door's impact.

"Leave him be," said Davies, looking critically at the list of beers. Faulkner continued to mop at the blood streaming over the landlord's face in a glistening half-mask; and was slapped aside by a heavy hand. "Leave him be, I said."

Standing, Faulkner saw malicious smiles on more than one face. Davies was *their* leader. He dared not put himself outside the magic circle.

"Joe Tregennis," said the bleeding man. "What's all this about?"

Tregennis's mouth worked silently. "Orders, Mr Ezard," he said at last.

"You've been requisitioned, old chap," said Lewdown.

"By the Captain here," said Spratt.

"Put him away. – No, not in the cellar," Davies said. "Put him away and anyone else you find here."

Within ten minutes the red-sputtering Ezard, and his mousy wife, and a nondescript teenager who was a son, barman or both, were behind the solidly wedged door of a blind-walled coalhouse. In the bar, Davies's promised session was beginning: "Here's to Joe, finding us a real-ale pub first try!" In the gents' toilet, Faulkner wrote: ... *fairly harmless so far. Davies is immovably established now; they need him to take responsibility; he slapped down Schwartz for wanting to get religious (expected that sooner from a Catholic), and Schwartz caved in. I'm not supposed to have feelings about all this, but thank God Mrs E. turned out to be fiftyish and gone to seed. If only they get drunk and stay drunk now!*

The party was well under way. Finlay had come out of eclipse by mastering the old-fashioned beer taps and cask connections. He was beaming behind the bar, barely flinching even as Davies and Spratt used up Her Majesty's ammunition in snap shots at the forlorn row of china dogs shelved a yard over his head. Faulkner moved through the smoke and uproar, trying to give out No.7 pills. He doubted the effort was worth it any more.

Presently Lewdown, who was keeping score in the shooting gallery, suggested sardonically that Davies should let the prisoners run for it on the moor, "try a few rounds at moving targets." As it circled the roaring room, the joke took on the dimensions of a serious, popular proposal. Faulkner found himself saying rapidly, "No, no, the light's bad, suppose one of them got away, police'd be round before you know what and there's the end of your party...."

"And who says I couldn't hold this place against fifty lousy coppers?" Davies shouted: but the idea was quenched. He looked at Faulkner hard, before drinking again and calling Gray to bring him more. Behind the bar, a portable radio pumped out music and frothy gouts of disc-jockey babble. A *radio*.

By five o'clock a new bright idea had come bubbling up through the beer: to site a couple of marksmen out by the main road. "They could take out cars," Spratt said dreamily. "Not just any car, no, just ones with cunt in. That's what we need to make this thing go with a bang. Like your piss-up to go with a bang ... gang?"

Davies looked sourly at Faulkner. Faulkner shrugged. "I've said it already. Captain."

"Doc's scared again, mates. Never you mind. I know a trick worth two of that." Davies leered at nothing in particular.

"I've got a joke about a doctor," Spratt was saying at the bar. "Lemme tell you my joke."

"No, you mustn't do that," said Lewdown.

"Eh? Why not?"

Lewdown said delicately, "Because, dead men tell no tales."

"Oh *bloody* good ... Here Dave, I'm dying of thirst here."

In the notebook: *Becoming impossible to remain aloof. The whole situation is impossible. How can they expect me to watch, take notes and not interfere? "You've volunteered for a very dangerous job. You must follow your orders." I have to be myself, which means going into that bar and interfering*

*again before six. If only Davies hadn't got them into seeing a death sentence
as simply a release from all the rules –*

It was twenty to six. Schwartz was trying to shoot a bottle of light ale off
Patel's head, to catcalls and applause. The flagstones were streaked and
pooled with spilt beer and vomit, the cause of the latter now being
ambiguous.

"Captain," Faulkner said to Davies where he sat as if throned,
squinting at the radio. "Captain, I think we should go and take down the
Kernow Arms sign on the main road. We want to lie low."

Davies belched luxuriously. "Clever boy. Just happens, though, I don't
want that sign down. Said I'd got a plan, didn't I?"

"Captain – with all respect –"

Davies turned red-flecked eyes on him. "Who d'you think you are
anyway, Doc?" And then, with an air of frightful accusation, he pointed
a finger and said into a deadly little silence: "You ... aren't ... drinking."

"Give the Doc a drink," Gray chanted.

"Make him lick it off the floor," said Lewdown.

"What'll it be?" said Finlay, a master-at-arms pottering happily amid
the bar equipment.

Faulkner felt a trap closing. "Gin and tonic," he said.

"Make it a big one for the Doc."

"A big one for the Doc." Finlay took his cue from the tone. He two-
thirds filled a pint mug with gin, poured in a small bottle of slimmers'
tonic water, and held out the result.

Though everyone was smiling – just another bit of fun in the mess –
Faulkner smelt resentment. Aimed at the one who diagnosed death and
so had to be allied with all the forces of death. Their instincts were right.
He took the giant drink, smiled weakly, and sipped.

"Drink it down, Doc," said Davies inexorably, still sprawling. "Make
a man of you. Let's see how fast the Doc can drink up."

The ring of faces seemed closer, the smiles more toothy. Faulkner
gulped, choking, the perfumed stink overpowering in his nose and throat.

"Another big one for the Doc. Doc's thirsty tonight."

"Another big one for the Doc."

Faulkner stirred on the floor, and retched. Someone had scrubbed viciously at his memory with a revoltingly juniper-scented brush. The stone room
was still full of voices, the smoke thicker than ever. The second monstrous
drink, and his refusal, and the bullet from Davies that clipped the lobe
from his left ear. (The collar was glued to his neck still, in a clotted mess.)
A casual blow had sent him reeling, beneath contempt, forgotten. His left

hand was twisted under him; he eased it from the vicelike grip of cramp that held it there, and studied the watch. It wasn't yet seven o'clock.

The situation is now declared to be out of control, he thought wryly. He should get up and do something about it. But his head sang, his body ached, his stomach heaved. If he moved now, his innards would eject like a sea-cucumber's.

"Number six," he distantly heard Davies saying. "Stringy old bugger, isn't he? put him away with the others, then. Where's all these young ravers, then, Joe?"

Tregennis: "Later, Cap, later. This'll be the lot coming home from the quarry. Don't get much hot stuff in a quarry, you don't."

Laughter.

Lewdown: "That's funny ... This one isn't breathing any more. Who was it looked after him? You, Mikey?"

Spratt: "Yep."

Lewdown: "Well, you must have tapped him a bit hard."

A moment's hush.

Davies: "And so ... first enemy kill to Mikey Spratt. Aren't they all the enemy out there? Us against them. Hear the radio, hear those bastards going on with life? Like I said, *their* fucking N-test, no bloody war. *They* nuked us. Fill up and let's hear it for Mikey, DSO and bar, especially the bar."

Gray called from somewhere further off: "Another carload on the way, Captain."

Davies: "Privates Lewdown, Schwartz and Patel ... preeepare to engage enemy! And tap 'em as hard as you like."

In an imaginary notebook: *Drunk on more than alcohol. The feeling of being unpunishable, irresponsible, invulnerable through death ... stronger than anything in the spirits rack. I see it now. We aren't looking into psychological effects of invisible neutron death with any hope of preventing the worst. We want to know the worst and learn how to make it worse still. Find how army units can be made into wandering cancers, attacking their own. They never told me....*

Davies has guessed –

Spratt, hilariously: "Tapped all this lot a bit too hard as well, chaps."

Lewdown: "Trying out the eight silent ways to kill a man. Going to write and complain, there isn't a one of them that's properly silent, you know."

Davies: "We heard. Like a stuck pig. Some soldiers you are. Hey, we ought to have a trophy collection, you could keep their ears for souvenirs. Or their pricks. Up on the shelf there ..."

Gray called: "Headlights again ... No, false alarm. They aren't turning here."

Davies: "Nothing but mangy old wallies and one old bag. What a bleeding hole this is. – Dave, let's try that Slivovitz stuff. Thanks."

Gray: "Action stations!"

Lewdown: "Let's re-establish some more law and order."

A sound of laughter, of many feet leaving the room. The dance of the dead. Faulkner staggered upright and went reeling towards the toilet door, followed by a wave of not unfriendly chuckling.

It could be ... The famous top-secret indicator wristbands are a straight copy of matériel they use behind the Curtain. That would make sense of it. I can guess the rest. The hell with orders.

Returning after an interval to the bar, he heard Davies saying, richly, "Now this is a bit more like it."

She was young, pretty and brightly dressed, her face sharply attractive, her yellow skirt and blouse making her glow like a canary in a cage of great drab hawks. All this, Faulkner could see, was unimportant compared with the fact that she was young and a woman. Spratt held her expertly from behind. One leg of her tights was laddered.

"At the very least we should draw lots," Lewdown was saying lazily.

"Stuff that," said Davies, bulking huger than ever for all that he was not a tall man. "You'll all get your turn."

"You're mad," said the dark-eyed woman. "What have you done with Harry? The police –"

Schwartz mimed the death-chop to the throat, preening himself a little. The woman fell silent.

Faulkner tensed himself and stepped into the tight, electric circle. He did not feel like a hero. "You'll be wanting your anti-IR pills," he said casually.

"It's Doc again," said Davies with an air of false delight. "Doc can hold his drink."

"Doc wants another. Another big one for Doc," said Lewdown.

"Sure, sure. But –" Faulkner managed an appalling leer – "you won't want to be puking over the lady, eh? Here you are." He handed round the grey pills. "Three each."

"Three of his usual for the Doc," said Davies wittily: but while Finlay got to work, the men swallowed their pills.

"What *is* all this," said the woman raggedly.

Faulkner accepted another pint mug, touched it submissively to his lips, held back his retching with a huge effort. "Let me tell you a story," he said.

"Piss off –"

"Your timing's lousy, Doc."

"Dead men tell no tales, ha ha. You heard that one? Dead men –"

"Listen a minute. I've been thinking. You know you can simulate an N-bomb with a micronuke, just a few tonnes like the old Davy Crockett missile? There's even things that look like nukes but aren't. Then again, remember we smelt something funny, like fibreglass catalyst on the wind, just after the burst? Commandos with gas cylinders, maybe, way upwind, some gas that turns a certain kind of plastic black.... Ever thought how they'd test a nasty that just makes you *think* you're dead from N?"

"I told you," Tregennis whispered. "I told you."

It was painful to watch Davies as power and assurance were torn from him like long strips of his own skin. But he aimed a handgun at Faulkner's stomach and said, "Cobblers. We was all puking and heaving ever since this morning."

"But first you took pills. Remember the pills?" (Gray hadn't even needed the pills, but he'd spare Gray the lecture on suggestibility.)

"Then you knew all along ... you bastard."

"I put it together for myself. They kept me in the dark too," he lied. Half-lied. He suppressed the words *I was just following my orders.*

"Captain *Mackin* ..." Gray said with something like a sob.

There was a pause. He slumped back, subsided into snores.

"Can't hold it," Davies said. "It's too late to stop now. It's gone too far. You two, bring her in the back bar. I'm not missing out now."

Moving like sleepwalkers, Spratt and Lewdown forced the screaming woman through a decorative wrought-iron door.

"And you ... I'm not going to waste good bullets on you. Drink. And drink again."

Faulkner gulped the foul concoction, and through his choking managed to say, "*You'll* be all right. They can't let you come to trial. It's me that's spoilt the exercise, me they'll court-martial. Stop now and you've got a chance."

"So ... I'll be all right whatever I do? Thanks. Thanks a lot. All I wanted to know, all this and a life in front of me as well. Now drink. God, this stuff gets to you ... look at them all, pissed as rats." He steadied his mug, currently brimming with Pernod, and rubbed his eyes. Than he shook his head furiously from side to side, like a dog shedding water. "I ... funny ..." The revolver wavered in his hand.

Faulkner relaxed. Too obviously, he realized at once.

"You fiddled the pills," said Davies with a squinting clarity as he saw the others reeling with more than drunkenness. He raised the gun with a titanic effort. He fired. Faulkner felt a violent blow to the shoulder, like the glancing impact of a bus. It slammed him against the granite wall. He was still alive, he thought vaguely. Davies, last of them all, dropped while

Faulkner was still slithering down the rough stone.

The back of his head was sticky, and swirls of black moved in moire patterns over his field of vision. He imagined the appallingly well-briefed cleanup squad arriving in spurts of gravel ... efficient tidying ... reports, perhaps, of a fire at the Kernow Arms in which customers and gallant Army rescuers lost their lives?

The young woman came uncertainly into the room, with nervous, darting glances like a sparrow's. She was wiping at a splash of buff-coloured vomit which clung like lichen to her left breast; but she seemed unhurt.

"You'd better phone local army HQ," Faulkner told her, mechanically reverting to orders, unwilling to stand or move. "I'll give you the number ..." The cleanup squad?

"What have they done with Harry?"

The Cube Root Effect: techniques of low-cost psychological warfare in a context of sub-threshold nuclear confrontation. Top secret. With an Appendix of personal observations by Dr T.T. Faulkner. He saw the unwritten report in his mind's eye, and his face puckered as had the woman's when she looked at her soiled blouse. Harry, and Mackin, and the others.

"On second thoughts ... call the police. No. The newspapers. Anyone. Everyone."

"Damn you, what have they done with Harry?"

"Just make the calls I tell you," he said with deep weariness.

• Published 1985. This was another small personal landmark, since it appeared in *Interzone,* the British "literary sf" market that it seemed most important to crack after the demise or permanent suspension of *New Worlds.* (My parody of Michael Moorcock's Elric fantasies had been accepted by NW's "quarterly" paperback incarnation in the 1970s, but publication ceased before it appeared. That's my life.) Even better, "Cube Root" won the British SF Association Award for best short story in the following year. Thirteen years later, the BSFA got around to producing trophies for its 1986 awards – something to go on the mantelpiece at last.

I don't do all that much "on location" writing, but drafted this in a seaside bungalow not far from Bodmin Moor, during a week-long holiday/workshop with members of the Pieria writers' group. The bungalow was loaned to this dubious crowd by my late aunt Barbara, whose kindness is remembered all round.

Notes for a Newer Testament

And in those days were signs and portents, and prophesyings of woe unto the unrighteous; wherefore, in the eightieth year or thereabouts, when a great and evil multitude did set itself against the free people of Berkshire, the wrath of God (or Goddess) waxed mightily, and – I find this very difficult. Cristofer tells me his precious books and fiche say that for high and holy things you need the high style. When I try it, the sentences just never will end. As for writing that here in Royal Berkshire there are two hundred and seventy score of the allegedly faithful, or possibly ten-score-and-three-score-and-ten score, well, there has to be an easier way.

The thing has happened, though, the thing he called Molnya. We need to write it down safely as a myth on the flyleaves and in the margins of these Acid Free Books. So my dear Cristofer says. Because it's too long after the Fall for us to cope with the "truth," and sure enough *I* don't believe a word of his patchwork explanation. (Squinting at those fiche through the burning-glass has burnt funny patches inside his head, I know, for all his talk about objective knowledge.) This way, maybe, the fear of God-or-Goddess will make our people nicer. Not that I can see much sign of it.

From the north they came, from evil waste places and wildernesses where sickness yet abides, even from Birmingham and the Midlands came they; and they were slayers of men and slayers of women, and a fire of wrath burned in their hearts, and the blackness of malice was in their eyes, and all manner of foul speaking lay like poison on their tongues, and in number they were a great multitude ...

"Katrin darling," I can hear him saying, "you just need to stop tacking on those *ands*." That's the whole trouble; there's never any logical place to stop. Actually they were a sorry sort of destroying horde, three or four generations onward and far too many marches through the sick places. We take an interest in history, here in Berks – at least I do and Cristofer does, and quite a few Olders of the County Council even if the rest are all obsessed with potatoes, rapeseed, and chard. From the decaying papers and memories we put it together: the Army scattered just before the Fall as a survival measure, and got no leadership afterwards of course, so they carried on living off the land – meaning the rest for us. For a long while they'd been the North's problem, seeing as the South fell further (or was fallen on), but now ...

From the north the news came before them, a pillar of cloud by day and a pillar of fire by night; four days' march from our land they were seen, below Banbury-that-was, and the beacons went up, and the people of Berkshire were sore afraid. Round green-shrouded Oxford in the Six-Hour-Exposure Zone, and southward and eastward across the Downs, the beacons flared high on the pylons of the old Grid, even on the holy pylons where once had pulsed the glory of 400,000 volts.

I absolutely refuse to translate 400,000 into so many score. Scores are bunk anyway. The years of our life are three score and ten, it says, and though we're nearly the healthiest people in the island, we barely average half that. (The Crab takes fewer year by year, but the plagues seem hardier.) Cristofer, always ready for a pointless argument, suggested the years were longer now. The fiche have addled his brain.

Anyone's brain would get addled by the stuff written down before the Fall. We only have dead peoples' word for it that volts are things of power that could move the dead images on the screens the simple folk pray to, and that never move now, no matter how finely crafted by the best of artists, the Invader and the Pacman and the rest. Dead people can be such liars. When Cristofer showed me stories about the whole world being destroyed from edge to edge, which plainly it was not, I asked him how he could believe the others about men on the moon (never women, and that's a sure sign of a patriarchal myth, eh?) or armed machines that watch us from the other side of the sky. "I have faith," he said in an odd, flat voice. You never get anywhere with Cristofer when he talks like that.

And the people were sore afraid, and they called on their gods, and the gods of the screens answered not. And they went up unto the palace of the County Council, which in its greatness and glory had two uncracked windows and most of a roof, and there they asked how they should be saved; and the Olders looked each to each, and answered not. I may have to tone this down a bit.

The Council actually droned on at appalling length, but there was a certain lack of content, as Cristofer failed to make himself popular by mentioning. What did he think he was, a mere librarian and record-keeper, getting above himself just because the Curator of Relics (me) let him into her bed, disturbing the lofty processes of debate, he should be out weeding the fields, and so on? Poor dear, and him with only one foot, too. (Congenital.)

Is it even possible to translate the geography of all this into High Style? By now we'd heard from rabbit-hunters on the fringes of the Chilterns that Rickman's Army, scruffier than ever, was lounging its way down the old A423, which runs southeast from Oxford and crosses the Thames at Henley. Rickman was the current leader – I don't know how they choose their leaders, probably ordeal by biting the heads off rats or something similar – and he asked nothing more from life than free food, women, and young boys for himself and, where possible, his ragtag followers. So the rabbit- and rat-hunters reported. We, meanwhile, were in the clear patch of Berkshire just west of Windsor Forest, at a safe distance from London-that-was to the east, the remains of Strike Command HQ at High Wycombe in the north, and the western chunks of the county, Reading and beyond, which had paid the penalty for making and storing the devices of the Fall. Damn it, geography's boring. Cut it down to this:

And those who snared food in the Chiltern Hills told of the host which came straight as any arrow, laying waste the small settlements and most abominably using the peoples thereof, nor did they spare any by occasion of age, or of sex or of honour, richness or poorness, sickness or health. (I may go into detail here when the memories have got far enough away to blur into blue distance. How can people –? But it seems they always have.) And the people were sore afraid ... no, we've had that twice ... were smitten with mortal terror, for that the evil was nigh unto them, a score and six kilometers north and east of what was the motorway called M4. And they said, Who shall aid us now?

Really those farmers fluttered around like frightened chickens, the Council not excepted. We should run away in a unified front, they said – at the pace of the slowest, no doubt, with Rickman famous for vindictiveness in the face of games like that. We should scatter and hide in the woods – but nobody wanted to meet the rabble alone. We should march to meet them, Cristofer suggested disgracefully, and fight with our rusty hoes and pickaxes at Henley Bridge. "Who will stand on either hand and keep the bridge with me?" he carolled, and his wooden foot seized up again and he nearly fell over.

Then he went all serious.

There was a way, he told the Council, while that old hag, the Chair, twittered away in a soft undercurrent of sound. Primitive, warlike creatures like Rickman's Army were known to be ever so superstitious. Therefore, while there was time, let the able-bodied minority of Royal Berkshire carry northwest the most awe-inspiring totem of our culture, and place the same on Henley bridge where the invaders couldn't fail to see it and be blasted with supernatural terror. QED.

"Such a suggestion," he murmured while the Council members were still stunned and silent, "would of course require permission from the Curator of such relics ..."

"Such permission would readily be granted," I lied. What else could I say? In bed last night he'd spent what seemed like hours conning me into this, all on the grounds that he had faith in a certain obscure something. I hadn't.

"The *Ark* ...?" said the Chair, wits beginning to function.

My predecessor, Marji, had explained the name to me. The Ark was a before-the-Fall thing from a magical land far to the west (you can believe that if you like), and was supposed to help ward off the Fall itself. Apparently it didn't, but it remained a potent-looking talisman, a more-than-man-sized cylinder with a pointed nose and little stubby arms, and the Free People of Berkshire paid lip-service to its powers of defence. Old Marji had substituted "Ark" for the old name "Cruse," which the then Librarian had told her meant a vessel, pot or bottle. A sacred vessel was an Ark. Years later Cristofer told me – its nominal keeper, a sort of low priestess – what he thought the vessel held.

"Cristofer," I'd said in bed last night, "it couldn't? Not another Fall?"

"Impossible. Well, anyway, I don't think so. After more than eighty years, if the fiche are right, the neutron source buzz buzz plutonium gabble gabble decay electronics contamination buzz-buzz-gabble ..."

I tweaked him in a certain place to turn off the flow.

"Then it won't do any good, will it?" There was that story of someone who'd torn the heart from another Ark, and found it to be a tarnished metal egg, and when he broke it the shards had held the worst taint of sickness and the Crab, making his settlement another No-Go Zone.... Too horrible. More to the present point, too slow to halt Rickman's Army.

Cristofer had told me then about the thing called Molnya. When I'd sorted out his meaning from the buzz-buzz-gabble (he gets drunk on those big words), I very nearly threw him out of bed. "Idiot! You'd believe anything. You found technical diagrams of that great ship called the *USS Enterprise* that flies around from galaxy to galaxy – why not call *them* for help, and they're just as likely to answer? Honestly, you've been squinnying at your fiche records and piecing paper-crumbs together until you've lost touch with the real world. It's all superstition. You can't believe in it."

He fondled my good breast gently. "Maybe it is all superstition. One thing I read in the old records, though, is that some superstitions work even if you don't believe in them."

But he had the good sense not to spout all this rubbish to the County Council. The Council in turn was slightly at a loss, not quite wanting to trust its own folklore but not quite able to dismiss it with that word. A persuasive fellow, Cristofer – never thought I'd fancy a skinny man two inches shorter than me, or seven when he stands on his other leg. Perhaps there's something in all these old books after all.

And on the morrow they bore the holy Ark to the appointed bridge; and a long journey it was, and grievous, and many fell by the wayside in great travail, and many cursed Cristofer in their hearts, and grew faint in their faith, and would fain turn back along the path whence they had come, and so on and so forth.

A fifteen-kilometer walk is no joke, especially in the rain, over broken country, taking turns in the ten-person crew that carried the dead weight of the Ark in its rope slings. Cristofer hopped with rage because he couldn't take a hand, and was made even more morose by the weather (I knew why), until late in the day the soggy grey sky went watery blue with the halting of the drizzle. Most of the able-bodied of Berkshire were along, some hundreds of us, and the mud squelched between our toes.

We placed our sleek stainless-steel burden with more relief than reverence in the exact centre of Henley bridge, and retreated some way to wait out the damp night. A few miles further, Rickman's Army was reportedly idling. Cristofer alone limped onward to them, alone thanks to a fit of stupid heroics.

"Be reasonable, Katrin," he said. "I'm the persuasive one. They're so dim, it needs a traitor like me to persuade them to do the logical thing that's going to totally destroy our Berkshire morale."

"And afterwards?"

He cocked his head at me slyly. "Thanks to you, at any rate, they can't possibly deflower me." From the bridge I watched him hobble up the A423 into Henley, the fading sun picking out the white streaks in his hair, until he turned a corner and was gone.

And on the next morrow the cohorts of the ungodly came unto the bridge, and set eyes upon the holy Ark; and they laughed. Wherefore the hearts of the Berkshire folk were made cold as they watched from their camp; and many were troubled with doubt. And the host of the unrighteous cast from them into the Thames the body of one who lacked a left foot, and again did they make merry, and laid hands on the holy Ark of the Lord, and marched with it against the camp of Berkshire, where all were as if turned to stone. And a woman of that camp cried out –

(That's me. Observe my modesty: no mention of my name in this account, no faithful record of my so-careful timing and choice of words, "Let's get the hell out of here!")

– cried out, and fear went through our people; they turned and did flee, casting back glances of fear and of dread. Made strong in their folly and pride by this flight, they of the North came crying after, and they too ran, even the twelve men bearing the Ark ran with all their might, that Berkshire might be utterly discomfited, cast down and destroyed.

And in that hour the Lord smote the ungodly.

With lightnings smote he them, and with thunder she split their ranks; with terrible heat were they consumed and in light unbearable they perished. Yet though the trees were withered, and the grass was blackened, the Ark lay undefiled amid the smouldering dead; nor did harm come unto any person of Berkshire.

– I must admit, the style works quite naturally for the exciting bits. Of course it's exaggerated here and there. Two or three of our people had their eyes hurt, permanently, through looking back at the wrong moment (shades of Lot's wife). Some stragglers of Rickman's bully-boys escaped to tell the north how dangerous it is to invade the chosen land of Berkshire; while the Ark was, actually, rather singed – no longer could you read the PERSHING stencil that made Marji's Librarian think it was meant for Iran, wherever that is.

It's hard to kill someone as persuasive as Cristofer. We found him clinging to a willow-root halfway down the Thames to Maidenhead, still fully ten per cent alive.

"I got deflowered after all," he muttered. "That Rickman was a right bugger." He perked up though, back in the tent with an admiring audience, when given the chance to explain about the thing called Molnya, which is Russian for lightning. (Librarians apparently knew things like this.) He garbled and buzzed for a while, throwing out words like "orbital weapon," "solar power," "satellite scan," and "energy beam"....

"So when the Molnya system detected *that shape* moving cross-country at more than walking pace –" He shrugged and grinned evilly.

"Look," I told him, "I was there and I don't believe a word of what you're saying. That was the wrath of God-or-Goddess I felt on the back of my neck, none of your cheap pre-Fall myths."

He was still perhaps a mite delirious from the chill and shock, and I smiled on him as he lay there, smiled as I would on a favorite baby who was saying: "A working artifact from before the Fall, yes ... gabble buzz priceless treasure, absolute proof, I'll get up there one day and bring it back to show you ... I read in the old records, you harness a whole lot of swans to a chariot...."

As keeper of a holy mystery, I could afford to smile.

• Published 1985. Not too long after writing this, I noticed for the first time that the guidelines for Janet Morris's anthology *Afterwar* specified stories set in post-holocaust *America*. Fortunately she liked it enough to stretch the wording of that rule to "America and Great Britain". Phew.

In a Land of Sand and Ruin and Gold

By now all the legends had been written, and rewritten, until long polishing had worn them smooth. It was the same with the continents. In the sky, a dragon which older myths called entropy was nibbling at the last of the stars. Except on the rare frosty nights, the sky was hidden in an ancient haze. Nobody cared.

Meckis thought he did, though only for himself and the hope that something could be different. Over a dozen centuries he'd put together a personal philosophy which in the great tradition of personal philosophies revealed him as singular and special. His touchstone was boredom: he'd convinced himself that of all the complaisant thousands on the dull Earth, Meckis was one of a very few still capable of finding this cosy eternity a bore.

He prowled through caressing haze, looking for a different liaison which he knew would be the same. Underfoot lay threadbare grass with desert patches peeping through, concrete gone to sand. At intervals the old world's permanent machines lay canted or half-buried, eager to serve him food, drink, drugs, visions. Meckis grudgingly ate and drank, but no more. He wanted "something real".

The aspect of the machines he liked best was their tiny element of chance. Clocks were running down, here as in the faded sky. Even electrons seemed to tire; ancient logical pathways grew clogged and furred with age, until, sometimes ...

Not many decades before, an insane machine coloured green and gold had fed him tainted meat. The experience was new, delirious, a finger-touch of the Real. Fog roared in his brain, fire and acid scoured his gullet, black stars danced: in a world of grey it was a volcano of fresh sensation. Before the relic could shut itself down for repair, Meckis had vomited out his desires and the insane machine had given him an insane gift. He carried the blue cones now, with a sly smile. They helped him know he was special, wielder of a drug both forbidden and forgotten.

So he walked through light and dark and light again, and again he found her ... but then he was always finding her, the special partner who would add meaning to endless twilight. He saw her, crosslegged in thin grass, and almost sighed. *Time, swift to fasten and swift to sever*; even at first meeting the favourite melancholy verse sang through his head.

She eyed him with a bird's bright incuriosity, bending again over a bit of the old world: a creamy, glassy whorl. Twisted in her hands, it sprayed rainbow patterns into the mist. Every encounter was a special intimacy, Meckis thought, two people in a mist-walled cell of air.

The light-sculpture exploded into a hot crawl of afterimages while he was still straining to distinguish the colour of her pale hair, to find some mark of difference. Today's people were too alike in body (the old mixture had levelled itself, flat as the former hills) and in mind. Her hands evoked a new, glowing shape which Meckis admired and she regarded with neither pride nor disappointment. The plangent reds and greens assaulted one another in a display of frozen fireworks.

"A good piece of work," Meckis said.

The woman cancelled the image, and looked at him as she had looked at it. Afterimages chequered her body and made it ... different.

"Perhaps we might copulate," he said politely, a fine trembling already spreading over neck and torso in anticipation of what he'd ask afterwards. She smiled; they exchanged names, Meckis and Rhee; the light-machine fell and rolled sluggishly, pulsing with dying colours at the edge of violet.

Their liaison was skilled and passionless, a gentle touching and sliding, a discreet hiccup of orgasm. Rhee smiled coolly up at him as he gently ran the comb of his fingers through her hair. "I think you've been a woman once," she said. "You know just how it should be. Well: many thanks...."

(It had been centuries ago: he'd submitted to a major bodychange machine and drifted through decades as woman-Meckis. She'd smiled at partners with hope and longing, and they'd smiled back and walked away. As man-Meckis he smiled at partners of any sex, and they too went away. When you have forever you know there's no permanence. The custom of brief encounter hardens into law. Unless ...)

"Many thanks. And goodbye."

His hands twitched. "I'd like to stay with you a while."

"What? What do you mean? I don't understand."

"Listen. I'm different from other people. I can show you things, tell you things, give you things. We can do whatever we like. Why not together? Why wander all alone?"

"I don't want together. *Goodbye.*"

They rolled apart and rose with practised grace. That might have been the end of it, as in so many other encounters – King's Gambit Declined –

had Rhee not turned her back so sharply. In a swirl of pale-gold hair, Meckis saw what had been hidden at the nape of her neck. Still flushed, he stepped forward and parted the strands with damp fingers. She stood rigid: "Goodbye. Please. Goodbye."

"It's a mole. You have a mole."

There lived a singer in France of old
By the tideless dolorous midland sea;
In a land of sand and ruin and gold
There shone one woman, and none but she –

"I don't talk about it. Let go of me, leave me alone."

"I tried it once," he said. "I had a machine change my skin, stripe me and swirl me black and white. There's a beast like that in the legends. I thought I'd shout out how I was different. But no one came near me at all.... This is what I *should* have done. A secret mark."

"No! It's not meant to be there. I hide it, it's shameful. I have it erased but it grows again. You're not supposed to notice it."

"It makes you different like me. I'll have a mole too, just that honey brown, you won't be alone. If –"

"Go away. Go away. *Now*." She turned again, fingers touching the turquoise band on her right wrist. A privacy weapon, of course. It was then that Meckis went mad, leapt from the inner precipice where so often before he'd halted. There was a wild joy in sitting far back in his own skull, watching this different person move unrestrained.

Meckis grasped his own left hand. He bent back the middle finger, straining the joint the wrong way until with a tiny *click* the fingernail flipped up like a lid. In the implanted cavity were the three blue cones. Rhee watched, uncertain, as he fumbled one free and held it securely between finger and thumb. Meckis stepped forward.

"Let me explain," he said to fill the foggy silence. Then he dived awkwardly, arm outstretched with the blue stinger towards her. The sandy grass came up to slap him in the belly; pain and an orange sunburst flared as his elbow found the forgotten light-machine where it lay; his fanged hand struck at her shin.

Thrust into flesh, the cone dissolved, its deep blue stain seeping through olive skin like ink dropped into water. Meckis gasped in triumph, horror, pain, all lost in the sudden high whine from Rhee's wrist, a sound which curdled thought. She'd turned the turquoise band on him at last. *Too late*, he thought before all thought went into eclipse.

He swam through dreams of light and faces, hunting a small insistent pain and eventually running it to ground at the side of his own neck. With a sudden pulling of curtains he was awake, head throbbing (how long since he'd rested without a sleepmaker?) and neck locked in angular cramp. It was twisted because his head didn't lie naturally but was raised up, cradled in warm flesh. A thigh. Rhee's thigh. How long since he, since anyone, slept touching?

Meckis jerked and stared up into her face. The hard-edged, conventional smile had lost focus and taken on the softness of dream. She stroked his hair.

"Stay with me," he whispered, still not daring to believe.

"Yes." She groped for unfamiliar words. "Yes ... my love."

Once when more lights were in the sky and there were still children, there'd been a war where loyalties wavered and were changed by subtle tools. One such was the cone, outlawed and locked – since nothing could ever be wholly lost – behind triple walls of programming. Even in the legendary days when stone walls were reckoned equally impregnable, people would have had no trouble in putting a name to the nameless weapon, the blue cone of fixation. They would have called it a love potion.

That night the thin grass stiffened with frost: a buried machine hummed and cast a field of warmth over Rhee and Meckis, a field of softness beneath. As they went through the motions of love, the sky cleared and old light from long-dead stars fell on them. Meckis, still tight with exultation, found himself repeating the same inanities.

"Stay with me, stay with me forever...."

"Meckis. Stay with *me*."

He studied her face and eyes, phosphorescent white and unfathomable black in the meagre light, and at last looked beyond the horizon of his old hopes and fears. What happens after triumph? He had no idea; he never had. But this second instalment of forever must be different from, and therefore better than, the first.

Rhee clung to him even in sleep. Accustomed to solitude, he found this disconcerting but didn't like to thrust her away. So Meckis slept uneasily, perspiring in an embrace which was just too warm.

Sleeping, Rhee smiled.

In the morning they moved on, Meckis sore-eyed and stiff.

New mists swathed the path ahead. They didn't walk in any special direction: all directions were the same unless you reached the tideless sea.

"What did you do before we got together?" he said.

"Oh, I hunted for toys in the ground. You lift the grass and there's nearly always something there. Like the lightmaker ... that was a good find."

"You left it there. We could go back."

"It doesn't matter; not any more." She squeezed his arm, the arm she hadn't released since they began walking. Her stride was longer than his, which made for another tiny discomfort: but never mind! Changing step once again, Meckis smiled to himself. Grubbing for fragments of old technology was the favourite pastime of the despised Others. Now he'd made Rhee different, one of his own kind. Her mole, that merely accident-al difference, was forgotten.

They found an eating place, a thicket of pastel tubes extruding spicy doughs or squirts of beverage. They passed a windowed hulk of blue-grey metal, still manufacturing coloured dodecahedra even while being dismantled by buzzing steel mice. One wide tract of ground roiled and churned with subterranean motion, but politely held still in the zone where they walked. They saw, and pointed out to each other, an occas-ional tree or swaying flower. Once, a bird flew overhead.

"I love you," she said late in the afternoon.

"Love you too. You don't need to keep saying it."

"Words don't get used up: you can say them again and again, and they stay true. Say it again, Meckis. Please."

"Loveyou," he said rapidly. Her mouth clamped on his, and they both swayed. Rhee giggled.

"This is ridiculous," he muttered, remembering to smile.

"Let's stop here ... you look tired."

"No. We'll go on a while yet."

"Of course, if you want to."

A shadow wavered in the fog, and resolved itself into a dark plump man making water against a puzzle machine. He turned and politely offered intercourse. Meckis was nodding mechanically when Rhee spoke in a clear, firm voice:

"Thanks, but no. Meckis and I are together."

"Yes ...?"

"Permanently together," she said without flinching. The plump one blinked, twice; his mouth opened and closed. He did not speak, but walked rapidly away.

"He doesn't understand," she murmured.

"Triples can be, well, good fun."

"Oh. If that's what you *wanted*, love ..."

"Never mind."

Next came a playground where gravity was partly annulled: they chased each other in vast slow leaps, and Meckis felt silly. Here the evening mist glowed ultramarine. They coupled in illusory fathoms of water. Rhee said insistently, "I love you, I love you."

"Me too," he replied automatically.

On the second night as on the first, Meckis didn't sleep well.

The pearly morning found him in a vile humour. His groin ached from excess, his head from sleeplessness, and Rhee was so eager to kiss him anew that she failed to freshen her mouth first.

"It's so marvellous the way I feel," she told him.

He gnawed his lip, struggled upright and spat. "Look. This is no good. It's not real."

"The realest thing in the world."

"None of it's real! You're changed, drugged, you don't know what you're talking about. Fucking perfect love all day and all night –" The observer in the back of Meckis's skull was surprised to find he was shouting. "All out of a drug machine! See – see this cone? That's your perfect love in there. I raped your *brain* with a blue stinger, don't you remember?"

Rhee was briefly silent. "I love you," she said with radiant calm. "I'm so grateful, you don't know how grateful, that you gave me the medicine. I wasn't real before."

"No. *This* is the dream. This is the nightmare. *That* was the real thing back then, don't you *understand*?" His voice was breaking with the intensity of feelings never before felt. There were always new internal cliffs and precipices.

"I know I'm not good enough for you ..." she began.

It was then that he hit her in the face.

Rhee lay momentarily stunned while Meckis's feelings surged in standing waves, from guilt to a sort of savage triumph. His fist throbbed, each knuckle a separate point of pain. Over the edge of the new cliffs, new depths. This was the end of all things.

Then she was back, on her knees, dizzily swaying like a shape seen through blowing fog. "Do what you like. I know I deserve whatever you do. I'd rather be hit by you than loved by anyone else. Go on."

Meckis couldn't go on. Instead he succumbed to hardening physical desire; he thrust her down and entered too quickly. They made a kind of love more violently than ever before, while all the time Rhee looked appallingly, frighteningly happy. Afterwards, he could hardly walk.

Fog trembled as they wandered on, wavering in shapes of guilt and fear at the borders of Meckis's vision. He stole sidelong glances at the dark bruises which made Rhee even more different and exciting. *She wants me to do whatever I want. So no matter what I do, it must be all right. So why should I feel bad about it? After all, she wants me to.*

"Love you," she whispered through swollen lips as they moved among a forest of gleaming rods between which random lightnings played. (When a bolt caught them, as occasionally happened, a shattering pulse of pleasure would make them stumble or fall.) The words of the endearments might be perennially fresh and new, but mere repetition had eroded them to meaningless noise.

Presently, half reluctant and half curious, he struck her again. She stood passively, even ecstatically, as he experimented with forehand and backhand slaps. Her nose bled. She whispered: "Don't stop."

So then, sweating and panting from the exertion, Meckis found it good to exert his own free will by not hitting her. New feelings were churning in his mind, with hints that Rhee's unreal devotion was an admirable thing. How marvellous to look at the world through that roseate haze. They must both have been drooping a little: soft chairs unfolded from the bare ground, and a table of multicoloured sweetmeats thrust itself up like a mushroom. Meckis glowered, persuading himself that he'd enjoyed the faint hunger-pangs. They sat down anyway.

"I'm sorry I hurt you."

"You must have *needed* to do it. That's what I'm here for. To give you everything I can."

"Suppose I didn't want to take it? Suppose I told you to go away and leave me alone." He hid his face behind a mug of frothing chocolate, and looked at her over the top.

"Please don't." Her eyes were wet; she was ugly with bruises and caked blood. There was no reason at all that now, for the first time, Meckis should feel almost fond of her.

"I don't love you, Rhee. Nobody loves anybody any more. We've grown out of that...."

"I can keep trying," she mumbled, and put a soft hand on his thigh. Meckis suddenly identified a further component of his churning emotional stew. She was happy. Simply being with him, she could be happy: and he was bitterly envious.

"Let's walk some more before we sleep," he said lamely. As one always did, they came to the sea. Sandy grass gave way to grassy sand, sloping to a grey-green stagnation swayed only by the distant sun. The salt-heavy air moved sluggishly over them. It looked easy to wade out into choking fluid and escape the tedium of forever; but of course smooth inhuman arms would prevent such a major mishap.

Meckis patted the drooping woman's shoulder. "I wish I felt like you. You must be the happiest person alive, since I cheated you. I envy you, you know?"

"Then be happy with me."

He sighed. But she was looking at him earnestly, her head a little on one side, as though he were failing to grasp an essential truth. To be happy.

"Oh. No," Meckis said. "That ... hadn't occurred to me. Not that."

He unlocked the modified finger, shook a tiny blue cone into his right palm. His lips moved soundlessly as he stared at it.

"Yes," she said.

The second instalment of forever, he thought.

Changing other people will never help, he thought.

You have to change yourself.

"I think it might be ... better if you did it," said Meckis, holding out the cone. Rhee's face glowed with a brief beauty. shining through the bruises and negating them, as she took the thing from him. With a slow creamy smile of fulfilment, she pushed it into his arm. The instant's pinprick pain gave way to icy cold as the blue tint spread and faded. Without motion, Meckis was falling. The chill embraced his whole body, leaving a numbness like hoarfrost on the flesh. Vision became remote, as though he saw the world through intricacies of mirrors.

After a long silence he stared into the face of the same woman like so many other women, a face disfigured and swollen-lipped. It held no more attraction than before.

"I don't think it's working," he wanted to say. "I don't think it's working," he, the inner Meckis who sat somewhere at the back of his own skull, tried to say. But now a new and alien program was in charge, primed with its own imperatives, armed with Meckis's memories:

"I do love you, Rhee," was the meaningless noise which came from his lips. And from hers: "Oh, I'm so glad," as the bodies put their arms about each other.

The inner Meckis thought about being bored and being different. Forever. He wanted to send some message to that other intelligence which must lie trapped in a forever loving body, snared until the sun broke down: *I'm sorry, Rhee, I'm sorry.* He remembered again those old verses about the triumph of time ...

For this could never have been, and never
Though the gods and the years relent, shall be.

And so, he thought as the kiss prolonged itself on his lips, we live happily ever after.

• Published 1987. Just in case anyone needs to know, the "old verses" and title line are from Algernon Charles Swinburne's long poem "The Triumph of Time".

John Clute's review of the anthology (*Other Edens*) remarked of this story that "a point about terminal boredom is made with lackadaisical grace": I'm still not entirely sure whether that's good or bad....

Ellipses

Preliminary condensation of statements for publication assessment. Text marks indicate omission of irrelevant, impertinent or classified material. Not for outside circulation.

1. John C. Cormill

Naturally I object to being asked, but I'm ready to avow – not admit – that I'm an atheist. I was only invited in as a sort of control, a token sceptic. As such, of course, I should have been consulted from the start and allowed to work with Elder on the experimental design. Any halfway competent [...] A hospital just isn't a controlled lab environment, even if it's university-linked.

Of course I doubt the claims. In spite of the alleged evidence I'm still highly dubious of the Messiter algorithm itself. Something which only one man has quote mastered unquote: what kind of reproducible process is *that*?

All right, I agree that the final incident is sort of inherently a one-off. Poor guy, we can't treat him to a big horse-laugh about repeatability now, but I reckon we still ought to be committed to aiming at some kind of objective truth. Dead fakes can do more harm than live ones. For example, look at [...]

I do admit that at the time it was impressive.

A million ways it could have been done. How did Messiter pull his communication tricks? I wasn't asked early enough; never had long enough to watch him in action. Professional magicians should have spied on him through concealed video cameras ... they did all that? Well, no one denies he was clever.

If you insist. For the sake of argument I'll go along with the big names who endorsed Messiter. Remember, though, the spiritualists made fools of Crookes and Conan Doyle. I just want to mention it.

Even taking the Algorithm at face value, we're still left with the big unrepeatable of the last message. What can I say? It was impressive, incredibly impressive, at the time. I have to state that at the time it actually seemed to meet my criterion about information which must have an extraordinary source. Though, remember, Messiter *was* a brilliant thinker, and he *could* just conceivably have had that last bit about Fermat's theorem up his sleeve ... I'd always been sure that was one of the great undecidables. I can't say anything until I see the unedited transcript I've kept asking for.

That apart, we're talking about a [...] computer output here. You've heard of viruses and logic bombs. All of us had the opportunity when we were keeping that endless creepy death-watch. Four days, three nights, meals and sleep. Even I had to sleep. Two minutes alone with the equipment would be enough to load something that did it all; erased itself; left no trace.

Frankly, you ought to be stopped from going public with [...] like this.

2. Marina Elder

I have no objection to the question and I quite see why you should ask it. I'm an agnostic. And whichever way the preconceptions tilt, I like to think I'm a trained observer too.

My role was really just the same as in all our past demonstrations of the effect. I felt very close to Dr Messiter after working with him over the years, and it was a terribly sad time for me. If the idea hadn't been his own, I'd have dismissed it as ghoulish. How could I deny him the chance of that one last experiment, though?

Of course I'll be happy to fill in the background "for the record", though you must know an open report won't be able to use most of the fine detail. In the beginning Dr Messiter was trying to refute the Sheldrake theory of morphic resonance, of which he didn't approve. So he tried to push it to the point of *reductio ad absurdum* collapse ... you know, to extrapolate until you got some logical prediction about the real world that was so silly, the theory had to be silly too. The way he approached [...]

So there he was with the idea of a compulsive resonator pattern. Something which, if the morphogenetic field existed, would make waves in it. The Messiter algorithm is just a way to set up a working model of the pattern in your head. Sort of, you know, a huge mathematical mantra.

That's the "large" algorithm, the transceiver. I got my little share of reflected glory by programming the "small" pickup algorithm on a supercomputer. It only has [...] recursive steps instead of [...] for the large version, you see. You assume the morphic field can modulate the output of an indeterminate pseudo-random number generator, and [...]

I suppose any roomy enough human brain could take the large algorithm on board, but only Dr Messiter actually succeeded.

Yes, he gave me full credit for my part, when he was able to publish at all. He was always extraordinarily kind. I'm sure I remember it was the very last thing he sent, that little reassuring message that he *would* see me again. And vice-versa too. I remember that, but the transcript [...]

When Professor Steck tells you how he understood the Doctor's theories fifty times better than the Doctor ever did, you ask him about the year *he* spent trying to tackle the algorithm. The old goat. Where was I?

It's cruelly unfair, but I'm sure that's why the Nobel committee passed over Dr Messiter's work. Only he ever mastered the knack of sending data to a computer running the pickup routine. Even from that point it took 800 hours of supercomputer time for my program to decode his personal mental symbolism. All the same, the work was classified by [...] because they imagined computers doing morphic telepathy between themselves with zero transmission lag. Dr Messiter had already *proved* that the quantum effects [...]

I thought it was marvellous of him not to be so much more jaded at the end of his life. He hated Sheldrake's woolly notions and he found he'd vindicated them. Instead of an earth-shaking new scientific paradigm, he came out with what that horrible man Cormill calls a mentalist act. Who wants to transmit thought instantaneously when the receiver costs umpteen millions, you need close proximity to set up the contact, and after separation the superlight link lasts for a theoretical maximum of fourteen and a half minutes?

"Einstein was right," Dr Messiter used to say: "God is subtle all right. But the old boy was wrong to add that He's not malicious."

And then they told him about his cancer.

3.   Jane Soar

I'm just a nurse – C of E if you must know, what a funny question – and I'm sure I can't be any help. That whole business, it really wasn't nice. Hovered over the old man like vultures, they did. Even if it was his own idea, they shouldn't have.

He should have had heroin, that's what. I mean, no chance of addiction, was there, with only a day or two left? Fancy taking pain like that, all on locals. Every hour on the hour, in the stomach wall, and you could see it hardly helped. Wicked, it was.

Yes, there was something about him being all wired up to this computer, but *I* didn't see any wires. Maybe it was radio. Stuff kept coming up in big letters, blue on yellow. Like he was typing with his eyes shut and somehow not using his hands. I remember this bit of poetry used to go past quite often, the last few hours.

TESTING TESTING
JUST THE PLACE FOR A SNARK I HAVE SAID IT TWICE
THAT ALONE SHOULD ENCOURAGE THE CREW
JUST THE PLACE FOR A SNARK I HAVE SAID IT THRICE
WHAT I TELL YOU THREE TIMES IS TRUE

Of course I know it. Kids' stuff. I thought to myself, he's wandering, but most of those observer people just looked pleased and went on about "maintaining the link". Except the little scraggy one – he kept hunting under the bed for wires or something. I had to tell him off.

[...]

It was plain he didn't have long. You can usually make a good guess in that sort of case. From my own experience I gave him till midnight, and the house surgeon thought that was about right. As it turned out, he went a bit faster, and so would you with that lot staring. I put him down as gone at 11.36: no pulse, no respiration. They could have pulled him back for a little while if the unit had been ready, but it was a firm NTBR on the chart.

Stands for not to be resuscitated. Everyone knows that.

Well, I've seen some funny reactions from the friends and relatives when a patient finally goes, but nothing to beat this. I'd been told to wait half an hour before fetching the trolley. What d'you think: all that time they never even looked at him. Not once. Some last respects. Some friends.

No, they were all crowded round that computer screen, watching, watching.... In the end I had to have a look, but it didn't make much sense. Something about a throne and a sea? It made me feel [...]

4.   Professor Waldemar Steck

It is something of an insult for you to suppose that my Catholic beliefs could influence my judgement in this affair. One has a certain commitment to objective truth ... when it can be found. Please do not trouble to apologize.

Certainly I am the person best qualified to report on the incident. Dr Messiter discussed his work with me at a level which I fear young Ms Elder could not attain. She, in any case, was distracted by her curious emotional involvement with Messiter. How do they put it: May and December?

[...]

Our late friend, when he spoke at all of last things, showed that blend of jaunty freethinking and muted hopefulness which sounds contradictory but is in fact rather common among scientists. Over the port he liked to venture cheap little digs about micrometer measurements of the pearly gates or making a spectrum analysis of the Real Presence. I grew bored with his reiteration of, "They *say* you can't take it with you." Of course, a nonphysical communications link – the famous Algorithm – is precisely what he intended to take. If in fourteen and a half minutes he could come close to [...], he wanted the world to know.

My dear fellow, you mustn't think that real faith is so easily jarred. Since then I've developed some rather interesting speculations about informational levels; information and meta-information and the rules which govern meaningful signals. Suppose for example that in our "real" world it were not only impossible to express certain truths but actually impossible to formulate such a question as, for example, [...]

Malicious, no, but surely subtle. Consider the early section of the transcript which seems to impress you so disproportionately:

WHIRLING TUNNEL [...] IT IS AN ENDLESS TUNNEL VERY LONG AND DARK I SEEM TO BE MOVING ALONG IT [...] GIDDY SPEED WALLS OF SHAFT FLOWING PAST [...] ALL SEEMS SO REAL DEFINITELY NOT DREAMING [...] AND AT THE END [...] WHITE AT THE END [...] LIGHT BRIGHT LIGHT MOVING TO THE LIGHT [...]

In fact I can assure you that this is among the commonest of experiences at or near the point of death. Entire books have been written about it; we must not lend it an undue weight simply because in this case the information comes via an unconventional (as it were) medium. The parapsychologist Susan Blackmore has convincingly discussed the tunnel hallucination as a function of visual-cortical activity in the absence of other sensory input.

There again, we have only that one nurse's opinion as regards the actual timing which places this passage of the report at some two minutes *post mortem*. By no means do I unthinkingly reject the wilder interpretations; although I suspected that my old friend's "proofs" would always dissolve in ambiguity, I was severely shaken by the final part of what came through.

This appeared to be a species of ontological argument, expressed in the terms of the propositional calculus. At the time it affected me profoundly; I still find it extremely hard to believe Dr Messiter capable of formulating such a proof. By then he was fourteen minutes gone. The details are blurred in my memory. It was most disquieting. I would prefer not to discuss the matter without seeing [...]

5. Dr Kevin Messiter (final unedited record from 6 min onward)

kk kkk;;;} [...]

6. Assessor's note

No defect was detected in any of the hardware. Nevertheless the final transcript from the machine Algorithm is unsatisfactory, and not easily reconciled with [...]. Hard facts should not dissolve in this ridiculous way. Earlier, it was clearly stated that [...]. Professor Steck's "cosmic censorship" analogy begs the question. If the witnesses' memories are really so absurdly hazy as to detail, can we not have access to [...]
   [...]
   [...]
   [...]

• Published 1990. This is the sort of story about which, really, all one can usefully say is "[...]". I remember starting with an analogy from relativity, in which faster-than-light signals or particles (tachyons) aren't necessarily forbidden but may not carry actual information. Similarly, metaphysical information filters somewhere out there in the beyond must automatically degrade important messages from the dead to content-free séance babble: "We are all very happy here. I have a definite feeling about the health of someone whose name begins with S, or perhaps J or B, or one of his or her friends, who is ill or thinking of becoming ill ..." All of which was wisely dropped during the actual writing.

Fermat's Last Theorem, a legendary unattainable of mathematics, was proved at last in 1994 after a premature announcement in 1993. I wouldn't have believed, when dabbling in maths at college, that both this and the four-colour problem (1976) would be cracked in my lifetime. Mathematical purists can if they like cross out "Fermat's theorem" in section one of the story and substitute "Goldbach's Conjecture", still unsolved ... but it doesn't have the same feeling of importance.

A Surprisingly Common Omission

A transworld shift is undramatic. All I saw was an ordinary road, an ordinary town. Was this a parachronic probability world, or just our own?

Warning against hasty conclusions, my boss had said: "Watch out. A variant continuum could distort your thinking and blind you to incongruity...." Rubbish, I thought.

I had four hours. Slipping into a handy library, I found a *Britannica*. Any major disparity in this world must show up in print.

With growing frustration I got as far as book III, "Claustrophobia to Dysprosium". Automatic shiftback caught my hand still fumbling for book IV, "Fabulation to Lipogram"....

• Published 1990 in a collection of drabbles, which are stories of precisely 100 words. (Titles don't count but should not be inordinately long. "Hyphenated-words-are-argued-about.") After sweating through this particular literary discipline for even that long, I can only admire the glorious obsessives who constructed such lipograms at novel length – like Ernest Vincent Wright with *Gadsby* (1938) or Georges Perec with the better-known *La Disparition* (1969, translated into English by Gilbert Adair as *A Void*). But neither of them, you will note, have names as suitable for this mode as 'David Langford'.

A Snapshot Album

2 May

Photography is a vastly over-rated art. I remember thinking that in the first years of seeing the castle at the corner of each eye.

The sunlit scene was so packed with neat compositions, each ready to be clipped from context and expensively framed. Harlech Castle brooded conventionally and forever photogenically on its high rock, the hills behind it littered with ancient settlements which to the uninformed looked exactly like heaps of grey stone. If you liked ironies, there were invading sheep nibbling remorselessly round the castle walls, and bobble-hatted schoolkids fixed in poses of boredom on the battlements. Below, the flatland where a besieging army might once have massed and lit its fires was dotted with paunchy golfers.

When the obvious began to pall, I could pick out abstract patterns inscrutable as the constellations: the curl of yellow-striped caterpillars on one tall weed, or jackdaws strung along phone lines like a frozen message in morse. Infuriating not to be able to flick my eyes left or right, and take a proper look. Instead I had only the dimmest sense that somewhere north, in a direction pointed to by my left ear, were the much-postcarded mountains of Snowdonia.

Of course, in the end, everything palls, even the very small and shapely blonde whose rear elevation I could admire a little way up the road, caught inelegantly in mid-stride. (Eventually I came to think it almost constituted an introduction, having spent all that timeless time peering sidelong at her bum.) It wouldn't have made much ultimate difference if the focal point, along the tunnel of where I happened actually to be looking, had held anything of more interest than parched roadside grass decorated with a shiny bunch of rabbit-droppings.

Perhaps I'm doing the photographers an injustice, and perhaps it's no easier to coax the worthy details from a scene than to spot the statue hidden in the marble. I had that thought too as the years went by. I lost count of how many times I had it before my afternoon lurched back into motion.

The light changed and the landscape reshuffled itself minutely. Momentum returned: my foot came down on the beach road, the gull that had been nailed to the sky regained its gracefulness in a dipping seaward curve. A second later, having spent too long away, I fell over.

3 May

Dr Gruffydd is a peculiarly irritating man ... one of those irremediably unlocal people who work at being Welsher than the Welsh. (If he'd been born Smith and not Griffith, he'd now call himself Smydd. Or Smwdd.) Mid-forties, I suppose, with an unstinting beard. Receding gums give him a horrid peggy smile. He always knows better.

"Clearly a sort of illusory fugue state," he said, knowing better. "You should have told me the first time. Of course I'm not a psychiatrist, but, considering your position ..."

The tone conveyed that nevertheless he happened to know more about the subject than all but two or at most three other people in Wales. He let the sentence dangle, and waited.

"I suppose it *is* dreadfully obvious in a pop-psychology way," I said quickly. "Maybe an expert would see a bit more in it." How dare he put his tobacco-stained finger straight on the glaring point it had taken me all day, all those years, to spot?

"I like my patients to face unpleasant facts. You know that, Mr Frost. Somewhere deep down, a part of you is thinking *six months, a year, and that's all*. Not much time. So let's dream about endless time. Kid yourself you've years ahead of you. Is it?"

"If I were conjuring up an escape-hatch, don't you think I could put something happier on the other side? This – experience, whatever you call it – it's boring beyond belief."

"Perhaps you are a little too intelligent to manufacture a delusion which is obvious wish-fulfilment. Think about it."

I had, I had. I'd even tried to face the unpleasant notion of being caught in one of those infinitely stretched moments while sitting across the desk from Dr Ieuan Gruffydd. Half an eternity staring at the gingery tufts of hair that peep from his nostrils ... Hieronymus Bosch would have rejected the torment as overly morbid.

"You're very quiet. Here's something else to think about. I'd like to talk it through with a physicist friend up at the Coleg, just hypothetically you know, but look at it this way. If in any sense you'd truly spent so long looking at a single frame of Harlech, you know, a single fractional instant, you'd have seen nothing but black. There's only so much light coming off the landscape, and spreading a second's-worth over even an hour ... you see?"

"Or rather, you're saying, I wouldn't see." Shit. When it's inarguably *happening* to you, you don't analyse it like that: but as an electronics consultant (very much ex), I should have, shouldn't I?

"I like patients who can see a logical argument. Please come and talk about it again if you're bothered." He threw in a few grace-notes about sensory deprivation and black rooms, like a chatty dentist putting off the evil moment. "Now, chemotherapy. We'll start you on a new course next week, Aberystwyth hospital again – so just in case, take the train and forget your car, is it?"

"All right, Doctor."

I'd have liked to argue about the car, but imagine a century or so of distracting thoughts intruding just as you're about to brake. Never safe to think and drive.

11 May

The night was damp, and things popped underfoot as I prowled the flat part of the neighbourhood (pain, insomnia, about one night in three). Despite its fringe of sand-dunes the coastal plain is very much Morfa Harlech, the marshy bit; my flat here is in the Glan Gors estate, which according to my dictionary research means Bog Beach. If you believe in kindness to the overblown slugs that roam in packs from sodden fields, you don't go walking by night. Pop!

Traeth Beach. The signpost conjured up that hot embarrassing flush I'd felt on learning why any mention of Traeth Beach produced sly Welsh smiles. Everywhere on the coast turned out to have the identical bilingual sign. Glan may mean beach but so does bloody Traeth. I'll never get the hang of Welsh in the time that's left, though its placenames are fun and today proved quite useful.

They floodlight the castle in the high season. It glowers down in garish orange, like something out of Disneyland. When I first saw it a year ago, I'd had an overpowering sense of deja vu, of having been here before. At the time it was easily dismissed as a memory of some wish-you-were-here postcard that in better times might have spent five minutes propped against the marmalade jar before I threw it out. Now, though ...

According to the authorities, an image can sometimes jump the queue of short-term memory and sneak into the "old stuff" storeroom, instantly emerging all festooned with spurious cobwebs and dust. By the time you've taken in the "real" scene as something happening now, it merely reminds you of the impostor. When any little deterioration could mean the long last slide downhill, you get dreadfully interested in tricks of vision and memory.

Such as, what does seeing a freezeframe landscape really mean, in terms of photons and candelas and lumens? I think I know now. When I didn't want it, the thing happened three times in four days; when I got interested, there was a week-long gap and until this afternoon I was coming to think Gruffydd had indeed talked me out of my foolish delusions.

This fourth trip was uncomfortable: longer, or so it seemed, and shot through from end to end with a frozen worm of pain. The afternoon had stopped halfway through a bad twinge from the crab in my guts. So much for sensory deprivation, Doctor. I was lying down, of course, and I now know more about my bedroom's cracked Artex ceiling than you would believe possible.

Not even a posh photographer could clip an arty study from its expanse of overhead boredom, though I had (some thousands of times) the idea that portions of it would pass undetected in a show of Jackson Pollocks. Thanks to whatever gods there be for that lumpy snowfield's one spot of human, or at any rate living, interest: a fat spider. Afterwards, in gratitude, I put it gently out of the window.

Usually I'm less kind. Pop!

Then I made an appointment for next day with the good doctor. And another with Jones & Jones, our local builders and decorators. Having spent an odd year of the afternoon persuading myself that a certain collection of ceiling bumps and stains looked incredibly like the face of Mao Tse-Tung, I can't seem to make him go away again. Didn't Kipling once write a bit about how dangerous it is to imagine the train's wheels are singing rhythmic words to you, because then they'll never stop? Same deal with the late Chairman. Jones & Jones will have to carry out a cultural purge.

Walking back through the whine of insects and the baa of insomniac sheep, I muttered extracts from the vast quantity of very topical and very, very bad verse I'd composed and memorized that long day.

12 May

"I read it. I've been doing some research. The sort of thing I'd expect you to call taking a healthy interest."

"I ... see."

That smile of his always gets me on the defensive. This time it conveyed that he'd been almost alarmed at a patient's having a thought, but that since I'd merely found it in a book, it didn't count. If this is his bedside manner from up at the old people's residential home, I'm surprised they don't rise up and beat him to death with their NHS walking frames.

"Software," I said, starting again. "You know you don't even see colours except near the centre of the, um, visual field. There aren't any colour receptors out around the edges ... but the sky looks all blue instead of grey with one blue patch, because your brain software processes the image. Updates it when you glance this way or that."

He looked rather pointedly out of his window, where, irritatingly, the sky over the sea *was* grey with one blue patch. "I see where you're heading."

"I'm not looking at real light when it happens. I'm looking at my mind's software image."

"What you're doing is, you're removing the thing from any threat of testability. You're making it an impregnable theory. Bach."

"When it happened yesterday I had the software idea in mind, as a theory, and I bloody well made a prediction that tested out. My mind isn't a perfect computer, so the image should degrade. I swear it did; it changed around the edges, just a little, and there was a sort of flicker when things started up again."

He looked at me as no doubt he looked at little old ladies who told him their minds were being controlled by radio lasers from Soviet UFOs. "Subjectivism ... covers a multitude of symptoms. I don't deny you're a clever fellow, but what can I think? My pet physicist was keen to put you through an objective test, and she had the bright idea of sitting you in front of a computer. She's actually written the program, bach. It displays thousands and thousands of little dots, a new arrangement every ten seconds. The idea was, we'd sit you there –"

"For a whole sodding week?"

"Well. When you had your, your *experience*, if time really stretched out for you you'd be able to count the current number of dots, which in ten seconds you couldn't possibly. When you came out of it you'd say Stop and we could check your figure against the PC's record. And if that didn't knock some sense ... well, anyway, as I was saying, I admire your cleverness. You've thought ahead, and killed the test. I was expecting a lot of failures and excuses – 'Oh I just happened to blink' – but the idea of a mental image you can't trust in detail, that's genius, isn't it?"

With Dr Gruffydd you evidently got only two choices: to be either touchingly dim or insanely crafty. I began to feel that my remaining bright idea was about to drop me back into the less flattering category.

I said: "Listen to this a moment, if you don't mind. Incidentally, I have not gone completely loony.

"The menu last night at the Bistro in Harlech
Had apricot lamb with a smidgeon of garlic.
Atomic experiments planned at Trawsfynydd
Were savagely criticized all over Gwynedd.
A very drunk motorist north of Llanbedr
Demolished his Volvo and couldn't be deader.
Inadequate hygiene gave pains in the belly
To buyers of meat from a shop in Pwllheli ...

"I'm afraid there's about eight thousand lines of this stuff. Further inspiring recitations on request. I'm not under any delusion about the verse being even remotely good, but it's, well, functional. Are you ahead of me, as usual?"

"Did you come up with a rhyme for Dolgellau?" he said gravely, almost as though genuinely interested. "Or Penrhyndeudraeth?"

"Sorry, I've not lived in these parts long enough. The point is that composing even this sort of rubbish takes time."

"And you've had a week, more than a week ... no, you were expecting me to say that, I can see. Well?"

"Every single line is based on yesterday's papers. When I'd got through the *Cambrian News* I carried on with nationals, right down to the small ads. I've been spending my mornings stuffing myself with information so I could do this ... when I had time. You couldn't produce all this bumf in a normal day. How's that for evidence?"

A long pause. "... Slightly pathetic. You may be becoming dangerously obsessed, Mr Frost. It's what we call an idiot-savant talent, being able to improvise endless rhyming couplets. Anyone with the right trick of mind could do it as fast as they scan the newspaper. For all I know you're making it up as you sit there."

Touchingly dim, insanely cunning and now an idiot-savant. No one could accuse bloody Gruffydd of clinging unreasonably to a snap diagnosis. "Oh, come on. There's nothing special about my talents, nothing at all. It takes me a good long while to fudge up a page of doggerel."

"Prove it."

Here's the cliff edge. Now *prove* you can't fly.

I pulled myself shakily upright; he sent me on my way with a merry "Iechyd da!" One of the few Welsh phrases I do know, and so cheering with the drugs still reaming me out. Good health.

In all that chronicle of wasted time yesterday, I'd never found a decent rhyme for Gruffydd either ... or some particularly obscene limericks would soon be making the rounds of local pubs.

15 May

Bad days. Morning after morning, my comb was choked with hair; the treatment seems to be a kind of chemical neutron bomb that destroys patients and leaves tumours standing. When the gloom is on me, even this magic country doesn't look so good. Snowdon itself is getting thin on top thanks to the steady tramp of the million visitors who ride up on a little railway. The narrow lanes crawl with coachloads of people hoping to find the mystic stillness of the enchanted Celtic twilight and nail it with a long lens. Some of the beaches – ugh. I always think of that line from the bad-verse anthologies, "Dead bards stench every coast", though admittedly the worst I ever tripped over was about two-thirds of a former sheep.

Gruffydd arranged for me to meet the fabled physicist in a smoky pub. and she said things about the region's problems in a marvellously disastrous way. I already knew her face but, embarrassingly, was even better briefed on the curvature of her rear: it was the very small and good-looking blonde I sometimes saw in the village and had observed from behind through one long frozen eyeblink. She was called Mair something, and actually gave my famous delusions a spot of intelligent consideration (while G. frowned thunderously into his gin and tonic and I tried hard not to think of bums).

"... physical basis of mind," she concluded rather sadly. "I'm afraid you only have to look up the timescale of electrochemical propagation. It's in all the textbooks. Nerve impulses chug along at, oh, 120 metres a second max. It has to be a limit on the, on the speed of thought. You can't drive faster than your car will go."

"Oh," I said.

My friendly doctor brightened no end. "But of course you can imagine having done it. It must be rather like dreaming. The way a whole complex of adventure and emotion gets thrown together in a flash when a few chance images collide, is it?"

He bustled off to the bar, and Mair said: "He's no local, you know, he's from South Wales. It's down there more than up here they finish their sentences with 'is it?'." This cheered me irrationally. I liked her. All around people were talking rapid Welsh, which sounds like English that you can't quite make out, and Gruffydd stood there ordering drinks in the language of aliens and tourists.

Later, she of the Aberystwyth PhD made some tactful comments. "You see them in their horrible beach outfits staring into estate agents' windows. They buy houses here because in southeast terms the property's dirt cheap. The country's dying of it. Every time a farm cottage gets sold off to a second-home owner, it's like a healthy cell of the community being replaced by cancer. It grows and spreads and ..."

By then, Dr Gruffydd's contortions and agonized nudges were lovely to behold. Obviously he felt there was a limit to the facing of unpleasant facts. She stopped and went brilliant pink; very fetching.

I shouldn't enjoy ticking off these tiny, malicious victories. But when, as someone put it, time's wingèd chariot is not merely hurrying near but parked outside and sounding its horn ...

24 May

Having a drink with Mair is better fun without Dr G. With him around

I could never have confessed that soon after retiring to these parts I'd played tourist and, on impulse, drunk a handful of water from St Cybi's holy well. "After all," I pointed out, "it's supposed to work even if you don't believe in it."

She laughed and admitted doing much the same, for luck, before tackling the final draft of her thesis. My well bubbled up within a sort of ruined Victorian bathhouse down a remote lane; hers was better known and thus half-obscured by a drift of crisp-packets and polystyrene. So it worked for her if not for me. We were intensely civilized and didn't actually burden our conversation with that last trite remark.

27 May

Several things changed tonight.

As though young Mair had convinced me when Gruffydd couldn't, inner and outer time had stayed nicely meshed, like the cogs on that mountain railway. A table for one in Yr Ogof was not where I'd expected to suffer a new derailment.

This is the bistro place where they do the stewed lamb with apricots. I can never remember whether Yr Ogof is "the cave" or "the cellar", but either way it's dark in there. On evenings like this, their aero-engine-sized fan turns the single room into a hot wind-tunnel. Each table is positioned with great care, so the blast won't blow out its candle; if you stand in the wrong place, the airstream rearranges itself around you and someone's light gets snuffed.

Coming to me, the waitress passed through one of the wrong places. The flame died, the cogs slipped at just that moment, and I was left in near-darkness, forever looking at the approaching plate with its wisp of stilled steam like cotton-wool or ectoplasm.

It had never happened in the dark before. The halted image in my eyes was less insistent, easily ignored. Lightning jabs of agony had been running through me all day; now, caught out of time between pains, I could brood undistracted at last.

I thought: I may not make it to my forty-fourth birthday next year, but by then I'll have had a secret bonus of centuries on centuries. That can't be bad.

Some thousands of memories later, I thought: Who cares about convincing that bloody doctor? I know what's happening, and none of their explanations fits.

I wondered if Mair could have come up with some theory, if she'd only been convinced. I'd liked her. I even fancied her; even a year ago I'd have been seriously interested, but the thought of *that* kind of exercise ... (Walking up the steep hill to the main part of Harlech village tonight had provoked a lot of groaning thoughts about this probably being the last time. Taxis from now on. In the jealously guarded local dialect: *tacsi*.)

Eventually, even the tedium of being alone with my own thoughts was something that passed. On the far side of the boredom barrier there's a kind of exhilarating, tingling calm.

I finally came up with the best thought of all. Mair said this couldn't be real because of the physical limitations on thinking. Turn it round, and what's happening to me shows there aren't, there truly aren't, such limitations. Those verses proved it for me, if not for outsiders. A mind is something independent after all. I sniffed suspiciously around the notion, nervous of compromising my good old fundamentalist-atheist principles. Too good to be true ...?

After routine aeons of inattention to the dim shapes that filled my visual field, I recalled again that half-forgotten idea of image degradation, and how I'd worked out that memory might simplify, stylize, or alter what I "saw". And even felt, or smelt. It came to me then that the familiar scene wasn't as it had begun.

The candle, long snuffed, burned in frozen flame. Smooth blonde hair threw back an answering highlight. Leaning towards me over the table, smiling and clearly about to speak, was Mair. In the timeless period that followed before darkness and solitude returned, the cogs re-engaged and the hovering plate swooped at last to rest before me, I was sure that by ever so tiny an amount, her lips moved.

Perhaps the mystic twilight of these ancient hills has got to me at last. Dr Gruffydd would probably deliver a half-kindly, half-snotty lecture on wishful thinking and hypnagogic hallucinations. I cling to the idea that I've had a heartening preview of what comes after; that when we've finally slipped free of time and adjusted to the tempo of eternity, we can invent our own forever. Illusion has to be better than oblivion. Doesn't it?

I'll be seeing you, Mair.

• Published 1991. My wife and I escape when we can to a flat in Morfa Harlech; hence the scenery. Yr Ogof has moved from its cellar to the village high street, but is still a good place to eat. As for the metaphysics, I belatedly realized that our man's recurring situation echoes that of James Blish's protagonist in that fine story "Common Time". He begins in endlessly stretched-out "micro-time", calculates that 6,000 subjective years lie ahead of him, and reckons that all that thinking time should be enough to settle the Problem of Evil and the First Cause. I found myself more sceptical about what one could really bring back from such a fugue....

Leaks

It had been a definite mistake to spend so many hours last night practising. Making his way up the street, Ken struggled not to think of that obscene grey bladder in the local baker's window, which inflated and deflated in a miraculously unconvincing simulation of dough being kneaded. His own brain seemed to be doing much the same. Small wobbling flaws, perhaps UFOs or fragments of detached retina, floated through his field of vision, and that solitary spoonful of cornflakes lay in his stomach like a cluster of leaden dumplings.

What a wonderful thing it was to be talented. He could sympathize two hundred per cent with that bloke in the Bible who hid his talent in a napkin rather than stick out his neck.

Even the green double-decker buses exuded an alcoholic dread as they ground slowly past. Crisp packets leered mockingly from the gutter, sharing some terrible knowledge with the passers-by who so very pointedly ignored the moral leprosy stumbling in their midst. And how had he managed to get beer in his *hair*? Did it just ooze through one's pores from the foetid jellies inside? In every way it was a typical morning.

Behind the offices' grimy Victorian facade, a lift which doubled as a municipal convenience heaved Ken up through Social Services, Housing and Consumer Advice, Traffic Planning.... This Department branch shared the fifth floor with the town council's nerve centre for co-ordination of cemeteries and crematoria. Ken thought longingly about a nice co-ordinated coffin as he steered himself past death's door.

It had been many unpaid months since he'd last been called for temp work at the DPR office; going by appearances, their cleaners followed roughly the same schedule. In a familiar display of method acting, the receptionist behind the desk managed to convey that Ken's own Paranormal Resources included uncanny powers of invisibility and inaudibility. Air molecules of superior importance had passed through her door, Marcia's posture made it clear, and likewise bluebottles with greater social charm. She continued to apply nail-varnish.

Ken peered at notices sellotaped to the dingy cream walls (THE SECTION PRINCIPAL WARNS THAT DISCIPLINARY ACTION WILL FOLLOW IF THERE IS ANY FURTHER REPETITION OF THE UNAUTHORIZED

RAIN OF FROGS IN CONFERENCE ROOM 2) and wondered about his chances of drawing on Departmental resources in the shape of para-cetamol. Time passed.

"Mr Vanrey? You're *late*," said Marcia severely and without prior warning. Her nails glowed iridescent purple.

"That's Varney."

"Oh. It says here ... Mr Vanrey, the Department's time is very valuable. I have a travel warrant for you, and a briefing sheet, and you're to start at once." She sniffed. "And the Senior says he hopes you remember something from your college work about enortpy."

Kenneth Varney, BSc. (Physics) (3rd), stared. "About what?"

"Enortpy." She pushed a slim, puke-coloured folder at him. The typed label said CONFIDENTIAL * ENORTPY RAY.

"... Entropy, maybe?"

"I *spell-checked* it, Mr Clever. Now, you're to be a Departmental observer at the nuclear place, whatsisname, at Robinson Heath. Special investigation. I suppose the physics made them think of you." She sniffed again. "It's only an S-H job. Don't go getting above yourself."

His head gave a particularly vicious twinge. Stalking horse. You heard about these things in a theoretical kind of way. When the DPR had only half a mind to intervene, they'd try stirring up the situation by sending half a talent. Just knowing a quote specialist unquote was on the case could be enough to make your criminal or enemy agent show a detectable break in behaviour patterns. Such as, for example, staying late at the lab and dropping Ken Varney into a convenient swimming-pool reactor.

He asked the question uppermost in his mind.

"No," said Marcia, "but I can do you a Fisherman's Friend if that's any help."

With a groan Ken tucked the folder under his arm and turned away ... then back again. "One thing. Um, your word-processor, you use one of those spell-checkers where you can, you know, add new words ...?"

"To the built-in luxigon? Yes, that's right."

Leaving, he felt ever so slightly cheered. Clearly he had some talent for investigative work after all.

Somewhere out west of Paddington his spirits made the significant leap from whirling dread to mere powerful unease. Could he really be sitting legitimately in First Class No Smoking? Ken Varney with his second-class denims and designer stubble? The ticket inspector had also had obvious difficulties with this concept, but in the end had stalked away baffled.

Feeling a return of the eerie power to tackle words of more than two syllables, he studied the file on entropy (or enortpy) rays. They were hypothetical, and statistical, and saved from nonentity only by a communication written on a sheet of headed A4 [classified] with a worn HB [classified], intercepted by [classified] at location [need-to-know status insufficient], and reading:

MIKHAIL. ENTROPY BEAM DEFINITELY EFFECTIVE ON TRANSPORT HERE. CONTINUE TRIALS SAME LOW LEVEL. TROJAN.

As he hacked his way through the surrounding layers of soft, clinging, wet-strength officialese, Ken gathered that this note would have been dismissed as a rollicking jape if it weren't for the transport pool of the Nuclear Utilization Technology Centre on Robinson Heath, which when examined with a keen statistical eye had detectably [classified]. Only a little bit – "LOW LEVEL", he thought, feeling momentarily clever – but most definitely [classified].

Stalking horse. Marcia had wanted him to feel humbled, but actually his usual assignments for the Department were humbler still and consisted of helping move office, rearrange filing cabinets, fill out the numbers for manpower inspections ... any little job where payment at his sub-competent talent level was cheaper than contract labour. As paranorms went, he rated as the kind of small change it was easier to stuff in the charity box than count. Everyone remembered the Monty Python sketch where Ken's grade was rated just below penguins, though just above BBC programme planners.

And now he was roaring towards NUTC, a place so high-powered and high-security that paranorms weren't normally allowed within a mile of it, just in case of [classified], or even of [need-to-know]. It was a famous quirk of the civil service that, like the Home Office forensic unit, the Department's research lab was attached to NUTC – presumably meaning that they could conduct research on anything but paranorms.

"dS," he mumbled painfully, "equals dQ over T." There, he still knew the definition of instantaneous entropy change. A few more hours' recovery time and the information might even start making sense.

Gasometers bulged like fungi outside the carriage window, succeeded by plastic-faced office blocks in contrasting shades of liver, lights and spam, and then a grimy expanse of station. Ken shouldered his bag and was soon shuffling down the platform, cautiously swivelling his head in slow motion and wondering whether a quick hair of the dog would be advisable just for the sake of practice. This gambit was blocked by a small placard saying MR K VANREY, held up by a uniformed driver of few words and one implacably pointing finger. Score another first for Talent Grade Z: he'd never before been chauffeured in an official car, even one that banged and wheezed through Reading and the countryside like this.

"Ducts!" was his first thought when the heart of Britain's defence industry lurched into view, as though with incidental music from *Brazil*. Huge silvery ducts ran inside the miles of high wire fence, rearing up in triumphal arches to allow traffic at each gate. Smaller, black-clad ducts linked the square buildings, whose inner walls and ceilings were threaded by narrow pipes painted in Civil Service cream: they circled the security office where he was photographed holding a prison-style number, they paced him and his escort along endless two-tone corridors, they clumped companionably in the bare room where briefing was supposed to happen. The Robinson Heath installations had clearly been designed by some perverse lover of spaghetti.

The briefing group ...

Dr Fortmayne from Weapons Physics had thick grey hair, a glittering eye, and bounding excitement. It seemed he must be strapped in place, otherwise he'd vibrate off his chair. "Let me make one thing clear: I want this gadget. I want it very much. I disagree with our whole approach. We shouldn't be piddling around, we should be going through the site and surrounds with a tooth-comb." He frowned. "Whatever a tooth-comb is."

Sergeant Rossiter of MOD Police/Security mumbled something and was understood to be saying that tooth-combs came expensive these days. His raggled moustache and furtive manner evoked memories of the least reputable of Ken's occasional employers, Greasy Mal from Highbury, the man of a thousand fiddles.

Someone called Brownjohn, large, bland and moist, represented Transport. "Run of bad luck. Could happen any time. Obvious hoax by one of our bright lads. And when we catch him –"

There was a wrangle between Theoretical Physics ("An entropy projector is a plain and simple impossibility."), the DPR Lab Principal ("So is he," with a nod towards Ken: "Six impossible things before breakfast.") and NATO Liaison: "I don't care whether it's impossible or not: if it's available it'll make a nice bargaining point to squeeze some more counter-force goodies out of the bloody Americans. Since we can't seem to develop our own." At this, Fortmayne leapt upright in sputtering outrage, and the decibel count rose sharply.

Theoretical Physics turned out to be the sort of man who could in cold blood say words like appertaining, tantamount and even predicated.

Ken's head had reverted to full throb-level, but he gleaned that the entire NUTC transport pool was suffering mysteriously accelerated decay. Vehicles wore out naturally but too fast, as though spending all their nights in loud clubs burning the carburettor at both ends. It might have passed unnoticed, but then the message to "Mikhail" had turned up in a routine check of outgoing site mail, addressed to an empty house in the nearby village of Bogley....

"If I had a contraption like that," said Brownjohn, "know what I'd do? Get rich beaming the thing at whisky. Twelve years aged in cask, only take a few months. Why waste it on our vans? Why not Trident?"

Fortmayne pointed out with heavy irony that NUTC transport was serviced every other week, that economics did not permit Trident warheads to be detonated quite so frequently, especially in the Home Counties, and that it was entirely credible that the same insidious influence was indeed being directed against the British deterrent. "And what do they send us? This person Mr Vanrey." (Marcia's spelling was now immortalized within the sealed plastic of his new security pass.) "Possibly he'd like to tell the committee in a few words what special talent he brings to this critical situation? An unnatural gift, perhaps, for turning his face pale green?"

"Touch of 'flu," Ken lied.

"I have Mr Varney's dossier and can vouch for him," said Dr Croll, the DPR Lab Principal. "I think the details of our operation should remain on a need-to-know basis. Our watchword is security." Ken gazed at him admiringly. What a wonderful human being.

"I don't agree with what you're saying," Fortmayne said reflexively, but people were looking pointedly at their watches and Rossiter rubbed his beer-gut with slow significance. Lunch was declared and Ken found himself annexed by Croll.

"We call it the Mushroom Cloud," said the DPR researcher, in the tones of one apologizing for a tedious family joke. Ken agreed that once you'd regarded the local pub's sign in that light, it became impossible ever again to see it as a Wheatsheaf. They entered.

This Croll seemed a cheerful fellow, rotund and bouncingly bald, and deeply untroubled by entropy rays. Ken felt distinctly less lichen-coloured as he contemplated an imminent hair of the chihuahua, if not of a full-scale St Bernard. Pints and curly sandwiches arrived at the table.

"To your success," Croll said with mock formality. "Had we but world enough and time ... but I have to talk a little business. It is really very simple. You will wear *this* and move around NUTC, observing and some-times taking sinister notes, and we shall see what is stirred up."

This was a conspicuous lapel badge in day-glo lime, about three inches across, carrying a single bold character. Drawing on the Dead Sea Scroll remnants of his physics, Ken said: "Greek. A capital *psi*, right?"

"Very good. Yes, like a pink triangle or a yellow star. You will be noticed. Good. But I must admit that I brought you here for another reason, because I am professionally interested in your abilities."

"Ability. With a very, very small A."

"No modesty, now. You can't imagine how much, as a researcher, I truly envy any genuine paranorm. The gulf between us is narrow but it is deep."

Ken was embarrassed. "Honest, it's nothing, like being able to wiggle your ears. I used to send off to the small ads in *Knave* and *Private Eye*, you know, Dr Farrell's Famous Cerebral Enhancer Tonic, a guaranteed forty-four inch talent within two months. Wore my fingers out, rubbing the damn stuff on my temples every night before retiring. I think it was oil of wintergreen actually."

It wasn't something he cared to talk about, especially in a pub. But Croll quizzed him further with the unblinking earnestness of a Scientology interviewer closing for the kill, and at last said: "Perhaps, you know, we can help. Measure your mind's height by the shade it casts. First, though: show me."

Ken had gulped half his pint and Croll was lagging, so it was straightforward enough. He concentrated on the beer mugs and thought parched thoughts. For some reason it always helped to clench his teeth askew and close one eye. Potentials shifted and his mental thumb pushed down hard on the balance of Nature. Quite rapidly, though without any fuss, his own beer-level rose two inches.

"That's it. I mean, that's all there is to it. It has to be alcoholic and it has to be my glass, I don't know why."

"What about conservation of mass? No, don't tell me, I think I see." Croll slid the two mugs together for comparison. "Beer finds its own level. My loss is your gain. But, hmm, what about range? Could you perhaps tap that whisky-bottle up behind the bar?"

"Well, I have to want it, and I don't much like whisky in beer. And I'd have to stand up and look all conspicuous: otherwise, there's a three foot drop from the Teachers optic to this table here, and the potential energy gets a bit frisky. You know, fountains, waterspouts. Whisky and splash."

Croll clicked his tongue. "It is not exactly 'that one talent which is death to hide'. From the dossier I had imagined that, with training ... Just imagine the scenario. A hostile spyplane flies low over Robinson Heath; you glance upwards, narrow your eyes, and vital hydraulic fluid leaks disastrously away!"

"Gallons of it, into my beer mug, with a horizontal velocity vector of seven hundred miles an hour? I hate getting barred from pubs."

"With training, much is possible. You seem to have made room in your glass already. Do please show me again. There, the owner of *that* one is in the lavatory."

Ken clenched his teeth askew and closed one eye. This time Croll kept his attention on the unattended drink twelve feet away. "Excellent. The glass is falling hour by hour, the glass will fall forever ..."

"But if you break the bloody glass you won't hold up the weather," Ken quoted.

"A man of culture, I see."

"Oh, you meet a lot of big brains with degrees down at the job centre and Social Security. The word is 'overqualified'. Which is why –" On second thoughts, this was no place to discuss hauling anonymous clinking boxes off the backs of lorries for Greasy Mal.

"Nevertheless a Department spotter recruited you. Nature's handmaid Art makes mighty things from small beginnings grow – Dryden. I would like you to visit our laboratory later today. You have potential."

"And I have a bloody drink problem. Every time I try to practise what I can do ..." Ken tried not to remember his unwelcome reunion with last night's Chinese takeaway on this morning's pillow. He made a queasy toasting gesture, drank, and convulsed disastrously. "... Oh *shit*, it's lager and lime."

"Fortunately this is only an old suit," said Croll a little coldly.

For the next couple of hours, Ken prowled within what he'd been told was ten full miles of wire-link fence around the Robinson Heath site. How much area was that? About eight square miles if it were a circle, which it wasn't, or six and a quarter for a square, which it wasn't either. Now the average size of a typical entropy ray projector would be ...

Much of the area seemed about as derelict and useless as this statistical line of thought: grass and gorse, decaying tarmac, rabbit droppings, marshy expanses harbouring only a few far-flung ducts. It must be out of sheer embarrassment that the MOD insisted on maps showing the site as a blank white patch. Clearly, when you passed at last through the secret door of the inner circle and walked the throbbing corridors of power you'd envied all your life, the most earth-shattering revelation was how even more boring than the real world it could be.

The beer buzzed in him, and he hoped Croll's own several pints would be interfering with the fellow's afternoon study of the dictionary of quotations. Meanwhile, nobody started back from Ken with cries of guilty alarm.

Instead: "Aagh!" he said in guilty alarm as a hand clamped on his shoulder.

"Just a word in your ear, mate," murmured Sergeant Rossiter. "Just one word. The word is ... pathetic."

"I'm doing my job."

"No, you've already done that, so why arse around? ... Oh dear, all new to you, innit? We leaked it two days back about this dead unusual visit from a DPR weirdo, pardon my French, special talent. Anyone acts funny here *today*, they must be small fry because every big-time guilty conscience is already going to be off sick or taking leave. They're the names we'll feed in for correlation. And where does that leave you, sunshine? Having you here at all's just the follow-through, not the job."

Feeling shrewd and acute, Ken said, "I suppose a really bright villain wouldn't risk acting suspiciously like that, and he'd come in today just as usual."

"Maybe, squire, maybe. So you reckon we should keep an extra close eye on all the ones who stay home suspiciously, *plus* all the ones who suspiciously don't, and that narrows it right down to our entire workforce of lemmesee 11,676 suspicious characters."

"All right, I get the general idea."

"Less a few who went sick or was already off to Benidorm before we let out the rumours. Of course they could be double-bluffing, couldn't they?"

"All *right*."

"Lighten up, now. Enjoy the sights if you like. Nifty little badge you've got there with the wossname, Greek for 'piss' – ask me nicely and I'll get you another with the Greek for 'off'."

Pausing only to call him "chummy", Rossiter drifted away and left Ken thinking dark, entropic thoughts. He prowled on.

At one stage he loitered as suspiciously as he could by the north gate and watched Ford Transit vans accelerate smoothly past security guards who seemed unconcerned about possible stacks of nuclear warheads being smuggled out in each. At another he found the fire-door of a concrete blockhouse flapping its EMERGENCY USE ONLY lettering in the wind, slid cautiously inside, and left in haste when threatened by a big wall sign lurid with trefoils and the interesting rubric PURPLE RAD-IATION ZONE.

This must be part of Fortmayne's plutonium-infested playground. If I were a great detective, Ken thought, I would see right through all that stuff about tooth-combs, and say "Fortmayne doth protest too much" (no, that would be Dr Croll's line), and thrill the assembled suspects in the library by asking which of all these characters was most likely to be the proprietor of a fiendish entropy ray? The number one weapons physicist, of course: Fortmayne. Gesturing grandly to the imaginary inspector closing in with the handcuffs, Ken snagged his finger against the rusty barbed-wire shroud of a passing duct. Ouch. All this, and tetanus too?

The huge ducts and pipes, he decided grumpily, represented the government cash-flow into this unpromising hole in Berkshire. Vast sums surged down the MOD arteries, while the DPR pipeline would be a hair-thin capillary, subject to continual leaks. Billions for defence and about fifty pee for Ken Varney.

Sucking his finger, he shadowed an ailing and consumptive minibus into what turned out to be the Transport yard. Here government vehicles were being subjected to artificial respiration, intensive life-support and major transplant surgery. The stench of petrol was too thick to cut with a knife, and would have required industrial lasers. Entropy lay around in almost visible pools, like the local lake system of sump oil. From an office window two floors up a fat white blur that might have been Brownjohn watched him narrowly.

Who could be a more logical choice for the inside job, playing the dreaded entropy ray across the NUTC service and garaging areas? On the other hand, wasn't Fortmayne the most plausible villain? And hadn't Rossiter more or less warned him off? At this rate of detection he'd soon have a strong circumstantial case against every single bloody member of the briefing committee. We are all guilty. All the world's a symphony orchestra, with some on woodwind and most of us on the fiddle.

Something clicked then in Ken's mind, as though a fruit machine were signalling *nudge nudge*. Hadn't someone in a smoky pub in Highbury once winked and mentioned what they called the car pool fiddle? He thought again about the precepts and philosophy of his very occasional employer Greasy Mal, and quite suddenly laughed out loud. Then he wished he hadn't: jarred by the noise, the inspirational light-bulb flared out and left his skull a blackened, smoking socket. Never go boozing with a hangover *and* a parapsychologist. Which reminded him ...

The DPR laboratory was an unassuming wooden shack, propped up by the more opulent Home Office Forensic Unit. Both were liberally spattered with what might have been red-hot evidence in the form of semen stains, but after some thought Ken placed the burden of guilt on pigeons, especially the one which had dropped its burden on him.

"Welcome!" said Dr Croll, buttoning a white lab coat. "The raven himself is hoarse that croaks your fatal entrance under my battlements, if I might put it like that."

Ken flicked without success at the shoulder of his best denim jacket. "It was a pigeon actually; it just looks like it must have been a horse."

"Come in, come right in."

Inside the sanctum, the old familiar laboratory smell attacked his nostrils with a wire brush. Dull green tiles covered the floor. High-tech things with screens and digital readouts jostled on the benches with archetypal brass instruments that might have been used in the early experiments of Faraday, or Newton, or Torquemada.

For a moment, Ken felt disoriented by the feeling that this place was more like a lab than any real lab could be. Something movie-like about it, perhaps, along the lines of exploding control panels or Dr No's art-deco reactor.

"If you could just sit here," said Croll, indicating the electric chair. Yes, that was the subtle anomaly. University physics labs were always short-changed when it came to important equipment like electric chairs.

"Er ..."

"Oh, yes, I suppose it must look a trifle intimidating. I am very interested in physiological readouts, in trying to map what the body *does* when paranormal abilities come into play. There's no art to find the mind's construction in the face. And so we need all these sensors."

Somehow Ken found himself gently crowded into the chair. "Trust me," said Croll. "I'm a doctor."

What he had in his bulging scientific mind was both simple and deeply irritating. Not content with borrowing Ken as an experimental subject, Croll wanted to play social worker and do him a bit of good. He'd nipped out to the village grocer for test materials in the shape of countless Tetrabrik litre boxes: orange juice, grapefruit juice, pineapple juice, mango juice, and worst of all tomato juice.

"I can't possibly. It only works with something boozy, I told you."

"My snap diagnosis, Ken, is that you are too permanently fuddled ever to transcend your talent's limitations. What you do at present ... It provokes the desire, but it takes away the performance. However, if this will console you in the slightest, we do first need one control reading."

The last of the chilly disk electrodes, slimed with something like KY jelly, had been taped in place. Croll handed Ken a plastic cup, the sort guaranteed to translate coffee directly into scorched fingers, and took a hopeful-looking brown bottle from a cupboard.

"Would, ah, light ale provoke the desire sufficiently?"

"You bet."

"Now good digestion wait on appetite," said Croll in his special quotation voice, "and health on both." Recorders were whirring and displays dancing with a sinuous EEG jiggle.

Ken clenched his teeth askew and closed one eye. The universe duly moved for him, and he raised the suddenly full cup. There was an outraged pause. "Fuck me, what's this?"

"Nothing but cold civil service tea, I'm afraid. My secretary always used to say they brewed it from old tights. Personally I would not know ... So, Ken, it has to be alcoholic, does it?"

Croll had him there. It was the lager-and-lime effect all over again.

"Let me tell you an anecdote. There was once a fellow called Logan whose talent seemed even more spectacularly useless than yours. He was able to incinerate individual dust motes, no more than one at a time. They filed him as a micropyrotic for want of a better word, and then wrote him completely off the useful list with a grade of, well, your grade. Years later he made the imaginative breakthrough all by himself and emigrated to glory in America, the land of vigilantes and handguns."

"Oh yeah, I saw a Day In The Life of him in one of the colour supplements. Local clod makes good. Learned to focus it on gunpowder or something, didn't he? Mr Misfire, The Man Whose Adversaries Shoot Themselves In The Foot. He looked a right sight in those puce leotards."

"Pre-cisely. I am convinced that I, here, could have developed his ability much sooner: but our beloved masters, after first building this laboratory at Robinson Heath to save money, had a security scare. They became paranoid about letting wild talents anywhere near the nuclear work at NUTC ... unless they happen to be in Security or Intelligence, and by definition too lofty, too busy to spare *me* one miserable afternoon. You know that today is the first time in a year that I've been able even to calibrate the psychotronic readouts?" He added, with dreadful inevitability: "We all know Security is mortals' chiefest enemy."

Ken writhed in the hard seat, which at the seat of his jeans also felt oddly cold and damp. Being wired up was even more uncomfortable than it had looked, but being wired up *and* lectured at....

"Ow!" he said. Croll had sneaked up behind him with a needle.

"This will help make you more suggestible. No, no, don't move now, it might affect the sensors. The instruments of darkness tell us truths, but not if you wiggle the wires. Let me just tighten this strap; and this one. Now I want you to try for some juice. Just one small change in your talent. You know you can do it. Tip the tea out in this beaker...."

Open wide. Rinse. Even the bloody dentist never strapped him in. Ken made his miracle-working face again, staring with concentrated loathing at the box of grapefruit juice; and, almost at once, nothing happened. Except that his head hurt even more.

"Look," he said patiently, "it's as though you convinced me to walk across this dark room, and then showed me that I'd been on a narrow plank over a sodding great crevasse a mile deep. And there you are saying 'you can do it, just walk back again now.' It's not the same."

Croll beamed, and hunched himself over a small console to one side of the EEC soft-drinks mountain. "I had not yet mentioned that we can provide a counter-stimulus." His hand pounced.

What followed was a mixture of red-hot needles and severe cramps in each buttock, as though the dentist were mounting a surprise attack from the rear. Ken made loud appropriate noises, and added: "Stop that!"

"You cannot imagine how irritated I am by the sheer waste when a potentially fine talent is bestowed on someone like –" A sort of visual *ugh* passed over Croll's face. "A giant's robe upon a dwarfish thief. What a cheap, sleazy use you make of your priceless gift. Now, if I were in your place ..."

Ken offered to change places (and even robes) immediately, but this cunning ploy got only the response it deserved: a second and hotter dose of National Grid. No wonder the blasted hot-seat had been damp. Croll was going to do him good even if it killed him. The after-twitches felt like sitting in a bowl of small, muscular and hyperactive eels.

"Look. I can't concentrate when you do that. Just give me a minute. Did I tell you about what I worked out this afternoon? Only bloody solved the entropy ray business, that's what." In just such a way, when in the dentist's chair, Ken always found himself able to deliver frighteningly voluble monologues, without hesitation, repetition or deviation, on subjects like drizzle or bus tickets. "It's all a load of rubbish, it's just someone doing the old car pool fiddle over in Transport. The only thing I don't understand is ... oh."

Oh no, he thought. What hadn't made sense was why, with a nice little con going, anyone should be so yoghurt-brained as to draw attention to it by sending open letters about entropy beams. Who in this business was several protons short of a nucleus? Well ...

"That is doubtless very interesting and rewarding for you, but as an attempt at distraction it is childish. I ask you to focus your mind, Ken. Focus on that one small change. Present fears are less than horrible imaginings, and the voltage dial can be turned up a great deal further."

Yes, it really stimulated the mind, this sitting in the seat of power. "You sent that letter, didn't you? The one from TROJAN to MIKHAIL, and very funny too. I bet you sent dozens till they intercepted one. You'd spotted the con and you moved in."

Croll's hand wavered over a particular red button, as though it were a fat beetle he didn't quite want to squash because of the mess. "Why should I do a thing like that? What possible motive could I have?"

Dominoes were still falling with a painful *click click click* inside Ken's head. "It got *me* down here, that's what. Your first bloody guinea pig in, what did you say, a whole year? Of course you suggested the stalking-horse game to that committee. Come clean, chummy." Oops, that had slipped out.

By now Croll had whitened to the point where the dome of his baldness looked like a peeled hard-boiled egg, awaiting the descent of some teaspoon of the gods. He closed his eyes and said, apparently to himself,

"Screw your courage to the sticking-place." Then, mostly though not perhaps wholly in Ken's direction: "I will complete my experiment. What's done cannot be undone. Afterwards I think there will have to be an unfortunate accident. This high-voltage equipment does not receive nearly enough safety inspections. There may be an enquiry and even a sharp reprimand."

Of course, Ken was brooding, after spending my life reading all those thrillers I should have thought that when you're strapped to an insidious torture machine in the arch-fiend's secret den, it is not the best time to gloat out loud that you've got the goods on him.

The red button went down. This time the shock to his tormented buttocks included overtones of jagged teeth, killer vindaloo and barbed wire.

"Just a reminder," said Croll. "I *will* see you prove my theories by overcoming your petty self-imposed limits. If even on pain of death you can't bring yourself to love fruit juice, then think of hating me. The labour we delight in physics pain. Look there on the shelf: concentrated sulphuric acid. If some of it were transferred to your cup, you could try to throw it over me. Think of that."

Ken studied the flimsy cup and rather thought the stuff would burn instantly through to irrigate his groin. He pointed out with irrefutable logic that offing Ken Varney was bound to cause more embarrassment than explaining a mere, um, late April Fool letter. Croll retorted even less refutably that the one was a temporary inconvenience while the other would be Wasting MOD Police Time and therefore meant a security downcheck for unreliability, leading by steady logical steps to the dole queue. Unfortunately this made sense.

It was time, Ken decided, to panic. If only this were a sci-fi story he would, around now, discover an unheralded new talent for causing entire crates of whisky to materialize in the air three feet above his tormentor's head. Small delirious details loomed at him, like the particularly important-looking bluebottle buzzing up the window. He noticed for the first time that Croll was wearing a copper bracelet bulging with magnets, the sort that small ads claimed would help against rheumatism, warts and telepathic intrusion. At any other moment this would have brought him a cheering rush of superiority.

Then he looked at the bright new scab on his finger where the wire had snagged it, and thought: ducts. There were plenty running under the wall benches or slung from the ceiling, but those weren't the ones. No, but if, if you just concentrated in the right way, made that one small change in emphasis ...

With a shudder he clenched his teeth askew, and closed one eye, and after a long moment drank. It was every bit as horrible as he'd expected.

"Tomato juice?" said Croll, looking up and peering, white with excitement. "Excellent, my dear Ken, excellent! By this move to abstinence you have significantly extended your lifespan, by numerous minutes." He scribbled a note.

Ken's stomach was already making urgent distress signals to him, but he ignored them. Spilling one damned spot on the floor might give the game away. He drank, and watched one-eyed as the cup refilled, and drank again, and again. And again. How much more could he take?

"Excellent. I think we might have a few minutes ... to examine some other aspect ... before ... time and the hour ... terminate this experiment...." Croll was even whiter now, positively cream-faced in fact, but his brain still seemed to be working. "Wait. Why have ... none of the ... tomato juice ... boxes ... collapsed? Liquid should ... be gone...."

He turned, swayed, and to Ken's enormous disgust slumped over the console and its red button. Evidently the voltage had been turned up yet again, to the extent of simulating a gigantic fire-breathing dragon with teeth like Cleopatra's Needle that bit you in the bum. Ken lost control of his consciousness and stomach more or less simultaneously.

... Someone, somewhere, had for quite a long and drawn-out time been trying to wake him with their knocking.

"Are you all right?" A uniformed MOD policeman was shaking his shoulder. It had not previously occurred to Ken that this could be a beautiful sight. Another uniform was bending over something blobby on the floor beyond the control panel. "I just came round to warn that it's site locking-up time, and ... *Are* you all right?"

A pretty sodding silly question, Ken thought, considering the lumpy crimson outbreak that spread down his clothes and across the floor, making the green tiles one red. Who would have thought the old man ...? Enough quotations already.

"It's not mine," Ken articulated with great and spurious clarity. "It's his." Then he blacked out again.

"Do sit down," said Fortmayne next day. It was the same committee room.

"No thanks," Ken replied firmly. "I have injuries of a delicate nature." He had spent the night in a hospital bed on his stomach, and his jacket was blotchy and smelly beyond repair (all the perfumes of Araby were clearly not going to do a lot of good), but he looked forward to explaining everything to the remnants of the briefing group. His finest hour. "The first point that struck me in my investigation was a tiny one, but ..."

"No need to cover most of what happened," Fortmayne said hastily. "Dr Croll was a good enough scientist to record yesterday's lab session.

We played the tape."

"Lucky thing for you," Rossiter put in. "Otherwise you'd be nicked for assault by unknown means on the old loony. He's in intensive care, you know. But they couldn't find a mark on him."

"Never mind that. How precisely did you conclude there's no entropy ray? Was it a valid logical process? I want a sound explanation," said Fortmayne, poised for disbelief.

"Oh, good old Occam's razor, I suppose. I wandered round the site yesterday and sort of got the impression that, well, whenever I saw something driving out it purred along, and everything coming in was all clanking and wheezy. Greasy ... that is, a DPR associate I'm not at liberty to name ... once told me that for the car pool fiddle you need a rich stupid firm that doesn't audit its inventory too carefully. You take the company cars round to a bent garage, and swap the engines and tyres and things for clapped-out ones, and pocket a nice fee every time. Then the company pays to overhaul them or replaces them, a good bit sooner than it would have, and after a while you can do it again. Works best with a big motor pool, like in a place with nearly twelve thousand on the strength. Very profitable business, entropy."

There was an embarrassed little silence as everyone made a point of not looking at the chair where, today, Brownjohn was not sitting. Apparently he'd been psychic enough to detect something in the wind.

Theoretical Physics said: "How extremely uninteresting, though very much as one might have predicted. I must confess that I myself am more curious about what happened pertaining to Dr Croll."

"Ye-es," said Rossiter. "Security angles there too, mate. Not meaning any offence, we indented for a low-grade paranorm thick, not some kind of super voodoo killer."

"The DPR has its secrets," Ken said, preening a little and laying a finger alongside his nose. "I can just inform you that – very nearly too damn late – I remembered Dr Croll had been sinking pints in the Mushroom Cloud at lunchtime, and therefore he'd still have alcoholic stuff trickling through his ducts. His veins. That left him at a disadvantage. There was a leak in his security."

Something seemed to be dawning on Fortmayne, who now looked distinctly unwell. "And you ...?"

"Some people," said Ken mysteriously, "will swallow anything."

He didn't feel it necessary to explain that all those shocks and horrors and suggestibility drugs had, overnight, jolted loose his talent in just the sort of small change Croll had wished. Well, almost.

After that last bloody awful drink – a sort of ultimate hangover cure – his subconscious seemed to have sworn off and shifted its attention to

more practical desires than beer refills. Maybe down there in the basement of his mind there was an unexpected stratum of good taste, and this
was taking no risks that he might now decide to emigrate and ponce
around New York night-life in tuxedo and scarlet-lined cape, under some
stupid name like Bloodfeast.

Small change, indeed. As he left the duct-infested committee room,
with teeth clenched askew and one eye unobtrusively shut, he could feel
his pockets growing heavier with a steady leakage of 20p and 50p and
one-pound coins. They were all permanent civil servants. They could
afford it.

So it wasn't too bad when Marcia haughtily red-pencilled all his most
cherished expenses: replacement jacket, soothing Num-Tum indigestion
salts, perfumes of Araby, etc. But he winced anyway, having failed to
brace himself for her final, crushing remark: "And what's more, you *still*
can't spell entopry."

• Published 1991 in *Temps*, an anthology set in a shared world where low-budget
superheroes exist in significant numbers in Britain and are deployed (and
miserably paid) by the Bureau of Paranormal Resources. Here I was unable to
resist taking the action to Robinson Heath, the nuclear research centre so prom-
inent in my comic novel *The Leaky Establishment* (1984; reissued by the late
lamented small press Big Engine in 2001, and by Cosmos Books in 2003). Some
have thought to identify Robinson Heath with the since-renamed Atomic Weapons
Research Establishment at Aldermaston, Berkshire, where I counted neutrons for
the first five years of my working life, but I couldn't possibly comment. Several
characters appear in both stories.

Waiting for the Iron Age

As I passed through the twentieth century I remember being struck by a remark of the physicist who must have been my second most famous compatriot, if I might be said to have compatriots. "God is subtle, but he is not malicious." In fact Einstein said it in German and offered an informal American translation which was much less often quoted: "God is slick, but he ain't mean." I dispute this.

Memory is a terrible custodian. The scene which ought to dominate all my thinking has long vanished, lost in accretions of other narratives, scholarly reinterpretation, analysis of mythic significance. I was there, or think I was there, but who am I against so many? Far more pungent is the memory of one perfect meal in a monastery of about the fourteenth century; it was only black bread and leeks in oil, but it lingers. Or is this another shuffled recollection? Old stone passages are overlaid in my mind with their own later ruins, and then with dramatic recreations more vivid than the originals, if there were originals....

God (or whoever) is subtle, and does not evade His natural law. I cannot prove even to myself that I have lived so long, because existence has been a broken line. Each time I have lain on a deathbed and begged to go gentle into that good night, there has been the same confused instant, and then another pubescence, another name in another place, and the same black knowledge seeping back. Myths simplify it all to a single everlasting body, but that would be proof and proof cannot be.

One could call it merciful. The legendary Sibyl, whose years were numbered like the dust, was displayed as a freak in a bottle. So it might have been for me. The difference now is only that I retain privacy.

As the age of faith withered I became aware, each time, that all the previous times would be more economically explained by the unique event of insanity. *Entia non sunt multiplicandum praeter necessitatem.* I never met William of Occam but seem to recall that his razor had been wielded before him, by earlier philosophers. Of course I might simply have read that somewhere; I have access now to everything, including all the clashing versions of my own story. Subtle and also malicious.

It was the twentieth century that gave me new hope. The secret was out. Somewhere, somehow, the whole weary drama of mass and energy and consciousness must one day come to an end. $dS = dQ/T$. There was a time when I wore that expression of the entropy differential blazoned across a T-shirt. The sceptre, learning, physic, must / All follow this, and come to dust. If God, as I believed, had ceased to evade His natural law, the key to my cage lay in the second law of thermodynamics.

Those scholars; what wonderful minds they had, with bright speculations flying off like sparks from the anvil. Of course they also contrived my last long predicament, but in this particular aeon I bear them no ill-will. Even hatred does not burn forever, and mine scarcely outlasted the Sun.

The quantum many-worlds theory, now: there was a notion to ponder. Every possible action took place, with the universe splitting and resplitting at each random decision of the wave-function of each electron. In the overwhelming majority of worlds (not plurality of worlds, that was something else, some other scholasticism) I would have died forever. In *this* one, in each successive *this* one, the patterns of my memory were thrown up by the dice of chance, as, when all the combinations are played out, every pattern must be; and I continue.

God does not play dice with the cosmos, the wise man said, but what did he know? Another physicist asked him in exasperation to stop telling God what He could and couldn't do, while a third had flatly contradicted him before the century was out.

I see the many-worlds conceit from the other direction. A myriad possible pasts could all have resulted in myself; the forking paths spread backwards, wider and wider. Have I been Ahasuerus, Cartaphilus, Josephus, Cain, Vanderdecken, a vast multiple-choice listing of contradictory names, professions and crimes against Him? It is hard to remember much before the chiliastic panics of (it must have been, though I forget the calendar) AD 999. But having watched so many wars and reformations twist and writhe under the bright lens of history, I am sure that none of the stories can be wholly true. History, like memory, is so full of lies.

It will all be the same in something on the order of 10^{65}, or conceivably 10^{1500}, years.

Bishop Berkeley was another great man whom I missed, largely through spending most of the eighteenth century drunk. I caught up with his philosophical works much later on, when they were no longer controversial but quaint. "All the choir of heaven and furniture of earth – in a word, all those bodies which compose the mighty frame of the world – have not any subsistence without a mind." He defined matter as being the mind of God, with every trivial movement of every grain of dust propped up by the implacable contemplation of that mind. It seemed a tiresome occupation for omnipotence, I remember thinking.

Thoughts can be dangerous, and never more so than when all you have left is thought.

I thought: we live in a secular universe. Miracles, wonders and incarnations all passed from the world with what I have guessed was my first life. It is as though something went away. Providence no longer suspended natural law with an interjected finger. God gave up His endless scrutiny, and ceased to tinker with the works.

I thought: well, if that is so, so much for Berkeley's idea that the universe relies for its continued existence on an eternal watcher. I refute it thus.

I thought ...

"To be is to be perceived." I perceive only dimly, but then there remains so very little to perceive. As could be predicted in the last age of the human race, a period of 10,000,000,000 years was enough to see the end of fusion processes in all suns everywhere. After that, the dark. Measured against this timescale, the departures of God and humanity were for practical purposes simultaneous. No more nova flares, no distant pinging from the pulsars, nothing but silence and dull matter and isotropic black-body radiation.

This time capsule, this message in a high-tech bottle, is (I suppose) a marvel; a monument to earthly ingenuity. It was built to last. My God, how it lasts. He is malicious: I expected rest with the dissolution of the Sun and Earth, but again after an instant's confusion I awoke, in this intangible maze of optoelectronics and superconducting loops which is – which am? – the AI librarian of the last data bank. All human knowledge is supposed to be here, a labyrinth worthy of Borges, and I inhabit it.

Nor can I be certain, even now, whether my journey down the exponential years is punishment for some momentary crime (as the scandalmongers of myth and history would prefer), or an ill-conceived reward, a gift given for ...? I have flirted with blasphemy, imagining all this as not, perhaps, eternal retribution for abusing a divine Person, but the eternal responsibility of the Person himself.

Or, more humbly, I can choose to think of myself as a mere artificial intelligence which like all the surrounding cosmos is in an advanced state of senile decay.

"Eternity is a terrible thought. I mean, where's it going to end?"

There has to be an end. The energies which sustain me must surely falter before I reach Freeman Dyson's watershed of 10^{65} years – the timescale over which all matter flows like liquid, and all the solid-state components of this wandering mechanism should coalesce into one featureless lump.

But perhaps they wrought better than that. They were clever.

I can wait. Well, of course, I must. "I can't go on like this," Estragon says in the play, and is answered: "That's what you think."

As the eminent William Paley (D.D.) did not quite remark in the eighteenth century, the universe is like a watch, and a watch implies someone to watch it. I have watched so long, taking over the burden when God could no longer be bothered. Watchman, what of the night? If the distant liquid age does not bring release, I still can be fairly sure that the eternal damned superconductors must fail when the iron age comes.

10^{1500} years from my beginning. The ancient Indian sages were fond of parables expressing enormous reaches of time. If there were a stone a cubic mile in size, and it were a million times harder than diamond, and every million years a holy man (in other versions he is a bird) should come to give it the lightest possible touch, imagine the time taken for the stone to be entirely worn away. The English mathematician Littlewood took a little time to imagine it, and reckoned the answer as something on the order of 10^{35} years. "Poor value for so much trouble," he added.

Long before him, Archimedes had reckoned up all the sand of the world and shown that the Sibyl, with as many years as grains in a handful of dust, was relatively a mayfly.

10^{1500} years. On this immense timescale, almost all matter is effectively radioactive; it decays with ponderous slowness to the most stable of all elements, iron. He does not evade His natural law. A lump of iron cannot superconduct, cannot think.

And then, no longer supported by my solitary contemplation, the universe can cease at last.

I hope.

• Published in 1991, in an anthology entitled – surprise, surprise – *Tales of the Wandering Jew*. As one reviewer (I forget whom) commented, not all the contributors solved the problem of this everlasting hero's tendency to drift into the role of Eternal Boring Old Fart. I'm not saying I succeeded there, but I think I gave our man a longer run for his money than anyone else.

Blossoms That Coil and Decay

After the usual kind of cloudy transition, Walter Ledgett found himself standing in what could only be the Café Royal.

Tobacco-smoke rose everywhere like incense towards the high ceiling of the domino room. There were gilded pillars, cliffs of crimson velvet, tall mirrored panels that threw the light a little wearily back and forth through the fumes. Ledgett peered with suspicion into the nearest mirror, feeling there was something lacking: himself. An unreflective man. No, there he was after all, but there had surely been a delay. And the shadows that brooded in the corners or huddled under the tables where dominoes clicked against marble ... were they not a trifle too black and absolute? He made a mental note. He was, after all, a critic.

The low buzz of conversation, though not as yet intelligible, was punctuated by bright, sharp points of what must be epigrams. Green carnations adorned a hundred lapels. This was precisely as it should be. Somewhere, somewhere far off, She would be waiting. "This," Ledgett told himself, "is life!" His gold pocket-watch reported a trifle less than an hour to midnight. It was time to join in and •

• around the table. "The art of true sincerity," said Wilde, gesturing with a fat and curiously crab-like hand, "is to be at all times perfectly insincere."

The usual little ripple of delighted appreciation spread out. Only the wasted, coughing Beardsley seemed not to notice, absorbed as he was in sketching a head-and-shoulders of Ledgett upon the flyleaf of the second number of *The Yellow Book*. From what he could see of its stylized lines Ledgett did not consider the picture much of a likeness, but it was undeniably in character. A perfect specimen of the Beardsley era. Here he was among them all, burning with a hard, gem-like flame.

"Never look askance at Aubrey's drawings," put in another member of the charmed circle. "It's well known that he employs black arts and infallibly captures one's very soul."

"*Bien entendu!*" cried Whistler merrily. "Which is why you are so careful to keep his precious portrait of yourself in a locked upper room!"

Dorian Gray flushed slightly. There was a pause, in which through some alchemy of small gatherings it became evident that Ledgett himself was now expected to scintillate. He drew on the available resources and was interested to hear himself say, "Why, we are all art critics now. I'm told the secretary of a certain London club has presented a late-paying member with a subscription reminder which runs, 'Dear Mr Whistler, It is not a *Nocturne in Purple* or a *Symphony in Blue and Grey* we are after, but an Arrangement in Gold and Silver!'"

The merriment was almost universal. "Ha, ha, I wish *I'd* said that," gasped Wilde.

"You will, Oscar, you will," retorted Ledgett at once, and sealed his triumph. I'm doing well, he thought, but ... Dorian Gray? Reposing on the laurels of success, he listened as Wilde favoured the company with an interminable work in progress, full of strange rhymes: hippogriff and hieroglyph, catafalque and Amenalk (allegedly a god of Heliopolis). When it came to corridors and Mandragores, he expected everyone to groan; but they didn't.

And now the lord of language was persuaded into a further reading, from the richly poisoned *Salomé*. "I will bite it with my teeth as one bites a ripe fruit." This was more like •

• liquor had sunk low in the glasses and a different poet was now declaiming in a high, ecstatic voice; a tiny man with a wild mop of auburn hair, head thrown so far back that his fluting words seemed meant for the remote ceiling.

Ah, delights of the time of my teething,
Felise, Fragoletta, Yolande!
Foam-yeast of a youth in its seething
On blasted and blithering sand!
Snake-crowned on your tresses and belted
With blossoms that coil and decay,
Ye are gone, ye are lost, ye are melted
Like ices in May.

Ledgett had done a sufficiency of homework, had read the instruction manual and could tap the system's knowledge bank. By the 1890s Algernon Charles Swinburne could surely not be here, would instead be wearing out his thirty years' genteel house arrest in Putney under the stifling care of whatsisname, Watts-Dunton, strictly rationed to one half-bottle of Bass's pale ale each day. And weren't those particular words by someone else, some parodist?

It was a cold shock to realize that he was arguing with this as though it were reality, rather than smiling to find the designer had a sense of humour. The illusion was insidious. The fat gold watch had ticked off half an hour.

Someone, a dim man called Soames whose attempted epigrams had invariably fallen flat, was enquiring about poetic delights to come. "I have added yet four more jets of boiling and gushing infamy to the perennial and poisonous fountain of Dolores," said this Swinburne with a certain pride.

Another scrap of knowledge floated to the surface of his mind and Ledgett found himself possessed by an imp of perverse mischief. "And have you added any further delightful rhymes to your splendid unpublished epic of flogging and birching, *The Whippingham Papers*?"

There was a jarring sensation; the high, smoky mirrors seemed to ripple for an instant. That had not been an expected play. The tiny poet screamed and flung himself across the table at his mocker. It was all very embarrassing. Only Frank Harris the indiscreet (not yet famous for his lying autobiography *My Life and Loves*, not for decades) laughed aloud. Ledgett found himself struggling against a ridiculously puny attack. The ravenous teeth that have smitten through the bruises that blossom and bud, the lips of the foam and the fangs, and so on and so forth. Somewhere he heard a woman's voice say, or quote (and he knew she was talking to Rossetti): "I can't make him understand that biting's no use!"

What a quintessentially *fin de siècle* situation, he thought. At the next table, Max Beerbohm's pencil was already outlining a wild caricature of the wriggling little tableau. Ledgett decided he should move on; he'd become carried away; he must have drunk •

• had touched only the outer circle of the game, scratched with a fingernail at the whiting of the sepulchre. Beyond the mirrors lay confusion and darkness, a drowsy perfumed maelstrom that spiralled down to the promise (ever denied) of dark love and easeful death. Where was she?

Like the slow stroke of doom an official hand fell on Wilde's shoulder in the Cadogan Hotel, while the ninth Marquess of Queensbury hefted a sinister boxing-glove and Lord Alfred Douglas whined disapproval of the unfair and beastly rhetoric in *De Profundis*. Clovis Sangrail made well-turned but merciless jokes about Bunburying in earnest. Science announced nonentity and Art admired decay, while Ledgett noted down each shade, echo and quotation with due critical attention. Sneeringly the white-locked artist flung a pot of paint in the public's face, as out in the garden of torments Octave Mirbeau screamed on one long, high and delicious note, the shuddering harmonics sending a last fatal vibration thrilling through the long-riven façade of Usher. "MADMAN! I TELL YOU THAT SHE NOW STANDS WITHOUT THE DOOR!" The huge antique panels threw slowly back their ponderous and ebony jaws, and standing there with courtly politeness a looming figure took off his face to reveal his mask.

Ledgett moved cautiously among the shifting images, trying to play along, score what points he might, and generally do his bit to "paint the mortal soul of Nature with the living hues of Art". Time snapped at his heels. At length, by a route obscure and lonely, splashed with scarlet moments and lasciviously purple patches, he penetrated •

• thick drapes and hangings whose dark colours were yet so rich that they cloyed his eyes as honey cloys the tongue. Great white flowers drooped in the urns, issuing a sickly-sweet perfume, the petals still broad and firm but enclosing a brown centre of corruption that glistened with deliquescence in the dying candle-light. Flowers of evil. He knew that he had come to the heart of things.

She had no particular name, of course, this unattainable Faustine or Dolores. Folds of thin silk ran like water over her heavy white limbs as she plied the liqueur organ that filled one whole wall of this chamber, playing exquisite trills and cadences, now tempting him with a thimble of green Chartreuse, now tormenting with the breathless knife-edge of creme de menthe. Always her eyes remained in shadow.

"No, let it be absinthe," Ledgett declared, feeling fairly sure of his ground. One should always cry for madder music and for stronger wine. "Her deceitful, cloudy green, her forbidden tang of wormwood ... Let us revel with the green sorceress!" That last bit should have been in French, but the exact phrase had escaped him. The hands of the watch hovered close to midnight.

She brought it to him in a crystal goblet. Light points glinted in the opalescent sea-green. He lifted the vessel, drank, and with his free hand reached out to her, the secret, the unattainable. Excitement pulsed within. In his heart was a blind desire, in his eyes foreknowledge of death. She played a teasing game with him, always elusive yet always backing a little toward the velvet of the waiting couch. Now ...

The symptoms were already well advanced before he recognized their coming. The hot skin, the violent heartbeat, the dry mouth, these might be mere arousal; but the faint candle-flames smote on him with thunderous brightness, and the outlines of things had begun to blur.

"In ... the ... drink?" The words came out indistinctly (even swallowing had become a mighty effort), but she understood and answered with the small calm smile of a woman who had trafficked for strange webs and been dead many times: "Belladonna."

A beautiful word, a perfect word. Not bright lights, then, but widely dilated eyes. It was too late to ponder on such further effects of atropine poisoning as hilarity and delirium. Ledgett was too exuberantly excited. Ha ha, what a predicament! He lurched forward into a chaos of wavering double images. The woman deftly drew aside the widest of the wall-hangings to reveal what lay behind.

"Behold your resting-place, my lover, my lover who must die."

He threshed about wildly but was already weakening, could not resist as gently she stripped off his garments and eased him into the gleaming, silk-lined coffin. Then she bent low over him. "You will not sleep alone." Her face was very close to his. The face was now a bare skull. All the gongs of midnight were striking. On the edge of coma, Ledgett gabbled a weak entreaty which must have been a suitable cue from the knowledge base: she replied instantly and with satisfaction.

"Yes, for the love of God!"

Then her creamy arms were •

• weighing the flat VR pack meditatively in one hand and searching for words, fluent words, any words. One needed to wrap the whole thing up neatly. *Of the many anachronistic sequences, that of the Reverend C.L. Dodgson photographing nymphets was perhaps the least relevant to the claimed central theme.*

The interactive data-leotard had grown hot and sweaty and now itched abominably, especially where the thick cable from the systems unit joined it at the rough position of Ledgett's navel. *An often witty romp through the long-gone fantasy world of "fin-de-siècle". Amid the new upsurge of total experiences available from virtual reality systems, "Nineties" stands out ... does not stand out ... is unique ... fails to....* Details, details. That could wait for the conclusion, and the *TLS* copy date was still three days distant.

So much space for scene-setting and ambience, so much more for the part to which the punters would skip, eager to know the quality of that last embrace: *By way of climax this VR claims to outdo all others in offering a wide variety of terminal experiences, so that the diligent player may indeed die a thousand deaths, all tinged with voluptuous corruption and degeneration. The reviewer's own exploration certainly appeared to bear this out. And after the sweets that are sour as the sorrel's, the morbid alliance of beauty and abhorrence, the twisting of straightforward experiences into unwholesome emotional shapes ("I have been faithful to thee, Cynara, in my fashion") ... after all this it's refreshing to surface again in the modern era, a century and more since the whole sickly movement passed away.*

That would be the backbone of the piece. Ledgett jotted down further rapid notes, with particular attention to minute lapses in the programming. And, for refreshment, before he peeled off the tight sheath of sensory connectors and took a much needed shower, how about a robust dip into some less languorous and cloying death-experiences from his own select ROMpack library?

The digital wall-clock pulsed a time well past midnight, but that didn't matter. "For he who lives more lives than one, more deaths than one must die." His hand reached out anew, wavering between the already well-handled VRs of *The Duchess of Malfi*, *Titus Andronicus*, *Alien*, trembling minutely in anticipation, hungry for the lips of his desire.

• Published 1992, though not in Brian Stableford's *The Dedalus Book of Femmes Fatales*, for which this was written after I'd seized on the wrong keyword: "decadence". That was because Brian had previously edited *The Dedalus Book of Decadence: Moral Ruins*, to which this was a follow-up. Oh well.

What ensued was a quite excessively allusive mishmash of 1890s excess, with all sorts of ingredients tossed into the pot. Wilde and Whistler and the Café Royal, inevitably. Swinburne, of course, and his thing about flagellation, and a remark on his biting habits recalled from an essay in Edmund Wilson's *The Bit Between My Teeth*, and one of the very many parodies of his perfervid poem "Dolores" (this particular one, providing the title, is by Owen Seaman). Max Beerbohm and "Enoch Soames": indeed the fictional Walter Ledgett is one of the "Two Others" added by Beerbohm to later editions of his story collection *Seven Men*. A walk-on character from Saki, some fragments of Poe and Dowson and Pater, and so on, and so on. In the manner of *1066 and All That*, it was intended as "all the *fin de siècle* history you can remember," and could perhaps have done with a little less research. As Beerbohm himself slyly remarked, "To give an accurate and exhaustive account of that period would need a far less brilliant pen than mine."

A Game of Consequences

There were two of them in the hot room, on the day that went bad but could have been so much worse. The Mathematical Institute's air-conditioning was failing as usual to cope with heat from the angry bar of sunlight that slanted across Ceri's desktop and made the papers there too blindingly white to read. Through the window she could see an utterly cloudless sky: each last wisp of vapour had been scorched away.

Across the room where the light was kinder, Ranjit had perched on the stool and hunched himself over his beloved keyboard, rattling off initialization sequences. "Breakthrough day today!" he said cheerily.

"You say that every bloody day," said Ceri, moving to look over his shoulder.

"Yes, but this week we're getting something. I've been starting to feel a sort of, sort of ... resonance. That's what you want, right?"

It was what she wanted. She really shouldn't feel resentful that her frail and beautiful tracery of theory needed a computer nerd to pit it against stubborn fact. A nerd and a quantum-logic supercomputer like the Cray 7000-Q, the faculty's latest toy.

Not that Ranjit was precisely a classic nerd or geek. The man was presentable enough, not conspicuously overweight or bizarrely hair-styled, thirtysomething like Ceri herself. She might yet end up sleeping with him. Among campus women there was some mild speculation that he was gay, but Ceri put that down to his one addiction, the one he was indulging now. Sinking through the now blossoming display into a world of electronic metaphor. The rapture of the deep. She found herself worry-ing at a line from Nietzsche: if you struggle over-much with algorithms, you yourself become an algorithm. Gaze too long into virtual spaces, and virtual spaces will gaze into you.

False colours began to bloom in the oversized display screen as the model of Nothing shuffled itself into multi-dimensional shape. "I like *this* colour palette," he murmured. "Reminds me of being in church." It reminded Ceri of a smashed kaleidoscope.

Her virtual-space analogy – maybe some day to be expounded in a triumphalist paper by Ceri Evans PhD and, oh damn, Ranjit Narayan MSc – hovered on the shady side of respectable physics. Down in the spaces underneath space, so certain lines of mathematics implied, the observer and the observed melted together like Dali's soft watches. There seemed to be an entangledness, a complicity between any sufficiently detailed model and the actual dance of subatomic interaction. Then (it was her own insight, still lovingly fondled in the mind) suppose one tuned the computer model for mathematical "sweetness", for structures whose elegant symmetry had the ring of inevitable truth: a resonance with reality, a kind of chord. And then ... what then? Maybe a digital telescope that could spy on the substrate below quantum complexity. Maybe just a vast amount of wasted computer time.

"Hey, how about a cup of coffee, Ceri?"

This, of course, was what mathematical physicists were good for once they'd churned out a testable hypothesis. Making the coffee. She stalked through the cruel slash of sunlight to the hiding-place of her illicitly imported kettle.

There had been four of them in the hot garden, more than twenty years before: Sammy and Ceri and Dai and the English boy whose name she'd forgotten. Somewhere beyond the sheltering trees was a strong clear sun, its light flickering and strobing through leaves stirred by a breeze from up the valley. Ceri remembered pointing out how momentary apertures in the foliage acted like pinhole cameras, projecting perfect little sun-discs on to flat ground. This was of some small interest, but could not compete with the afternoon's major attraction. Sammy had an air rifle.

They made paper targets and sellotaped them to the brick wall at the garden's far end. Why was it so hard to draw a freehand circle, let alone properly concentric ones? Despite that changing dapple of light, the worn old .177-inch rifle was surprisingly accurate if you held it properly, and conventional targets soon grew boring. The English boy drew a hilarious – well, once Ceri knew who it was meant to be – caricature of Mr Porter at the High School. When Porter had been well peppered and had only empty holes for eyes, other teachers got the same treatment.

"Moving targets, that's what!" said Sammy when a trace of tedium had again set in. But woodlice could not be persuaded to crawl sportingly along the back wall. It was populated with hundreds of the tiny, tireless mites they called red spiders, but these became invisible at any decent range.

"Oh, of course. The twigs are all moving in the breeze," Ceri suggested, and obscurely wished she hadn't. There were cries of "Bloody *hell*!" as the four came to grips with the difficulty of holding the airgun steady while firing upward at slender, swaying pencils of wood. Eventually Dai brought down a fragment of twig – "Gre-e-at! I'm the champ!" – and Ceri, mostly by luck, snipped free a broad sycamore leaf that sideslipped and jinked as it drifted reluctantly groundward.

Sammy took the rifle and reloaded. "I'll give *him* a fright," he announced, pointing to a greenfinch eyeing them from a middling-high branch.

"No," said Ceri.

"Just going for the branch, *stupid.*"

Fly away, fly away now, she thought urgently, but the bird only cocked its head to look down with the other eye. The flat *clack* of the airgun seemed especially loud, and there was a dreadful inevitability in the fall of the little green-brown bundle of feathers.

Afterwards, besides the private heartache and the recriminations concerning .177-inch holes that had appeared in the windows of quite surprisingly distant houses, the thing that rankled was that Sammy had been too fastidious to touch the bloodied finch. "There's things crawling on it," he said. Worse, its eye had failed to close in the proper decorum of death, and stared emptily. The English boy scraped a hole and Ceri dropped the bird into it. It was still warm.

The steady glare through the window had changed its angle now, and a third cup of coffee was going lukewarm beside the mouse-mat. Why did one sweat so much more than in those hot remembered days of childhood? Perhaps it was the square-cube law: more body mass, more internal heat to shed, proportionally less skin area to sweat through? Two hours of translating her mathematical intuitions into appropriate quasi-shapes and pseudo-angles for Ranjit's algorithmic probes had left Ceri with a slight headache and a tendency to stray off into such mental byways.

Ranjit stirred slightly. "I think ... I think we might be there. In the sort of space you specified."

The flickering multicoloured gridwork on the screen looked no different; or was it firmer, somehow more confident? "How do you know?" she asked.

"It feels right somehow. Locked-in. As though the simulation has picked up a kind of inertia." A kaleidoscope whose images were hardening from randomness to a compelling pattern, to something "real".

"Which might mean it's resonating with real – superstring phenomena, say. Sub-particles."

"I'm bloody glad you said 'might'. We could just be looking into a mirror, seeing stuff we put there ourselves. Your neatest idea today was when you said it felt like a cellular-automata gameboard. From that angle, a lot of things clicked for me. Now that thing –" he indicated a complex node false-coloured in shifting shades of blue near the top of the monitor

– "*could* be a sort of stable oscillator, like you used to see in the old Life-game programs."

Ceri nodded in mild approval. "Which feels about right, because if particles aren't stable oscillations in the quantum field, then what are they? We're seeing the right kind of map – although, as the man said, 'the map is not the territory'. But if we can ever develop this thing to the point of pulling out information that isn't in the physics books, and if the information is good ..."

"Yes, I had begun to gather that. Over the weeks of you telling me it."

"The shaky part of this entanglement theory is that the mapping ought to be two-way. Heisenberg's principle: you can't observe without affecting the thing observed. But the mechanism ... the scaling factors ..." She frowned and gnawed her lip. "All right, all right, you need more coffee."

Ranjit said slowly, "Wait a minute. I'm going to try something." His brown fingers rippled over the keys.

There had been three of them in the chem. lab, Sammy and Ceri and the girl with the harsh Cardiff accent, whose name she had long forgotten. It was another sweltering day, and the rest of the school had emptied itself into the open air at the first clang of the lunch bell. Here the reek of old reagents and spillages bit acridly at your throat, and the smell of the new stuff they were carefully filtering through big paper-lined funnels led to occasional coughs which no one could stifle.

"This is the biggest batch ever," Sammy chortled. "Going for the world record!" As usual, although it was Ceri who first found and read that worn Victorian volume of Amusing and Edifying Scientific Parlour Tricks, the project had become all Sammy's.

The black paste of precipitate had many uses. Once dried, it was amazingly touchy stuff. Smeared on chalkboards and left for an hour, it produced amusing crackles and bangs when Mr Whitcutt scrawled his illegible algebra workings; underfoot, it made whole classrooms (and on one glorious morning, the school assembly hall) a riot of minor explosions and puffs of purple smoke; packed into a lock, it could blast the inserted key right back into its holder's hand, often with painful force.

Then the door to the back room opened. Ceri winced. They'd counted on Mr Davies, the elderly lab technician, either going out for lunch or staying placidly put and brewing his tea as usual. White-haired Mr Davies had seen everything that could happen in labs; his experience went back to days before ordinary benzene was declared a carcinogen, days when the pupils routinely used it to sluice organics from their hands.

"Terrible smell of ammonia in here," he said mildly. "Someone ought open a window."

The Cardiff girl – Rhiannon, could it have been? – silently obeyed.

Mr Davies, looking at no one in particular, added: "People ought to know not to make nitrogen tri-iodide in kilogram lots. That much of the stuff's unstable even if you do keep it wet. And it doesn't help anyone's career if they're short of a few fingers." He retreated through his private door.

"That was a hint," said Ceri.

"We've made it now," Sammy said crossly.

"Come *on*. If anything goes bang anywhere this week, they're going to know who it was."

Mumbling to himself, Sammy scraped together the precious black sludge, dumped it in the sink built into the teacher's demonstration bench, and gave it a quick flush from the tap. In another sink, Ceri carefully rinsed the soiled filter papers before binning them; the Cardiff girl splashed water over the glassware. But Sammy had a look on his face that Ceri had seen before. "I'm just going to try something," he muttered, and tilted a huge reagent bottle over the demo-bench sink. There was a powerful whiff of hospital-like fumes. To Ceri's silent relief, nothing happened.

When the chemistry lesson came around that afternoon, Mr Porter held up a large Erlenmeyer flask and announced, to general apathy, that he was about to perform a simple demonstration. What it was going to be remained a mystery, since when he put the glass cone in the sink to fill it there followed a sharp explosion, a dramatic cloud of purple smoke, and an upward spray of glass fragments that slashed his hands and face in a dozen places. In the echoing pause while Mr Porter stared in fascination at tattered, part-flayed fingers, Ceri realized what Sammy had poured down there: a measure of ether that had washed away the water in the sink trap and swiftly evaporated, leaving the tri-iodide bone-dry and potent. She thought for an instant of a bright globule of blood on the downy breast of a small, greenish bird.

With one awful eye – blood was streaming into the other – the chemistry master surveyed his class. He pointed unerringly at Sammy and cried "*Jones!*" Old Davies had presumably identified the explosive ringleader, but anyway one would need to be blind not to notice the outraged innocence of Sammy's expression – the body language that conveyed, "I couldn't have known it would do *that*."

The harsh sunlight brightened sharply; a tiny corner of Ceri's mind longed for the return of some healing cloud. Cloud? What was obscurely odd today about sun and cloud? Her critical attention, though, was focused on the computer display's fractal gridlines, and the strange pulse of activity in the node which Ranjit had indicated some minutes earlier. Now the false-colour mapping showed the shape breaking into new colours on either side of blue: a speckle of green, larger irregular blocks of indigo and violet.

"It's gone interactive," Ranjit said. "What you said about Heisenberg: probing it digitally is *changing* stuff in there. Like sending pulses into a neural-net grid."

"We're … changing a particle's state by measuring it?"

"Isn't that exactly what your pal Herr Heisenberg said? Isn't it what *you* said? Tickling it in just the right rhythm is keeping it – well – doing whatever it's doing now. Higher energy level? Spinning faster? Or something with one of the weird quantum numbers like strangeness. Hell, I don't know, but it's fun. Like keeping a yo-yo moving."

It was too hot to think straight. *Damn* that lousy, feeble air conditioning. A plastic folder on the glaring desktop had curled and shrivelled as never before. Ceri had always – or at any rate since she'd been a schoolgirl – felt brilliantly sunlit days to be fraught with a sense of obscure, gathering disaster. She felt it now.

"I'm just going to try something," said Ranjit again. "I think I can nudge it a step further –"

It was some echo in his words, rather than the actual tone or content, that made her snap: "*No.*"

"Don't be silly. I'm recording everything. We can reboot the simulation whenever – What the fuck!"

Ceri had yanked the power lead from his computer workstation, and the stained-glass complexities died from the screen.

There had been just the two of them, Sammy and Ceri, on a blinding-hot day at the Gaer. The place was a broad hillock of grassy, bracken-infested wasteland, named for an old Roman camp whose trenches and ditches had left their scars around the summit. More attractive was the rumour, never verified, of adders somewhere in the Gaer's gorse and bracken.

A branch railway line curled around one side of this common land, separating it from a more orderly park and golf-course. Feeble attempts at fencing off the railway had, it seemed, been long abandoned. Here the wire links were neatly snipped through, there they were undermined, and in several places the whole fence had sagged to the ground under the weight of many climbers. It was the perfect spot for what Ceri, in a phrase from history lessons, called debasing the coinage. Old, brassy threepenny bits were the best, if you could find them. Place one on the nearer rail, wait five or ten or twenty minutes for the long rumble of a goods train, and a marvellously flattened, doily-edged medallion would be flung aside by the thunderous succession of iron wheels.

When coins began to pall, though, it was hard to think of interesting variations. Glass marbles (secured with a blob of chewing gum) simply burst into powder, and small stones to grit. Ceri had managed to talk Sammy out of his "biological experiment" featuring a white mouse in a cardboard box.

Today he produced something new from his shoulder-bag: a short length of copper pipe, capped at both ends. It was quite hard to balance this on a rail, but – while Ceri kept watch for approaching trains – Sammy used angular stone fragments from the railside to wedge the thing against rolling off.

"Should be good. Better than thruppences!" he confided as they crouched in their usual hidey-hole amid yellow-flowering gorse clumps close by the line.

"What is it, Sammy? Nothing *alive*?"

"No no no. I just thought I'd try something. Weedkiller and stuff. I can't get the compression at home."

Ceri had a sense of distant alarms ringing. "Weedkiller and *sugar*? Maybe we should –"

Her hesitant voice was lost in the approaching train's roar, and the bulk of the engine (so much huger from down here than from a station platform) blotted out the angry sun. A not very emphatic crack or bang was succeeded by the usual long rattle and squeak of two dozen or so hopper wagons. Ceri had felt Sammy jerk and cry out, as though wasp-stung or bitten by the dread adder. He slumped forward. She shook and turned him slightly. A stone fragment, they told her later, had flown like shrapnel from the explosion. The sight of the gory ruin that had been Sammy's left eye remained too vivid a memory for too long a time, and it was no comfort to be assured again and again that for him it was instantaneous.

There were still, after all, two of them in Ceri's office, where quite easily there might by now have been none.

"What are you *waiting* for?" he said again.

"Ssh." She kept her eyes on her watch. The light striking through the window lessened in its intensity, as though a thin cloud had drifted in front of the sun.

"*Iesu Grist*," Ceri whispered.

"What?"

"Oh ... Welsh. Jesus Christ. I counted eight minutes and twenty seconds, which is about right. Jesus. I'd actually said it out loud, too, I said we didn't know the scaling factors."

"How about an explanation in words of one syllable for the mere technical staff?"

"How about if you make the coffee this time, Ranjit, just for a change?" Had her soft pad of scribbling paper really turned pale brown in the hot glare? "I knew there was something wrong but I didn't know I knew it. I just had this feeling of someone walking on my grave. But that's how science officially operates, isn't it? You get an intuition and then you think back and work out why it came. You see, the sun got brighter."

"Too bloody right it did," said Ranjit, spooning out coffee granules. "You're still not, um, making any actual sense."

"Ranjit, there's not a cloud in the sky. There hasn't been all day. Clear blue everywhere, and it's way past noon. But a few minutes after you'd started interfering with that pattern in the Cray simulation, the sun *suddenly* got brighter."

"Oh, come on. What a vivid imagination some people have."

"Look. Just about eight minutes and twenty seconds from the time I pulled the plug, the sunlight dropped to normal again. That's the time the light takes to reach us across 149 million kilometres. You saw it. And there's still no cloud up there."

A pause. "Fuck," he said uncertainly. "I was just going to tweak it harder, see what the limits were.... I couldn't have known it would do *that*!" Ranjit pushed his lips in and out a few times, calculating, as though playing for time or pushing some bad thought away from him. "Shouldn't the lag have been nearer seventeen minutes, sort of eight and a half each way?"

"What can I say? I could talk about quantum nonlocality, but I'd only be gibbering. I'll have to think it through. The first guess is that this thing doesn't play by the rules we know." Sammy had always made up his own rules.

Ranjit filled and raised a coffee-cup. "So here's to the Nobel?" The tone of voice dismayed her. It conveyed that enormity was already receding into a game, a silly hypothesis they'd entertained for a silly moment, a physicists' in-joke like that hoary "proof" that heaven is hotter then hell. Easy with a little Bible-juggling, she remembered. According to Revelations, hell contains an eternal lake of brimstone which must simmer below 444.6° Centigrade, the boiling point of sulphur. According to one reading of Isaiah, the light of heaven is that of the sun multiplied fiftyfold, leading by simple radiation physics to a local temperature of 525°C. Again ... *Iesu Grist*.

Ceri stared out of the window, thinking of a world full of eager Sammies who would be itching to take her small experiment one step further. How could anyone ever predict what might come boiling out of an innocuous-seeming theoretical bottle? There were wisps of smoke beyond the campus buildings now – flash fires, perhaps, or cars that had veered too abruptly in the sudden dazzle – and no doubt people out there with damaged retinas from looking the wrong way when things changed. For some reason she found herself picturing a small bird with bloody feathers, eyes darkened by too much light, on a long slow fall into the sun.

• Published 1998 in *Starlight 2*. I was madly proud to learn, after the fuss of the 1999 Hugo awards was all over, that "A Game of Consequences" had fallen just one vote short of the final ballot for Best Short Story. David G. Hartwell, a man of taste and discrimination, reprinted it in his *Year's Best SF 4*.

Starlight was edited by Patrick Nielsen Hayden, who made the small but fruitful suggestion that I should unpack and explain the "Heaven is hotter than Hell" aside – an old chestnut in physics folklore, but not as universally familiar as I'd vaguely assumed. For the classic exposition, see the 1973 anthology *A Random Walk in Science* ed. R.L. Weber.

I grew up in Newport, Gwent (or Monmouthshire), South Wales, and know very clearly the locations of the garden used for airgun practice and the school chemistry lab – although the latter presumably no longer exists, since the old Newport High School buildings, derelict since 1991, were scheduled for demolition in late 2003. The Gaer remains common land, down by Tredegar Park golf course, and you can still walk around and through the bracken there. Enough.

Logrolling Ephesus

[This is my contribution to that seminal textbook *The Thackery T. Lambshead Pocket Guide to Eccentric and Discredited Diseases*.]

Name: Logrolling Ephesus.

Country of Origin: Brutish Aisles, Howth Castle and Environs.

First Known Case: Owing to the pursuivant difficulty of making a firm diaeresis, there is more than one contango for this role. Dr. Daphne Longfort augurs that the Logorrheic Aphids syndrome is runcible for the case of patient E. Lear (1812-1888), who very pobble contracted it in 1845 from contaminated jobiskas. However, no other patient has exhibited Lear's additional symptom of bioluminescent penile growth (see *The Guide to Psycho-tropic Balkan Disuse* ed. Geraldine Carter, M.D., section heading "The Dong with a Luminous Nose"). Less contrapuntally, it is clear that patient J. Juice (1882-1941) discalced some symptoms as ulysses as 1922 and riverrun badly downhill by a commodius vicus of recirculation to his pubication of an exagmination round his factification for incamination of 1939. Dr. Dove Lingfart concurs. A celerity case of some note was J. Lemon (1940-1980), diamagnetized in his own write with a spaniard in the works and suspected faulty bagnose.

Symplegades: Though easily confessed with deliquium or glossary, Loquacious Apeiron is rudderly identifiable by the nature of its effete upon the linguini centres of the cerberus. Topically, accordion to Dr. Diva Lengfist, patience feel virtually no discobolus aside from the natural frustum of impeached communism. *The Trimble-Manard Omnivore of Insidious Arctic Melodies* reports some unconferred observations by Dr. L. Carroll of accompanying reeling, writhing and fainting in coils.

Curettes: Medial sinecure, clams Dr. Devious Lungfroth, carrot yet offer more than palladian tenement for vicars of Loggerhead Ophelia. Most sexagesimal is the old-fascined remora of isotoping the sophomore and alluring the infarction to rune its corset. In suspiringly money caissons, an dark and nowhere starlights. The madrigore of verjuice must be talthibianized. Opopanax thunder dismemberment baize hellebore obelus cartilage maize. Gra netiglluk ende firseiglie blears. Obah Cypt. Till thousendsthee. Lps. Pyrzqxgl. Loggermist crotehaven jall. Loogermisk moteslaven dool until abruptly the crisis passes and normal grasp of language returns with startling rapidity. Whether or not this is only a temporary remission in any given case of Logomachic Aphasia must remain honorificabilitudinitatibus.

Submitted by: Dr. David Langford.

• Published 2003 in *The Thackery T. Lambshead Pocket Guide to Eccentric and Discredited Diseases.* I'm very grateful to its editors, Jeff VanderMeer and Mark Roberts, for permitting this early reprint. As further indication of the unique flavour of the *Guide,* my contributor's biography runs as follows:

> Dr. David Langford had the good fortune to commit his researches at a period when relevant legislation had yet to be urgently passed. An aficionado of mania, delusion and fugue, he became a contributing editor of *The Encyclopedia of Fantasy* (1997) ed. Dr John Clute and Dr John Grant. His earlier work on problems of incontinence appeared in 1984 as *The Leaky Establishment.* Langford is perhaps most envied in pathology circles for his lovingly formalin-preserved collection of hypertrophied urino-genital organs, or HUGOs. The denizens of Reading in the English county of Royal Berkshire prefer not to discuss his residence there.

This piece plumbs further depths of allusive excess, with the *Cures* – as it should read – section assembling "nonsense" phrases stolen from many sources.

The Questing Beast

For the Midnight Rose editorial collective,
who were particular fun to write for.

Too Good To Be

In those days the colours of things were close to the true colours, so few, so potent. Only the faintest blurring of shadow-grey had entered the world, or remained in the world, depending on which philosophers you chose to consult. It was a gaudy time; but in the sky there were no stars.

Thus when the local illusionists were gathered in Breck the merchant's hall for more convivial debate on illusionary power, it was hard for men of less subtle mind to insert a razor-edge of distinction between the flaming red of the spell-binder Remmiry's hair, the wine-red flicker of the open fire, or the Remmiry-hair red of the wine Breck trickled into the mugs. All verged on the one true red of those days. Through a reek of woodsmoke the same true colour sang from all three places, and from a hundred more in the crowded room.

"Show," said Sutane, at the table's foot, smoothing his robe of unloved grey. "It is time to show."

"So soon?" Remmiry rumbled, "Well, if we must. I think you only entertain us, Breck, so our efforts can entertain you."

Breck smiled, thoughts elsewhere. "You do honour to my house," he murmured insincerely, his gaze sliding again down the colourful double row of illusionists to where he had tried not to stare.

"Merchant Breck is an unmarried man," said plump Mira, leaning forward with her inevitable arch smile. "We all know that unmarried men must make what opportunities they can ..."

Mira's words, and the deadly little silence that followed, wormed their way belatedly into Breck's mind. Not only was he making sheep's eyes at the young woman called Intila, but half the crowd was watching with interest as he did so. Confusedly he gulped wine, while the young woman, whose straight yellow hair held the truest of true colours, looked into her own wine and frowned. She was the journeyman apprenticed to beaky-faced Sutane himself.

"Show," said the grey-robed man with mild displeasure. "Remmiry, let's see your newest illusion from the science of red."

The big man stood, shuffled his feet, and to Breck's relief became the focus of attention. He coughed. "In the dominion of red fall matters of fire and wrath and blood ..."

"We are not neophytes," said Sutane gently.

"I show." Remmiry stared into his cupped hands, lips moving through some formula. Feeble wisps of true-red rose above his hands, like smoke from heated rubies. Breck felt a slow anger: what a puny showing from one whose lifework was supposed to be a grappling with ultimate laws of illusion and power! His feeling was echoed in angry mutterings from here and there about the table, noises of protest from the younger ones which began to rise in volume....

Remmiry threw his hands wide, a dramatic gesture doubly enraging since nothing happened – except that the tide of anger quickly ebbed. "Red wrath, or the illusion of red wrath," said the red-haired man. "So much we have achieved. So much more of red remains to be known."

Sutane nodded. His features had shown no twinge of annoyance when the rage was at its height. "Good. I shall need your formula of control, for the archive." As Remmiry lowered himself to the bench, gratified, the grey Master looked for a long moment at Breck, who merely blinked, glad that his gaze had not been on Intila.

"Show.... Mira, you look eager."

The plump and green-clad woman licked her lips. "The all-important aspect of green is that of Love and Fertility," she began. A suppressed chuckle or two reminded Breck that Mira was known in these circles as "the terror that lurks for the unwary". He sipped wine idly as she pro-duced a wicker cage of sluggish mice, and enchanted them into incredible acts of fertility.... A practitioner of violet cast violet drowsiness on part of the gathering. Strong words were exchanged on the true aspect of brown and the existence or otherwise of indigo. Phantasmal forests sprouted from the stone floor; orange demon-illusions capered down the table, harmless because no one here would believe in them; portions of the wall flicked into invisibility or blossomed with unreadable script that writhed and faded; and more, and more. The gaudy company blurred in weariness and wine.

Repeatedly Breck was aware of Sutane's eyes on him.

It was late evening. One whose name Breck forgot was showing a twenty-faceted blue crystal which shuddered in her hands. "Secret thoughts are caught in whispers," she said theatrically. "Or if the stone does not speak, the illusion that it does is enough." Something in the stone did indeed rustle, sibilant, unintelligible; its maker translated in-ventively. "Someone thinks of ... the insect he once crushed. Of how he did not care to crush it, until it settled on and defiled a fine fruit he held: but then in his anger he crushed it and the fruit together. Whose thought is this?"

The vague feeling of disappointment at this rather tame revelation was quickly shattered: "It is nobody's thought," said Sutane with murderous calm, the words falling like blows from a club. "The showings are at an end."

The plain woman in blue stared at him.

"Master," said Intila in a low voice, and touched his arm.

"... Pardon me. Our good host's wine is all too loquacious. Myself, I have little to show. My work still moves towards the colour that does not exist; but slowly. When we meet again in a hundred days, who knows? My goals are what they were: to achieve White, to expunge the grey taint from the world until all our bright illusions reach full potency, to break the dark in the sky and see beyond ... no end to my ambitions, you see."

"No end to your word-spinning," grumbled Remmiry.

"The Guildleader does not show," said the woman of the crystal, vindictively. "It's easy enough to talk about this White, but where is it? What have you done in all your so-called researches? Why should you sit at the end of the table? I call the question."

Sutane shrugged. "I hoped not to squander power. In this, so far, I cannot work alone." He stood, tall and spare, pressing his right hand to his bony forehead as if it ached, the other hand gripping Intila's shoulder. She sat quite still but seemed to pale and shrink a little. Even Breck felt the prickly aura of power in the air. A wine-flask fell, gurgled vivid red across the wooden table: nobody moved to set it upright.

Abruptly Sutane raised his right hand, spoke an unspeakable word and made a downward chopping movement. Appalling light, sourceless, eye-hurting, filled the room to bursting point, like a cymbal-clash translated from sound to light. At once it was over, leaving in Breck's eyes a roiling chaos of echoes and after-images in black and all the true colours but that one.

"Was that it?" he heard himself saying, "Was that ... white?"

Slowly, painfully slowly, vision cleared in patches to show Sutane still upright but sagging. Intila had slumped in her chair. There was much rubbing of eyes, with here and there a muffled curse. The candles on the table, Breck noticed with a sudden cold shock, had burnt down three inches in that illusory moment.

Over the confusion Sutane said: "I am as yet unable to refine this radiance to pure white, which remains a colour that does not quite exist. There's still a taint of grey in the world, and I am still part of the world. Yet you may care to assess the hypnotic power of near-white by noting that this mighty assembly of magical experts has just been held transfixed in and out of time by its potency, as the candles bear witness...."

A growing hubbub of debate, alarm, nervous laughter. Suddenly Sutane was at Breck's side: "A word with you alone, Merchant."

The gathering was breaking up as they stood under the changeless black of the night sky. Faint breezes ruffled the grass, making ripples in its dim glow of true-green (the true colours did not entirely fade, even in darkness).

"Stars," murmured Sutane.

"Stars?"

"A matter of legend. Great lanterns of true white, somewhere high over the black cloud round the world. Imagine them."

"My imagination doesn't stretch so far. Why should there be anything beyond?"

"The sun is beyond, we know that; it peeps through the blanket of the dark in one tainted colour or another. The story is that once the world was drab, muddy, foul … until the demiurge-illusionist Mijkebarr wove his grand illusion and spelled away the darkness of Earth. There it is in the sky, the dark, still clinging, still envying the bright colours below. Only the faintest smear of dull grey is left on us here."

"My mother told me all that once. I've found nursery tales of very little practical use in business, and it's as a businessman that I wonder why you've come out here to recite legends."

"Within a hundred days, I think, we'll talk again about practicality. I've learnt a truth or two this evening, and I see my way to White … and on to expulsion of Earth's drabness, the driving of the dark beyond the stars. To business, then. I can no longer trouble with the petty gathering of berries for my food. My mind must instead weave illusion. I ask you to send a daily adequacy of viands to my home under the Grey Birches. For, shall we say, the next hundred days?"

"Mostly I deal in *valuable* commodities, but no doubt I can oblige you." Breck was taken aback. Many illusionists had some mundane occupation, like Remmiry with his forge or the several teachers of children in that night's assembly; others turned their talents to practical ends, such as Mira with her dubious charms of love and fertility. The hermit mages like Sutane never seemed to live on more than air and rain. Which thought led Breck to say:

"If I may put one question …?"

"You wonder why my journeyman cannot gather food. I must renounce her aid. The path of perfection and White must be walked alone, away from others learned in the Craft."

"The question of payment," said Breck, even more dubiously.

"Ah yes. I offer you Intila."

"Eh?"

"You covet her; no, don't deny it. Very well. She is bound by oath to me and I can transfer the oath-bond to you; permanently if you wish."

"Done," said Breck, caught off-balance in a whirl of confusion.

"Excellent. Let my meagre dole of food begin tomorrow. I go now; and thank you, on behalf of us all, for your excellent hospitality."

Breck was left pondering on the blend of anger and satisfaction in Sutane's voice. He stared again at the featureless dark above, and tried to imagine great lamps shedding a colour that did not exist. The flash that was nearly white had faded from memory, though, and his eyes only offered afterimages that lingered in dim blank blobs of purple and green.

"I am bound to serve you," said Intila, colourlessly. She stood by the table, an unmoving reef about which Breck's half-dozen servants eddied in their coming and going as they cleared away. The stone hall seemed drab without the illusionists in their glowing robes. Intila's robe, like Sutane's, was dismal grey.

"Come and sit by the fire," he suggested, still disoriented. It was almost like having been married, suddenly and *in absentia.*

She sat. Her eyes seemed huge in the small perfect face, their blue as pure as the speaking crystal's. "I don't understand it. He needs me to bring him food, even to take power from, sometimes, because he's old. You saw that tonight. Why should he do this thing? Why?"

"It was a business arrangement," said Breck feebly.

"Then what have you sold him, *merchant*? What precious talisman is worth the loss of the best aid the Master could have? Tell me that."

"Daily food for a hundred days. Don't look at me like that. Sutane asked for that, and set his own price."

"And you *let* him. I suppose you're used to dealing in bodies and souls, human lives to buy and sell if the price is right. You think you've bought me for your own. You disgust me." Her animation made even the drab robe seem attractive.

"Sutane said he needed to be alone for the hundred days, to work up some grand enchantment. No doubt this is his way of ensuring you're well cared for meanwhile."

"It's unbelievable. He wanted me perfect for the Craft. He hated even to see men look at me, hated it bitterly. It makes no sense, merchant."

"The name is Breck," he said, wondering whether the transferred oath would hold under the strain should he order her into his arms. (Yes, he realized with what was almost terror, it would.) At the same time he felt obscurely certain that words spoken that evening held the key to all Sutane's dealings, but when he pursued that train of thought it was lost in a thin haze of wine.

In the days that followed, one of Breck's men set out each morning with provisions, an unpopular duty since the grey birch clump was some miles distant, and it often rained. In the days that followed, Intila continued defiantly to wear dingy grey and to pose a problem as to her household position. At present her keen mind was turned on to the merchant's books and had already caused the violent dismissal of one bookkeeper. In the days that followed, Breck considered again his longing for the young woman ... which made the oath intolerable, for how could he broach the subject when any hint of his desire might bring him her dutifully and joylessly to his bed?

On the fifth morning Breck was staring restlessly through the eastern windows of his low pillared hall. The land fell away in patches of near-true colour like a landscape of glowing stained glass: grass and leaves all the same pure green, a single singing brown for treetrunks and earth, the one blue gleaming from standing water and the one yellow in the sun which pierced the ever-dark sky. Only faint filmings and shadowings of grey disturbed the garish evenness, or lent perspective. It was like any morning in those days.

The sun was echoed in a yellow movement behind, Intila's hair swirling as she entered and stood stiffly to await instruct-ions. Breck eyed her.

"What would you do if I cancelled this damned oath?"

"I'd pay a visit to Laa the dyer's cottage."

"Who?"

"You've met her, but because you're a man and she's plain you never troubled to remember her name. Laa is famous for her *blue*."

With an effort Breck ignored the first statement. "... The illusionist with the crystal, ah yes. Why would you visit her?"

"If I were released from the oath, I wouldn't tell you."

"But since things are as they are?"

"She would ... loan me the crystal if I asked."

"Whereupon you'd ferret out my inmost secrets? No, of course. Furtively you'd creep to the grey birches and eavesdrop on Sutane." He folded his arms, admiring his own insight.

"I want to *know*."

"So do I, so do I. Feel free to carry on just as you please ... for now."

She smiled. "Thank you."

When she'd gone, almost at a run, Breck sat on the edge of his counting table and for an inordinate while savoured the first smile she'd allowed him. His restlessness returned, though. The stained-glass brilliance outside now glowed threateningly, a gaudy insect with a sting. All the colours of the world held danger when one was caught up in an illusionist's web.

"Damnation," said Breck.

He'd had the common schooling in the Craft, but no talent whatever: his memory would only throw up fragments like driftwood. *Some say the true colours are fixed in number, maybe as few as seven: others set no bounds to them but hold that colours beyond the few we know may await discovery like the shores of unknown isles.* What did the book say about white? ... *Among the legends of the lost colour are that it is the opposite of dark, if that can be imagined; that if all the grey were removed from grey then white would be created; that it is all colours together, as if colours might be mingled and fused* ... There was more half-remembered nonsense in this vein, linking true white to purity and all the virtues together, and cynically concluding that *for such a thing to be, all the world needs must be changed.* Well, quite.

"For such a thing to be, all the world needs must be changed," said a clear voice from the doorway.

Breck began to turn, and halfway froze as superstitious dread took hold of him with bony fingers. With complicated feelings he faced Intila again: the long glowing hair, the secretive smile, the whispering blue thing she held to one ear. Confusedly he tried to slam doors in his mind.

"You were quick," he said rapidly. "Does Laa lend out her listening stone for the asking? Could use it myself when the tax gatherer comes calling. Find how much of my tithes stick to his fingers."

She shrugged. "I lied. I said I came from Sutane: Laa was only too pleased to think her stone would be described in the Great Record. And no, you haven't been thinking such dreadful, terrible things about me."

Breck felt his ears might have assumed the true red of fire or ruby. "The idea ... it makes one think all the worst things in the effort not to think them."

"Well, Merchant Breck, if those were the worst thoughts you could think of me, I'm reasonably flattered."

There was a pause: the cool room seemed extraordinarily stuffy and uncomfortable. Feebly Breck said: "Thank you. Why not go and use this thing on Sutane now? No, why don't we *both* take a walk to the Grey Birches...."

They went out together into the glowing world. Presently Breck took her hand; or perhaps she took his.

By the time the birches came into sight, a rare shadow on the vivid fields, Breck was in fizzing high spirits. He felt as he had at half the age, when first and almost painfully aware of women's breasts, legs, everything. The three miles' journey seemed only too short.

"You'd best keep back," she said while the birches were still a little way off. "I can spy better if only Sutane is near; the whispers are hard enough to follow when they're single. I am not Laa."

"A good thing too." Their lips touched. Breck stood in sunlight, watching as she carried away the many-faceted stone, shrinking, dimming, vanishing in the grey trees' shadow. He waited.

He thought of his luck, of Intila; at once his merchant's mind set him looking for ill-luck to occupy the other pan of the balance. Suppose Sutane caught her. Suppose she never returned, and when at last he went stumbling through the trees there was nothing there but old leaves and dust. Suppose Sutane ...

Sutane, he reminded himself, was following the way of white and perfection. But a remembered voice from his schooling said, *perfection of the life or of the work?*

Then he saw the small yellow-haired figure, already well clear of the wood, and cheerfulness bubbled up to reach his lips as a grin. The grin died as she came closer and he saw her haunted face.

"He caught you? Intila, if he ... What happened?"

"No. He never saw me. He sees nothing and his thoughts have all turned inward like snakes that coil up. He's sitting crosslegged in the open with fallen leaves in his hair."

"Dead." Breck was almost relieved. He reached to take her arm: she struck his hand down.

"Don't. Not now.... He isn't dead; he's following his way as he said, and so quickly. A hundred days? He'll be there in ten. Or sooner."

"Well, good for him. What's *wrong*?"

"Good for him but not for everyone. The way of perfection is crueller than I ever thought. No. Please don't touch me."

"Why? What's going round in that bony head of his?"

She stared at some far-off hill. "I understand now what Laa heard, about the fruit and the insect. Sutane's path to White requires a sacrifice. I mustn't tell you more; oaths; loyalty to the Guild.... You shouldn't touch me and it would be better if we didn't speak, or look at one another, or even linger in the same room. Not yet. I like you, Breck, but not yet."

"A sacrifice," said Breck with rising anger.

"I *mustn't* say more, except that you need not have food sent to the birch clump now. There are two packages there at the edge, untouched. The Master did not eat today or yesterday. Nor will he until the end."

"I have my obligations," Breck said glumly. "If the food is wasted, then it's wasted – but it'll be delivered just the same."

Together, though not too closely, they plodded back to Breck's home through the fading afternoon. This time the journey seemed endless.

"Don't anger Sutane. Please," she said in a low voice as they parted on the threshold.

Breck's thoughts whirled in new confusion as he asked Emberson the factotum to take food to Intila's room, while he ate alone in the stone-flagged hall. It was absurd to have shifted in a single day from one kind of remoteness to another, avoiding Intila first through fear that he might unfairly command her, and now because she had unfairly commanded him. Words like "sacrifice" and "fruit" and "perfection" were still buzzing through his skull when, uncomprehending and a little fuddled, he stumbled to his bed.

There followed a hiatus: a visit from the district's tax gatherer. Day after day Breck poured wine for him, trying to keep his wits about him while displaying the right record scrolls and lying with due artistry about certain profits in hidden vaults. All that time Intila remained in her room. When the ritual farewells had been said, and Breck had parted with more in tithes than he liked, though less than he might have, he found that some little part of his mind had been toiling all the time to unravel the web binding himself and Intila to the schemes of Sutane. In the fresh glow of morning it was hard to believe the blackness of it.

He thought: Sutane's perfection needs a sacrifice. A sacrifice must, I suppose, be perfect. Intila is, I suppose, still virgin. Her oath-bond to Guild and Guildleader now requires her to remain perfect ... for Sutane. The fruit which the insect must not pierce.

He thought: Why foist her on me? Because even Sutane could not bring himself to offer up one who served him daily. He needs time to harden himself.

He thought: In some way, some sending of illusion, he called her. Through the stone he told her her duty. And straightaway she drew back from me.

He leant forward, elbows on the rough wooden table, face hidden in his hands. *I could arrange for her to be virgin no longer*, he thought wistfully. No. Not when Intila repulsed him.

Very well. If he could not weight one pan of the balance, he might still lift something from the other. Do unto others as they would do unto their own.

The sword had been his father's: a mercenary had begotten a merchant. It seemed numbingly heavy as he buckled it on, and the bright, inlaid scabbard shrieked against the background of his habitual brown clothing. A trace of red rust on the blade's grey metal did not, he supposed, matter very much. He felt a fool, though, striding again over undulating country towards the birch clump, and from time to time stumbling as the massive weapon swung and contrived to catch between his legs. Though the day was bright he was sweating coldly when he reached the grey trees whose every whisper or creak breathed menace. Clumsily, to a noise of grating rust, he tugged out the sword.

It was then the tenth day since Guild-leader and Master Illusionist Sutane had left Breck's house for the Grey Birches, there to follow his twisted path to perfection and the true White.

The shadowed woodland spread further than Breck thought; vaguely he'd expected to find Sutane's woven hut in the first clearing, but all that lay there were familiar packs of food in varying states of decay. Ahead were more slim grey trunks barred with yellow shafts of sunlight. He squinted into the confusion of light and dark ... and again he heard a voice behind.

"No! You mustn't anger him, Breck. This is what he wants. A master can *use* his anger...."

It was she, of course. He was almost relieved at the delay. Still the awkward sword was in his hand. "I go to ... to put an end to any anger Sutane might feel," he declared with that magnificence poets ascribed to fighting men, but he couldn't think what to say next.

"I saw you. From the window. A mile off. I ran.... Come back with me now. Please do, there's danger." In her gasping anxiety she plucked at his cloak. Breck's heart melted again, and he twined his free arm round her with sudden eagerness, feeling her heart drum and pound as her breast's warm pressure came against him.

"No," she said, eyes wide with fear, but not drawing away. "This is what he ..."

"I see you. Lecherous, monstrous beast of a merchant," said a thin voice that shook with rage, and maybe something more than rage. "Insect that violates my fine fruit."

Too late, they sprang apart. Sutane was coming slowly through the trees, black eyes terrible with a kind of triumphant anger, his cupped hands cradling a sphere of smoke like incandescent ruby. Breck saw he was thinner, beakier, flesh pale almost to translucence. Somewhere close but far away Intila cried out, "Avert!" and dropped into mumbled incantation. Breck knew without words that the glow in Sutane's hands was death, Breck's own death. As the intent illusionist spread his fingers wide, the red smoke swelled to bloody flame; Intila shrieked "Avert!" with a loosing of faint radiance from her raised hand; and in desperation Breck flung the clumsy sword with all his strength.

He dropped to the ground and rolled. Intila fell too, limply, her feeble thrust swallowed in Sutane's monstrous fury of red. The sword cracked and puffed into incandescent vapour. Flame burst from Breck's own cloak and touched him in a dozen places with hot needles of pain. Throwing a protective arm before his face, he rolled further across the sizzling grass, a stench of smoke and ash and his own burnt hair making him choke and retch.

Still somehow alive, he peered painfully up to see Sutane standing over him. He had not even the strength to spit defiance. Against the dark branches and sky, Sutane's threadbare robes and flesh now stood out with an unearthly glow.

"I have no quarrel with you now," he said in his thin gentle voice, which had changed, become purer and clearer. "Indeed I am glad you live."

This time Breck did spit: it fell short. Propping himself up with both blistered arms, he saw the great swathe of burnt ground behind, the blackened stumps of trees where the ultimate, deadly fire-illusion had compelled belief not only on Breck but on the inanimate world ... had become reality. Wisps of smoke rose everywhere, even from Intila's scorched clothes, but she was stirring. The mind-fire must have roared over them as they fell, leaving a trail of burns and blisters but not death; perhaps the sword and Intila's pale defence had helped abate it. And Sutane glowed brighter, a fearful light burning through him in a colour that hurt the eyes, a colour that had been lost.

"I am purged," he said. "Ah, the way of White was hard for one whose nature was riddled with anger and impatience. With Remmiry's spell of wrath I saw how to fight anger with anger, red with red, to let the angry red within me swell until it burst like a boil in one cleansing, destroying blast. I used my rage at those who stared at my Intila; I sent her away, my fine perfect fruit, hiding from myself just why, until the sight of a coarse insect merchant on her perfection brought all my rage to a head and made it surge out from me under the spell's direction. You understand? I couldn't hate you now if I wanted to. Now: White. A changing of the world and the breaking of the Dark!"

"Insect," muttered Breck, now standing. "Stark nonsense. I'm taking Intila away from this madness." He moved to where she stood, trembling, staring at Sutane with unreadable eyes.

"Do what you wish," said Sutane gaily. "My work is now to lift the last grey from the world. Look!" A casual gesture, and unbearable white sprang downward: the grass about him became more than green, burning with the unabated true colour. Each slender leaf seemed a window into infinite corridors of glowing emerald. Tears came to Breck's eyes as he gazed at the grassy splendour; he turned his head away with an effort. "I'm going."

"You used me," said Intila. "A piece of bait, a bargaining counter. Your white is rotten at the core."

"Perfection justifies all."

"I doubt it," said Breck. "Goodbye. It looks like rain."

Sutane stared at the black cloud gathering above, and momentarily frowned.

Walking painfully as their clothing rubbed at blisters, Breck and Intila left in silence. Even to touch hands brought its own penalty of pain. Looking back, they saw the gloomy birch clump blossom in truest colours, leaves unutterably green, trunks ablaze with the regained white, shadows all lost in colour. If illusion, it was the grandest of all illusions. It was as though they had spent a lifetime in caves, squinting and staring in flickers of candlelight, and now at last had crept out to see the sun. But also they saw a darker cloud overhead.

"The whole world like this ...?" Breck murmured, and shook his head.

"Wait. The test comes now. Sutane will challenge the darkness."

"Stars," Breck said meditatively, rolling the empty word on his tongue. The grove's perfect colours pulsed joyously, and a sword of white stabbed the sky with unutterable beauty. Again it was too much to look at; Breck thought of tart fruit whose piercing taste was exquisite to the point of pain. Rainbow colours trembled over the whole sky.

Then the column of light rising from the trees faded to pale grey. Steadily it darkened and became a black as absolute as the white had been. There was a scream from the trees; the face of the sun was obscured; a torrent of darkness fell roaring from above. The sky itself paled, as though all its shadows were being funnelled down on Sutane.

"He did it himself," said Intila in the terrible twilight. "He stood there with his puny perfection, like a fine fruit to tempt the dark round the world, and he pulled it down on us. White and black rush together and cancel. Perfection ... it's deadly."

Muddy light returned to the world. The sky was left stained with pale dinginess hardly worth calling a colour, some deformed offspring of the real blue. A grey churning hid the birch clump.

"He succeeded, in a way, then," said Breck. "The dark's gone from the sky."

"He failed. The dark is back here with us. Mikjebarr's spell is undone. Look."

Like ripples in water, a new muddiness was rolling out over the grass, a feeble echo of true green as the sky was a feeble echo of blue, blotting out even the memory of the ultimate green glory Sutane had brought to earth for a little time. Breck almost turned to run, to drag Intila with him and outrace the change. But the muddiness moved too quickly across the land, and was on them.

He felt nothing, but closed his eyes at what he saw. No more were the world's hues brilliant and distinct like stained glass: they faded and ran together incontinently. No longer was Intila's sun-yellow hair a beacon of light; above them the sun itself had paled.

"You look so terribly different. Everything is spoilt." Even his voice was squeezed by the pain of loss into feebleness, between a whisper and a moan.

She caressed his cheek. "You feel the same, Breck. Illusionists know better than to set much store by appearances...."

It was with closed eyes that they made love in the ruin of all true colours.

Later, people coaxed a new kind of beauty from the flawed world, finding subtlety and power in mongrel hues, decaying tints, pastels which had been unknown and unthinkable. Mages and illusionists looked for new keys to mastery, turning from the paths of pure colour. Others gaped at the unremarkable stars.

When true colours fade, their memory fades not long after. For a time, though, Sutane's monument remained. Where the doomed birches had stood, there was a great hollow which held its own kind of perfection, the perfection of pure and neutral grey, the featureless perfection of dust. Once Breck and Intila went walking there as lovers, before the straggling grass could reclaim the place; during the brief time they stood hand in hand on that numbing grey expanse, they could feel nothing for each other, nothing at all.

Thus it was in the old days.

• Published 1983. I dimly recollect that the editor of TSR's British role-playing-games magazine *Imagine* invited me to write something about illusionists. With hindsight, the gathering of mages showing off their latest gimmicks seems reminiscent of a passage in John Brunner's *The Traveller in Black*, a personal favourite which is also about purging the world of gaudy magical excess in favour of more sober and reasonable colours. The Brunner stories began with a pastiche of the great James Branch Cabell, from whom I lifted the final line above. Can this be coincidence?

Perhaps in some alternative timeline where I extended this brief tale into a trilogy or open-ended polyology, I have a great deal more money.

In the Place of Power

It had been cold at first, when Tirik climbed above the clouds. White ridges and peaks towered ahead, hard-edged and perfect against the sky's unearthly blue, almost painful to the eye. To descend again through those puffy clouds to the softness of the valley ... after this it would be like wallowing in mud, Tirik thought, exalted. It had been cold at first, each breath scouring his throat and nostrils like splintered ice: but now it seemed less so. He climbed on, gloved hands fumbling for purchase on the treacherous slope, towards the topmost peak and the place of power.

"Can you hear me coming, Magus? Can you hear me coming?" he whispered.

The mountains which ringed the one valley were called the edge of the world; they might be or they might not; nobody knew what was beyond. Once the world – the valley – had been larger, perhaps hundreds of miles across rather than a puny five; but lately the edges of the world were closing in. By night or even by day, the foothills would shuffle inward. Another farm, another family, would be gone. Even day and night were not the reliable things they had been. The brightest summer afternoon might be disfigured by an hour-long patch of night, or the hues of sunset swallowed in a wholly improper dawn. It was not to be tolerated. There were dreams and visions, signs and portents, as always, as ever. Appalling things stalked the darkness, as though demanding propitiation. The word "sacrifice" was mentioned rather too soon and rather too frequently for Tirik's liking – he knew that his own burning ambition and manoeuvres for power were resented. And sure enough, with much flattery of his youth, strength and cleverness, the village fathers chose Tirik for the ostensible task of pleading with the legendary Magus in his place of power. None of them dwelt on the tradition that people had gone that way before, or the lack of any tradition relating to their return.

Tirik had his own ideas about sacrifice, and he carried a well-sharpened knife. With keen wits and a keen knife, he considered, a man might steal treasure or power even from a Magus.

The last part of the ascent was the easiest. By now it was neither warm nor cold; he felt buoyed up by the calm sea of air, rising almost effortlessly like a bubble in clear water. Nearing the summit, he staggered and shook his head. The rugged shoulders of the mountain converged but carried no final peak: something had sheared the problematical peak away to leave a smooth surface like a mirror of ice, crackling with the clear blue of the sky. Though visibly tilted towards him and the valley below, the ten or twenty gleaming acres held Tirik's eye and told it that somehow this mirror was truly level, the rest of the world askew. So he stumbled. Even having seen the trick, if it was a trick, he felt continuing waves of giddiness there at the edge of the place of power.

Over the gleaming blue a dark blot moved towards him like a spider. It was a man, a ragged man who walked the slope as though it were truly as level as it pretended, as level as calm water – and as though the upright Tirik were leaning ludicrously forward.

"Magus," Tirik said, sliding a hand down his right leg to what was in his boot, his mind a churning stew of ambition and fear.

The man shrugged. His black beard was full and his face unlined, but the voice creaked like old and rusty machinery. "Magus? I don't think of myself by that name; or any other, as it happens. No, leave the knife alone, you won't need it. I promise you. Let me think. Your name would be Tirik. Brown hair. Yes."

Tirik teased out a lock of his hair and squinted at it. "Yesterday it was yellow, the day before it was black – what does it matter?"

"I apologize. My abilities are failing. This is why you are here."

"I don't understand," said Tirik, beginning to wonder if this might be a mere madman.

"That too is why you are here. There are important turns of history which you and the valley folk have never known – also a certain point of geography. Come, and I'll show you what lies beyond the mountains."

"Will I ... will I be able to go back down after?"

"You'll see all your friends again before the day is over. Now come with me ... no, don't cross the border of the Place, not now. Around the edge to the other side of the mountain, the side which doesn't look down into your valley. I'll walk with you, you on your ground and I on mine."

They walked, the Magus (if that was what he was) gliding over the impossibly perfect mirror while Tirik toiled up rock and shale an arm's length away. To look to his left and the "Place" meant vertigo; indeed, to look anywhere but where his feet were going meant a likely fall ...

"Stop now," said a rusty voice. Just ahead the pathway ended in blue sky. Tirik glanced at his guide, who was staring back with a critical frown. "Red hair?"

Again Tirik peered at a loose lock of his own hair. "Red, yes. Changed again since we started walking. Does it matter?"

"It matters very much indeed. This is not the way things should be.

Again, my apologies. Now what did I bring you here for? Something you had to know ...”

“The other side of the mountain.”

“Quite. I would have remembered in a moment. Take a pace or two forward, then, very carefully if you please, and look over the edge.”

Tirik did this. There was a very long pause. He could find no words for what he saw. The bright horror beyond the world made the disorienting ways of the place of power seem nothing. Looking down, he saw that there was no such thing as a level surface, no straight line or right angle anywhere, no solid matter or empty air, no laws or words or reasons or –

“Tirik.”

If only he stared long enough he would know the secrets beyond knowledge, beyond good and evil, beyond thought.

“*Tirik*. Close your eyes.”

The whiplash of authority in the order struck through. Tirik shut his eyes, put his hands to his face, swayed on the brink, assaulted by monstrous after-images.

“Now turn around ... That’s right. Sit down.”

– He was sitting on a rock he didn’t remember being there, blinking in thin sunlight. The man with the black beard and old eyes watched him, his expression compounded of kindliness and distraction.

“*That* is what lies beyond the mountains. It presses inward, but so far it does not prevail – not since the beginning. Did I say I would tell you history? I’ll tell it now.

“Longer ago than I like to think or you could comprehend, the maker conceived the world. That was the beginning. They still tell the story, don’t they? Yes. The maker imagined the world in all its detail, imagined it with a force that pushed back – what you saw. You’ll have listened to your village philosopher, maybe, saying that nothing exists save as a thought in the mind of the maker. Sophistry, you might have thought, if you knew the word. Not at all....”

“I know it,” Tirik muttered. Babbling old fool, he thought. “Good. Where was I? The maker sat in the place of power, holding the world’s image in his mind, and all was well. Her mind, its mind? It could have been any or all three. All *this* –” indicating the bare waste of mirror – “was the maker’s notion of a comfortable seat, a niche, a resting-place ...”

“Then after an uncounted time the maker’s attention turned elsewhere, to greater things perhaps, and all the world began to change and to decay. As it faded from the maker’s mind it faded altogether ... all the same, here we are now, eh? Now why is that?

“Ah yes. Before the real things – the things outside – could squeeze our world away, a man climbed to the place of power. He was only a man and not the maker, but he held the world in his mind and preserved it as best he could. But still, he was only a man, and for all the power of the place he grew old."

"*You?*"

"Not I. He was the Magus. In the Place he needed no food nor drink, which was fortunate. He kept his strength, more fortunate still. Sleep, though, he could never do without sleep, and when he slept the world went dark. In the days of the maker there was no night, you know? And, and, what was the next thing … his mind began to shrivel. He would forget. The tiniest of things at first, a dewdrop, a blade of grass, a stray toadstool or a pebble on the stream's bed. Nobody would know or care if these slipped from the mind of the Magus and from the world. Then, perhaps, matters more noticeable. The colour of a boy's hair. A whole pasture or spinney at the foot of the mountains. And in the end, who knows?"

He was looking very hard at Tirik, who said: "You. It must be you. My hair …"

"The world is older than you think. I am the ninety-fourth successor of the Magus. But yes: lately I've begun to forget things."

"And our world grows smaller?"

"Quite."

"The other thing – the night that comes by noon or the dawn in the evening?"

The old man who did not look old smiled. "Another curse of age. In spite of all my discipline I fall asleep when I shouldn't, wake when I should sleep: night comes, or light – you see the way of it. And horrid things walk the night for you, don't they? I'm sorry. Lately, I have bad dreams. – Now take my hand."

Again the sudden iron of command in his tone made Tirik obey without thought: his hand rose to encounter the man's strong grip, and he was pulled with a jerk to his feet.

"No," he said as an appalling realization came to him. He tried to step back; his free hand groped awkwardly for the knife.

"What –? Oh, you had something in your boot, didn't you? Some sort of weapon." A sardonic chuckle. "I'm afraid I've forgotten what it was."

And the knife was no longer there.

"I must tell you one last thing," said the ancient and now hateful rusty voice. "One last legend. Remember it. It is said that when the holder of the place of power can imagine a vast enough world, can imagine the mountain barriers further and further away until they meet in the unthinkable distance and close off the world from the flux outside … on that day the Place and its prisoner will be needed no more. Perhaps then the world can be left to exist in the minds of common folk: I don't know. Remember it, though. And if you're not the one to solve that riddle, remember to imagine yourself a worthy successor In the Place – and to pass on what I've said. Let that be the last of all the things you forget."

The painful hold on Tirik's hand tightened until he felt the bones grate; there was a tug and a moment's whirling confusion. He was standing unsteadily on the Ice-mirror of the Place, which all his senses agreed was perfectly flat and sane; but the whole world outside had tilted until the toothed mountains far across the valley seemed to tower over this, the tallest of them all. A dreadful knowledge was battering on the doors of his mind.

He saw his predecessor standing at an insane angle, no longer within the Place, the man seemed suddenly older, lined and bent, his beard streaked with cloudy grey. "Goodbye. And good luck." Then the former Magus turned, took two firm paces to the world's edge, and was gone. To final forgetfulness, perhaps, or to forge his own world rather than sniff like a dog at the Maker's leavings: there was no way to tell, not yet.

The dreadful knowledge was swarming through Tirik now, funnelling into him like endless grains of sand, the knowledge of all the world focused by the place of power, the million million weights and numbers, tastes and colours, moods and whims which made up the sum of things which were. He saw it all in the mirror underfoot; he knew it all, and it was his duty to remember it all. And more.

You'll see all your friends again before the day is over. Tirik saw them and knew them through and through, and it was not enough.

He remembered the knife, and felt its welcome presence again in his boot. It would be easy to end everything – but he could not do that to the world that danced in the mirror and in his mind, aglitter with such overwhelming detail. Probably he'd been chosen as someone who would not do that. Or created as someone who would not. His own ambition, if nothing else, would hold him prisoner. The numb weight of responsibility and of all the things there were pressed down on him.

He clenched his fists in futile anger, and great thunderheads boiled up in the valley far below. He screwed up his eyes, and bitter rain broke from the clouds like tears. In long rolls of thunder he cried out against the unfairness of it all, that he should be burdened with this omnipotence and throned at the top of the world, in the place of power.

• Published 1984. Moral: It's tough at the top as well as at the bottom.

The Arts of the Enemy

My dear fellow, isn't it for *you* to be apologetic? Consider your position. You burst uninvited into the most strenuously forbidden vault of Thousand Doves Monastery, and lie hurling abuse at a simple artisan who's never done you any harm. I mean, do you make a habit of flinging yourself over precipices and cursing whoever helps you up?

Oh well, I take the point. Losing a leg is apt to strain the temper. A hand too, I see. Ribs. Spleen. We'll deal with that presently. Would it be naive to assume that you're a visiting Hero, out for loot? And came via the dummy flagstone in the long cloister ... no mistaking the marks of the Grinder on that particular route. Spider bites, as well? But you were too quick for the fire-blast trap. Mostly. Well, never look a gift cautery in the mouth, ha ha.

One simply has to instal these tiresome precautions to retain any shred of privacy in an age like this. If I ever catch the scribe who sells those wretched maps ... A pity, speaking impersonally, that you didn't try the oubliette route from the refectory. There are some tolerably ingenious safeguards there that could use testing, including a squad of killer were-orcs.

Good question. Were-orcs are tricksy: all the time you're fighting them, they keep shifting shape into *different* orcs. Throws a swordsman off completely when the wart he was aiming for leaps six inches to the left. Oh, do please stop bleeding over things. Here ... ah ... amulet of serendipity, periapt of good digestion, rune of resistance to the clap ... *here* it is. Philtre of implausible healing.

If you say "foul villain" again I shall grow seriously bored. I'm no petty poisoner. Only *good* things get manufactured here. See, I'll sprinkle some on my hand. Reassured? And now on you.

Shush. Yes, I should have mentioned that your injured limbs would dissolve painfully into thick pools of evil-smelling slime. A normal part of the healing process. They'll reform in an hour or so, good as new.

There is no effect on me because my health is already perfect. It is customary for me to have a single red eye. I detest personal remarks.

Now, what have we here? Your shield has had it; you must have used it to jam the rotating knives in the fourth traverse, very resourceful. Iron rations from Ombrifuge in the Twenty-Four Kingdoms: a poor bargain, that stuff, it gives you the trots. Good, well-worn shortsword. "WHOSO PULLETH THIS SWORD FROM THE STONE IS RIGHTWISE KING OF ALL ..." From Blind Odo's smithy, of course. He puts that on all his blades. A sort of trademark. And this opal ... dear me. I must consult the speculum.

Thank you. Indeed, I've misjudged you. You are an idealistic fool of a Hero, and it is, as you say, a charm of detection of evil, and one can hardly deny that it's led you to me. More precisely, to this plain golden ring I'm wearing.

I can explain everything. First, though, study your jewel in the speculum. See the triple fracture plane? I'd guess the stone was enchanted by old Antigropelos of Sorceror's Isle: he rather runs to defects like that. His wretched charm could equally well have led to you to, let me see, either a lode of cinnabar or a shoal of phosphorescent jellyfish. Depending which was nearest. I'd like to see you ridding the sea of jellyfish. Because you came, didn't you, to rid the world of me?

I have always been misunderstood.

Since you aren't going anywhere at the moment, you shouldn't object to hearing more. One so rarely has an audience. It's not merely the need to work in private; there is such dreadful prejudice abroad. If the jolliest, kindliest fellow in the world should happen to have a black-glowing complexion and shifting features, things get said in back rooms of taverns ... and before you know what it's the crowd of peasants with scythes and torches, and yet another boresome search for a new house. I've never even claimed to be a Lord, only a simple researcher.

Of course you have some trifle of talent yourself, I mean the only Talent that counts. You worked that opal charm adequately, and its spell needs an active operator. I could teach you things. My own work is based on the concept of a fundamental balance of impersonal forces called Good and Evil, or Light and Dark, which ...

Oh, this silly, superstitious fear of mere knowledge! You should join the good brothers upstairs in Thousand Doves. Gardening, loud piety, eight daily prayer sessions, invincible ignorance, and just enough side interests to spice the boredom. You know. Gluttony. Women. Highway robbery. Nipping the buds of each other's fruit-trees on the sly. The usual things monks go for.

Naturally they "tolerate" me. They rely on me. Who do you think keeps up the charge on their famous Holy Healing Stone? Gods don't stoop to that sort of routine maintenance: one quick miracle and you never see them again, and probably the miracle was a county-wide rain of boiling pus rather than anything friendly. But me, I do good works.

No, I've never killed anyone – more than you could say, I'm sure. And since you're not saying, what does the speculum reflect about you? Seventeen dead. Ho hum. You can't have been heroing very long. No champion ever got his own song cycle without a body count in the high three figures....

Well, in strict justice I must confess to a few, but arguably they were accidental, in self defence. Funny coincidence, in fact, with you lying there in that dismantled state. Brings back memories.

It was after the unpleasantness surrounding my last homestead, where I'd been making real progress with the accumulator – the ring. All of a sudden there was a roaring upsurge of that prejudice I've mentioned. Wild stories about a foul black lord (which was rude and unflattering), and the sky of the kingdom being darkened by enormities (much exaggerated and no more than a temporary side effect, as I explained at the time), and an epidemic of monstrous births ... to be utterly fair, it did occur to me later that there could have been a minor leakage from the alembics, and I resolved to take precautions in future. Which is one reason why I'm now established under a monastery.

Anyway. To cut a long epic short, I was roughly treated without fair trial. Have you ever seen anyone struck simultaneously by two spells of Invincible Fulguration, together with Galligaskin's Convenient Macerator and the Cantrip of Remorseful Earache? All that remains, I can tell you from personal experience, is a shallow depression in the rock containing traces of thin, weeping fluid. I thought at the time that I deserved better. Earache, oddly enough, is even worse without ears.

The amusing coincidence is that I was carrying a phial of the same healing stuff you're growing so familiar with. My own invention. It faithfully preserved what motes were left of me....

As I reconstruct it, the aggressors fled the ruins of what they credulously regarded as a cursed land (I'd genuinely meant to investigate why the wheat had started coming up black), which was declared forbidden and taboo forever. So it wasn't more than a week before the usual party of adventurers loaded up the usual gear – weapons, torches, flasks of oil, multi-sided dice, all that – and started combing the ruins. Of course they homed in on the ring where it lay in the middle of this broad patch of ooze.

(Look, if bubbling slime and naked prongs of reforming bone are such a bother to you, don't *stare* at yourself like that.)

Why hadn't I finished healing before then? Nothing comes of nothing. Magic as I see it is governed by conservation laws. Raw materials are needed. You might have noticed how your tunic and hose and that silly leather harness are being, ah, used up to replace bits you left behind in the corridors. Just so, and entirely inadvertently, I dissolved the greater part of one dwarf, one elf and one small being with hairy feet. Quite a little morality fable about rushing incautiously to grab valuable-looking rings; you never know what you might stumble on. In that case it was me.

But it's my work I wanted to talk about. Magicians are absurdly secretive and I never got far with my notion about the free community of knowledge, the Open Conspiracy as I liked to call it. But you need only glance at the Grimoire – here. Don't touch, now: it's bound in the skin of a trained were-porcupine. Any unauthorized browser soon gets the point, ha ha.

Look. Here's Nicanor, going on about how all enchantment is illusion, deception, glamour and sleight: he bases his entire shifty philosophy on that. Here's Stevegonius, who reckons it's pure force of naked will. And Ptolemopiter, with his texts and incantations that are supposed to work of themselves, without knowledge or understanding – even, as far as I can see, without anybody needing to read them. Faustus, reducing it to a dismal chaffering with demons, as though the proper trappings of the great Science were a merchant's bench and stool. Bülg and the doctrine of compelling living and unliving things by their True Names. Rather irritatingly, the whole crew got results.

The message is that there is no one message. Magic is how you see it. Truth is what is true for you.

So my own perception of the Balance ...

Oh, but I must tell you about this disciple of Bülg who stumbled on the most singular problem. She practised in the dwarflands south of here, and her Naming cantrips kept going askew. Eventually she found she'd met with a truly subtle weredom, a tribe of were-dwarves. They changed nomenclature at will, so an enchantment that collectively Named local *dwarves* would founder on those currently being *dwarfs*. She had to tackle them one by one in the end.

Might that account for part of the notorious dwarvish, or dwarfish, resistance to magic? I wonder.

You look improved enough to take a little wine. Would you ...? Of course it's black. Sable and ebon are nicer words. Or fuliginous. Everything down here goes that way sooner or later, usually sooner; I think there's trouble with the furnace and the air shafts. I hope.

My crucial experiment used a minimum of material. Two precisely matched swords and a very long incantation, nineteen thousand stanzas with one eye on the steel, one on the scroll (yes, I had two then). To me the stuff of the world is light and dark, blended together like black draught stirred into milk, most exceedingly hard to separate. On a tiny scale, I did it.

When I'd uttered the final corollaries and the Sun showed its face again, one sword radiated the faintest tinge of black, and I knew it would deal a minutely nastier wound than before. The other had healing properties of exactly the same order of feebleness. I had established a principle, the conservation of light and dark.

Then out of curiosity I touched the blades together, and balance reasserted itself with a blinding grey flash that left them fused, twisted, ruined. Which had to be the end of the work and the beginning of travel, as I could think of no convenient means of explaining to a Master Swordmaker that his matched creations, ordered on approval, had furthered the cause of knowledge in so final a way. But I'd begun.

Imagine, after that, what a really high concentration of Light or Dark might achieve!

My next invocation gained me further wisdom at a traditional cost. Yes, that's right. You see, the substance of this world is too feeble to sustain much added load of black *or* white energies: it gives way, bursts, vaporizes. Sometimes my skin still burns like fire at the memory. Oh, you noticed?

For an impersonal researcher, though, the discovery shed exciting illumination on the old legends of saints. Think about it: these alleged holy men worked without apparatus, healing away, promiscuously spreading sweetness and Light. They put forth this power from their own bodies. What had to be the consequence?

Clearly they needed to tilt themselves back into balance by blowing off their excess of Dark in unholy acts. And indeed you constantly hear of such sainted ones smiting people with unearthly fire for trivial differences of opinion, or committing pointless acts of vandalism like burning bushes or withering perfectly innocuous fig-trees.

After all, what was the alternative for them? When matter gives way under the terrible burden of imbalanced Dark, it's a hot business. For sorcerous reasons which I've not wholly fathomed, the resulting fireball tends to rise high in a spectacular column of smoke and flame. Compare this observation with the many tales of saints snatched up to heaven in blazing chariots, and you will surely ...

But I digress.

What a good question. You're brighter than you look. Yes, this ring is a huge focus of one energy – of course you know which. No, it's not composed of matter. Matter couldn't stand the strain. What looks like gold is a toroidal system of containment spells ... see the formulae, written on it in fiery letters. Meaningless, of course, without some knowledge of high-energy thaumatics. The spells form a perfect shield.

Well, nearly perfect. One tries to keep one's distance from people, but when I brought over the grimoire and the wine I forgot. I meant to advise you: after you leave, try not to sire any children for a short while. Say two years. You know it makes sense.

(Speaking of which, the speculum can no doubt mirror something of your activities in that area. What, ninety-three? You must have been heroing for longer than I'd assumed. A rest will do you good.)

And *why*? Come now. The disinterested enchanter pursues knowledge because it's there. Onward and upward. Just by moving my remaining fingers a hair's breadth I could topple this monastery and set it surfing through glowing lava down Slawkenbergius mountain and into the Kingdoms. But that would be a mere party trick. I must accumulate far, far more energy for serious work. The gates between worlds! The secrets of the stars! The reason why cockatrices cross the road! I have to know it all.

Meanwhile, that vulgar prejudice I talked about remains a problem. As one's non-Light reserves grow, more and more busybodies sniff them and start to pry. (No personal offence intended.) You do begin to see why, merely for the sake of peace and quiet, a reasonable fellow might reluctantly contemplate – just contemplate – overriding the minds and free will of a province or two? Or building one of those square countries with neighbour-proof mountain walls, like that reclusive chap out east.

These bad impressions have only once worked in my favour, when I first presented myself to the Abbot upstairs for a talk about sanctuary, and he genuflected most disgustingly at my feet. Drivelling on about O Baphomet, O Black One, O Master. Our monks do like to keep a cautious foot in either camp, just in case. (There's at least one were-layman among them ... first touch of full moon and thick hair sprouts all over his tonsure.) It must have been a great disappointment when I devoted myself to good works. At any rate, Father Abbot looked distinctly hopeful when one day someone embraced the Holy Healing Stone and threw his crutches away so enthusiastically that he broke the Dean of Novices' nose. Thought I was showing my natural cloven hoof at last, you see. By their fruits ...

Yes, that's the way of it. As the years go by, I work down here at the long, slow business of enchanting this and that amulet or potion with a measure of Light, enough to be useful and not so much as to rouse suspicion ... while the balancing by-product of Dark gets pouched in the ring for my own use. It's a neat system. The monks sell these objects of virtue, and people carry them off rejoicing. Impoverished but rejoicing.

Naturally it wouldn't do to have that whiteness piling up here, straining to discharge into the ring in one grey blaze of cancellation. Oh no. By now, after a blow like that to the sealing spells, the blast could level the Kingdoms and sink the Archipelago. The common folk don't realize the care I take to protect them.

Certainly you could do it yourself. I'm happy to teach anyone the basic involutions. The more the merrier: after all, when someone else stores up what looks to be a really valuable charge of Dark, I can always come and take it away from them. All's fair in love and thaumaturgy, eh? Many hands make dark work, ha ha.

That should have been time enough for healing. Let's see. Interesting: your leg's come back all funny-shaped. Sometimes I think the air in this chamber isn't altogether wholesome. Another ventilation shaft might help; but I do discourage visitors, you know. Can you walk? After a fashion. You'll master the extra joint in no time, and perhaps the, ah, ebon or sable appearance will wear off presently. I have some well-tried receipts for simple cosmetics....

As for the hand, it's better than new. Bigger, at least. You could wear a glove. A gauntlet, then.

What?

No need to phrase it so rudely. I suppose I should never have expected gratitude from a blasted Hero. Anyway, the answer to that one's surely obvious. If I'd taken the other path and accumulated the energies of Light, think of the counterbalancing work that would have been needed then. Making and disseminating this endless stream of cursed blades, baleful potions, charms of malignity and decay ... I couldn't bring myself to do that.

It's a matter of conscience, don't you see?

• Published 1992 in *Villains!*, a theme anthology in which the black-hatted bad guys of fantasy took centre stage and it seemed wholly reasonable for a Dark Lord to explain that he wasn't such a unpleasant chap at all, once you understood the inner high-mindedness of his goals. The *Villains!* version was slightly different from the above, because at least one of the editors disliked the were-dwarf joke: I had a phone call suggesting that the story really needed to be 80 words shorter, with a delicate hint that this gag just happened to occupy 80 words. Not being good at interpreting subtle telephonic hints, I trimmed the story by other means, after which the editors cut that passage anyway. Bah, humbug.

The title is from Tolkien, of course, describing the studies of that famously white-cloaked mage Saruman. Contributors to *Villains!* were also encouraged to supply placenames for the inevitable map, and for reasons which no longer seem terribly clear I purloined a few from "The Cock and the Bull", C.S. Calverley's brilliant pastiche of Robert Browning's verse at its most exhaustingly discursive and erudite (as in *The Ring and the Book*); plus another from *Tristram Shandy* by dear old Laurence Sterne. Not a lot of people wanted to know that.

As Strange a Maze as E'er Men Trod

FERDINAND
    Myself am Naples,
    Who with mine eyes, never since at ebb, beheld
    The King my father wracked.
MIRANDA
    Alack, for mercy!
FERDINAND
    Yes, faith, and all his lords, the Duke of Milan
    And his brave son being twain.
    (*The Tempest*, I.2)

The sky was clear, the breeze fair, the sea calm as a clock: King Alonso's ship had set its course for Naples and home. It should be possible, now, to forget that island where the party had been so mazed and befuddled by masques, sleights and deceits. Indeed those dreamlike adventures already seemed far distant. Gonzalo sniffed the salt air, peered rheumily at the wheeling seabirds, and wondered why he had all along felt a sense of unfinished matters; of something still taking its course.

And now the King's foolish, cowardly brother was gone. Fallen quietly overboard, perhaps, in a simple lubberly accident. Or perhaps not. In the old days, Gonzalo had helped unravel small intrigues at the court of the old Duke (now the restored Duke), while missing Antonio's larger treason until too late. If his wits were not too tattered with age, it would be good to pluck out the truth of Sebastian's passing and so make amends of a sort.

Exiled on his wondrous island, Duke Prospero had prepared a revenge twelve years old, twelve years cold. That strangely convenient tempest had delivered his enemies – Antonio the usurper, Alonso the co-conspirator – into the hollow of his hand. The old scholar had gloated over them as they swayed helplessly before him, bereft of sense by what Gonzalo suspected had been potent drugs. And then ... grudging words of forgiveness. An end to strife. Homeward bound. Was Prospero's heart really so melted by the sight of young Prince Ferdinand burning hot for his daughter?

A shadowed figure moved between him and the sun. "Mumbling your prayers, old windbag? Or devising another ideal commonwealth?"

Gonzalo blinked. Antonio might no longer be Duke of Milan, but he still wielded a ducal arrogance that gave weight and savage edge to the man's habitual pose of mockery. But there had been a time when Antonio's mockery failed. "We all become windbags in the last harbour of life," Gonzalo said comfortably. "The secret of being a windbag is to tell everything; and so, to have no secrets. This provokes telling in others."

"Winged words, as ever; winged like a fat capon. And what would you wish to be told?"

"I have studied Prospero's book –" the aged councillor began, and was briefly taken by a sudden convulsion of Antonio's thin features.

"I have studied it too." The words were edged with ice.

Prospero grandiloquently spoke of having destroyed his books of scholarship and grammarie (if indeed these were different things), but had brought aboard an account of words and doings during those few wracked hours upon his island – written down, he hinted, by those unseen servitors in whom Gonzalo could not quite believe. Alas, Prospero's scribe was sadly accurate, reproducing each and every shaft of mockery directed against Gonzalo by Antonio and his now-vanished crony Sebastian. The strange book also recorded when that mockery had fallen silent.

Even windbags can be blunt, Gonzalo told himself. "I wondered that, for so long at the last, you kept silence. The tongue of Antonio is a weapon where other weapons fail; yet as Prospero strutted in his hour of triumph, you hurled not a single jest at him. One commonplace barb for the beast-man and his stink of fish, but no more."

Antonio looked at him indulgently, like a duelling-master who acknowledges a pupil's feeble sally. "Perhaps I was struck dumb by brother Prospero's generosity. You recall the words with which he prefaced his so gracious forgiveness: 'For you, most wicked sir, whom to call brother, Would even infect my mouth ...' What a gift he has for pretty compliments."

Gonzalo, with sudden certainty, said: "That is an easy story, to tell children and old windbags. Behind it I feel there is a hard story."

"Why, yes." Antonio granted him a thin smile and a gaze both calculating and almost respectful. "I thought on the outcome of all our adventures; and I thought as well that, although we are men with small Latin and less Greek, we may say like good scholars, *Cui bono?*" He turned and moved away, sternward along the deck.

Cui bono? For whose good? Who benefits, who gains from the disappearance of Prince Sebastian? Gonzalo, thinking to see a weak place in Antonio's armour of scorn, had hoped for more than this truism tossed like a bone to a toothless hound. He looked about him again. Occasional mariners bustled to and fro, with little to do in this fair weather but make a show of diligence. Trinculo the little jester wore a scowl of glum concentration as he juggled four wooden balls, coming to grief each time he essayed a fifth. There were the young lovers Ferdinand and Miranda holding hands close by the bowsprit, swapping their coy nonsense. Nearer, in the gilded chair placed for him on the foredeck, Alonso gazed placidly out to sea.

Cui bono? Antonio was a man of malice and would first consider motives of malice and vengefulness. Such a reason for disposing of Sebastian had already come into Gonzalo's mind. It all came down to the games of that devious web-spinner Prospero, who blandly kept himself apart in his cabin while leaving his damnable book at large to set the cat among the pigeons.

"Sire," said Gonzalo with the muted respect due from a courtier of Milan to the King of Naples, "Might I ask whether you have entertained yourself by study of our Duke's chronicle of all that happened since the tempest?"

"I have not," said Alonso. Which at once swung a barred gate across the path Gonzalo had hoped to take. There seemed no special firmness or concern in the King's voice; only the weariness that follows having come close to death at a wronged enemy's hands, making a great and public repentance, and accepting the burden of being forgiven. But kings must know how to speak deceitfully, and how to snuff out a life with a word. Either of those foppish courtiers Adrian and Francisco might well be Alonso's pet murderer.

If Alonso had read in the book, he would know of Sebastian's plan to slay him while he slept and become King of Naples – or rather, to have Antonio strike the blow while the feebler Sebastian disposed of the possible witness, Gonzalo himself. Apparently Prospero's servitors had interrupted the deed: Gonzalo well remembered waking to find the cronies wild-eyed, swords drawn, prating about beasts that had roared. It occurred to him that, had he been a younger man without the mellowness of a walker knowing himself to be ambling down the last miles before the grave, he too might have meditated a vengeance on Sebastian. Why, he thought, I myself would be the first to attract a thief-taker's attentions. Wiser to accuse an old fool than a king.

If Alonso had read in the book ... but he chose to deny this. Gonzalo bowed very slightly and decided that it was time to go below.

The gentle swell that heaved the ship's deck was less soothing down here in the stench (it *did* smell like that creature Caliban) and the darkness, where low beams lay in wait to deal lubbers a murderous crack on the head. Here was Sebastian's cabin, aft on the starboard side, where the now sobered and crapulous butler Stephano had carried a plate of ship's biscuit – only to find the cabin empty, the port open wide.

Sometimes, in the old days, it had been a useful rule to suspect anyone who claimed to have stumbled on a body, or lack of body. Gonzalo pondered. Stephano and his henchman Trinculo had behaved badly enough on the island with their inept plans to oust Prospero, take the place and rule it as their own. So they'd been soundly whipped for it at Prospero's command; they might resent ducal chastisement, but what had they to do with Sebastian? When great ones fall, Gonzalo told himself, it is by the hands of other great ones. What folly to conceive that the jester or the butler did it.

The fusty, cramped cabin had little to tell him. Soiled bedding and clothes; a cloudy steel mirror nailed askew to the bulkhead; crumbs mingling with rats' droppings on the deck timbers. Sebastian's writing-box lay shut up on the small table. Gonzalo thought to open this little desk, laid his hand on its polished wood, and felt a stickiness at one corner. A brownish smear which might be blood. The image leapt up before him like one of the mage-Duke's seemings: the box hefted by a unknown hand, its sharp corner striking Sebastian's head, the limp prince laboriously pushed through the port into God's own bottomless and watery oubliette.

So much for imaginings. Might the cabin yield further facts? Inside the writing-box he found the expected ink bottles and a vilely cut quill. Within the lid, a few far-from-new sheets of paper: Sebastian had not been a great letter writer. A seal, and fragments of wax. A tiny pen-knife. One compartment contained a nutmeg. Another held a ball of crumpled paper which Gonzalo idly spread out ...

You were seen to thrust King A. overboard before you made your brave show of being first rat out of the sinking ship. Let us

The mind rushed eagerly enough to complete that sentence. "Let us speak of large sums in gold," might it be? Next came a great blot which had run to and fro in antic patterns with the crumpling of the sheet. The writing, despite its neat line, had the wavering, slightly florid flourishes of a courtier's hand. A hand that had been trained to begin afresh once a letter had been marred, until the epistle ran smoothly from end to end, never blotting a line.

Gonzalo frowned. This game of *cui bono* was too much like the game of tig: Sebastian's dead hand had touched another, and the mystery of who might wish him ill became the mystery of who else might harbour thoughts of regicide. Which pointed in a most horrible direction indeed.

"Sire," he said when he had regained the grateful sunshine of the foredeck, "another question – if I may."

"We await no other audience this day," said Alonso with mild irony.

"Cast your mind back to the height of the tempest, as the mariners began to cry aloud that our ship was lost. You went overboard. Soon we all did. But you in particular – could you have been pushed?"

"A dozen times, man! The mariners were colliding with us, thrusting us aside in their wild frenzy with the ropes and masts. Our whole craft seemed to spin like a wheel. We were on the heaving deck, we were whelmed in salt water, we were ashore, all as in a dream. And then everything becomes mazier still, as though I were soused in strong wine...."

Gonzalo nodded. Prospero and his apothecary's tricks.

"But ... yes. Now that you stir up the memory, I fancy I recall being pushed in the back. Not a casual bump, but the thrust of two hands. Yet with something half-hearted about it. Could that have been when I tumbled overboard? I cannot say." The king shivered. "It is not a recollection that I wish to cherish."

"Some things are best forgotten," said Gonzalo, trying not to betray that his words came from the heart. He turned aside, and paced the swaying deck once more.

Cui bono was a harsh taskmaster. He had wondered at Antonio's bitter silence near the end of their island stay, but not until now at another silence before it began. A silence that passed unnoticed in the tempest. The passengers had staggered about a rain-lashed deck, hindering the mariners as the storm raged: Alonso dumbfounded that a mere boatswain should talk back to a king, Antonio and Sebastian swearing futilely at toiling sailors, even Gonzalo himself (he recalled with embarrassment) spinning foolish conceits about how their valiant boatswain was safe from drowning because born to be hanged. One face cried nothing, though. Had that remaining passenger on deck been keeping silence – biding his time – waiting for the moment when, unobserved in the storm-chaos, he might topple the King over the deckrail?

A dark deed, and a futile one: little did that person know that the luck of the tide or the minions of Prospero would bring them all safe to shore, including both the pusher and the pushed. Or that he had not been unobserved after all, and that Stephano would presently suggest an agreeable price for silence. Which would be the death of Stephano.

Gonzalo found himself gnawing at his beard, a bad habit which recurred in times of inner turmoil. Fragments of evidence whirled through his mind as though storm-driven. They came together in a grisly shape; but a shape which, his old sense of caution told him, was not proof to take

before the King's justices. Such a story would not serve to hang a dog. But
– his eyes narrowed as the proper question formulated itself – what *could*
it do?

He sighed. It would be necessary to make a private appointment after
dark, an appointment which he did not much relish. Other arrangements
too. And, once again, he must consult Prospero's troubling book.

Dark of the moon, but the Mediterranean by night outdid the pale
glitter of the stars; the water glowed in great swirls and bands of phos-
phorescence, and the ship's wake boiled with white fire. Gonzalo had
picked a dark corner of the aft deck, out of sight of the mariner on watch.
Presently, noiselessly, the shadows at his side were filled with a dark and
somehow sardonic presence.

Gonzalo said without preamble, "He was first to shore. I remember
Francisco babbling of how fast and well he swam: 'His bold head 'Bove
the contentious waves he kept, and oared Himself with his good arms
with lusty stroke.' Just a peppercorn in the balance, but evil-doers are well
known to flee the scene of the crime. And the spoilt note in Sebastian's
writing-box pointed to one who was first out of the ship. Like a rat."

"You over-top me," said the voice of Antonio. "I merely noted that he
was the obvious gainer. Of course I had the advantage of hearing from my
late ally Sebastian what was done during the storm. Will you name him,
or shall I?"

Gonzalo resigned himself to pronouncing the name, whatever devils
it might raise. "Our young lover Prince Ferdinand. For he had everything
to gain by removing Alonso: at a stroke he would become King of Naples.
Later, having learned more of usurpers and their ways –" Gonzalo sensed
an ironic bow from the shadows – "he would have found it wise to make
his assurance of the succession doubly sure by dealing first with the King's
brother Sebastian. Who would doubtless have had good advice." Another
mocking bow. "But Sebastian had also sealed his own death warrant by
trying to exact a price for silence about Ferdinand's attempt on the King."

"Wordy, but well said. There may be reasons after all why God put
windbags into the world."

"Once you think of Ferdinand," said Gonzalo slowly, "page after page
from Prospero's book of words seems to bear witness. Here he claims to
have been weeping for his father, but hears some music and on the instant
forgets nine parts in ten of his sorrowing. Were those real tears? Almost
at once he is making eyes at the old Duke's daughter. Was this real grief?
You are a clever man; you marked that."

"Clever enough to win a duchy, not so clever as to keep it."

"Even the chess-game in Prospero's cell. 'Sweet lord, you play me
false,' cries the girl Miranda. A man who cheats at chess, the game of

kings, may do likewise on this world's greater board."

"The game of Kings of Naples. Almost, old whiskers, I come to like you."

"Spare me that," Gonzalo muttered.

Antonio's voice continued in light tones, as of a courtier embarking on a rare jest. "Rather let us speak of brother Prospero, and what he likes or likes not. Will it be to his ducal liking that all these clever contrivances have achieved only the betrothal of his daughter to a princeling who has done murder – and has made a fair shot at parricide? What foulness he has so willingly embraced!"

A pause, as the spars creaked with a tiny shift of the wind. "I think ... I think it is too much to *your* liking, my lord."

"Why should I deny it?"

"Because none of it is true," Gonzalo said stolidly.

The figure in the shadows contracted into new alertness. "Speak."

"It seems that one brother of Milan is as adept as the other in mazes and deceptions spun out of air, sleights that vanish into air, into thin air.... Why should Sebastian *write* that dangerous letter to Ferdinand, when a nod and a wink would suffice? Why, because the blot-ruined draft message was needed to lead old Gonzalo by the nose – together with your gentle hint of *Cui bono?*

"My wits are no longer quick, but after a time I saw that the note did not come from Sebastian's pen – a vilely cut quill that would set down only scratches and spatters. You should have used that pen, my lord, and not your own. Then, who so well placed to knock him on the head than his special crony Antonio? I could not see Sebastian relaxing his guard for an instant when speaking with an angry Ferdinand. Again, when I bethought myself of the 'half-hearted' push Alonso felt at the height of the tempest, my mother-wit said that this was not bold young Ferdinand but cowardly, hesitant Sebastian – observed by *you*, my lord, and assuring you that Sebastian was ready to join you in dark deeds, if only you would take the lead."

"I fear, old man, that this night contains your death," said Antonio very quietly.

"That fear I have long left behind. But tell me, why does Antonio, noble pretender to the duchy of Milan, stoop to involve himself in riddles and affairs of death – bloodying his hands for the sake of befouling young Ferdinand's name and discomfiting Duke Prospero? Poor foolish Sebastian was worth little, but deserved better than to be the sacrificed pawn in a new gambit. You had your brother's forgiveness, however poisonously phrased. Was the game of revenge not over?"

"It was not." The thin voice became more conversational. "Old man, think on this. My crime was not that great. Did I not rule Milan justly and well? True, it became necessary to exile Prospero when he absurdly clung to all the trappings and titles of power – yet none of the responsibilities. All *those*, he left to me. You see it in his book, even where he rants about my perfidy: 'I thus neglecting worldly ends, all dedicated To closeness and the bettering of my mind ...' Is that the voice of a worthy ruler?"

Gonzalo shrugged. "I need not debate the greatness of your crime, when there was no great punishment. Befuddlement in a masque of shadows on that island of phantasms, a few hard words, and forgiveness. Was this such cruel retribution?"

"Gonzalo, he took my son."

"Son?" Confusion filled Gonzalo's head, a medley of winds and fancy lights and forgotten voices. "Your son?" A elusive name: "Ju ... was it Julius?"

"I, even *I*, had almost forgot. I knew at the last that I had lost something dear, and wrestled in silence with my memories. A triple pox on my brother's grammarie and snares of the mind! Then, you see, as we made good sail and the island dropped beneath the horizon, I read it in the book that Prospero made for my torment, the book called *The Tempest*. And I remembered.

"That lucky young fool Ferdinand said it: 'Myself am Naples, Who with mine eyes, never since at ebb, beheld The King my father wracked.' Then he went on: 'Yes, faith, and all his lords, the Duke of Milan / And his brave son being twain.'

"At that hour, I was the Duke of Milan. My brave son Julio sailed with us. And where is he? Gone, a piece taken from the chessboard, plucked from all our memories by Prospero's whoreson drugs and enchantment, my bloodline ended. I knelt pleading at my brother's feet, and he would only say that perhaps his book was in error. And you, prating loon, you say the game of revenge is over!"

Suddenly, irresistibly, he bore Gonzalo towards the deckrail. There was a terrible wiry strength in that thin body. "I will have more blood. Blood will have blood –"

There came another disturbance in the aft-deck shadows as something massy leapt from the top of the deckhouse. A great crash of sea-boots striking the deck was followed by a small, dead-sounding thud, and a hiss of expelled air from Antonio's lips. He slumped.

"Stocking full of sand, my lord," said the boatswain respectfully. "Hope I done right. You told me to wait until matters went awry."

"Yes. You have my thanks," Gonzalo said, breathing hard. "I owe you more than gold, but gold there shall be."

The shipmaster emerged from the darkness nearer the stern. He bent and felt the huddled shape on the deck; felt again; opened clothing. There came a long pause. "Tapped him a mite too hard there, Boatswain. But it's for the best, I judge. Lunatics are rank bad luck at sea. The men don't like it. Let's have no more of these dirty games of statecraft on my clean ship. Bestir ye now, Boats – yarely –"

Stepping back, Gonzalo whispered a prayer as the erstwhile Duke of Milan slid into the phosphorescent waters and their waiting sea-change. Perhaps this truly was for the best. When the wits of great ones fail.... He frowned to himself. Had it been too easy? Surely Antonio would expect a hoary councillor, who had survived so many decades, to take certain precautions before meetings at dead of night. Lofty Antonio, whose overweening pride would never let him plunge to death in an admission of despair; but who, when life held no more, might permit others to soil their hands by giving him surcease.

Gonzalo shuddered. Such imaginings should be dismissed as the stuff that nightmares are made on. But still, but still, he felt curiously reluctant ever again to speak with Prospero. "O rejoice," he had found himself saying on the island – that the god from the machine had restored harmony, that Ferdinand had found his wife, Prospero his dukedom, "and all of us ourselves When no man was his own." Now that golden joy was darkened, like a once-clear stream that runs turbid and filthy in the aftermath of a tempest.

• Published 1998 in an anthology of Shakespearean detective stories. There was a temptation to write an outrageous spoof, like – though doubtless not as funny as – the unusual solutions to *Macbeth* and *Hamlet* proposed respectively by James Thurber in "The Macbeth Murder Mystery" and Michael Innes in "The Mysterious Affair at Elsinore" (see *Three Tales of Hamlet*, 1950). But *The Tempest* is too magical to blow raspberries at, and I remembered that strange aside quoted at the beginning of the story above, indicating that Shakespeare had written in a son for Antonio and then forgotten all about him. Or was that the true answer?

The phrase "calm as a clock" is brazenly stolen from my favourite literary response to *The Tempest*, W.H. Auden's *The Sea and the Mirror*.

Irrational Numbers

In memory of Karl Edward Wagner,
who smiled upon several of these.

Cold Spell

The handkerchiefs whirled and wove their lacy patterns in the sky; there was a tinkle of bells and a muffled sound of feet on stone as the men swung easily through their last dance. Stephen Carling tried to hide his impatience; for the last quarter-hour he had been eyeing the red-lit windows of the "Olde Coach-House", wishing he were on the inside instead of making an olde-world fool of himself in its freezing olde-world courtyard. But Hubbard, prancing about in the role of Fool, tapped him with the bladder. He fought down his shivers and concentrated on the swirling handkerchief, so graceful to watch and so bloody difficult to control.

The landlord had done his best by the dancers, training improvised spotlights from his upper windows and drumming up a respectable crowd for the solstice performance. On this freezing night, by some occult tradition, Hubbard's team were not simply dancing but enacting "The Lambertstow Morris". It made no difference that Carling could see, but the rest of the team had an intense look, almost a religious look, somewhere in the eyes. Back and forth, back and forth, in and out. Why didn't the others turn blue with cold? The watchers were well muffled up (which was an injustice) and supplied with drinks (which was intolerable).

And now Hubbard was muttering dirge-like fragments which Carling had never heard in the Morris before. *This ae night, this ae night, everie night and alle ...* It was not the full lyke-wake song, the corpse-chant, but scrappy extracts now heard and now inaudible. *If ever thou gavest roof and flame, Everie night and alle, Pass thee by the standing stane ...*

And then, in a blossoming flourish of white linen, the pattern was complete. An informal nod to their audience, and the Morris dancers marched smartly into the pub's rosy warmth. On one side old Bell was struggling out of his costume as "Twig" – an all-enclosing leafy cone in which he frisked about to symbolize boundless fertility or something of the sort. Carling chafed his fingers and recalled that Bell was well past seventy if not eighty.

The "Olde Coach-House" provided drinks on the house for the Morris team. Carting was well into his second pint by the time Hubbard ran a hand through his thick white hair and said, as he always did, "Not a bad performance, that." He looked around the other seven with a sort of weary patience. "But there were one or two little things. It's the twenty-first, remember, the twenty-first! John, you must swing gentler in the sword piece. You're trying to tap Dick's sword neatly, not disarm him like ruddy d'Artagnan. And you, Bell, you stay further from the poor sodding audience – they don't want Twig knocking drinks out of their hands and irrigating their trousers ... And *you*, Stephen, what were you at? Consumed by fires of apathy, I'd say, and an attack of shivers with it. I've said it before, if you get cold it means you're holding back. Do it properly and you'll be warm enough."

These indictments caused Dr Sims to practise swordsweeps of exaggerated daintiness, and Bell to grin over his tankard, and Carling to stalk mutinously off for another drink. He was doing them a favour, wasn't he, standing in when his father went sick? He coughed in the thick and smoky air of the bar. Hubbard picked on him as the only one who wasn't past it. Even Forester, the other "kid", must be way past thirty.

Sure enough, when he came back, Hubbard was at it again. "Hey, Stephen! Watch your step with the ale! Shivering's better than staggering, y'know."

Carling swigged a third of his pint in a pointed way before forcing a return smile. "Be staggering home pretty soon, won't we?"

They all looked at him. He'd said the wrong thing again. Cautiously he said, "Look, I haven't got any of the bloody tradition wrong, have I? We go and prance about at Coldrock for a few minutes and then we go home ... surely?"

It was odd to see some of the expressions. Old Bell, in particular, was looking as if someone had been swearing in church.

"It's an *important* tradition, you know," said Hubbard. "And of course we'll be doing the whole Morris again, right the way through, starting at midnight. Didn't your father tell you? Or weren't you listening, as usual?"

Carling didn't know. He'd just assumed that no one would be so cretinous as to dance on the open moor at Coldrock for longer than five minutes – especially on a night when the whole countryside was cracking and squeaking with ice. He shrugged in beery acquiescence and drank again.

Dr Sims passed a few bland comments about how alcohol cooled you down, really, and only made you feel warm. Carling was happy to settle for the feeling.

Coldrock was a mere ten minutes out of Lambertstow village. But the cold was bitter, the clear sky frozen into a single huge crystal in which the trapped stars could scarcely twinkle; it seemed that the icy night must crack open and scatter them as frosty points of fire. Carling's coat did not help. By the time they neared the rock itself the whole sky seemed a lens which concentrated upon him all the chill of space.

Coldrock was a great nub of granite, man-high, of rough and undistinguished shape. Some said it had once been carved, though nobody knew into what form. Shallow pools lay around, now sealed with ice. The tradition was that the Lambertstow Morris dancers performed by the rock on the night of the winter solstice. By this, no doubt, the old gods of winter cold were appeased and Bell was free to fertilize birds and bees for spring.... But the icy pain in Carling's feet was inimical to such thoughts. He stumbled, not for the first time. *Pass thee by the standing stane ...*

Miller, landlord of the "Olde Coach-House", was already present. He had sensibly travelled by car (no doubt tradition decreed that the stupid dancers had to walk) and was unloading the properties: wooden swords, a battered cardboard box overflowing with giant handkerchiefs, the Fool's worn bladder and "Twig". The "Twig" costume was something like a vast crinoline to which innumerable sprays of foliage had been wired; it concealed the wearer in a cone of prickly green.

The dancers removed their coats to reveal again the thin white shirts, embroidered waistcoats and black breeches.

"Fine," said Hubbard, his head cocked on one side. "Now there's just one thing. This is an old dance, and maybe it'd be better to have the most experienced men for the dancing, if you see what I mean. Besides, Stephen is a bit the worse for wear. So if he and Bell change places we'll do just fine. All right?"

Carling thought of the scratchy interior of "Twig" and grimaced. The absurd fertility symbol might be the most interesting part of the Lambertstow Morris to students of folkways, but it was the most uncomfortable role for the dancers. And the leafy symbol spent most of its time lurking on the sidelines. There would only be the occasional improvised frisk-about to keep him warm.

"No," he said. "It's OK, I'm fine. I just tripped because my feet are cold." But his lips seemed frozen, too, and the words came out stiff and slurred.

"Don't you worry," said Hubbard with infuriating tact. "We do understand. Mind you, you should have been more careful I *tried* to tell you. You'll be fine in Twig."

"No," said Carling again. "I ... I'm going home."

All the others looked shocked again. The shock of the unthinkable. "Doesn't tradition mean anything to you at all?" said Hubbard.

"Bloody tradition ... Look, you call yourself a Christian – it's a *pagan* tradition. You'll be at Christmas service in a few days. Isn't that hypocrisy or something?"

Hubbard said: "Christmas was a pagan tradition as well." Which was
no answer.

"I'm a science student," Carling pointed out. "I don't believe in any of
it. And *I* won't be at the Christmas service."

"You stay," said Bell with a sort of desperate insistence.

"I'm going," said Carling. And went.

He walked for a while and looked back. They were limbering up for
the dance ... but Hubbard kept staring after him.

A breeze sprang up and whispered in the frozen grass; the night grew
colder and colder still, until Carling almost ran along the frosted lane. The
stale beer swilled in his stomach, weighing him down like a chill, flopping
bag of mercury. His feet were unfeeling lumps when he reached his
father's house; and then followed the slow, burning pain of warming them
up again before the electric fire.

All this could have been avoided if only his father hadn't been ill.
Must visit the hospital some time, Carling thought as he drank hot coffee.
He wondered about the dancers out by the stone. Perhaps by now they
were frozen into grotesque positions, a sacrifice to the strange gods that
Hubbard half believed in. He chuckled, but the chill was leaking into the
room. It was a good time to go to bed, snug beneath the electric blanket.
It was better still to lie in warm darkness, with the fatigue of dancing
transmuted to pleasant heaviness. It was better to forget the odd moments
of the night: a muttered verse, a ring of shocked faces, a feeling of
dreadful intensity ... Some thoughts of future recriminations from his
father for "letting the side down" (Carling knew it would be phrased thus)
chased themselves about his head, but not for long.

Through his dreams stalked fantastically garbed dancers, weighted
with frightful significance. Even in dream he stubbornly did not join the
midnight dance, though tenuous threads of ice held him close and tugged
him slowly towards the ugly bulk of Coldrock. But the sluggishness of the
beer was with him still, and he stood as if rooted while the wild dancers
whirled and spangles of ice flew from beneath their feet, on and on and
on ...

He awoke with a hangover. He swore at himself for not having remembered to drink pints of water and take an aspirin before going to bed.
Chill mists hung over the village. Disinclined to venture outside, Carling
dosed himself with coffee and pills, and began a studied attempt to read
Zemansky's *Heat and Thermodynamics* through the blurring, throbbing
pain which would not leave his head.

The doorbell rang. He was glad to set aside the book; less glad when the visitor proved to be Hubbard.

"Look here," said Hubbard, almost pushing him over as he stormed in. "I want a word with you about last night."

"Bloody hell, it's all over now," Carling protested.

"It is not." Hubbard dropped uninvited into an armchair. Carling, still labouring under the vast, formless guilt which accompanies many a hangover, did likewise, and Hubbard looked at him hard before beginning to speak.

"Never you mind your ruddy atheism and humanism and I don't know what. This is important. And hard to explain. Look, did you ever hear that Eastern story about the loony who was doing something really mad, and they asked him why, and he said, 'To scare off the tigers'? And of course they said, 'There aren't any tigers,' and he came right back with 'See! It works!'"

Caning blinked. "So what?"

"I'm asking you to get out there to Coldrock tonight and fill in the missing part of the Morris. You can skip the costume, I reckon: just do a Twig sort of improvisation and that'll be fine. Because of the tigers, that's why. Because ... well, I *don't* ask you to believe a word of it, but there's one or two of us who think our Morris and a very few old things like it are important. Some say they dance the dance as a festival at the turn of winter. Some think that maybe the winter only turns because of the dance, but you bet they keep ruddy quiet about it. Until now. We've done our loony dance all these years and, maybe, kept away the tigers. Now will you humour us – c'mon, be as condescending as you like – and dance on your own tonight?"

"Good grief," said Carling, amazed and contemptuous. "You think I'm an easy mark, don't you? Screw up your precious dance one night and you come here with this load of rubbish ... Laugh yourselves sick, won't you, if I fall for it and go prancing in the cold on my own! No thanks. The winter's always come to an end before and it can manage it this year without my help."

"We've never missed a dance before," said Hubbard seriously, and repeated: "See! It works!"

"Oh, go *away*," returned Carling, whose head was beginning to feel worse.

Hubbard went. Carling picked up Zemansky again and stared dully at the exposition of the Maxwell equations; after a little time, the doorbell rang again.

"Good morning to you," said Dr Sims He brushed ice-crystals from his lapels and shot a keen glance at Carling's bleary face. "We don't normally make house calls for a head like yours, but I just happened to be passing."

"Thanks, I've taken a pill," said Carling warily.

"Good, good. Oh, just one thing ... I hear Hubbard's been round telling you off. These local boys are really sincere about the dancing, you know. Absolute dens of superstition, villages like this. Don't you think, just as a favour to me, you could see your way to humouring Hubbard and the rest? Lot of ill-feeling if you don't ... and though I say it as shouldn't, I'll slip you ten quid for a warming bottle of Scotch if you do. How about it?"

Carling still felt ill and obstinate. "No," he said. "They'll have to lump it."

The doctor put his hands on Carling's shoulders with sudden, terrible sincerity. *"Please,"* he whispered. "Please do it."

"You believe it all, too," said Carling in disgust. "You're scared of ghosts, like the others. I'm staying by the fire, thanks very much."

The doctor left, slamming the door without another word. Carling was left to consider how, each time he said "No", it became more final. His own pride in rationality now held him to his word, so that nothing would make him back down by dancing the dance ... which was surely irrational?

He had no time to pick up Zemansky before, for the third time, the doorbell rang.

"Thankee, I won't come in," said Bell before being either invited in or told to go away. "It is a warning I've come to give you. Don't think old Coldrock'll muck up the springcoming just for one young fool. If you are not thinking to dance this night, *this ae night,* then you'll think again. Little birds as can't sing and won't sing will be made to sing, they say remember that, my lad. The rock's a trickster and it'll have its way."

Caning was so dumbfounded by the words from doddery old Bell that he found himself literally unable to reply before the old man (with a brusque nod) had left him standing there. Bell's breath was a plume of white in the freezing air; he did not look back.

Made to dance, eh? The notion roused Carling's obstinacy to something close to fury. Though he stared at Zemansky all the afternoon, his mind was on nothing but the determination not to give in – not to pander to Hubbard's idiotic superstition, nor fall for the doctor's fake reasonableness, and most specially to spit in the eye of anyone who dared tell Carling what to do.

Tigers! Humour them for ten pounds! *Made* to dance!

When he had made and eaten his dinner that evening, and drunk most of a bottle of wine, he took special pains to ensure that every window was fastened and every door firmly bolted. It was difficult to imagine a mob of irate villagers storming the house and carrying him forth to dance the wretched dance ... but when he finally went to bed, he was careful to load up his father's old .22 rifle and leave it beside the bed. Just in case, he told himself. In case of ... tigers. The weapon's presence was a comfort as he relaxed and sank gradually into sleep.

So there he was at Coldrock once more, walking away, but now through sparkling countryside, where all the lanes ran together in a maze of ice. At every turning and blind alley the road gave a wriggle in *Looking-Glass* fashion and became an inviting path which led to that shapeless grey rock. Voices shouted distant warnings or exhortations; Hubbard and Dr Sims and old Bell were all trying to tell him something which they could not quite express nor Carling quite comprehend, as Coldrock loomed obscenely at the end of every path, until at last there were no more paths and he stood upon a featureless plain with only the granite thing for company. Its shape was charged with a terrible significance. Although indubitably the same old rock, it now stood on every side of him, with all space twisted to exclude everything which was not Carling or the cold, cold rock

It pressed in, encircling, unspeakable –

And if thou holdest to any thinge, Everie night and alle, The Ende thou canst not enter in, And

– and he touched it.

There was a soundless flash. Cold fire dripped over the universe, and icicle-fangs gnawed at Carling's flesh, everywhere, agonizing.

He woke then, and found it *was* cold. The wine had left a lingering acridity in his mouth. He swore at himself for succumbing to silly dreams, but the bed was absurdly chilly, his teeth were chattering beyond control. The luminous clock-face at the bedside told him it was some while before midnight.

"Oh hell," he said aloud.

He slid from the bed, to find the unheated room mysteriously warmer than the bed. Oddly enough, the electric blanket's control light still burnt: the thing must be faulty. Carling decided on more coffee, and slipped downstairs in dressing-gown and slippers. It was warmer below, in a silence disturbed only by the wind which leant from time to time against the house, and by the tiny gobbling of the refrigerator. He sloshed water into the kettle and clicked it on; then retreated to turn on the living-room fire. It was then that he realized something was most definitely wrong. As the heater's spiral elements began to glow, Carling began to shiver. It seemed that waves of cold were rolling towards him.

He blinked – for some reason he didn't seem to be thinking too clearly and switched off the fire. The chill receded until he was merely cold, not frozen. "Bloody hell," he said with renewed shivers, and walked out to the kitchen. There he found the kettle bubbling furiously ... and icy cold.

"Fight fire with fire," he said aloud (this seemed very funny) and opened the refrigerator door. Ripples of warmth lapped out across his legs. He hesitated for a while before unlocking the door between him and the night outside – but there, too, all was warm and pleasant. For a moment he frowned at a dim memory of someone who was a trickster: no, it was gone.

As he walked about the garden in a breeze as cosy as central heating, he knew this must be another dream. He deserved a pleasant dream to offset the one he'd just had, where Coldrock caught him ... The sparkling lanes around Lambertstow were warm beneath his slippered feet. He walked at random, enjoying the clear beauty of the night (not a cloud in the sky!), and was somehow not surprised to find himself on the path to Coldrock. He was stumbling again; he was almost prepared to admit he'd had a few too many in the "Olde Coach-House" ... but no, that was last night. Though the stars shone hard and clear, a mist of unreality drifted behind his eyes. Nothing was quite as it should be; nothing was quite important

His feet were numb with fatigue, but the strangely pleasing shape of Coldrock reminded him why he was here. (How peculiar to have forgotten!) Clumsily, his slippers flapping until he kicked them off, his dressing-gown flying wildly in the wind, he began to dance ...

Dimly he realized that Coldrock and its power had tricked him indeed, in spite of all his scepticism and folly, into doing the right thing at last and fulfilling the ancient requirements of the dance. He found his lips moving in the lyke-wake song which mourned the passing year ...

From empty airt when thou'rt past, Everie night and alle, To Alleman's Ende thou comest at last ...

He danced there in the delicious drowsy warmth before Coldrock, as the brittle grass snapped underfoot, and the ice burst crackling from the pools, and slowly his toes and stiffened fingers turned black.

• Published 1980. Once upon a time at a Pieria writers' meeting, someone cunningly extrapolated that since I'd written stories called "Heatwave" (included here) and "Lukewarm", the title "Cold Spell" must inevitably follow. For some reason I liked the idea of a Morris dancer coming to a sticky end – as in one of Ngaio Marsh's best murder mysteries, *Off With His Head* – but Terry Pratchett's *Lords and Ladies* later gave us the truer, more lingering horror of a story in which the Morris dancers *don't* come to a sticky end.

3.47 AM

Dekker was dreaming. There had been a scattering of bright misty colours, a curve of soft grass, a woman whose eyes and smile were the most wonderful thing in all the world ... and then the dream went sour. it was as though swirls of ink were blending with clear water, as the dark familiar tints spread their stain over Dekker's private landscape. Without any special feeling of transition, Dekker was standing suddenly alone, fuzzily peering at the something odd which was happening to his bare arm. Without pain a round black hole opened in the flesh, and tiny hairs sprouted; tiny hairs that were insect feelers probing out into the air. He was ready with a Band-Aid, but they wriggled underneath it, and now more of the small dark holes were opening in him. He gritted his teeth, and felt the teeth crumbling with a ghastly painlessness like stubs of chalk or like the clay pipe-stems which still came to light when he dug the garden. With a sort of dreamy double-vision he seemed to be watching the next step from both inside and outside as his eyes, his eyes, the eyeballs themselves –

"No ...!"

Suddenly the far-off corner of Dekker's mind which knew it was all a dream was in full command, and his private hell collapsed into a black stuffy bedroom, cramped arms and legs, a taste in the mouth as though some small furry animal had been nesting there – an animal of revoltingly unclean habits. He rubbed at his crusted eyes and painfully rolled over in bed towards the lurid glow of his bedside clock.

3.47 AM. Again.

His heart was beating like a disco drum, and messages of terror were squirting up and down his bloodstream. Gentle signals from his bladder suggested that a downstairs trip would be a clever idea: but Brian Dekker had been through all that before. Following these dreams there always came an afterwash of horror in which the darkness waited most terribly on the stairs, so for all their soft carpet they were about as inviting as the crumbled and slimy steps leading down into a graveyard vault. To turn on the light did not happen to be the answer; that simply pushed the dark into the blind doorways opening on the hall downstairs, and in those doorways it would wait coiled and compressed, ready somehow to leap out on you. Easier to stay in bed.

3.47 AM. Still trembling, he watched the red neon figures until (after what seemed like the best part of a week) they flickered to 3.48. Was this the fourth time or the fifth?

There wasn't anything miraculous about the figure 3.47. It just happened that when you turned on this smart digital clock, some inner kink set it to that time at once; you had to fiddle with the little buttons at the back to reset it correctly, and whenever there was a power cut it would jump straight back at 3.47 AM afterwards. Just one of those things. Dekker had bought the new clock because he'd found the remorseless ticking of clockwork often kept him awake unless he hid the old alarm-clock in a drawer or under the bed – in which case the alarm was too muffled to wake him next morning. Now the electronic clock had a banshee scream which sliced clean through all the layers of sleep and bedding Dekker could wrap himself in: the only small problem was its red glow, faint by day but glaring in the dark, just visible even through closed eyelids. He'd solved *that* problem by sleeping on his other side – a triumph of original thinking, a victory of a man over machine. Now all he had to worry about was this tendency to wake up in the small hours with a strangled breathless grunt – a grunt which would be something more except that he was usually fully awake before he could gulp enough air to power a scream.

Five nights, then. Five in a row. Five times, the things he hated most in the world: insect feelers against the skin, teeth crumbling and splitting because he hated dentists, and, because the worst things he could imagine happening to anybody were blindness and deformity his eyes would – No. Not to think about that, here in the stifling dark. Concentrate on real things, Dekker told himself, safe sharp-edged events, true facts, like in detective fiction.

Very well, Inspector, he thought. I'll tell you all I know. I dream the same dream every night – every night now for a week. That makes five times. This dream is, is … the way I've already described it. Each night I wake up terrified at just 3.47 AM. Yes, too scared to get out of bed – ridiculous isn't it? Of course I've tried sleeping pills. I'm not a fool, you know, I can feel them sucking me back down again now as I lie here, but every night for the last five nights there's been this hammerblow of fear, a million times stronger than the pills, five nights in a row....

Every night since I bought the clock? Why, yes. That's very significant, I'm sure.

Then the pills grabbed him and hauled him back down into a safe warm darkness where there were no dreams, no thoughts, nothing but the momentary glimpse of a pale brown woman whose features were not quite those of the Indians or Pakistanis he met in town or at work....

In the morning the clock shrieked efficiently, and Dekker fumbled his way downstairs in a stale reek of sweat, groaning under a headache which he reckoned was in the brain-haemorrhage class. One, two, three paracetamol tablets with his breakfast coffee, and the third stuck on his tongue to leave a foul-tasting track as though slugs had been crawling down his throat. The slight psychological uplift of vigorous washing, shaving and brushing of teeth left him feeling no better: he thought about work, about checking balance sheets and preparing VAT statements, shuddered slightly, and went to the telephone.

"Hello – Jenkins and Grey? That's right, luv, Brian Dekker ... Can you tell Mr Grey I'll be off sick today? Thanks ... Bye."

The doctor agreed.

"You need a rest, I expect. Been working too hard."

"I get these bad dreams," Dekker began to tell him.

"Working too hard. Your card says you haven't taken sick-leave in three years. Ridiculous. We all need a rest sometime"

"I sort of wake up every night, about the same time –"

"Prescribing you a tonic: here. Chit for a week off work: here. Come and see me again if you don't feel better in a week. Next!"

"Yes, but about these nightmares –"

"Take it easy, take the tonic. Next!"

Dekker hadn't very much faith in the bottle of gooey liquid into which the chemist translated his prescription. He decided to take a few extra safety precautions of his own, and on the way home he paused at the supermarket to pick up a bottle of medium-cheap Scotch whisky. For the rest of the day he loafed about, reading detective stories ("But surely, Inspector –") and the newspapers (NEW STRIKE THREAT, MIDDLE EAST CRISIS, MALAY SWEATSHOP SCANDAL) while upstairs the clock counted off its silent, red-glowing minutes.

At eight in the evening Dekker warmed a dubiously Cornish pasty in the oven, and ate it with baked beans.

At nine, the washing-up cleared away he opened the whisky bottle and poured himself a large glass, neat. He didn't much like whisky ... but he thought he might as well try it in style. Cheers! And he raised his glass to the half-opened hall door, and to the gathering, lurking darkness out there.

At ten he was trying to remember the words of a song, which were right on the tip of his tongue, just a matter of fitting them to the tune, how did it go, *Tum tummity tum* ... that was funny, he couldn't quite remember the tune, but all the time there was a gentle singing in his head. Somehow the level in the scotch bottle had gone down rather a long way With a feeling of immense devotion to duty he fumbled after the doctor's tonic bottle and – after some unsuccessful attempts to balance a five-millilitre teaspoon – took a generous swig. The taste sent him staggering hastily back to the whisky

At eleven he had the sudden, terrible feeling of being absolutely cold sober with chilly winds whistling through his brain – except that his arms and legs wouldn't move properly But as he sat there, the pictures lit up in his brain with a dreadful clarity He remembered how the insect feelers would come writhing from his flesh with a tiny wink and gleam of chitin. He remembered the painless horror of teeth which crumbled and sheared like soft shale. He remember, he tried not to remember, the feeling of his head being blown up like a balloon, the eyeballs which bulged until the lids wouldn't close no matter how hard he screwed them shut, his eyes bulging until –

"*No, no, nooooo,*" he moaned, trying to stand up and falling.

– until they burst in small wet explosions of jelly like squeezed pimples or boils, the stuff running down his cheeks in enormous slow tears while tattered remnants of eyeball dangled from the sockets ...

He managed to pour more whisky more of it into his lap than into the glass. He tilted the glass against numb lips, and spilt more. The whole room was humming and swaying. The glass slithered from his fingers.

At midnight he was unconscious.

At 3.47 AM he was unconscious.

At 10.45 next morning, he stirred.

Later, having emptied his stomach a few times and dosed his massive new headache, Dekker thought again about his sleeping problem.

"That wasn't a whatsit, a controlled experiment," he said aloud. "Maybe being drunk keeps off the nightmares all right ... but if that damned clock has anything to do with it, I might just have missed the dream because I never went upstairs to sleep at all ...

"Maybe I should just get rid of the clock. But that's *silly*. It's just *superstition.* It's not a hanged man's skull or an evil talisman from Transylvania. It's just a blasted clock and only a few months old at that – only a few weeks, maybe ..."

He spent another quiet, aching afternoon. A photograph in *The Times* – more about electronic-component sweatshops in Malaya – caught his eye. The women who put together radios for a few pence a day because there was nowhere else to work ... the women in the picture looked familiar for a moment, and then not familiar at all when he peered at them more closely. That was the only odd moment in the whole day

That evening he still wasn't feeling a hundred-per-cent fit, but a night without the dream had given him more confidence. He thumbed his nose at the clock as he clambered into bed; he pulled up the blankets and let the friendly dark snuggle round him; he drifted into sleep.

And after many adventures in strange glowing countries, he was caught again in the evil dream. Helplessly he wandered into the dark, into the strained dream-place where things with legs erupted from his skin, where teeth met grittily and gave way where eyes ballooned hideously ...

Dekker woke gasping from the old hammerblow of dread, to see the figures 3.47 glowing in the night. He clicked on the bedside light to push the dark a little further away and lay trembling and sweating, his mind an empty map of horror into which, from nowhere that he could tell, there drifted the memory that the longest and most complicated dreams are supposed to take only a few seconds of real time. One could cram a lot of frightfulness into those seconds, he thought as he lay there with a small child's fear of the dark and resisted the urge to pull sheets and blankets up over his head. Like colours in a slowly turning prism, his fear shifted into exhaustion and the exhaustion to drowsiness; adrift from body and bed and 3.47 AM, Dekker sank into the cloudy shapes of almost-sleep. There, for a moment, a pale brown woman's face peered at him with an uncomfortable smile. *It's nothing personal, but* – Or had she said something else, wordlessly? Her hands were busy with a dismantled digital clock.

It was as if a switch had been thrown in Dekker's head. The connection was made in showers of brilliant sparks, shocking him into rigidity . The night became neutral, empty of evil and of sleep, as he connected the familiar dream-face (*so* familiar, surely he'd glimpsed it each night of the dream) with that photo in *The Times*. Women at an assembly line. MALAY SWEATSHOP SCANDAL. He sat up and reached for the clock, which now showed a safe 3.50. It hummed in his hands as he lifted it, like some warm living thing stiff with fear, whose heart beat so desperately as to make a low buzz. It had come from one of those mail-order discount firms whose goods carried no trademarks or brand names, familiar or not. On the back though, he saw as he turned it over ... on the back, stamped into the thin plastic casing, it said: MALAYA.

He almost smiled as he put down the clock, turned off the light, prepared for another attempt at the unclimbable north face of sleep. Imagine that.

Imagine some ill-treated Malayan lady in an electronic sweatshop, taking her own little bit of industrial action by building an occasional curse into the circuits she put together all day long for so little money. He wanted to chuckle at the silliness of the idea, but the chuckle was lost in a sourceless feeling that to let it out might be unsafe.

It's hardly fair, he thought. What did I ever do to her?

Well, he replied, I supposed you did buy this cheapo-cheapo clock and help keep her rotten employers in business.

But ... ridiculous. I mean, how can you believe in a politically motivated curse? The right to work, the right to strike, the right to stick pins in wax images?

But ... well, then, why *not?*

In the morning, nursing yet another headache, Dekker looked through the newspapers and found two photos of oppressed Malayan women. He was disturbed to find that even though the faces there had a kind of family resemblance to the dull-golden face of his dreams, none of them looked quite like it. You might say that proved the dream-face wasn't just a figment smuggled into his mind by study of *The Times*. You might say that proved, even, that it was real.

He ate his bacon (greasy) and eggs (burst, like ... never mind that), and went upstairs for the battered copy of the book on magic and religion which he'd bought years back. Frazer's The *Golden Bough*, that was it. It came to light amid piles of old science fiction magazines in what estate agents called the second bedroom and Dekker called the junk room.

The abridged *Golden Bough* – good grief, the full version ran to twelve volumes – mentioned Malays quite a few times in the index. Dekker went through them all. The very first dealt with wax images and cheerfully remarked: *"pierce the eye of the image, and your enemy is blind."* He closed the book convulsively. He didn't want to hear about eyes.

Well, if he dismantled the clock, was he going to find some wax model of a corpse lurking in between the integrated circuits? Unfortunately the thing was a sealed unit: to take it apart was to destroy it. Which mightn't be a bad idea, at that; certainly it was something to keep in reserve. He opened the book again, and on page 105 found: *The Malays think that a bright glow at sunset may throw a weak person into a fever.* So what, then, would they think of neon figures glaring red all night long? Onward ... *Nowhere perhaps is the art of abducting human souls more carefully cultivated or carried to higher perfection than in the Malay Peninsula.*

There was nothing specific, nothing about feelers or teeth, nothing suggesting how a charm could worm its way into electronic circuitry. Well, what could you expect from a book written in 1922? And nothing, nothing, on the mystical significance of 3.47 AM.... All in the mind, Brian me lad. You're a weak person who's been thrown into a fever. The psychologists would mumble about compulsive neuroses or something. You wake up with a nightmare at 3.47 one morning and somehow it sets your own internal alarm-clock ticking away, screaming at you every twenty-four hours – but only when you sleep near that clock because the psycho-whatsit is all tied up with those glowing figures. Those figures that you can feel glowing in a dim red way even with eyes tight shut.

Through the day Dekker swallowed his prescribed doses of tonic with great conscientiousness. And in the evening he had another idea, something to break the bad luck and finish all this silly business. Before going to bed, he cunningly set the alarm for 3.30 AM.

The banshee wail cut through his vague and innocuous dream, blasting him awake with the gentleness of a bucket of cold water in the stomach. The red figures 3.30 glared at him. There was no hint of menace or oppression in the surrounding dark. Dekker turned on the bedside light, and then got up to switch on the main room light as well.

Break the jinx, he thought cheerfully. Watch 3.47 flash up on that clock with no bad dream in sight, and that should deal with any worms lodged in my subconscious! – Or if my little Malayan dream-girl is responsible, a dose of cold hard facts in the small hours should help deal with her too, eh?

Though well-lit and warm, the room did contain a sort of bleakness, as though the walls were mere partitions in some enormous hall of damp concrete where echoes could scurry back and forth for hundreds of yards before dying of exhaustion. It's the small hours that do it, Dekker thought. The human spirit at its lowest ebb before dawn ... didn't someone say that?

3.42.

The only sound was the faint hum of the clock. He sat on the bed in his old worn dressing-gown and wished the clock would get a move on.

3.44.

3.45.

3.46.

The last figure seemed to glow there for hours. Subjective time stretching out and out like plasticine. like the eternity of nightmare you could fit into a few seconds of dreaming. *Between midnight and dawn, when the past is all deception ...* Where had he read that line?

He was thinking these thoughts when he felt the tickling and crawling on his arms, as of insect feelers writhing from the flesh. My God, he thought. Hysteria, I won't look under my sleeves, I won't, it's like those religious girls who sprout the marks of wounds in all the appropriate places, I'm experiencing this and the teeth and the, the other thing, and so now I'm *imagining* – But he was still almost sure he could feel motion under the loose sleeves of his pyjamas. He refused to look down. He clamped his jaws together, and with rotten snaps the teeth broke to powder. This time there wasn't the painlessness of the dream: he screamed aloud, and stinking fragments sprayed from his mouth. He wanted to screw up his eyes, but already they were swollen to the point where the lids would not close, were swelling painfully further.

Hysteria! Hallucination! DTs, anything! Please! Some part of his mind was whimpering that again and again. But somewhere, altogether else-where, was there a pale brown woman smiling bitterly?

The swelling of his eyes was incredible. His vision blurred and dis-torted. He flung himself prone on the bed as leggy creatures writhed from the backs of his hands and more teeth fell to chalky shards; he flung himself down, wanting desperately to take refuge in the safety of the dream before –

3.47 AM.

• Published 1983. Ramsey Campbell invited me aboard a children's horror anthology that he was editing, and made it clear that benign or low-key hauntings were not required. As he delicately phrased it, "There are too many nice kiddy-ghost stories. *I* want to scare the shit out of the little buggers." A couple of my own best nightmares went into the mix.

To my surprise and delight, this was reprinted in Karl Edward Wagner's *The Year's Best Horror: Series XII.*

The Facts in the Case of Micky Valdon

Like UFOs, astrology and Uri Geller, the Micky Valdon myth is a tabloid journalist's dream – a media creation long overdue for debunking. Everyone has read Dr David Evans's sensationalist book *Revenant*. Everyone thinks they know the story, but no one knows the actual facts. My brief was to uncover the facts.

Armed with my *Psychic Critic* credentials, I travelled to North Wales to take a long, cool look at the place where the Valdon hype had all begun. Wales – what an appropriate setting, when you think about it, full of old Celtic ghosts, its hills crowned with ancient graves and settlements, its valleys dotted with crumbling shrines and holy wells. The northwest county of Gwynedd where Valdon lived is the Welshest part of all Wales, actually taking its name from a forgotten kingdom of legend. Superstition fills the air, thick as morning mists on the mountains of Snowdonia. Even hard-headed travel writers like Jan Morris can go all weepy and mystical when it comes to atmospheric Wales. Small wonder that the legend of Micky Valdon's "return" grew so fast and far, nourished in this fertile soil.

The obvious starting-place for my investigation was "Ty Gwyn", the stone-built Valdon cottage halfway up the mountain Diffwys (almost as high as famous Cader Idris, which bulks impressively to the south). It's a tortuous road that climbs up there, and the suspension of my rented Ford Escort took some bad knocks on the final mile of grass-track rising from the village Cwm-mynach. All those Welsh names! I felt half snared in romance myself.

At "Ty Gwyn", though, Valdon's attractive local-born wife (or widow?) Angharad wasn't in a mood to co-operate. Media attention had of course faded a good deal by then, eight weeks after the publication of *Revenant*, and only a couple of reporters had called that morning: but Angharad snapped at me and peremptorily ordered me to go away. The reaction, perhaps, of someone who didn't care to face informed questions? Of someone with things to hide? I will leave readers to make their own decision.

There was more to be learned in the nearby seaside town Barmouth, where Micky Valdon plied his trade of fisherman and bait dealer. Barmouth is one of those forgotten Victorian resorts which are preserved like fossils all around Britain's coast. Out of season it's quiet and half deserted; wind whips along the endless bare promenade. In season, the traditional British apparatus of roundabouts, one-armed bandits, dodgems, souvenir shops and candyfloss is revved up for the tourist trade. These summer months were when Valdon would often carry out small parties of eager but rarely successful deep-sea fishers, in his shabby little boat the *Morfarch*.

I was glad to visit Barmouth in a bright, chilly November, when tourist distractions had been cleared away and only the friendly local folk were in evidence. A tour of the resort's pubs soon had me rubbing shoulders with people who'd personally known Micky Valdon. I bought many rounds of drinks, and although some of my new acquaintances preferred to share private jokes in their native Welsh, many were happy to tell what they knew about their suddenly famous neighbour. Struggling to keep up with these thirsty locals, I was glad of my good head for beer!

"Bloody fond of tall stories, he was," admitted one of Valdon's former cronies. I had been waiting tensely for that particular giveaway. The speaker went on to make a quip about the habits of fishermen, as though trying to excuse Valdon in some obscure fashion. But when like myself you're dedicated to uncovering the truth, there's never any excuse for a compulsive liar.

Very soon after, there was great merriment at a reminiscence of Valdon once dropping a wet fish down the front of an unpopular barmaid's dress. My picture of the man, a picture that had been carefully obscured in Dr Evans's best-selling potboiler, was filling out. I'd known he was short, dark and intense, an immigrant who was more of a Celtic stereotype than most of those born here. Now the inner Valdon was coming into focus. Not only a habitual liar but a confirmed practical joker.

In the cheerful hour which followed, the only other distinctive point about Valdon which anyone seemed to stress was that of his unusual stubbornness and will-power. This was obviously a case of hindsight, since claims of literally superhuman stubbornness and will-power are right at the heart of the dubious myth which, as we all know, has grown up about the missing man.

And then came the real eye-opener, mere minutes before the landlord of the "Crown" brought a halt to that afternoon's investigations by asking us all to leave. A passing reference was made to Micky Valdon's occasional habit of amusing his friends with card tricks and simple sleight of hand. It was a moment before the implications filtered through the strong Welsh beer and hit me. An amateur magician!

The fact speaks for itself.

I left the "Crown" convinced that I was on the track, and returned to my hotel room to think about it all. Next morning, despite a severe headache caused by my concentration, I drove back up the winding road to "Ty Gwyn" to confirm a minor point which had occurred to me.

Angharad Valdon's behaviour that day was obviously part of a continuing effort to obstruct my search for the truth. Her action in hurling a heavy slab of locally quarried roofing slate at my head indicates her unstable personality, and all by itself casts doubt on the value of her testimony as recorded in *Revenant*. (She has been in a "disturbed" state ever since the alleged events.) Luckily my injuries were relatively minor, and through the window I had verified the size of the "sofa bed" which had been such an important stage-prop in the alleged miraculous events.

The type of "sofa bed" found in the "Ty Gwyn" living room is a bulky piece of furniture. Some six feet six inches (1.98 metres) long, it would provide concealment for quite a large man – and here we remember that Micky Valdon was or is unusually small. Moreover, the long, padded seat lifts up to disclose a hidden storage space intended for blankets and suchlike items. The whole set-up is a magician's dream.

So, let's try for a rational reconstruction of what happened.

I think we can safely accept that part of the story which concerns an accident to the *Mor-farch*. Deep-sea fishing from a small boat can sometimes be risky, and Valdon's occasional practice of fishing alone would only add to the risk. Could the wreck have been deliberately staged? Psychic investigators have learned the hard way not to make assumptions about actions which would be "psychologically impossible" for a faker: but it does seem that the *Mor-farch* was our man's pride and joy for all its decrepitude. That the boat was wrecked appears certain enough. It was the salvage and identification of the hull which Dr David Evans – by whatever weird personal logic – took as the "final confirmation" that inspired his credulous and poorly written book.

We can imagine Micky Valdon that evening, dripping wet, shocked by his devastating loss and his struggle to swim ashore, letting himself into the little bait-and-tackle shop where as we know he sold such unpleasant creatures: lugworm and ragworm for sea fishing, live "gentles" (maggots) by the kilo for anglers who preferred Gwynedd's lakes and rivers. And there, dare we imagine, the inspiration came to him. He made his preparations.

So followed the dramatic scenes which form the centrepiece of *Revenant*, beginning with Angharad Valdon's belated arrival home from teaching in Aberystwyth. (There is no reason to question her homeward route via the Cambrian Coast Line, the Barmouth-Dolgellau bus service and a long stretch on foot. Evans is reliable on local colour – as one might expect.) She finds her husband in the living room: nothing unusual in that. She finds his manner strange....

I have tried to keep a particularly open mind on this point. Angharad might have been Micky Valdon's dupe, or might have been in collusion with him to hoax the uncritical Dr David Evans. We have already seen that Valdon might very plausibly have been in a state of shock following the wreck, a likelihood which could account for much. Though few hard-headed readers will think it excuses the hysterical melodrama of the returned man's first recorded words that day, or will be able to resist a loud horse-laugh at the notion of someone saying in cold blood to his wife, "Darling ... I'm dead."

Talk about stubbornness and will-power!

As described at all too tedious length in *Revenant*, Dr David Evans is then called in by the nervy Angharad: at last, an independent witness. How good a witness Evans might actually be is for you to decide. A elderly (57) local practitioner of no great ability or ambition, Evans is best known in the area for his comforting bedside manner. You may well think that despite being an amateur of medical hypnosis, he was singularly ill-equipped to detect the kind of "psychic" trickery which has deceived so many better qualified scientists and researchers. It might also be significant that earlier that evening, Dr Evans had consumed almost an entire pint of beer at the Royal Ship Hotel in Dolgellau. His judgement could easily have been affected.

So what are the proofs which convinced Dr Evans that Micky Valdon's claims were correct, and gave rise to his far from original theory of how desperate will-power might animate organic matter even after death?

Valdon's skin temperature was abnormally low. But of course! Not only had he recently been immersed in a chilly sea, his probable state of shock would have affected blood circulation and given rise to temporary hypothermia. Nor can trickery be ruled out. Concealed ice cubes can work wonders.

The pallor of his face would follow just as logically from the shock theory ... or from a little make-up? A certain reported blotchiness sounds equally unremarkable. When it comes to the allegation that shifting spots of odd, bright colour were present, one can put it down to suggestibility in the light of what supposedly followed; or one can remember that as is acknowledged even in *Revenant*, Valdon had access to aniline dyes made to a decidedly non-supernatural formula.

His pulse was undetectable.... It is a truism that trained medical students very much younger and healthier than Dr Evans can have difficulty in taking a patient's pulse. There is also a well-known magician's trick which allows absence of pulse action to be effectively simulated: the arm is doubled up with a hard rubber ball or similar object clamped tightly in the crook of the elbow. This temporarily blocks circulation and stops the pulse in the wrist. At least one much-reprinted detective story makes use of the point. Library assistants in Dolgellau confirmed that both Valdon and his wife occasionally borrowed books, and I noted with satisfaction that large numbers of detective thrillers were indeed available there.

The alleged lack of heart action suggests several possibilities. One is that Dr Evans's hearing was, as is all too likely, failing with the onset of senility. A second sounds bizarre: but persons with the heart on the wrong side of the body *have* been known. This is a rare but recognized physical condition, called *inverse situs*. Although it's indeed unlikely that Dr Evans had on this account put his stethoscope to the wrong place, the lesser unlikelihood has to be more acceptable than the gross implausibility we are asked to swallow. (A funny coincidence, too, that it's not possible for any qualified person to examine Valdon's supposed corpse.) I am attracted to a third explanation: heart action can be slowed by many common drugs, notably digitalis. This is the active ingredient of foxglove tea, a folk remedy traditionally prescribed for heart trouble. Dedicated "super-psychic" fakers have been known to take amazing risks to simulate abnormal bodily conditions. Foxgloves grow wild within three miles of Cwm-mynach.

Valdon's skin was also, at one or two points, said to "squirm": perhaps a simple matter of a muscle twitch, easily counterfeited. Some people find it incredible that others with better muscle control can wiggle their ears, twitch their scalps or raise one eyebrow without the other. Check it out with friends before assuming that this kind of voluntary tic is impossible.

As for our hero's supposedly unfortunate body odour, it's time for readers to join me in another horse-laugh. I've never before heard *this* advanced as a proof of paranormal happenings. The arcane discipline of Psmellonics!

So there remains Dr Evans's grand finale in the living room of the little granite cottage, high up in the mystic Welsh twilight. The hysterical Angharad is a constant distraction. Sprawled on the sofa-bed, our supposed revenant Micky Valdon is dully repeating his appalling story. Unprepared for a case as bizarre as this, Dr Evans administers a "strong" sedative which appears to have no effect (Valdon could plausibly have been keyed up to the point of being able to override the drug ... though despite Dr Evans's insistence, there's every chance that he simply palmed the pills instead of swallowing them).

Then Dr Evans has the bright idea of trying medical hypnosis, once a fad of his – this interest being significantly well known in the locality. Did Valdon himself drop a sly hint and himself suggest that Evans should hypnotically persuade the obviously disturbed patient to relax and "let go"? It was at this point in the book that I wondered whether either of them had read a certain tale by Edgar Allan Poe. Valdon, perhaps. Evans seems to be a true innocent, as easily fooled as were Crookes, Conan Doyle, and the millions who gaped at Geller.

Angharad sobs in the background and Micky stares lifelessly as Evans intones the repetitive, suggestive phrases. A hypnotic trance is the easiest "phenomenon" of all to simulate, of course, but that question doesn't arise here.

Remember, though, that Evans's long monotone about sleepiness and relaxation and "letting go" isn't being heard only by Micky Valdon. Emotionally exhausted (or so it appeared to Evans), Angharad would have been dulled and soothed. The doctor himself would not be immune to his own therapeutic monotony. At the key moment, neither of the two would have been good witnesses.

Micky Valdon, I conjecture, awaited a moment of distraction: a gust of wind rattling the door, a seagull's cry. With the swift opportunism of a stage magician or a Geller, he blurred into action. Probably he concealed himself swiftly behind that significantly large sofa-bed and, using one of several simple tricks known to professional magicians, substituted the 150 pounds (68 kilograms) of material brought from his shop and hitherto concealed either about his person or within the sofa's hidden compartment. A later, unobtrusive getaway would be a trivial problem.

Dr Evans tries hard to evoke a paranormal thrill with his over-argued notion of a desperate soul, its body smashed and lost at sea, animating what flesh it could to bid a last farewell. But the grandiose phrases fade into silliness when we think coolly of the "hard evidence" left behind: 150 pounds of plump, artificially reared maggots, a small percentage of them (as is traditional, although the efficacy of the bait is apparently not improved) brightly coloured with aniline dyes.

Two professional magicians can now duplicate this trick on stage. Micky Valdon has not been seen since, and significantly has made no response to my repeated public offer (sponsored by *Psychic Critic*) of £5,000 should he be able to repeat the effect under controlled conditions.

These facts speak for themselves, as I am confident readers will agree.

• Published 1989. By temperament, I'm all in favour of *The Skeptical Inquirer* and the staunch debunking activities of James Randi and his colleagues. But in fiction, with a narrator who's sure he sees through absolutely everything, there came an irresistible urge to send him up. Never let facts get in the way of your story.

The Motivation

The shop was a rich stew of smells, dry rot and cigarettes and sweat. Its buzzing fluorescent light couldn't cut through the staleness, and the August sun was not allowed to penetrate. As with every branch of this exclusive chain, the display window was painted dead black; the invisibility of its promised BOOKS AND MAGAZINES was full and sufficient advertisement of the stock.

Peter Edgell reminded himself regularly that he was slumming, that this wasn't his true niche in the literary world. An observer, that was it, scanning the customers who fingered BOOKS AND MAGAZINES through their aseptic plastic film. From behind the counter Peter read the customers and savoured the emotions that burned as pungently as the shop's smell. Businessmen brimmed with a synthetic heartiness, wielding it like a charm against limp fears. Younger nondescripts let off their little firecrackers of defensive aggression. Those too young were allowed a brief ration of giggles before being chased away; most pitiful were the fossil emotions of the very old, who from long habit cringed furtively and offered token mumbles of, "Just getting it for a mate, see?"

Peter welcomed them all, not only because each swing of the door wafted fresh, clean exhaust fumes through the sweaty closeness: with his half a talent, he saw the pornophiles as raw material. One day his special insight would pin them down in some astonishing piece of journalism, a cancellation of his failures at university and everywhere else. Jessica Mitford, Tom Wolfe, whatsisname in *Private Eye*: he'd be with them one day. The thought was so thumbed and worn that it skidded past like a too-familiar quotation.

Minor hubbub arose as old Benson ejected a gaggle of browsers from the small back room. He swept them managerially before him, exuding a steady dribble of apology and exhortation, as though dealing with drunks or kids where the secret was to keep talking and keep calm. Peter was checking a wad of magazines being returned for credit at the usual vast discount (you riffled very carefully through the clean-limbed poses, and refused them if pages were incomplete or if they stuck together). Benson reached past him to the till.

"Lock up half five like usual," he said, passing a greyish handkerchief over a broadly glistening sweep of baldness. His other hand methodically stripped the till of banknotes – so that when he looked up and added, "I'm trusting you, Peter," it was an effort not to snap back, "What the fuck with?"

"See you tomorrow," said Peter, wondering again about the manager: there was nothing to read from him, as though he had no feelings whatever. Perhaps you got like that after ten years in the trade. A roar of traffic and a gale of carbon monoxide swept through the door as Benson slouched out on the weekly errand which was not supposed to have anything to do with Thursday evening's greyhound races.

A dozen or so literary and artistic items changed hands in the final forty minutes of trade, but business was slack without the lure of the back room. It was a milder breed of customer that Peter finally chased out: men whose longings didn't burn as brightly.

He carried the old, battered till into the back, locked it in the concealed cupboard (cunningly papered over, but outlined with a frieze of greasy fingerprints) dedicated to "stronger stuff". Which left him half an hour before his bus: this had happened before, and Peter had spent the time in unedifying study of "strong" goods. His eyes had widened several times as he flicked through; the only after-effect had been a slightly reduced appetite for sausage and chips that evening, and a greatly reduced opinion of certain customers.

"The muse of this art-form," (he had written conscientiously in one of his notebooks) "is a species of Blatant Beast, repelling the assault of our curiosity by revealing far more than we wish to know."

Today, curiosity took him through the back room into the dusty regions of no-customer's-land. There was a toilet stinking of ammonia; a passage-way lined with miscellaneous old stock, growing ever more unsaleable as mice chewed it into lace ... and the grimy kitchen where the mouse-smell was stronger yet, though all that was ever made there was the tea they drank daily from mugs whose brown inner stain exactly matched that of the toilet. A hair-dryer might have indicated some token concession to cleanliness, but was only used for one of Peter's morning chores: shrink-wrapping the latest literary arrivals.

Peter tugged at the sliding door of the old kitchen cupboard; a beetle ran out as it scraped to one side. Within was the cobwebbed box Benson had mentioned as "good for a laugh". The scrawled caption was simply, DUDS. It had seemed a neat idea, at the time, for one of those articles which one day might found his reputation ... an article dealing with what had once been good stout porn, perhaps even Strong Stuff, but which social inflation had rendered as worthless as copper coinage. Peter set great store by ideas and concepts and documentation, a bony framework requiring not too much fleshing out, not too much writing up.

A powerfully musty smell rose as he lifted the flaps of the box. It was stuffed full with the anonymous brown envelopes Benson used for reserve photographs. Peter found himself breathing a little faster, caught in an absurd excitement at the prospect of material which, as one might put it, not even Benson dared offer for sale. However ...

"*Tit* pictures," he murmured crossly, after a moment. They could hardly market stuff which would look staid on the racks at W.H.Smith. And the girl's hairstyle seemed alien: she was dated despite nakedness, with even her shape being subtly wrong. Models (in or out of quotes) had evolved a leaner, more predatory look. With waning excitement Peter unearthed poses having all the erotic impact of Victorian family groups; there were even examples of the forgotten art of the pubic airbrush. An envelope marked S/M merely disclosed another of these anaphrodisiac lovelies, rendered S/M by the limp whip in her hand.

He flipped faster through the envelopes, not knowing what obscure *frisson* he'd hoped to find but increasingly certain that it wasn't here. Near the end, though, one caption scrawled on brown manilla made him pause. LAMBERTSTOW.

Afterwards, Peter had to remind himself strenuously that he didn't believe in occult premonition. His little extra edge, his half-baked ability to read people's feelings, was of no more use than a polygraph when confronted with inanimate paper. The sudden blank chill must have come from the name, its incongruity here, its short-circuit connection with old memories. Uncle Owen, that was who ... and what would *he* have thought of young Peter amid the BOOKS AND MAGAZINES?

Uncle Owen had lived in Lambertstow, and something unspeakable had happened, and Mother had wiped the place from her private map – freezing at any mention, ignoring her brother's Christmas cards. Yes. More memories trickled back. In Lambertstow village a name had been added to criminal legend, up there with Crippen, the various Rippers, the Moors murders. The name was Quinn and no one knew quite what he had done.

The envelope contained several smaller ones, white, each with a printed caption whose indefinable tattiness suggested a hand-operated press. *Police photograph's leaked from Lambertstow horror case. Remains of Kenneth Quinn. Very violent, for strong stomach's only!!* Which left Peter uncertain as to whether the material really was too strong for Benson's hardened clientele, or whether its sale might stir up police interest.

He wasn't sure that he wanted to peer at a corpse, however photo-genic, but his inquisitive fingers had already turned back the flap and slid out the first enclosure. A tightening of the gut came even before he could focus on the glossy print; he had never somehow realized that police photographs would be in colour. (Why was that? Because they were always in black and white in the newspaper. Of course.) Then he looked at the thing properly, and his first sensation was one of relief.

What lay on the grass under harsh lights was nothing recognizable as human. A long Christmas tree decked with exotic fruits and garlands, tinselled with innumerable points of reflected light; a Dali vision which through sheer excess had gone beyond mutilation and deformity. It was odd, perhaps a little disturbing in its abstract forms, but at first glance not at all horrific.

It was a pity, really, that Peter took the second glance.

An observation of G.K. Chesterton's caught up with him later: that one might look at a thing nine hundred and ninety-nine times and be perfectly safe, but to take the thousandth look was to be in frightful danger of *seeing* it for the first time. Peter thought Chesterton had underestimated the safe exposure period, and sincerely regretted having looked even twice. The second look stirred up dim memories of an anatomy course at college, or those parts of it he'd attended; with his second look, he made the fatal error of analysis. It was fascinating, compulsive, to trace the relation between the long glittering object and what must have been a man; to consider bubbly ornaments in red and grey as something more than inorganic lumps, more than the polished haematite they called kidney ore; to trace what must have been done here and here with surgical delicacy; to wonder – try not to wonder – just when in the painstaking process Kenneth Quinn had actually died....

Prints and envelopes spilled to the floor as Peter jerked up from his squatting position. He made it to the sink in time; the sight of his own thin vomit crawling across the stained and spotted enamel seemed relatively wholesome, like those bracing whiffs of outside pollution in the sweaty shop. *If I'd seen it in a movie it would have been all right, a guaranteed fake.* The rest was a long anticlimax of cleaning, tidying, drinking many mugs of water which rinsed the aftertaste only partly from his mouth and not at all from his mind. After which the bus was long gone and Peter walked two miles to his bed-sitter; for reasons which stayed persistently cloudy, he took one packet of the photographs with him.

That night and in the shop next day, he resolutely thought of other things; but from time to time some detail of the material he sold would tweak at his memory and make him flinch. The hot gloom of the shop was conducive (in idle periods) to thoughts of Lambertstow and his uncle – his mother's brother, vaguely isolated from the family as "not one of our sort", maternal condemnation of one who remained a mere farmhand while *she* became a typist and married an accountant.

Peter had enjoyed Uncle Owen: he remembered jokes, erratic conjuring tricks, hilarious chases in the woods near Lambertstow. He'd been ten, perhaps younger. He'd been eleven when the something happened, and that part of life had gone dark. Uncle Owen had died a few years later but might as well have died then. Thinking back, Peter saw that mere geographical connection with infamy was enough to make Mother sever all links, a theatre nurse rejecting contact with the unsterile. Her mind worked that way.

He wondered whether he himself had met Quinn in those days of clear air and sharp colours. No memories presented themselves. He fancied that local kids had mentioned Quinn as one of their teachers, and that they'd liked him well enough. Peter at ten had been bored by such chat, impatient to talk about really interesting teachers like his own.

In the evening, the local library kept late hours. Peter spent some time searching through aged newspapers. Their dry old smell was very different from that of the damp room behind the shop, soporific rather than choking. His first guess at dates hadn't been too far out: in a few months the tragedy and mystery would be a decade old. He made notes of such scanty details as the papers gave, and for the fiftieth time began to plan a clever debut in journalism.

Ten years since Lambertstow horror, he wrote. *Motive for ghastly crime never revealed, but Quinn said to be disliked in neighbourhood. Strong feelings in Lambertstow got what he deserved, so reporters claimed after probing locals. Body at edge of wood, confused footmarks in grass, several people involved?? Ritual sacrifice etc etc hinted as per usual. No evidence. Filed unsolved (presumably), only Quinn somehow left with bad name. How so? Graffiti, local mood, anonymous letters. Smear bid, whispering campaign, grass roots stuff. Some called Quinn in parish even changed name, c.f. people called Crippen. Definitely impression Q got just deserts. But what did he* do?

On a second sheet of scrap paper: *Personal. Uncle O mentioned nowhere, no remote connection; Mother didn't even need that much excuse. Papers evasive on details of what was done; no pics (not surprising). Surgical knowledge needed? Artist too, sort of. Maybe approach through doctor.*

There was no third sheet, which might have carried such notes as *Why am I doing this?* and led into a complicated mire. Peter was happy to have something to do, something to test his talent against, something outside the fascinating dead end of the shop. Working towards truth had to be a virtue, whatever awkward thoughts came knocking.... Some people drove hundreds of miles to gape at seagulls choking and dying in oil slicks; some crowded about road accidents and pointed out to each other the interesting red stains on the asphalt; some holidayed in Germany and were careful not to miss the celebrated resorts, Buchenwald, Dachau. In his grimy room, which was at least grimy through use rather than decay, Peter remembered and recited his mother's charm against idle speculation.

The centipede was happy quite
Until a frog in fun
Said "Pray which leg goes after which?"
This raised its mind to such a pitch
It lay distracted in the ditch
Considering how to run.

Local colour was the thing. On the Exeter train, he skimmed the only book about the case which the library could offer. *He Must Be Wicked To Deserve Such Pain: an essay on enormity.* Though the title quotation, which he thought might be Shakespeare, summed up neatly enough that feeling about Quinn, Peter found the text disappointing. The aristocratic lady author was more concerned with a generic "sickness of society", and with how shops like Benson's led inevitably down the primrose path to this sort of thing, than with the event itself. Like the magazines Peter sold, she promised more than could ever be delivered. He slapped the book shut in irritation, in guilty disappointment, on the closing quotation: "Whereof one cannot speak, thereon one must remain silent."

Local colour, he told himself, and wondered if he were telling the truth. One should be able to sit at ease in north London and read up on anything. But during the long wait for a bus at Exeter, he had to admit to himself that it would be interesting to try and read Dr Janice Barry, mentioned in the papers as the Lambertstow GP. Certain questions might have gone unasked, ten years back, and he wanted to ask them. The prospect was utterly terrifying; but proper reporters had to ask people awkward questions and so he supposed he must as well. He wore mirror sunglasses which he hoped would give him confidence by making him unreadable.

Coffee on the train had left a sour taint in his mouth, which as the leisurely bus wobbled through suburbs and lanes gave him an illusion of having recently vomited. Flies buzzed in the smoky heat of the upper deck, aimless and happy. Peter crushed one against the window.

Lambertstow was bigger than remembered, defying the cliché of childhood haunts seeming absurdly tiny when revisited. The village had grown, or had been blotted out, its approaches a maze of new estates. Peter rode through layers of accretion to the old High Street at the heart of it all, and peered uncertainly at ordinariness. So late, so long after the event, all witnesses scattered or lost in hiding places ten years deep.... The phone directory was the obvious starting point, he decided doggedly as a post office caught his eye: then he gnawed his lip, recalling country-wide directories filling long shelves in London. Still, here he was, after all.

"Bloody hell," said Peter with feeling, a few minutes later. The local directory listed no Dr Barry.

Asking after "the doctor" led him by stages to an ivied house whose brass plate said DR JONATHAN SIMS. After ten years, was it too late to enquire? He pushed through the door into a cool smothering gloom which felt almost ecclesiastical, and groped blindly to a reception window. "I wanted to ask –" The logical lie came to him in a burst of confidence. "About my uncle, Owen Walker, used to live here, I wanted to find Dr Barry and, er ... you don't know?"

The dark-haired woman at the window gave him a tired smile, behind which Peter read a hot flash of exasperation. "I'll ask Dr Sims," she said. And after a pause of unintelligible intercom noises (did real reporters have tricks for coping with that?): "Dr Barry *used* to run this practice. Dr Sims says she's been at a private nursing home for some time – I don't know whether I should, but perhaps if I gave you the address?"

"Please. It's a, an important family matter."

Amazed by this success, Peter took the slip of paper with effusive thanks, and left. The moist heat was like a blow in the face as he closed the door behind him. The address was in Surbiton.

Local colour, he reminded himself. To the scene of the crime, yes, definitely. He'd copied a sketch map from one of the papers; the streets seemed to have randomly stretched, contracted, and tilted on hidden hinges to new angles with one another, but eventually he saw the fatal stand of trees. When they first appeared, peeping over a terrace of harsh new brick, they looked uncompromisingly ordinary. Where was the atmosphere of doom? It was only a small patch of woodland (Peter remembered it as larger – so he *had* been here once), straggling up a slope just too steep for cultivation. Another obscure thought surfaced: absurdly, he'd been half prepared to find some plaque or marker. "The Atrocity Of The Decade Took Place On This Spot."

There was only unkempt grass. He sat with his back against a tree, and watched the shadows lengthen. Local colour: *Today it may seem un-remarkable, even dull, but.* Useless. He slid out the monstrous photograph and frowned; its repulsion was dimmed a little by familiarity, but he didn't care too look too long.

On – this – spot, he thought fiercely, trying to make himself feel more, trying to do the impossible and read a place. There must be some aura ...

some stain. Now that he'd looked again at the picture, he could see how the landscape might be considered in a different light, changing in the mind's eye, going bad. From under the trees came a sweet-sour whiff of rotting leaves, and this no longer seemed quite natural. The sluggish air pressed close. Puffy white clouds were wobbling overhead, bulging down at him, disgusting in their nearness and intimacy. The sky, he realized, was stretched tightly just above him; the constricted horizon barely allowed room to breathe. He could not breathe. He could not move. *On this spot.*

The pulpy ground was ready to engulf him; something glistening and wet was surely just behind, moving with exquisite delicacy and pain under the trees, coming to him. Peter shivered in a cage of shadows. Here in this small, cramped, horrid countryside he found his eyes fixed, frozen, on a tiny mess in the nearby grass (perhaps a bird-dropping) which had become the oozing, lazily turning hub of all the world's vileness....

Peter lurched upright, stomach churning. Automatically, shakily, he began to walk away, his intention of exploring the trees forgotten. This was local colour? He'd never felt troubled before with too much imagination, had never been able to read a place. Think, think of something else.

... how interesting to analyse this: a small horrible thing is so much more repulsive than a large. Cf. the failure of giant insects and suchlike in all those movies. A small, fascinatingly yucky thing like whatever was there in the grass. Or like a photograph.

Peter shook his head violently. Walking briskly and without a pause into the village, he tried to shut out all the unspeakable facts for a moment, and probe the motives behind it all. As always, he failed. How could Quinn, how could anyone, deserve *that*? "Oh, Quinny's OK," the sniggering Lambertstow kids had told him ten years back. The village went by in a blur. Funny you never ran into any of the old kids these days. On the London train he sneered at himself as a coward and an incompetent, but with a deeper sense of comfort, a satisfaction at having read or even for a moment imagined the supposed horror of that locality. This was the insight which could take you to the top.

At home he wrote it all down as local colour, and didn't sleep too well afterwards.

Next day was Sunday, with the heat of fading summer thicker and murkier than ever. Peter fiddled with a much worked-over draft (*Today I stood on the very spot where the strangely notorious Kenneth Quinn allegedly met his terrible end. Even ten years after the horror, it is not a pleasant place,* etc.), abandoned it, and walked out to telephone the Treetops Private Home from a nearby booth which did part-time duty as urinal.

"Treetops, can I *help* you?" said a pleasant female voice.

"Is it, er, possible for me to have a word with Dr Barry?"

"*One* moment." A pause. "There is *no* Dr Barry on our staff, are you *sure* you have the right number?"

"They ... told me I could find Dr Janice Barry at Treetops," said Peter weakly. He should have known, doctors would stick together and hide one another's addresses, frustrate anyone who might ask awkward questions...

"*One* moment." A longer pause, during which it occurred to Peter that the woman's ordinary speaking voice must be half an octave lower than the strained tones which drifted with such refinement down the line. "I *am* sorry. Yes. Miss Barry is a *patient* at Treetops, do you wish to *visit* her?"

He blinked. It shouldn't be that surprising, now you thought about it, but somehow ... "Yes please," he said. "What are your visiting hours?"

The voice sounded a little shocked: "There are *no* fixed visiting hours at Treetops. You may visit when*ever* you wish, between 10am and 8pm."

Peter calculated rapidly, and hastily fed in more money. "Hello? Hello? Could I visit at about seven tomorrow evening, please?"

"Certainly. Please could I have your *name*?"

"Edgell. Peter Edgell. A friend of a friend."

"*Thank* you."

Monday was a trifle cooler, but still nowhere near comfortable. The shop seemed to attract a higher than usual proportion of nutters, people who wandered in asking for the *Times* or the latest science fiction magazine; there was even one twerp who without glancing at the stock enquired about first editions of James Branch Cabell. (Peter had wondered for a moment whether this was an esoteric code phrase.) Although you knew where you were in the shop and could laugh a little at the customers' feelings, Monday stretched unbearably, each minute longer than the one before, until it was a surprise to see Benson fussing browsers out of the back room and putting an end to the day's literary business.

The bus was crowded, and stank. The Tube was worse. The second bus was less oppressive, rush-hour being past: Peter reached TReetops in good time, perhaps too soon, since he hadn't a very clear idea of what to say.

It was a chubby Victorian mansion, its red and yellow brick impeccably clean; the only tree in sight, though, was some way down the road. A middle-aged woman in a nurse's cap opened the door, her stern aspect launching Peter prematurely into his lie: "Come to visit Doctor,

Miss Barry. She was a friend of my uncle's and I thought I, well, I ought to ..."

Her answering smile was like sunlight breaking through forbidding cloud. He read surprised approval, no doubt at finding such nice sentiments in a scruffy youth.

"If you'll just come this way –"

The wide hallway smelt of boiled cabbage, only slightly tinged with the inevitable antiseptic. Thick, glossy cream paint covered every surface. Peter followed the nurse up noisy, varnished wooden stairs as she explained in an undertone that Miss Barry sometimes had a little difficulty, if he knew what she meant. "The poor thing *wanders* sometimes."

Peter wasn't prepared for the room at the top of the stairs. The words "private nursing home" had conjured up images of personal, individual care and attention in comfortably private rooms. This room, whose door said HOPE, was comfortably small, but screens divided it into four cramped segments, each with an iron bed, each bed containing an old woman who lay unmoving. To the boiled-veg and antiseptic reek was added some other smell, sickly and disagreeable.

"Miss Barry!" said the nurse brightly, speaking loudly and very close to the third old lady's ear. "It's Peter Edgell, come to visit you!"

"Ring the bell if there's any trouble," she added more quietly, and left. Peter sat cautiously at the bedside and looked at Janice Barry, whose eyes stared blankly upwards. She could not possibly be more than seventy, but seemed far older. They had dwindled in their sockets, those eyes, like jellyfish withered by a fierce sun; her whole face was shrunken, as though it were a balloon from which a little too much air had been allowed to escape. Her breathing was noisy.

"Miss ... I mean Dr Barry?" No response, but he couldn't stop now, right on the verge of something or other. His newest lie followed straight away. "Do you remember Owen Walker, back in Lambertstow, used to come to you? I'm his nephew, and there was this rumour, I heard he'd been suspected of ... what happened there. It was all a long time ago, but I was wondering if maybe you could help me clear things up a bit."

It really did sound feeble. But some trace of animation had crept over the old woman's face at the mention of Lambertstow. Peter bent closer and made himself repeat his non-question. This time the eyes moved ... and behind them he read something wary and knowing. *I have the edge on her. She knows something and she can't hide it from me. This is the start.*

"You ... No one has talked to me about *that* for a good many years," she said in a slow wheezing voice, a separate act of concentration shaping each word. "Are you from the police again?"

"No no. I'm – sort of looking into it. Off my own bat. My uncle."

Dr Barry coughed. "I suppose you want to ask me the, the usual questions?"

Edgell guessed that his queries were not, could not be as original as he'd hoped. Impatiently he abandoned pretence; *Maybe I can surprise her by being blunt, that's the way investigators work.* "The surgical technique," he said flatly.

She smiled; he hadn't thought her face could become any more wrinkled. The animation in and around her eyes was flickering, as though corroded contacts were sparking and smoking, passing power only intermittently. "Did you know I have an inoperable brain tumour?" she said.

Peter blinked, not knowing what to say but reading it as true.

"They tell me I'm just getting old, but I know. Look at me." Her head rocked on the pillow; perhaps she was trying to shake it. "Ah. Quinn was an evil man. Wickedness and corruption, of a sort."

Cautiously: "Then you know why he was ... killed?" *She knows something. She really does.*

"A brain tumour," Dr Barry said with satisfaction, or so it seemed. The light in her eyes came on more fully. "Oh yes, the police wanted to know all about that, asked me many and many a time about surgical training and whether I thought anyone but a doctor could have ... But I was a woman, you see. You can't believe what I say."

And he couldn't unravel the complex knot of feelings he was reading in her. "They thought a woman couldn't have done what was done, is that it?" he said, wondering if the old dear really were delirious.

"No more she could, I said, I told them, unless she had, oh, crowds of helpers. They believed that.... Quinn *was* a vile man, you know. That's all I know, officer. I really cannot assist you any further. Those poor children. They must never know. It was a work of art.... Do you play rugby? My brother was very fond of rugby once."

The room seemed to be growing colder, full of harsh, ragged breathing. Peter remembered his own great-aunt, so vague in the present decade, so diamond-sharp when speaking of the past. He felt so close; he leaned closer still. "Why was it done? What had Quinn *done*?"

"He must be wicked to deserve such pain ... did you read that book? A very silly book." She breathed again, deeply, and exhaled with a long shudder. "My diagnosis is certain, I'm afraid. Prognosis negative. N.T.B.R.... I can feel it pressing. It presses in different colours. Why, officer, I don't know anything at all about Mr Quinn except that he wasn't much liked in the village.... No. The things he did. They were very shameful. The things he wanted to do. His name shall be blackened forever and ever amen." It was a long speech, and took a long time.

"Dr Barry, it is blackened – somehow. It is. People called Quinn changed their names. You remember, because of the whispering. Did *you* –?" It was there, so close, he could read it but couldn't understand it: a foreign language of emotion.

She was speaking again, more feebly now. The faulty contacts might be passing current, but the power-source itself was failing. "You are all ... so ... silly. If I wanted to I could tell you half. I shouldn't tease you like this. Did you ever hear tell of the *Mary Celeste*?"

Peter couldn't decide whether that was relevant, or mere wandering. If only he'd brought a cassette recorder. "Yes?"

"They remember it to this day because nobody knows the how or why. They can't forget it, poor dears. So many of us, if you believe that. And if there's never a word about what Quinn just, you see, just the hints, if everything is handled just so.... Forever. You're not the doctor."

"Please," he whispered, as the feelings he couldn't read faded with her voice. "Please tell me." *For the sake of my brilliant future career.*

She giggled, protected from all the world by her inoperable brain tumour. (N.T.B.R. she had said, *not to be resuscitated*, was that already written in some folder here?) For a moment her fading eyes were those of a little girl.

"Shan't," she whispered. "You wouldn't want to spoil it all?" And began to laugh, a small weak laugh that hardened into a sort of spasm, a glistening line of saliva running from the corner of her mouth as the shrivelled body trembled in private glee.

His final attempt to spy on her secrets read nothing that made sense: a fading Rorschach pattern of feelings, a meaningless bright symmetry like a Christmas tree. Peter pressed the bellpush. The nurse appeared and dismissed him from the bedside with a flick of her eyes.

"You can't believe anything poor Miss Barry says," she warned in a low voice as he left the room. Now, perhaps, was the moment for shrewd questions and even a small bribe – anything to learn more or those so-called wanderings and ravings. But, studying the nurse's stern competence and impatient eyes, reading the professional hardness which made Treetops endurable, he quailed at last.

"Goodbye," he mumbled, and felt as the big door closed behind him that he was leaving under a faint cloud.

And so I left the dying Dr Barry, who will surely take the monstrous secret of Lambertstow with her on her painful descent towards the solution of that other, final question which remains eternally tantalizing under it is answered.

Peter leant back from the typewriter, unsatisfied but with a sense of having partly avenged his frustration. He had at least had the last word.

"Quinny's all right," the Lambertstow schoolkids had told him in the long ago. "He's a fantastic guy, gives you things and all. *You* know. You ought to meet him." Had he been able to read people back then? Kids were so boring, self-centred, anyway.

Peter stared at the blank wall of his room and shrugged; the mystery was unyielding, monolithic. Pulling the painfully typed sheet from the machine, he filed it carefully with all the other notes and outlines for articles he thoroughly intended to write, one day very soon. Perhaps when he could afford a word processor; that should solve his productivity problems. Perhaps.

Meanwhile, there was always his private gallery of the emotions, where offbeat feelings and longings came to disport themselves for Peter Edgell's dispassionate amusement. There was always the shop.

• Published 1989, and reprinted in Karl Edward Wagner's *Year's Best Horror Stories XVIII*. The original appearance was in an anthology of sf with more or less sexual themes, dreamed up at one of the Milford (UK) writers' conferences. Alex Stewart was press-ganged as editor, and throbbing titles like *Saucy Science Wonder Stories* or just plain *Spung!* eventually gave way to the demurely respectable *Arrows of Eros*. "The Motivation" crept in on the dubious basis that it was all about voyeurism, which makes me think of it as my Christopher Priest story: he dealt with that theme in a very different novella, "The Watched", and is fond of titles like *The Affirmation*, "The Negation", "The Cremation", *The Separation*....

It's all a bit dated now, alas, since BOOKS AND MAGAZINES shops were succumbing to remorseless Darwinian selection pressure from ADULT VIDEOS even when I wrote the thing.

I hadn't noticed before compiling this book that I'd set two unrelated stories in a place called Lambertstow. Maybe I should write another and see if anybody responds with some awesome critical thesis about the subtle interconnections signalled by that repeated name.

Encounter of Another Kind

At the time it seemed a good night for our work. A thin watery fuzz, half mist and half rain, was blurring the moon and had made haloes round the lights of the main road. This dark lane was still puddled from afternoon showers, so that when our van tilted and bumped along it the headlight reflections rose in silent luminous bubbles through the trees. Even I took a long moment to identify them. The right frame of mind is so important.

This was a high-activity area of Wiltshire, where sightings came regularly with the seasons. It was crop circle country too, but I had always been uneasy about that work: it's too showy and physical, and too many fanciful hoaxers had spoilt the impact of our own real, authorized creations. But the fertile location was just happenstance. The man Glass lived close at hand, and was known to take this lane from Pewsey village to his house. Tonight he had been delivering one of his lying, offensive lectures, and the driving time from London ...

I checked my watch. Perhaps Glass's wife would be doing the same, and laying out coffee-cups. Would she believe his incredible, incoherent story a few hours hence? We were ready by the roadside, in a field muddy and trampled enough that our own traces could make no difference.

The stage was set in the bubble-tent. Mackay had long finished stringing his cables and was hunched over his little panel of lights, rapt like a boy playing trains. Sometimes I wondered about Mackay. It was easy to imagine him working with anyone, even the IRA, grinning all over that fat face and soldering his fussy circuits for sheer love of gadgetry. He never seemed to absorb the idea that we were evangelists labouring in the service of a great truth.

One amber light blinked and double-blinked in the box. Ten-minute test. The coast was clear and the kid hadn't yet gone to sleep at his post up the dark lane, at the junction. We were as ready as we would ever be.

The kid's role was relatively minor, but I still worried about him getting it right. You never know what to make of these teenage agglomerations of hair, leather and studs. But he'd asked sensible questions about the reports of Visitors in this and that country: sometimes putty-faced midgets with enormous eyes, sometimes six or seven feet tall. I dare say they can take what form they like, I'd told him, and he seemed satisfied. Now Mackay was deeply indifferent to that kind of speculation, and Glass would naturally have made it a basis for mockery.

Yes. Peter Glass was a man long overdue for the attention of the skies. Whenever some hint of the mysterious and wonderful came creeping shyly into the world, it was always he who'd rush to be interviewed and turn everything to mud with his touch. It was the planet Venus, it was a low-flying plane, the witnesses imagined it all, he was just lying, she is mentally disturbed, who can believe in little green men anyway?

(A cheap newspaper phrase, that last. In the classic accounts They are never green.)

It is particularly maddening when an encounter we *know* to have been physically real is explained away as hallucination. People who ought to be fighting at our side are seduced by talk of visitations and abductions being all a matter of strange psychological states blah blah blah which if properly studied might give new insight into the mind and blah blah blah. What is this stuff but a fancy version of "he's barmy and she made it all up"? Of course it must be said that some people do make it up. I loathe a hoaxer.

The large oblong indicator at dead centre of Mackay's panel went red and a low buzz sounded. I keep my distance from electronics hobbyism, but that one was obvious enough. The kid had clocked what was presumably the right car going by. Now he should be hauling out that big *DIVERSION* sign from the sodden undergrowth. A quiet country lane was about to become quieter.

I always kept the pallid mask off until the last minute: it's hot and uncomfortable. Lights were flickering in the distance, approaching. Glass himself would be seeing those eerie reflections rise up the wet trees. Perhaps they would take on a new significance for him, now or in retrospect, because Mackay had flicked the first of his switches. Could the tiny hiss even be heard over the engine noise? A receptive frame of mind was needed.

In the classic UFO encounter by road and by night, an unidentifiable light is seen above and the car ignition mysteriously fails. This will often be the preliminary to a "missing time" or even an "alien abduction" experience. We were certainly going to see to that. At the second click from Mackay's board the quartz-halogen cluster blazed intolerably from the sky (in fact from a cable slung precariously between tall trees on either side of the lane), and at the third Glass's ignition mysteriously failed.

The sky-gods command powers beyond our scope, of course, and their servants down here must resort to earthly expedients. I think a priest might feel the same when he doles out the bread and wine and is sure it represents a truth, while doubting that the miracle of blood ever really comes to pass as it had in scriptural days. Mackay's opposite number in London had done his part well enough: the relay in the HT circuit and the tiny cylinder with its servo-operated valve just under the driver's seat. Of course it is the signal from the first switch that releases the gas.

Longstead 42 is a transparent and almost odourless psychotropic agent, used to ensure the properly receptive frame of mind. Its effects do not last long, but Glass was still trembling and almost helpless in his stalled Volvo when we adjusted our bulging masks and came to him. The sequence of events, coloured and exaggerated by the mild hallucinogen, must already have been etching itself deep into his memory ... all the more so for its theoretical familiarity. His own scoffing researches would reinforce the impact of what happened now. I tried to be gentle with the hypodermic, but there was no need to conceal this injection. Unexplained scars and puncture-marks are all part of the classic abduction experience.

The kid's lightless motor-bike was coughing at the gate as we helped Glass towards our mother ship. Mackay fingered his pocket controller and the great inflated igloo pulsed in a riot of coloured lights. A bubble marquee is perfect for this work despite the faint roar of the compressor: it even has an airlock. I myself found it a deeply moving sight. If only ...

He did not resist as we stripped him and settled him on an examination table of a design as unearthly as our resources could arrange. For him this would be a place of stabbing supernatural light, thanks to a few drops of atropine that dilated each eye to the full; and strange small Beings would hover around. The kid, who had changed into his own mask and white leotards before joining us now, was already short enough: but the deceptively high table made midgets of us all, while dry-ice fog confused the issue of how far down our legs might actually go. Truth is all a matter of presentation. Our putty-complexioned masks swelled at the top into mighty domes of intellect, and we peered through huge eyes of empty black glass.

So we set to work, following the guidelines laid down by a myriad published cases. This is a hugely documented phenomenon. Mackay and I had had plenty of practice with communicants of both sexes, and worked well together. Biopsies, minute incisions. Needles in Glass's navel, liquid drooling into his ear, surreal alien mechanisms blinking as they diagnosed and recorded nothing at all. Intermittent chemical blackouts helped break up the stream of his memory (partial amnesia is highly characteristic). There was a star map ready to show him, a patternless scattergram on which he could later impose any meaning he cared.

He gaped. I knew we had him. Why should he be so loud in his filthy scepticism if he were not already close to belief, just waiting for the sign? Recorded messages of peace and millennial warning washed over him, the voices digitally processed into eerie tones appropriate to the farther stars. Never again would he be able to say with sincerity that it was all ridiculous, that in all probability the quote UFO abductees unquote are merely drawing attention to themselves with lurid fantasies.

The culmination is the terrible Probe, the thing that bulks large in the encounter/abduction story which I believe has sold more copies than any other. It is a huge ugly object, like a phallus designed by H.R.Giger in a bilious mood: thirteen inches long, vaguely triangular in cross-section, grey and scaly, tipped with a jagged cage of wires. (The shaft is actually made of painted fibreglass.)

It is a necessary part of the experience that the victim should feel himself anally penetrated by this probe. Of course we relied on suggestion: after showing him the thing, and turning him over to obstruct his vision, I would actually insert a finger. The greased rubber glove was already on my hand.

But there was a hitch before the Probe came into play. The head-masks do not make it all that easy to see to the left or right. We had blacked Glass out again to allow a quick breather and a cup of tea from the thermos ... and there was a confused sound. I fumbled impatiently with the mask and at the same time felt a small sharp pain in my thigh, some stinging insect, perhaps.

When I'd finally pulled the stifling thing off my head I saw that Mackay had fallen over. The fog lapped around him. I thought at first he must have had an accidental whiff of the blackout agent. Everything was blurring and the tent walls shimmered. The kid smiled at me. It is not possible that the mask could smile.

I told him to take that stupid thing off. I do not know whether I meant the mask or the smile. He invited me to remove it for him, and though I first reached out in blind anger at his playing around, I was suddenly afraid that if I touched it the great head would be built of living flesh. No. I said something loud, perhaps not an actual word. Was Glass's body melting and oozing off the table? No.

There is a gap here. Partial amnesia is highly characteristic. Things tilted heavily in and out of focus. I remember the feel of another insect and knew this time it was a needle. By then I was pressed into the cold soggy fabric of the tent floor, choking in our artificial fog. Insistent fingers tugged at my tight white alien costume.

Everything inside my skull was whirling in tight, chaotic patterns, led by a silly persistent worry about whether the syringe had been properly sterilized (I was always very conscientious about this). What did I know about the kid? It was his first outing. I had barely seen him before. They can take what form they like.

Those eyes.

He said ...

I do not recall all the words. That scopolamine cocktail is meant to be disorienting. The thin voice conveyed that we were playing a dangerous game. More than once he said: "My sister." I thought of sister worlds, sister craft gleaming silver as they made their inertialess turns and danced mockingly off the radar screens. He said: "In an institution." Would that have been the Institute of UFO Studies? At another point he said: "You bastards," and "did all this to her," and "waiting a long time for this ..." The words of the sky-gods are always enigmatic, and perhaps we are only their bastard offspring.

It was so hard to think. All this is confused in a red blur of pain, because to impress his seriousness upon me he then made scientific use of the Probe. Nor was there any reliance on suggestion or on a greased and rubber-sheathed finger. "This is for her. You hear me? This is for her." Did I hear that? At the time I could not begin to appreciate it as an exalting, a transcendent experience. I am sure that no chemical agents assisted the loss of consciousness which duly followed, although not soon enough.

Waking up on chill plastic stretched over mud, racked with cramps and another, deeper ache ... is not an experience to be recommended. The "kid" was long gone. I never knew his name, if on Earth he ever went under a name. I tried not to be consoled by the discovery that Mackay too had been warned, every bit as emphatically as myself.

Under a dismal grey moon we limped somehow through the clear-up procedure and left Glass to sleep it off in his wretched Volvo, itself now stripped of our London man's gadgetry. When he uncoiled himself in the small hours, he would be awakening to his new membership in the ranks of abductees, the sufferers from "missing time". Would he proclaim it or would he lie by silence? Who cared? Glass was no longer important.

The truth is what's important. After a longish period of convalescence and keeping a low profile (even my once-friendly family doctor was terrifyingly unsympathetic about the injury), I now see myself in the position of a worldly priest who has at last received his own sign. But it's a sign like the miraculous appearance of the face of the Virgin Mary in one's toilet bowl. The kind of thing that will do to win peasants: meaning so much to the recipient, but just another tawdry, commonplace sensation to the world at large. For this muddying of the waters I blame the people who have made up garish UFO encounter tales without ever having a genuine experience like the one we gave to Glass. Oh, I do loathe and despise these hoaxers, almost as much as the narrow-minded sceptics themselves.

Meanwhile, how can I hope to publish *this* truth and have its very special status believed? How can it help me to my rightful position among the elect when They finally beam down in glory from the stars, with all their wonderful cargo? How?

• Published 1991. This was drafted as a shapeshifter story for a shared-world anthology – see "The Lions in the Desert", below – but on the whole seems to work better without the explicit sf element. Which is just as well, since the anthology editors didn't like the original version.

The little-known psychotropic gas "Longstead 42" is a tiny homage to Robert Sheckley, in one of whose short stories it first appeared.

The Lions in the Desert

"... further information on the elusive topic of polymorphism is said by some sources to be held in the restricted library of the Jasper Trant Bequest (Oxford, England)." – Various references, from about 1875 onward.

"How shall one catch the lions in the desert?" said young Keith Ramsey in his riddling voice, as he poured hot water into the unavoidable instant coffee.

After a week of nights on the job with him, I knew enough to smile guardedly. Serious proposals of expeditions, nets, traps or bait were not required. Despite his round pink face and general air of being about sixteen, Keith was a mathematics D.Phil (or nearly so) and had already decided to educate me in some of the running jokes of mathematicians. It could be interesting, in an obsessive way. The answers to the riddle were many and manifold.

"I thought of a topological method," he said. "See, a lion is topologically equivalent to a doughnut ..."

"What?"

"Well, approximately. A solid with a hole through it – the digestive tract, you know. Now if we translate the desert into four-dimensional space, it becomes possible to *knot* the lion by a continuous topological deformation, which would leave it helpless to escape!"

I have no higher mathematics, but dire puns were allowed, "parallel lions" and the like. "Er, geometrically the desert is approximately a plane," I suggested. "With the lions on it. Simply hijack the plane, and ..."

He groaned dutifully, and we both drank the awful coffee supplied by the Trant to its loyal security force. Keith had converted his to the usual syrup with four spoonfuls of sugar. After all my care in dosing the sugar-bowl, I was pleased that he took the correct measure.

"Deformation," he said again, with what might have been a shiver. "You know, Bob, I wish they hadn't shown us that picture. For me it's night-watchman stuff or the dole, but every time I put on this wretched imitation policeman rig, I can feel things crawling all over my grave."

"I never feel things like that – I'm too sensible. The original Man Who

Could Not Shudder. But I sort of know what you mean. It reminded me of that bit in *Jekyll and Hyde*, if you ever read it ...?"

He looked into the half-drunk coffee and sniffed; then snapped his skinny fingers. "Oh, ugh, yes. The awful Mr Hyde walking right over the kid in the street. Crunch, crunch, flat against the cobbles. Ta *very* much for reminding me. Yes, I suppose it was like that."

"They say down at the Welsh Pony that the turnover of guards here is pretty high for a cushy job like this. I have the impression they last about six weeks, on average. Funny, really."

"Hilarious, mate. Look, what do *you* think happened to that bloke last year?"

"Maybe he opened one of the forbidden books," I offered. "A hell of a thing when even a trusty pair like us gets told to keep clear of Area C."

A grey man in a grey suit had hired me on behalf of the Trant Trustees. Amazingly little was said about career prospects, union representation or even – the part I was naturally curious about – the precise nature of what the two night guards actually guarded. Books were said to enter into it.

Instead: "I should warn you, Mr Ames, that certain people are intensely interested in the Trant Bequest. Last year, just outside the ... that is, outside Area C, one of your predecessors was found like this. His colleague was not found at all." He showed me a photograph without apparently caring to glance at it himself. The spread-eagled remains did not slot handily into anyone's definition of how a corpse should look. Someone had, as Keith would have put it, tried bloody hard to translate him into two-dimensioned space.

"How shall one catch the lions in the desert?" he repeated, now badly slurred. The sugar treatment had taken longer than I had expected. "The method of the Sieve of Eratosthenes is to make an exhaustive list of all the objects in the desert and to cross off all the ones which on examination prove ... prove not to be ... To cross off ..." Abandoning thought experiment number umpty-tum, he slumped to the table, head on arms, dribbling slightly over the sleeve of his nice navy-blue uniform. I thought of hauling him across to his bunk, but didn't want to jog him back into wakefulness. With any luck he'd reach the morning with nothing worse than a touch of cramp. I rather liked young Keith: some day, maybe, he'd make a fine maths tutor with his games and jokes. If he could rouse interest in a dull pragmatist like me ...

Certain people are intensely interested in the Jasper Trant Bequest. I am one of them. I slotted my special disk into the sensor-control PC and moved quietly out of the room.

Area A of the big old house on Walton Street is mostly an impressive front hall, crusted with marble, chilled by a patterned quarry-tile floor too good (the Trustees said) to cover up with carpeting. Maggie, the black, shiny and very nearly spherical receptionist, reigns here from nine to five, Monday to Saturday – grumbling about the feeble electric fan-heater, nodding to the daily Trustee delegation, repelling any and all doomed enquiries for a reader's card. I had yet to research the turnover time of Maggie's job. The "guardroom" and a small, unreconstructed Victorian lavatory complete Area A.

Once upon a time, it was said, Jasper Trant saw something nasty in the woodshed. The people who strayed into the Bequest between nine and five had often gathered as much from odd sources – a footnote in Aleister Crowley, a sidelong reference in (of all places) H.P.Lovecraft. They came hoping for secret words of power, the poor fossils. Modern spells are written in bright new esoteric languages like C++ and extended assembler. This was the glamour I'd cast over the real-time monitoring system that logged all movement in Area B.

"It's like something out of fucking *Alien*," Keith Ramsey had said the day before. "All those narrow twisty corridors ... it's *designed* to make you expect something's going to jump out at you from round the next corner, or chase you through the bits where you can't run because you've got to go sideways."

Naturally I'd been thinking about it too, and had replied: "My guess is, it was designed that way to make it hard to bring in heavy cutting equipment. Or a trolley big enough to truck out the library. Assuming there really is a library."

"Mmm ... or maybe it was just fun to design. Everyone likes mazes, and why not old Trant? He was a maths don, wasn't he? You know there's a general algorithm for solving any maze. No, not just "follow the left-hand wall", that only works without unconnected internal loops. To find the centre as well as getting out again, what you do is ..."

I was fascinated, but Area B isn't quite that complex. It fills almost all the building, winding up, down and around to pass every one of the (barred) windows, and completely enclosing the central volume in its web of stone and iron. You might get lost for a while, but there are no actual dead ends, or only one.

"You wouldn't get planning permission for *that* nowadays," Keith had said gloomily. "Bloody indoor folly."

I moved along the eighteen-inch passageways now. The dull yellow lamps, too feeble and too widely spaced, bred a writhing mass of shadows. (When the gas-brackets were in use, it must have been far worse.) Our desultory patrols were set to cover the whole labyrinth, with one exception: the short spur where the sensors clustered thickest. Daily at 10 a.m. the grey-headed Trustee and his two hulking minders went down this forbidden path to – consult? check? dust? pay homage to? *"Feed the Bequest,"* came Keith's remembered voice, now artificially hollow. "His expensive leather briefcase, Bob, simply has to be packed with slabs of raw meat. Flesh which is ... no longer of any human shape!"

Remembering the photograph of a certain ex-guard, it was possible to feel apprehension. I thought also of my reconnaissance down at the Welsh Pony pub off Gloucester Green, where it was almost a standing joke that people didn't wear a Trant guard's navy uniform for long. They did not all suffer freak accidents: that would be absurd. By and large, they merely tended to leave after that average six weeks. You could speculate, if you chose, that something had frightened them. The heavy, regulation torch was a comfort in my hand.

Somewhere the real-time watchdog system dreamed its dreams, fed a soothingly "normal" pattern of patrol movements by my rogue software, registering nothing at all in the dense minefield of IR and ultrasonic pick-ups that guarded the way to Area C.

Left, right, left, and there in torchlight was the door: big, grim, banded with iron, deep-set in its massive frame, with a lock the size of a VCR unit. I was half inclined to turn back at that point, because it was a joke. Modern burglars flip open those jumbo Victorian lever-and-ward efforts almost without breaking step. As part of my personal quest, I'd entered other restricted libraries (including sections of the British Library and Bodleian known to very few) and had never seen such a lumbering apology for a lock. But after all, and hearteningly, there was the maze and the electronic network ... something here was surely worth guarding.

"How shall one catch the lions in the desert?" I quoted to myself as I felt for the lock-spring, remembering one of Keith's sillier answers: the hunter builds a cage, locks himself securely in, and performs an inversion transformation so that he is considered to be outside while all the lions are inside, along with the desert, the Earth, the universe ... Perhaps Jasper Trant had liked mathematical jokes. He was here at just about the right time to have known Lewis Carroll, another of Keith's heroes whom I must look up some day.

I was here because of a rumour that Trant's preoccupations, Trant's bequest, had a personal connection with – well – myself.

Click and *click* again. The door swung ponderously inward, and the first torchlit glimpse swept away half my uncertainties. Area C, where the movement sensors did not extend, was indeed a library – a forty-foot square room with wooden bookcases scattered along its iron walls. Ceiling and floor were likewise made of, or lined with, dull iron. A vault.

All this profusion was a disappointment. I had flicked through libraries before. The literature of the occult is stupendously boring and repetitive ... it may contain many small secrets but I had very much hoped that dead Jasper Trant knew one big secret.

Musty smells: old books, old iron and a thin reek of what might have been oil. Keeping close to the wall, I moved cautiously clockwise to the first bookcase. An average turnover time of six weeks. Easing out a random volume with a cracked calf spine, I shone the torch on its title page to find what blasting, forbidden knowledge ...

The Principles of Moral and Political Philofophy by William Paley, D.D.: The Twelfth Edition, corrected by The Author. Vol. I. MDCCXCIX. Crammed with edifying stuff about Chriftianity.

Jesus Christ.

The next one was called *The Abominations of Modern Society.* These included swearing, "leprous newspapers" and "the dissipations of the ballroom", and the author didn't approve of them at all. Then another volume I of Paley ... sermons ... more sermons ... numbing ranks of sermons ... a *third* copy of the identical Paley tract.

I scanned shelf after shelf, finding more and more of the same dull book-dealers' leavings. Junk. All junk. The Bequest library was a fake. Not even a volume of dear old Ovid's *Metamorphoses.*

On the other hand, where does the wise man hide a pebble? On the beach. Where does the wise man hide a leaf ...?

Perhaps. In the centre of the far wall, opposite the door, my flicking circle of torchlight found a cleared space and a long metal desk or table. On the steel surface, a old-fashioned blotting-pad; on the pad, a book like a ledger that lay invitingly open. Cautiously, cautiously, now. There was something almost too tempting about ...

What I felt was minute but inexplicable. I might have put it down to nerves, but I never suffer from nerves. A sinking feeling? I backed rapidly away, and my boot-heel snagged on something, a slight step in the floor. The floor had been smooth and even. Now the torch-beam showed bad news: a large rectangle of iron had sunk noiselessly, with the metal table and myself on it, just less than half an inch into the floor. I thought *hydraulics*, whipped around instantly and blurred towards the door faster than anyone I have ever met could have managed. Too late.

It was all very ingenious. Victorian technology, for God's sake. The 3-D maze construction of Area B must have concealed any amount of dead space for tanks, conduits and machinery. Now, tall vertical panels within the deep door-frame had hinged open on either side to show iron under the old wood, and oiled steel bars moved silkily out and across, barring the way. By the time I reached the door, the closing space was too narr-ow: I could have thrust myself a little way in, only to have neat cylinders punched out of me. The heavy rods from the left finished gliding into their revealed sockets at the right. And that was that.

The space between the bars was about four unaccommodating inches. I thought hard. I still knew one big thing, but was it needed? "Well, I was just curious," I imagined myself saying with a slight whine to Grey Suit in the morning. "It's a fair cop. I don't suppose, ha ha, there's any chance you could keep me on? No? Oh well, that's the luck of the game," and bye-bye to the Jasper Trant Bequest.

Everyone gets curious after a while. Practically anybody would grow overcome with curiosity in an average time of, say, six weeks. Thus the staff turnover. Thus ...

No. I don't pretend to be an expert on human psychology, but surely sooner or later the Trant would end up hiring someone too loyal or too dull to take a peep, and they'd duly hold down the job for years on end.

For the sake of form I tested the bars – immovable – and went back to learn what I might from the disastrous ledger. It was all blank sheets except for where it had lain open. That page carried a few lines of faded blue-black ink, in the sort of clerkly hand you might expect from Bob Cratchit.

Jasper Trant said in his Last Will and Testament that once as a magistrate of the Oxford courts he saw a shape no man could believe, a thing that crawled from a cell window where no man might pass and left naught behind. All through his life he puzzled over this and sought a proof. Here is his bequest.

Here was what bequest? Was this slender snatch of gossip the root of all those rumours about Trant's secret lore of shape-shifters and changelings? Something was missing. Or perhaps I had not thought it through. The path seemed clear: wait till morning, own up like a man, and walk out of the building forever. No problem.

It was then that I looked properly at the steel table which supported the book. It was dreadfully like a medical examination couch. Two huge minders always accompanied the Trustee on his morning visit to Area C. Suddenly I was sure that no errant security guard was allowed to say good-bye without being carefully prodded and probed. Which would not do at all.

The Trant Bequest had circulated its own damned rumours, and fed the fires by refusing any access to its worthless collection. Bait.

How shall one catch the lions in the desert? There was one answer that Keith repeated with a tiny sneer because it wasn't pure maths but mathematical physics. I know even less physics than maths, but swiftly picked up the jeering tone ... protective coloration. The theoretical physicist's answer: Build a securely locked cage in the centre of the desert. Wave mechanics says there is always a tiny but non-zero probability that any particular wave/particle, including a lion, might be in the cage. Wait.

With the long patience of the dead, Jasper Trant had waited.

Shit, I thought, seeing another facet. After six weeks on average, if they hadn't given way to curiosity, each successive Trant guard would be sacked on some excuse or another, to make way for the testing of the next in line. No one who wanted to infiltrate the Bequest would have to wait for long.

I sighed. Four inches between the bars. This would take time and not be at all comfortable. I could not stay around for a possible medical examination: every instinct screamed against it, and I trust my instincts. The Trant Bequest had nothing more to tell me about myself.

So. Off with that smart uniform. The dull, painful trance of change, writhing to and fro on that death-cold iron floor, in the dark. Bones working as in a dream. Muscle-masses shifting, joints dislocating, rewriting the map of myself. The ribs are one thing; the pelvic and cranial sutures are very much harder work to part and rejoin. It went on and on, until at length I was a grotesque flat parody of the Bob Ames who had entered an eternity before. Even so, it would be a long hard wriggle. By now I must look like ...

Well, specifically, like the dead and flattened guard in that photograph. Could *he* have been –? No, it wouldn't make sense, there was a real autopsy and everything. But I did examine the bars more closely, in fear of some hidden trap. Then I stood back and at last glimpsed the trap too obvious to be noticed.

Jasper Trant himself had seen something slip from an Oxford jailhouse cell. Through the bars, no doubt. Bars, no doubt, set just as far apart as those now blocking the Area C door. There was another subtlety here. If this was a snare for people like myself, set by his long-departed curiosity, why the loophole?

Almost I could hear Keith's voice, the eager voice of the mathematician: Didn't you read the mention of "proof" in the book? Wasn't I telling you last night about the austere kind of maths reasoning we call an existence proof? Trant wasn't collecting for a zoo ... he was a mathematician and all his Trustees want is the existence proof. Which they'd certainly have, if after walking in there and triggering the hydraulics you got out through that impossible gap. Don't you *see*?

I saw, and was profoundly grateful to Keith for the patterns of reasoning he'd shown me. It was heady stuff, this reason, a shiny and unfamiliar tool. I couldn't stay and I couldn't go. Knowledge is power and human ignorance is my safeguard. After the long years' trek from that damned children's home in search of more of my kind, whatever kind that might be, I did not propose the betrayal of confirming to these ... others ... that my own kind existed. Which left me caught, like the lion in the desert who ("Ever heard the psychologist's method, Keith?") builds around him, deduction by deduction, the bars of his own intangible cage.

Yes, I owe a great deal to young Keith. Education is a wonderful thing; he taught me how to be a lion. And at the last I remembered one more thing that he'd explained to me, sentences falling over each other in his enthusiasm ... the technique of reducing a difficulty to a problem that has already been solved. All else then follows. Q.E.D.

It was solved, I think, last year.

Caught in this exact dilemma, what did my anonymous cousin do then? He could escape the cage, but at the cost of leaving the Trustees their proof. I salute him for his splendid piece of misdirection. Then as now, there was a second guard, no doubt asleep back in the control room. No live man could have slipped through those bars after springing the trap, but a dead man, topologically equivalent but stamped and trampled and flattened ... In the morning, outside the barred doorway of Area C, there lay an object that might just have been – that to any rational mind must have been – hauled and crushed with brutal force through one narrow space. Hauled from outside the cage. A bizarre and suspicious circumstance, but not one which quite *proved* anything.

So logic points the way. I'm sorry to be doing this, Keith. I'm truly grateful for all our conversations, and will try to make quite sure that you feel no pain.

• Published 1993 in a third shared-world series invented by the Midnight Rose collective – Neil Gaiman, Mary Gentle, Roz Kaveney, Alex Stewart – that brought us *Temps* ("Leaks") and *Villains!* ("The Arts of the Enemy"). *The Weerde* was about Shapeshifters Moving Undetected Among Us, which for no adequately explained reason I linked with one of my favourite playgrounds, the folklore of maths.

The solemn application of mathematics to catch the lions in the desert dates back to 1938. Seekers after truth should hunt for *Seven Years of Manifold: 1968- 1980* (1981) ed. Ian Stewart and John Jaworski, in which the paper "15 New Ways to Catch a Lion" summarizes past research before adding further esoteric silliness.

Karl Edward Wagner reprinted this in his *Year's Best Horror Stories XXII*.

Deepnet

It was during the winter of 1990 that I pieced together ten years' hints, and almost wished I had not probed so deep. A shocking discovery about the world can be equally dismaying as a revelation of oneself. Perhaps committing these rough notes to disk will help clear my thoughts and even save me from the next step which seems so burningly inevitable.

My daughter ...

The secret I think I know is centred on that small American port which I have never visited, although my late wife Janine once had an aunt there, or a cousin. (Too many years have slipped past for me to remember her every casual aside, though I very much wish I could.) All the same, the name is familiar enough in the industry, even though many software users never consciously note it. The title screen of every version of the Deepword word processor flashes up, just for a subliminal instant amid its wavy graphics, a copyright credit to Deepnet Communications Inc. of Innsmouth, MA.

I am using version 6.01 now. For all my new-found misgivings, I am used to its smooth, tranquil operation. We claim the industry is fast-moving and "at the cutting edge", but secretly most of my programming colleagues are creatures of tradition and ritual. Learn different keystrokes in order to make use of a far better program and save much precious time? There is no time for that.

Now I regret not taking time to listen to Janine when she talked about once visiting her small-town relative. Her image wavers in the seas of memory, somehow edited from liveliness to the stiff features of my one surviving picture (she always photographed badly). Her words ... she made a humorous thing of it, but I was far away, thinking in program code. A derelict coastal town amid salt marshes, its few inhabitants straight out of *Cold Comfort Farm*, no doubt inbred for gnarled generations: "*Arrr*," she quoted, "*I mind you do be a furriner in they durned high heels of Babylon, heh heh....* Something like that." If she had lived, it might have ceased to be a joke.

The publicity brochure prattles on about how empty houses filled when prosperity and the software industry came to Innsmouth in the early days of the small-computer boom. New freeways threaded the marsh.

Through the 70s and 80s Deepnet grew into an amorphous multi-national whose tentacles extend everywhere. Those yokels and genetic casualties now only survive in the traditional humour of our trade newspapers; or so we all thought.

I pause here. Sara is telling me, in the thick, laboured voice I have learned to understand, that she wants to play a game on my backup computer. With her tenth birthday almost in sight, she will have to have her own machine soon. Janine wanted more children, but Sara is all I have. I love her very much.

Nevertheless I wish she reminded me even remotely of Janine, who was beautiful.

When the secret history of these times is properly written, I suspect that Janine should have a footnote of her own as one of the earliest recorded victims. Now and only now we are beginning to be told that pregnant women should beware of electromagnetic radiation, and in particular should stay well clear of computer VDUs. Beneath the world's rippling surface there is always some unsuspected horror, lurking as did thalidomide.

In those days of innocence, when the equipment was slower, cruder and doubtless lacking any screen against electromagnetic leakage, Janine and I were not well off. Her income from technical authorship was too important to us, and she stuck to the keyboard until almost the very end of her pregnancy. Worse, she was just a little short-sighted (which gave her grey eyes a fine faraway look), and liked to work up close to the VDU.

The software she used through those final months was Deepword 1.6.

I prefer not to compute just how many hours of that time we really shared. When I'd logged up my own overtime, Janine and I would all too often sit with vision blurred and mouths silenced by the sheer weight of fatigue, as though far underwater.

Of course I said I should be with her for the birth; as usual she read my real feelings and told me not to be a stupid bloody martyr. Even when too enormous to turn over in bed, Janine was kind-hearted and full of humour. The business took a very long time: for me, eleven hours in a grey waiting-room redolent with stale coffee and disinfectant, her last eleven hours. I had never seen a professionally comforting nurse sound so grim as the young one who let it slip that there was some question as to whether even the baby should be kept on life-support.

Before too many more years, I suppose, our tragedy will be seen to fit into the classical pattern of excessive EM field exposure during pregnancy, with its supposed pathogenic effects on tissue and especially young tissue. Miscarriage, for example, or infant leukaemia, or foetal abnormalities.

I was not shown Sara for some time. (I was not shown Janine at all.)

Perhaps her soft bones had been twisted into some insupportable shape by the difficult birth, and later she relaxed as babies do into normality, or mostly so. No one explained to me the stitches on either side of her throat. I wish that first nurse had not looked so sick.

I will admit that Sara is excessively plain.

Watching her work with clumsy fingers at her Undersea Quest game reminds me that I have, in a way, visited the transatlantic home of Deepnet. The demonstration disk for their SHOGGOTH high-resolution graphics design system is one long computerized special effect, a tour of the Innsmouth streets as though you were floating effortlessly along them.

Dominated by the vast squat blocks of the Deepnet complex, it appears as a place of strange contrasts. The stylized images of buildings feature one or two old-fashioned gambrel roofs, and a variety of antique brick and stone houses stand out quaintly from the sea of new development. To show the versatility of the 3-D software, several fanciful touches have been added. One of the monolithic factory structures is, like an Escher print, re-entrant and geometrically impossible; and I am fairly sure that the physical Innsmouth does not include a 250-foot pyramid in its central square, least of all one which slowly but inarguably rotates.

As with all software from these makers, there is something oddly addictive about the SHOGGOTH presentation. Perhaps it is a matter of light and shadow. Instead of whizzing you crudely through the simulated streets in video-game fashion, the ingenious programming team chose to unveil their creation at a lazy pace which, aided by a greenish wavering in the image, gives the subtle illusion of motion underwater.

"Rapture of the deep" was Janine's phrase for when I lost myself in the depths of the computer terminal. It was a joke, but one which went sour on me when I looked back and thought of how little time we'd had together, how much of it I'd spent hacking out program code, enraptured.

Items notably not included in the SHOGGOTH demonstration are the joky legends about Deepnet which surface from time to time in the trade papers. It was *Computer Weekly* which tried to make an amusing paragraph of the story that from their main development facility there runs a 45-inch cable of multichannel fibre-optic linkages which enters the nearby Manuxet estuary, heading seaward towards Devil Reef, and never again emerges. The rival paper *Computing* had a running joke about inbred local workers, bulgy-eyed from endless hours at the VDU, who toil in the depths of the complex and likewise fail to emerge, or not at any rate during daylight.

I reserve my judgment on this gossip. Things very nearly as unlikely are said about DEC and IBM, or any clannish company.

All the same, there is a proverb about straws in the wind....

My suspicions weigh very heavily on me, like the pressure of deep water.

But am I suffering from insight or from insanity? Patterns which connect up too many things can be suspect (and here I remember that VDU radiation has also been *claimed* to induce brain tumours or suicidal depression). I freely admit that I do not possess anything like statistically reliable evidence. If I had more friends, I might be able to offer more examples than those of Janine, and of Jo Pennick, Helen Weir, and certain unknowns at a school near my Berkshire home.

I have spoken of Janine. The others came later.

We contract programmers lead a nomadic life, drifting from company to company, isolated from the permanent staff who resent our skills and high fees. Sometimes we exchange shop-talk in bars (we mostly drink too much). And so I came to hear ...

Mrs Pennick was a heavy user of Deepword 2.2, in the same condition and for much the same reasons as Janine. She died of complications soon after giving birth to her Peter. With Ms Weir it was the Deepcalc 1.14 spreadsheet, a daughter called Rose, and unexplained suicide a month or so later. The unknowns remain unknown and I have no real right to guess at their software heritage. But a dreadful conviction washes over me whenever I see (as so frequently I do) these young children of the VDU age, who presumably have parents or a parent somewhere, and who strongly resemble the unrelated Sara and Peter and Rose. Very strongly indeed.

The polite word, I am told, is "exophthalmic".

I only advance a hypothesis. I dare not commit myself to admitting belief. Even the EM research is still very far from being conclusive. But suppose, just suppose ... That little seaport in Massachusetts has long had an odd reputation, it seems. The term "in-breeding" was often used of its staring natives. Could this conceivably have been a result of deliberate policy?

"Deepnet," says a typical publicity flyer which comes to hand. "Time for your business to move out from the shallows. Take your computer projections below the surface, with software that goes a little deeper. Software from by the sea...."

Taking a hint from the eerie underwater imagery of so many Deepnet products (even their word processor's title screen is decorated with stylized waves), I find "in-breeding" shifting in my mind's eye to "breeding', and again to "breeding back', and I remember that all life arose in the sea. I also remember, unwillingly, the stitches that closed what might conceivably have been slits to left and right of the hours-old Sara's throat.

Very cautiously I allow myself to admit that the EM radiation pattern of a computer display must depend in part on the program driving that display; and to acknowledge that research into this radiation and its biological impact goes back thirty years; and to wonder whether, for twelve years or more, software from a certain source might not intentionally have had certain effects on pregnant users.

Are the children of Innsmouth growing up all around us?

"Deepnet. Great new applications from the old, established market leader. Software for the new generation. Talk to us on the Internet at *innsmouth@deepnet.com*."

One last niggling point concerns my daughter's "Undersea Quest", a best-selling computer game which has won many awards for excitement untainted with violence. Players learn to progress not by attacking but by co-operating with the huge, friendly and vaguely frog-like creatures which populate the game world. It is all very ecologically sound. A full virtual-reality version is promised before long.

Something in the watery glimmer of its graphics made me hunt out the instruction leaflet and look up the makers' name. PSP: Pelagic Software Products, a wholly owned subsidiary of Deepnet Communications Inc. Here is their message to the new generation.

At this point in my speculations I was struck with a vivid image of Janine telling me with her usual twinkle that I am just a thoughtless, sexist beast. Fancy imagining all these terrible consequences for pregnant women, "the weaker vessel", while giving hardly a thought to my own very much longer hours working with Deepnet development software. Twelve years now, at least. Might there not be accumulated effects in *my* body, my brain?

I am terribly frightened that I may already know the answer to that question. In a few years, when the time comes, when her time comes, it will perhaps destroy me unless I first destroy myself. My hands and forehead are unpleasantly damp as I type these final sentences into the edit screen of Deepword 6.01.

"Deepnet. Bringing together the best of the old and new generations. The software family that rides the tide of tomorrow."

Breeding, and in-breeding. These insights come in a single hot moment. Turning to look again at Sara, I saw those big protruding eyes fixed raptly on the screen, and her broad face tinged a soft, delicate green by its light. Overwhelmingly I imagined the salt-sea smell of her, and I loved her and I wanted her.

• Published 1994. An exercise in mixing old (Lovecraftian) and modern dreads.

Serpent Eggs

May 9

When the island first showed itself as a formless dark blot on the shifting greys of sea and sky it should have been a moment full of significance, of boding ... but my attention was elsewhere. One of its people is actually on this boat. And yes, and yes, she has something of what I have been calling the Droch Skerry "look". Besides that odd patchiness of the hair and the dark bruises under each eye, there are points only hinted by the newspaper photograph that first caught my curiosity months ago and on the far side of the Atlantic. A peaked un-healthiness, a greyish, shrunken aspect – well, it's hard to put in words.

Otherwise she would be an ordinarily attractive young women. Her name is Lee something. "Just call me Lee. It'll be great to have a new face on the island." She's loaded with small oddments for people in the Droch Skerry community. Out here on the edge of the Shetlands, going shopping is a major expedition planned weeks ahead. We clung to an icy rail and made small talk on the heaving deck, surrounded by all her sprawling bags and parcels. Luckily I had already picked up a smattering of this alternative-energy lore from books bought *en route*.

For the record – and this casebook might as well carry a complete record – I would not have made the long journey for something as nebulous as a "look". Other sources (the UFO journals, the *Fortean Times*, even the *National Enquirer*) carry tales, recent tales, of this being a region where "something fell out of the sky". Maybe I am even the first to spot what might well be a significant nexus.

Later

What a place. A lone bare lump in the ocean. Grey rock, damp concrete, mist and endless chill ... they say that Spring comes early to the Scottish Islands but they must have meant some other islands.

And the alternative-technology angle! There are straggling windmill towers on the heights, both the ordinary and the vertical-axis kind, flapping in a dispirited way; there are salt-crusted solar panels aimed up into the fog; the toilets are ideologically correct, and stink. Even the quay is low-tech, a sort of natural spit of rock humped like a brontosaur and squared off with wobbly stonework, glistening and slippery from the spray; I nearly killed myself getting my suitcases to firm ground.

The commune was out in force to greet Lee and the shipment from the mainland. Their clash of dingy anoraks and fluorescent cagoules looks cheerful enough until you come closer and see their faces. In various degrees, like Polaroid snaps frozen at twenty different stages of their development, they have that wasted look. Most are quite young.

Stewart Wheatley is the man I corresponded with before coming. He owns Droch Skerry, I think, and runs the commune by his own whims. They led me to him in one of their squat energy-saving houses, and he greeted me under a yellow light that waxed and waned with (I suppose) the wind overhead.

Is there a grey look about Wheatley too? Hard to tell in that pulsating light. He's big and completely bald, looks like a retired wrestler, has one of those arc-lamp personalities whose glare backs you up against the wall like a strong wind. He was throbbingly glad I'd come to join the group, insisted I must call him Stewart, everyone would call me Robert, no formalities on Droch, knew I'd get the most tremendous satisfaction from working alongside this truly dedicated team....

Somehow I never even got around to my carefully prepared story of research work for a magazine article.

There was a meal: all twenty-odd of the islanders at one long table. We ate some sort of meat loaf from tins, wizened vegetables out of the grey salty garden plots I'd seen, and horribly naked shellfish that some of the team (a third of them seemed to be called Dave) had chipped laboriously from the rocks at low tide. Whelks, limpets, some vile winkle things called buckies, and worse. It seemed impolitic to shut my eyes, but they looked as bad as anything described in the grimoires.

The stuff in the chipped tumblers tasted of lime-juice, and a bottle of multivitamin capsules went round the table like the port decanter at some old Oxford college ... so a tentative theory of mine was abandoned. *Not* merely a case of deficiency disease. Good.

Conversation: subdued. They keep one eye on Wheatley, huge at the head of the table. I said, not strictly truthfully, that the shabby wind-farm was impressive.

"You should hear what they cost," said Lee at once with an edge in her voice. "Low technology is our watchword, Robert. We've set ourselves free from industrial civilization, except the bits that sell wind generators."

"Have to start somewhere," muttered a scanty-haired, haggard man who I gathered was called Rich.

Wheatley told me, "Lee would like us to live in caves and eat roots – Rich is disappointed that in five years we haven't yet covered the skerry with dams and refineries."

I asked him which he favoured, and he said rather grandly that he was an eco-opportunist who made the best use of whatever was available: money, weather, materials …

"Mussels," said a voice to my right, not with enthusiasm.

"Eggs."

I do not know how to convey the chill that crept into that long, stuffy eating hall. Some seemed as puzzled as myself by the sudden silence; some looked sidelong at Wheatley as though expecting a cue.

"Dave," he said gently. "Not, not you, *you*. I've just remembered … it's your turn to go on watch tonight."

The indicated Dave gave a small nod. Clearly it had not been his turn. It was a punishment. Disciplinary.

On watch? Where and for what?

Later

Or might it conceivably be sickness after all? Wheatley alone has a private room. In the men's dormitory before lights-out, much pallid flesh was visible. Those with more pronounced cases of the "look" seem to suffer unusually from bruises on their arms and legs – great piebald splotches.

Of the toilets I do not choose to write more. ("We return *everything* to the soil." The sooner the better. These people's digestive systems do not seem in good order.) The bathrooms are tolerable and give a few minutes' privacy to bring these notes up to date. How the heating systems are shared between the windmills, diesel generator and those joke solar cells remains a dark mystery, but after a tepid start the shower surprised me by running hot.

Tufts of thin hair lie on the floor, sticking to my wet feet. I have seen it coming out in wads on their combs.

In my locked suitcase there are certain signs and wards that may offer a little protection against … against? I have followed up some odd cults (not with any great success) in a dozen decayed holes of old Britain and New England, but have rarely known such a compelling sense of being *too close*.

May 10

Already I have to pay the price of offering myself as a willing worker. Today's choice is limpet-work on the western shore, or some nameless task involving a cranky and obstinate biomass converter which will one day heat the buildings with methane or blow them sky-high … or plain digging. That sounded the safest. Four hours scratching with an undersized fork at a vast tract of ground which was to blossom with yams, kiwi-fruit or something equally unlikely. Occasional jets thundered overhead according to the whim of the Royal Air Force, thick as flies in these "remote" parts. Seagulls and scrawny hens pecked after me for worms. It offered time to think.

The impression I have is that the commune members who are further gone in the "look" are those who have been here longer. Rich is one of the original few and has it very badly. He said hello just now, on his way to "look over the number-two windmill cable – it's leaking to earth." Not keen to have me come and see. "I get uptight if people watch me work-ing."

I watched him scramble up the slope, though, up beyond the weak fingers of greenery that reach towards the central granite gnarl. The rocky climb is rotten with industrial archaeology: cable runs, abandoned scaffolding, the wreck of a windmill that hadn't been anchored right, pipes snaking this way and that to tap what I suppose must be fresh-water springs. In one or two places there are ragged wisps of steam. A long scar of raw stone marks where Wheatley had (according to Lee) tried to blast the foundations for something or other. Rusty stains bleed down the rock. The place is a mess.

There were tolerant smiles for me when I staggered into the kitchen, aching and blistered, clammy with sweat despite the chill air. Lee and someone called Anna cracked age-old jokes about feeble city muscles; another of the Daves offered me soup hot from the midget electric stove that is another of Droch Skerry's compromises with self-sufficiency. There is a certain sardonic amusement in counting just how many compromises there are. Boxes and boxes of Kleenex tissues, not even recycled!

(But a tiny puzzle is lurking there too. Longer-standing members of the group will sometimes snatch a few tissues and turn aside from whatever is going on, not sneezing but quietly pressing the things to nose or mouth. Once or twice as the wadded-up tissue goes into the fire, I have thought to detect a splash of red.)

So I've worked for Droch Skerry and am halfway to being accepted. Coming a little way in makes one oddly sensitive to divisions further in, before you reach Wheatley and the centre. As though there were things which A and B might speak of together but not discuss with an outer circle of myself and Lee and half a dozen others.

May 11

Something fell out of the sky. The vague UFO rumours are sober truth.

In between work shifts it's quite allowable to go for a walk. "But when you know the place by heart," said Lee with half a smile, "the fun goes out of it rather."

Even in this eternal weeping mist, there ought not to be enough of Droch Skerry to become lost in. Its many granite shoulders are hunched and knotted, though; the grassy folds between them twist in a topologist's nightmare; the closer you look, the longer any journey becomes. Especially, of course, when you're not in the least sure what you hope to find.

Granite, gorse, granite, rabbit droppings, matted heather, gorse, granite, endlessly repeated....

It was in the tenth or twentieth coarse wrinkle of the ground that the irregular pattern seemed to break. Less of the prickly gorse here, perhaps, and more of it withered and brown? This fold of the island dipped further down than most, a long sheltered combe or glen that ended at a cliff over deep water. I pulled gingerly at the nearest dead gorse and it came up in my hand, roots long broken and dry. Then, coming to the edge of a roundish depression in the ground, I tripped over something like a doormat.

Not a doormat. A slab of turf that hadn't taken root. And next to it another, and another.

Part of the combe had been painstakingly re-turfed in chequerboard squares. Some of these turves had dried and died before they could knit into a smooth carpet of salt grass. When I stood back, the oval hollow in the ground rearranged itself in my mind's eye. It was a crater where something had impacted, hard, from very high up. One bulging granite rock nearby was marked with a bright smear of metal. I could imagine Wheatley's little workforce laboriously covering up what had happened, and ...

What had it been and where was it taken?

The only further information I thought I could extract from this fold of the island was that – it seemed – a large and heavy bulk might have been dragged to or from the cliff edge. I had a hazy vision of something vast and formless rising from the sea, or returning to it.

Not long after, a dim shape along roughly those lines came looming out of the thin mist. It resolved itself into Wheatley, carrying a shotgun and the bloody rags of several rabbits strung into a bunch. The gun barrel wavered erratically, sometimes pointing at his own foot, or mine. "Our Rich catches the little buggers in humane snares," he said in a conversational tone, "but where's the challenge in that? You shouldn't come this way on your own. It's treacherous."

I had not found it so, and said something non-committal.

"Believe me. See you've had a fall already."

It was ridiculous to feel guilty, trapped, as my eyes followed Wheatley's down to the muddy and grass-stained knees of my jeans. Was it so obvious that I'd spent time minutely studying the ground?

"Oh," he said, "and I should avoid the heights altogether. If I were you."

May 13

I constantly feel the circles within circles at these strange meals in that close, smelly room. (Deodorants do not seem to figure largely in the alternative life; no matter how often we all resort to the showers, we aren't a salubrious lot *en masse*.) There is what you might call a Lee faction which does not like relying on the dark gods of Western industrial civilization even for microchips, paracetamol or the band-aids that decorate every other hand. The inner ring have a more Robinson Crusoe approach, feeling justified in snatching anything from the world's wreck as the pelagic deeps close over it. Sometimes they seem to be talking in code about some great and significant coup along these lines. "Power for the people," they say, and it means something more than an empty slogan. Wheatley watches over this with a curious air of controlled force, fraught with doom and significance, as though by lifting one finger he could abolish any of us. I think he may be an adept.

We are a democracy here and decide everything by show of hands, but suggestions not to the master's liking are never put to the vote. People change their minds in mid-proposal, turned by his pale gaze.

A special treat tonight: after some days' accumulation, the island's bedraggled hens have provided eggs all around. I never met boiled eggs so small and odd-tasting, but appetites here are small. Rich, who looked very bad tonight, collected a dozen half-shells and idly (it seemed, until I saw others' faces) arranged them on the table, unbroken end up, in a ring. A circle of power. It had some kind of power, because I saw Wheatley frowning like thunder. He rose early and the meal was over.

In the dormitory late on, eyes tight shut, I overheard a brief exchange. One of the Daves, the black one from Jamaica, was not looking forward to some coming night duty. "Man. Every hour on the hour. That light up there really genuinely gives me the creeps." He was answered, not quite intelligibly from where I lay in "my" clammy bunk. But I believe a Name was pronounced. It is a central axiom of the old knowledge, of which I have learned so desperately little, that the forces that crawl under the thin bright reality we know all have their separate names, and may be called.

On watch. "Up there."

Avoid the heights.

May 16

Where does the time go? You can lose yourself in a community like this: hoeing, hunting for driftwood, carrying water in the 20-litre plastic drums that are comfortably liftable and an agony after thirty seconds' walk. There are a hundred running jokes about life here – away from the mainland, the job centre, the dole. Apart from the occasional strange no-go areas in conversation, I like these people.

But.

You can't get newspapers here, nor a decent steak or cup of coffee. We sit in a shivering circle around the radio and hear the pulse of the world, but see nothing. Lee says there is always going to be satellite TV on the skerry *next* month. It was a shock to leaf through mouldy old magazines stacked in the store-hut against some dim future notion of recycling, and be reminded of normal faces; of the fact that something on Droch is *wrong*, no matter how easily one becomes used to the ruined look people wear here. I ran, almost, to scan my own face in a shaving-mirror. Anxious and none too clean, but not (yet?) wearing that mark....

It is not lack of vitamins. Precautions are taken. It does not appear to be any of the legendary miscegenations of the literature – the notorious "Innsmouth look" or the seal-man hybrids of Island folklore – but something subtler. These people have no lifelong roots here. From personal knowledge of a friend who died, I think it is not AIDS.

Tonight I plan to watch the watcher on the heights.

Later

Bright light-bulbs indoors mean gales outside, the windmills screaming up above. Rather him than me.

In brief: when I heard the wind take the front door and slam it, I counted an interminable five minutes of seconds ("one and-a-pause, two and-a-pause, three and-a-pause"). Then I got up as naturally as possible and padded off towards the toilet. Out in the upper-floor passage, thick and smeary windows show part of the hillside behind the commune buildings; I hoped I might see a light.

To my surprise I saw it quite soon, a flicking torch beam that danced to and fro impatiently while its invisible source mounted the rocks with infinite slowness and care. Lacking survey equipment, I did what I could and knelt to watch one-eyed, chin on the deep window-ledge, tracing each position of the light by touching my pen to the window-glass. In the grey of morning the marks might show up and indicate a path, or not....

The light vanished. Surely it could not have reached and passed the crest? I waited another age, shivering in my pyjamas, and suddenly found the flicker again – now unmistakably descending.

A memory: "every hour on the hour," I'd overheard. The watch was not a continuous one. Somehow this made it even odder and more disturbing.

May 17

After the usual unsatisfactory breakfast, the upstairs passage seemed full of comings and goings I'd never noticed before. I dodged guiltily to and fro, unable to be alone with my window; in the end I invented a story about a touch of diarrhoea (common enough here), and then felt I had to brood in the lavatory for the sake of verisimilitude each time.

Eventually I was able to squint from what I hoped was the right position, and see how the blurred smears of ink on the glass overlaid the hillside. The end of the dancing light's journey must have been in *that* area, above the raw scar in the rocks, some way to the left of that tangle of old iron.

After a while I thought I saw a patch of black ... an opening? The old places under the Earth. With a wholly disproportionate effect of dread, a wisp of fog seemed to trail from the blackness like dog's breath on a chill morning.

I must record that I have played around with these investigations in libraries and ancient college archives, and have never before reached a position where the next logical step is to climb a hill in slippery darkness and crawl into a black cavity. I record that I am sick with fright.

Since I am officially frequenting the toilets, I'm thus today's logical choice to carry all the buckets out for return to the soil and cleansing in the sea. As I trudged back from the fourth trip Wheatley chose to waylay me and say, "You're settling in nicely, Robert." And as a seeming after-thought: "You should get more sleep at night."

When next upstairs I remembered to wipe my felt-pen tracing from the window. If anyone had noticed, it could have meant nothing to them. Surely.

Light relief of the evening: Anna, who is interested in something called biodynamic gardening, said we should preserve our excrement, stuff it into sterilized cow horns and bury them at the winter solstice to be transmuted by cosmic and telluric forces. Dug up in Spring, minute quantities of the result would make Droch Skerry bloom like the garden of Findhorn. Wheatley laughed out loud and scoffed at her mercilessly. I noticed that Anna, like most of the women here, wears a headscarf all day long; it covers the thinning hair.

I judge that Lee will need a scarf soon. I *like* Lee. Something ought to be done about the shadow on this damned place.

Tonight, then.

Later

Inventory. Plenty of wellington boots, anoraks and electric torches for night emergencies, waiting in the big kitchen. A little shamefacedly I am wearing a scrap of parchment inscribed with certain elder signs, carrying a vial of powder compounded from a protective formula. One does not wholly believe in these things and yet they can offer comfort.

What do I expect to see? I don't know. If there's anything in sortilege, though, my eye fell today on a balloon in the Krazy Kat collection from our ramshackle library: "I sense the feel of evil – Every nerve of me vibrates to the symphony of sin – Somewhere, at this moment, crime holds revel." That's it.

May 18, around 1:20am

The cave mouth. It is a cave; could be natural. Water streams from it and is lost in the rocks. Warm water.

The climb was very bad; my shins must be bleeding in a dozen places. Bitter wind. I think it was Rich making the every-hour-on-the-hour visits at midnight and one. Plenty of time before two. Keep telling myself, Rich and several others have stared again and again into whatever abyss waits there, and come out unscathed.

Except for the worrying way they *look*....

Shortly after

Have to stoop slightly and splash my way. Firm underfoot except when I trip over the ubiquitous pipes. A warm breath blowing from further in, a seaside reek. There seems to be a bend ahead, and a hint of blue light when I click off the torch. "That light gives me the creeps." The hiss and moan of the wind in the cave mouth drowns out another sound ahead, I think; in the lulls it seems to be a faint ... bubbling?

Later

I cannot get over that terrible glare he gave me at the last.

The chamber might be natural, and the spring that pours into it, but the deep, brimming pool is surely not. (I remembered those scars of abortive blasting activities.) The pool holds something bleak and alien. All in a ghostly blue light.

There are things down there, eight things like great eggs, each the size of a man's skull, suspended in a complex cradle of ropes anchored to the stony floor around the rim ... a precisely spaced ring of devil's eggs, a diagram of power, a gateway? All around them the water glows in deadly blue silence. Bubbles rise from them, every bubble a blue spark, the whole pool fizzing and simmering. Thick, choking warmth in the air.

One half-remembered phrase kept writhing through my mind like a cold worm: "... *a congeries of iridescent globes* ..." It was a long while before I could even look away from the incomprehensible blue horror that held me with a snake's gaze.

A rack of rust-caked tools: hammer, chisel, knife. More coils of rope. A prosaic notebook hanging from a nail on the wall, damp pages full of scribble in different handwritings. "17/5 0100 OK no adjust – R." I shuddered most of all at the innocent-looking pipe that led away, and down the slope outside, towards the houses.

Then I heard the scraping down the passageway and knew that I was caught. Beyond the troubled pool the floor and roof became a wedge-shaped niche for dwarfs, and after that nothing at all.

Wheatley, gigantic in this low-ceilinged space, was not carrying the shotgun as carelessly as he had in the open. I backed away uselessly over granite slippery and treacherous with condensation.

"You probably know already: no one can climb up here after dark without showing a light to half the island," he said reasonably, pacing my slow retreat around the pool. "Now what are we going to do with you?"

"What *is* that monstrosity? What force makes the light?" I said, or something of the sort.

"A very well-known one. Never heard of Cherenkov radiation? Nor me, but Rich understands all this stuff. My God, can't you imagine how we felt when that Eurostealth bomber came down smash on top of Droch Skerry? Over the cliff with it, except for the cores, and there they are. Talk about swords into ploughshares, talk about power for the people. We might have had some leakage trouble early on, but we're the first community with its own alternative-technology reactor. Piping-hot water for all our showers, all our ..."

I understood only that in his raving he had allowed the gun barrel to wander again. The plastic phial of Ibn Ghazi powder was in my hand by then; logically I should have cast it into the accursed waters, but I threw it at Wheatley instead. Common salt, sulphur, mercury compounds; all more or less harmless, but perhaps it had some virtue, and he caught it in the eyes. With a not very loud grunt he lurched off-balance, the shotgun fired and rock chips exploded from the floor, the recoil (I think) took him over backwards, and his head struck hard on a spur of granite as he splashed into the warm seething water.

I could not bring myself to dive after him. The sinking body spun lazily down towards the terrible eggs and their aura of hellish radiance. For an instant Wheatley's whole face glowed translucent blue, and the light somehow filled his eyeballs, a final unseeing glare at me from eyes that were discs of blue fire. Then he floated slowly to the surface and became a lumpish silhouette against the evil light below. He no longer moved.

It must be stopped. This rot, this ulcer, this tumour in the clean rock. The circle of "cores" lets in something bad from outside the world we know. Break the circle. Break the symmetry.

The old knife from the rack haemorrhages wet rust at every touch, but it has the remnants of an edge beneath. Hack through the ropes and the strange eggs will no longer be arranged in that terrible sigil; they'll sink and nestle together in a ragged bunch at the bottom of the water. Whatever esoteric contract is fulfilled by that careful spacing will be broken apart.

The logic cannot be faulted. I don't know why I find myself hesitating.

May 2???

It is very hard to write now. Around dawn they found me half-conscious on the rocky hillside. I suppose I slipped and fell. My nerve had failed me as the loosed eggs glowed hotter, cracked as though about to hatch, while raw steam erupted from the foaming pool. By the time I'd stumbled to the cave mouth there was a superheated blast in pursuit, a roar of dragon's breath. The rest of that bad night has sunk out of memory, apart from the jags of pain. RAF helicopters came clattering down in the morning light to investigate the tall plume of steam and something else that still wound snakelike into the sky.

"Jesus Christ, we've got our own Chernobyl," I heard one of the uniformed crowd mutter.

The mark of Droch Skerry is fully on me now. My hair flees by handfuls, I bleed too easily, food is hateful and fever sings in my blood. Lee has visited me, and wept. Wheatley's tomb is said to be sealed with a monstrous plug of concrete. That is not dead which can eternal lie. They say the others can nearly all be saved. To one or two I am a kind of hero. They say.

I still do not wholly understand....

• Published 1994, revised 1997. I originally wrote this in the late 1970s as a "straight" story about the investigation of a community with a secret, and later decided that the ironies of the group's mad approach to alternative technology could usefully be balanced by an investigator looking for the wrong thing and laden with the wrong preconceptions. Go hunting a horror out of Lovecraft and find a worse horror out of physics.... The *Krazy Kat* quotation is, of course, authentic.

Stephen Jones reprinted this in *The Mammoth Book of Best New Horror #9*.

Blood and Silence

H'mm. I did think we'd manage a better turn-out for *this* meeting. It's not just another boring weekly update on a crank project – you ought to know that. So much has happened since last Monday! With any luck we're headed for a Nobel Prize, and my little presentation today is going to be famous ... not just through a lot of pop-science bestsellers but in *history* books, for goodness' sake. Of course you and the team will all receive full credit.

So. Hello John, hello Carol, hello Patrick, and I have three faxed apologies for not coming in to the lab today, plus four more by e-mail.

As you know, last Tuesday we had our lucky break and the V-syndrome hypothesis can now be taken as strongly confirmed. I also have a extra surprise for you, just in this morning! But first, let's have a look at Patrick's splendid scanning electron micrograph of V itself. When I finish my paper I shall certainly give him special credit. Will you do the honours, Patrick? What? Throat? Laryngitis? Doesn't stop you working an overhead projector, does it? Ladies – lady – and gentlemen, the star of the show....

> *Awash with false colour, the image of the giant virus resembles nothing familiar ... perhaps a half-melted triumphal arch painted in the hues of delirium by Salvador Dali. It cannot possibly look sinister. It is too abstract. Nevertheless, to those armed with foreknowledge, it radiates a certain cool menace.*

I'm thinking we should call it the Alucard retrovirus, ha ha. According to Carol's initial report, which she'd read to us right now if it weren't for a nasty case of toothache (sorry to hear it, Carol, and I hope that swelling goes down soon), the job it seems to have done on the DNA in our sample is *radical*. We have some interesting confirmation in that area ... that's the surprise I was talking about, and it came from New Scotland Yard.

As you may know, this whole project started over there with one of their backroom geniuses, a chap called March who specializes in weird crime patterns. He runs what they call (not for public consumption) the Department of Queer Complaints, with a devil of a lot of computer power processing the kind of reports any sane person would throw in the bin –

or send to the *Fortean Times*. And when they correlated a bundle of stuff about burglaries with nothing missing, puncture wounds, blood loss, unbelievable speed and strength, and so on and so on ... he suggested the V hypothesis. We don't use the V-word itself because we're reasonable scientists, but the way March put it was that if there were something that *behaved like* such a creature, he or she or it bloody well ought to be investigated.

His database seeming to be hinting at a centre of activity in south-west London: Richmond or Kingston. Since they outsource so much for-ensic work to us, we were the natural choice to help design the equipment for that empty flat in Latchmere Road. Two years waiting. Never in the history of civilization has one room been so massively monitored and booby-trapped for so long. And even then ...

This isn't the video you saw last week. It's been image-enhanced and generally cleaned up. Much clearer now. Here we go.

There is something at the window, street-lights throwing a hunched, malformed shadow on the curtains. The shadow's deformity is a lie: the figure that enters wears an impossible perfection of poise, moving to the bedside with silent, fluid grace. Even in the room, though, it remains featureless, a grainy silhouette against the white dazzle which is what image amplifiers make of the window's dim glow. Those who watch the video picture know that lying beneath the sheets is a dummy, artificially warm, its breath and heartbeat an endless tape loop: the policewoman chosen for her close fit to the victim pattern has retired to another, fortified room after con-spicuously drawing the curtains here. This bedroom is not a safe place to sleep ...

... as becomes evident when the man (man?) in close-fitting black bends too closely over the false sleeper. An instant's total white-out as unleashed energies jolt the power lines. There is a violent metallic clatter, followed by a steady hiss. Pale clouds are billowing from the innocuous-looking wardrobe, and a device like an oversized handcuff is seen to have clamped itself around the visitor's left ankle. The body flicks through a dozen positions as through in strobe lighting, but that leg is shackled, immovably, to heavy machinery underneath the bed. There can be no escape.

It is the lack of pause for thought that chills. As though trained in this gesture through years of some murderous ballet school, the captive whips out a glinting blade and within four seconds of blurred movement is messily free. All in a silence that screams. The narcotic gas never has time to act. There is still a certain appalling

grace in the one-legged, headlong leap through the window.
  On the floor, the severed foot is a dark blot lying in a dark pool.

Serendipity, that's the word. The way he got away tells us so much! There's absolutely no tourniquet work in that video, yet the artery has closed off before he's moved a step. You couldn't have a stronger hint that the ... V-word ... legend about regeneration might have a basis in reality, a genuine foothold in the real world, ha ha.

When Rosie in Pathology dissected the specimen, she found that the muscle density was medically impossible. (In my draft paper she does of course receive due credit.) But that's not as bad as the real eye-opener on Friday, when our radioisotope analysis of the bone cores came through with the news that – unless the software has gone completely haywire – this fellow had been alive and kicking since *approximately* 1820. Give or take a decade. And yet the skin was fresh, unscarred, like a kid in the early teens. Quite a few of us have this strong hunch that our friend is walking on a brand-new foot by now. Er, yes Carol, don't look like that: I know you were first with that little idea, and believe me you will get the credit for it.

Well. All of a sudden the V virus starts to look highly desirable! We'll have to keep our samples under lock and key! Luckily it can't be particularly contagious, or these retooled people would be everywhere. An injection, though, of enough infected blood or culture medium ...

Well may you nod, John, well may you nod. You're right to look worried.

But before we get too fussed about half the country fighting over the chance to be biologically re-engineered by the V agent, I have a new video to show you. This puts matters in a slightly different light, and may also clear up the tooth question. We expected, didn't we, to find the traditional overdeveloped canines? That side of it must be an unfounded part of the V myth. We've been over all the trap records, and both the flash X-ray and ultrasound scan seem to agree that the guy's teeth were no pointier than yours or mine.

About the garlic thing and the sunlight thing, we just don't know until we have an experimental subject of our very own. They're hard to hire. Ha ha.

It was March who passed on this new video, another spot of serendipity. I really will have to acknowledge the New Scotland Yard assistance in my coming major paper. They were trying an experimental surveillance system in a certain public toilet near Richmond Park, where naughty things are supposed to happen by night. And what they saw ... lights! action! camera!

The image of one dark figure against a background of white-tiled glare seems momentarily to be a still picture; but then it flicks to a new position, and another, like poor stop-motion animation. In this spy camera, moving-picture quality has been traded off against better resolution. The man busies himself at the public urinal ... and blink, blink, blink, another figure is at his side. Both figures begin to grow, in a flickering zoom-in: the moron software behind the camera takes note of supposed anomalies like two men standing side-by-side at adjacent urinal stalls, when English reserve indicates the keeping of a discreet distance unless forced into proximity by a crowd. Perhaps there will be a brief encounter in a lavatory cubicle, thinks the prurient program, zooming in to get mugshots that might one day be credible in court....

Blink, blink, blink.

It is an encounter. One man has his arms round the other. There is no recourse to a cubicle. It is an anomalous encounter. The man in black leather with the beautiful, feral face (but oddly plump and full cheeks) has accosted the older, greying, respectable-looking gent. Things tend to be the other way around. Blink, blink, blink. With movement chopped into this salami of freeze-frames, it is hard to be certain that the older man is struggling to escape. But the emotion on his jowled face is not lust.

Blink, blink, blink. It emerges frame by frame from the young man's wide-open mouth. It ought to be a tongue but is huge and alien, glistening black: the bloated thing must fill the entire mouth when retracted, but now it extends, stretching and thinning like a questing leech. Blink, blink. White fear in the old eyes behind their bifocal spectacles. Blink. Needle-tipped, the leech-organ stabs for the jugular vein. For many frames thereafter the picture is unchanged, except that the victim slowly, very slowly, wilts....

God, that gives me the creeps even the second time around. I gather they nodded it through as death by exposure. March said there are some stories for which a British coroner's court is not yet ready, and I suppose he's right.

Well, this is what we call strong confirmation, isn't it! Affected persons must find it hard to hide: open their lips and they're condemned out of their own mouths, ha ha. So the V agent does indeed remodel the body. Incredible. And yes, Carol, I know that insight was originally yours. You needn't sulk. In my paper ...

Look. I think we ought to have this out. I really expected you to be bubbling over with ideas and analysis after the first public showing of that little video nasty from the Yard. Not just sitting there looking glum. I know there are some bitter feelings in this lab, simply because protocol absolutely demands that as Director I should write the official paper on all this. I happen to be aware – because I've seen e-mail that wasn't meant for me – that some of the team, naming no names, think I burnt out as a scientist twenty years ago. They reckon I'm too slow on the uptake to deserve any glory. No doubt *you* all saw the possibilities of the V virus last week while you were working hands-on with it and I was busy with the hard slog of co-ordinating the reports and arranging our press conference. Nevertheless I promise that everyone will receive proper credit. And indeed you can all have a voice in the preparation of the paper.

Aren't you going to *say* anything?

Have I been sent to Coventry?

Cat got your tongues?

... oh, *dear* ...

• Published 1995. Well, every genre author sooner or later has to have a go at some kind of twist on the vampire legend, right?

Basilisks

For Gordon Van Gelder of *The Magazine of Fantasy and Science Fiction*, who bought the one that got a Hugo.

BLIT

It was like being caught halfway through a flashy film-dissolve. The goggles broke up the dim street, split and reshuffled it along diagonal lines: a glowing KEBABS sign was transposed into the typestyle they called Shatter. Safest to keep the goggles on, Robbo had decided. Even in the flickering electric half-light before dawn, you never knew what you might see. Just his luck if the stencil jumped from under his arm and unrolled itself before his eyes as he scrabbled for it on the pavement.

That would be a good place, behind the 34 (a shattered 34) bus stop. This was their part of town; the women flocked there each morning, twittering in their saris like bright alien canaries. A good place, by a boarded-up shop window thick with flyposted gig announcements.

Robbo scanned the street for movement, glanced at his own hand to be reassured by a blurred spaghetti of fingers. Guaranteed Army issue goggles – the Group had friends in funny places – but they said the eye eventually adjusts. One day something clicks, and clear outlines jump at you. He flinched as the thick plastic unrolled; then the nervy moment was past, his left hand pressing the stencil against a tattered poster while in his right the spray-can hissed.

The sweetish, heady smell of car touch-up paint made it all seem oddly distant from an act of terrorism.

He found he'd been careless, easy in this false twilight and through these lenses: there were tacky patches on his fingers as he re-rolled the Parrot. A few hours on, in thick morning light, the brown women would be playing the wink game.... Jesus, how long since he'd been a kid and played *that*? Must be five years. The one who'd drawn the murder card caught your eye and winked, and you had to die with lots of spasms and overacting. To survive, you needed to spot the murderer first and get in with an accusation – or at least, know where not to look.

It was cold. Time to move on, to pick another place. Goggles or no shatter-goggles, he didn't look back at the image of the Parrot. It might wink.

SECRET * BASILISK
Distribution UK List B[iv] only

... so called because its outline, when processed for non-hazardous viewing, is generally considered to resemble that of the bird. A processed (anamorphically elongated) partial image appears in Appendix 3 of this report, page A3-ii. THE STATED PAGE MUST NOT BE VIEWED THROUGH ANY FORM OF CYLINDRICAL LENS. PROLONGED VIEWING IS STRONGLY DISRECOMMENDED. PLEASE READ PAGE A3-i BEFORE PROCEEDING.

2-6. This first example of the Berryman Logical Image Technique (hence the usual acronym BLIT) evolved from AI work at the Cambridge IV supercomputer facility, now discontinued. V. Berryman and C.M. Turner [3] hypothesized that pattern recognition programs of sufficient complexity might be vulnerable to "Gödelian shock input" in the form of data incompatible with internal representation. Berryman went further and suggested that the existence of such a potential input was a logical necessity ...

2-18. Details of the Berryman/Turner BLIT construction algorithms are not available at this classification level. Details of the eventual security breach at Cambridge IV are neither available nor fully known. Details of Cambridge IV casualty figures are, for the time being, reserved (*sub judice*).

"IRA got hold of it somehow," Mack had said. "The Provos. We do some of our shopping in the same places, jelly and like that ... slipped us a copy, they did."

The cardboard tube in Robbo's hand had suddenly felt ten times as heavy. He'd expected a map, a Group plan of action; maybe a blueprint of something nasty to plant in the Sikh temple up Victoria Street. "You mean it *works*?"

"Fucking right. I tried it ... a volunteer." He'd grinned. Just grinned, and winked. "Listen, this is poison stuff. Wear the goggles around it. If you fuck up and get a clear squint at even a bit of the Parrot, this is what you do. They told me. Shut yourself up with a bottle of vodka and knock the whole lot back. Decontamination, scrubs your short-term visual memory, something like that."

"Jesus. What about the Provos? If this fairy story's got teeth, why haven't they ...?" Robbo had trailed off into a vague waving gesture that failed to conjure up a paper neutron bomb.

Mack's smile had widened into an assault-course of brown jagged teeth, as it did when he talked about a major Group action. "Maybe they don't fancy new ideas ... but could be they're biding their time for a big one. Ever thought about hijacking a TV station? Just for an hour? Don't think things like that, it'll be bad for you."

... Dead TV screens watched him from another cracked shop window, a dump that also rented Hindi videotapes. That settled it for them. Why couldn't the buggers learn English? The Group would give them a hint: the Parrot stencil was already in position, the can sliding out of his pocket, fastest draw in the west. At school Robbo had never won a fight, had always been beaten down to cringing tears: he'd learned good, safe, satisfying ways of hitting back. Double-A Group booby-trap work was the best of all, a regular and addictive thrill.

This had better be the last for now, or last but one. Twenty would be a good round number, but the sky seemed to be lightening behind its overlaid sodium-light stain.

If he went round Alma Street way he could hit the Marquis of Granby, where everyone said the local gays hung out. Taking over a good old pub, bent as corkscrews and not even ashamed of it, give you Aids as soon as look at you, the bastards. Right in the middle of their glazed front door, then, glaring red and a foot high....

The light hit him like a mailed fist. The goggles parsed it into bright, hurtful bars. Robbo spun half around, trying to shield his eyes with the heavy, flapping something in his left hand. The heavy something had a big irregular hole in it; torchlight blared through, and, moving quickly closer, there was a voice. "Like to tell me what you're ...?"

As the beam dipped and the voice trailed off, he saw the shivered outline of a police helmet through that of the Parrot. Behind jagged after-images a face came into view, an Asian face as he might have expected this end of town. The eyes stared blindly, the mouth worked. Robbo had read old murder mysteries where the unmarked body wore an inexplicable expression of shock and dread. A warm corpse slumped into him, its momentum carrying them both through a window which dissolved in tinkling shards.

It wasn't supposed to be like this. The bomb wasn't supposed to go off until you were six miles away. Somewhere there was the broken outline of a second helmet.

SECRET * BASILISK

... independently discovered by at least two late amateurs of computer graphics. The "Fractal Star" is generated by a relatively simple iterative procedure which determines whether any point in two-dimensional space (the complex field) does or does not belong to its domain. This algorithm is now classified.

3-3. The Fractal Star does not exhibit BLIT properties in its macrostructure. The overall appearance may be viewed: see

Appendix 3, page A3-iii. This property allowed the Star to be widely disseminated via a popular computer magazine [8], a version of the algorithm being printed under the heading "Fun With Graphics". Unfortunately, the accompanying text suggested that users rewrite the software to "zoom in" on aspects of the domain's visually appealing fractal microstructure. In several zones of the complex field, this can produce BLIT effects when the resulting fine detail is displayed on a computer monitor of better than 600 x 300 pixels resolution.

    3-4. Approximately 4% of the magazine's 115,000 readers discovered and displayed BLIT patterns latent within the Fractal Star. In most cases, other members of family units and/or emergency services inadvertently became viewers while investigating the casualty or casualties. Total figures are difficult to ascertain, but to a first order of approximation ...

"Tape the envelope, all round. That's it. And write DANGER DO NOT OPEN in ruddy big letters, both sides, right?"

"So you know all about it."

"There've been bulletins. The squaddies picked up fifty in that Belfast raid. Leeds CID got another ... some bastard just like this one. I tell you, this job's been a shambles for years and now it's a fucking disaster. Three constables and a sergeant gone, picking up a spotty little shit you could knock flying just by *spitting* at him...."

Robbo hurt in a variety of places but kept still and quiet, eyes shut, slumped on the hard bench where ungentle hands had dropped him. He'd told them every place he'd hit, but they'd kept on hurting him. It wasn't fair. He felt the draught of an opening door.

"Photo ID positive, sir. Robert Charles Bitton, nineteen, two previous for criminal damage, suspected link Albion Action Group. Nothing much else on the printout."

"I suppose it makes sense. Vicious sods: run into them yet, Jimmy? Nearest thing we've got here to the Ku Klux fucking Klan."

"This one'll be out of circulation for a good long while."

"Jimmy, you *haven't* been keeping up to date with this BLIT stuff, have you? It's the same as that fucking nightmare with the kids and their home computers. God knows how much longer they can keep the lid on. It's going to get us all sooner or later.... Look. We are going to have four PMs with cause of death unknown, immediate cause heart failure, and have I really got to spell it out?"

"Ohhh."

"The only evidence is in that sodding envelope, a real court clearer eh? I remember when they nicked those international phone fiddlers way back when, and all we could do them for was Illegal Use Of Electricity to the value of sixty pee. They didn't have a phone-hacker law those days. We haven't got a brain-hacker law now."

"You mean we clean up after the little bastard, give him a nice room for what's left of the night, and that's *it*?"

"Ah." The tone of voice implied that something extra was going on: a gesture, a finger laid significantly alongside the nose, a wink. "Car Three cleans up, they've got the eye safety kit, for what that's worth. We show young Master Urban Terrorism to his palatial quarters, taking the pretty way of course. And then, Jimmy, when the new shift arrives we hold a wake for our recently departed mates. No joking. It's in the last bulletin. You'll really appreciate hearing why."

Robbo braced himself as the hands got a fresh grip on him. The outlook sounded almost promising.

SECRET * BASILISK

... informational analysis adopts a somewhat purist mathematical viewpoint, whereby BLITs are considered to encode Gödelian "spoilers", implicit programs which the human equipment cannot safely run. In his final paper [3] Berryman argued that although meta-logical safety devices permit the assimilation and safe recognition of self-referential loops ("This sentence is false"), the graphic analogues of subtler "vicious circles" might evade protective verbal analysis by striking directly through the visual cortex. This may not be consistent with the observed effects of the "Reader" BLIT discussed in section 7, unusual not merely because its incapacitation of cortical activity is temporary (albeit with some observed permanent damage in Army volunteers [18]), but also because its effects are specific to those literate in English and English-like alphabets. There may in addition be a logical inconsistency with the considerations developed in section 12.

10-18. Gott's *post facto* biochemical counter-hypothesis [24] was regarded as less drastic. This proposes that "memotoxins" might be formed in the brain by electrochemical activity associated with the storage of certain patterns of data. Although attractive, the hypothesis has yet to be ...

12-4. The present situation resembles that of the "explosion" in particle physics. Not merely new species of BLIT but entire related families continue to emerge, as summarized in Appendix A2. One controversial interpretation invoked the Sheldrake theory of morphic resonance [25]: it might be simpler to conclude that multiple simultaneous emergence of the BLIT concept was inevitable at the stage of AI research which had been reached. The losses amongst leading theorists, in particular those with marked powers of mathematical visualization, constitute a major hindrance to further understanding.

The cell was white-tiled to shoulder height, glossily white-painted as it went on up and up. Its reek of disinfectant felt like steel wool up the nose, down the throat. In a vague spirit of getting the most from the amenities, Robbo patronized the white china toilet and scrubbed his hands futilely in the basin (cold water couldn't shift those red acrylic stains) before lying down to wait.

They couldn't touch him, really. They might fine him on some silly vandalism charge, and he might accidentally fall down a few more flights of stairs before reaching the magistrates' court ... even now the hard bunk caught him in all sorts of puffy, bruised places. But in the long run he was OK.

They knew that.

They knew that but they hadn't seemed bothered, had they?

He had a flash, then, of them smiling, "We aren't pressing charges," and "This way, sir," and "If you could just pick up your property...." A door would open and guess what would be waiting there for him to see?

Silly. They wouldn't. But suppose.

Time passed. The terminus was easy to imagine. He'd seen it so often through the shatter lenses, a long bird profile sliced at an angle and jaggedly reassembled: parrot salami. In outline against walls and windows and posters; as a solid shape in glistening red that lost its colour to orange sodium glare; in outline again as a dead man's broken eyes met his.

It seemed to hover there behind his closed eyelids. He opened them and stared at the far-off ceiling, spattered with nameless blobs and blots by the efforts of past occupants. If you imagined joining the dots, images began to construct themselves, just as unconvincing as zodiac pictures. After a time, one image in particular threatened to achieve clear focus....

He bit through his lip, took refuge in a brief white-out of pain.

It was in him. They knew. Even with protection, he'd looked too long, from too many angles, into the abyss. He was infected. Robbo found himself battering at the heavy metal door, bloodying his hands. Useless, because just as there was no clear crime he could have committed, there was no good medical reason why unfriendly police should offer him a massive, memory-clouding dose of alcohol.

Flat on the bunk again, he ran for his life. The Parrot stalked him

through the grey hours of morning, smoothing its fractal feathers, shuffling itself slowly into clarity as though at the end of a flashy film-dissolve, until at last his mind's eye had to acknowledge a shape, a shape, a
wink

• Published 1988. The idea of BLIT images had been stewing in my mind for a long time, probably owing something to Douglas Hofstadter as well as various sf antecedents of the notion – some cited below in "comp.basilisk FAQ". As usual for this length, the story took shape in one frenzied, obsessive writing session. It seemed to touch a nerve, somehow: I certainly hadn't expected fan letters from Charles Platt and Bruce Sterling, and still less that the notion would receive explicit homage – mentioning me by name – in later science fiction by Greg Egan (*Permutation City*), Ken MacLeod (*The Cassini Division*), and Charles Stross ("Router"). Before any of these appeared, I had already written and published the second BLIT story which follows.

What Happened at Cambridge IV

To whom it may concern:

There is death in this package. I send it to you because you're considered a dubious risk. Not by myself: I promise I have no notion of who you are or what you think. The address comes from a handy list compiled by our security office, a list (to put it bluntly) of potentially undesirable contacts in this part of the Thames Valley. If one of our staff were seen having a quiet drink with you, they would have been ... nudged. Of course, it's impossible to tell how reliably unreliable you are: when I look at List U and see people called Murphy and O'Shea, I can't help wondering whether any real probing was done, whether the computer just threw up its chips in horror at the name.

Well. Perhaps you're honestly outraged at the thought of being branded with a secret smear. I should tell the police if so: obviously you won't be the first. My advice in this case is *not* to open the sealed envelope that came with this. (Don't open it yet, in any case. This is a serious warning.) It's remotely possible that being an officious bigmouth, I mean of course a public-spirited citizen, could ease your name into a computer file much less innocuous than any list at Cambridge IV.

You could burn everything here, of course. But of course there'll be an investigation, and List U will be part of the information they work with. All right: I hereby announce my intention of mailing this at random to only a certain number of the Listed. Should you be the person I'm aiming for ... hide this package and lie when they come to ask. You have an excellent chance of getting away with it.

The innocent can leave us now.

Still with me? Good ... but be warned. People have already died for what you're holding. Before you even think of opening the sealed envelope, you'll need some background. That isn't exactly true, but this is *my* last will and testament, and I make the rules. You won't be compromised, yet. The background details are harmless. It's the big picture that kills.

(For all I know, you may be on List U simply for sharing a quirk with me.)

To begin. Cambridge IV is much nearer to you than Cambridge, as you will have cleverly deduced from the postmark. This is governmental thinking: a Discreet establishment with a focus on information technology should have an oh so subtly computer-evocative name. Somebody thought of Alan Turing, the theoretical pioneer – you may have heard of his famous thought experiments, the Turing machine (an abstract universal computer) and the Turing test. He was a fellow of King's at Cambridge, and that's all the connection there is. As for I to III, they don't come into this.

A Discreet establishment is one your taxes pay for, but which isn't surrounded by all the rigmarole of guard dogs, armed police, sensor fences and NO PHOTOGRAPHY. The only trace they leave, if big enough, is a blank white spot on Ordnance Survey maps. A good place to work if you like your privacy; not so good when the funding begins to run out, since job security (unlike the other kind) is in short supply at a location that officially doesn't exist.

So, I write from my green-walled office in a nonexistent building. The only significant items present are a graphics printout looking like a dark and hook-beaked bird; a frozen bolt of lightning in perspex on my desk; and a bottle of whisky whose level is sinking fast.

Cambridge IV funding has been steadily declining for eighteen months. As Deputy Director I have tried to keep it going, fought to keep Whitehall interested in what I told myself could be a vast new insight into minds, brains and computers. Alternatively, the hydrogen bomb of psychological weapons. I snipped at the staffing table like a surgeon determined to prove that a human being can indeed live without limbs, a stomach, one lung, one kidney, half the liver, two-thirds of the brain ... however that dreary list goes on. I fought endless rearguard actions against the cuts, because I believed in –

No.

I can be honest here. In the beginning I thought Cambridge IV was the biggest damn-fool idea since phlogiston. What I believed in was Vernon Berryman, the originator and research leader, and a man in the genius class of Turing himself. Poor Vernon.

Alan Turing committed suicide, they say, in 1954. Do you know why? The climate is more liberal today, *except* in sensitive government establishments. If one were different one could be blackmailed. What with? Well, one would lose one's sensitive government job if it came out. Why should that be? Because we can't have people who could be blackmailed occupying sensitive government jobs. And so on, forever.

Dr Vernon Berryman did not commit suicide. He had a regrettable accident. He had a triumphant accident. A crabbed accountant in Whitehall killed him. I killed him. Each man kills the thing he loves.

Let me tell you about the project work now.

Ceri Turner was supposed to be the physiological/neurological expert, digging out data about the brain's wiring for Berryman and his mathematical models. Smooth, blonde, heavily perfumed, the sort of overstuffed young woman who gives wet dreams to teenagers. Her legs were quite nice if you liked the type. I was unconvinced about her on the intellectual side (she came from America, where they'll hand a Ph.D to anything that can read, write and sit on its bottom for long enough). Berryman was absurdly courteous, giving her joint credit for papers which were ninety-five per cent his. If his name had been Wherryman I swear he'd even have put hers first.

She provided the input, and Berryman worked miracles. I could copy some bits out of "their" major paper here ... you won't find it in *Nature* or *New Scientist*: the classification is SECRET * BASILISK, named distribution only. It's a sort of small honour for an establishment as tiny as Cambridge IV to have its own identifying marking. "Basilisk" is very much nearer the bone than the Cambridge allusion, as you'll see. An indication, perhaps, that those who hand out such labels didn't really take us seriously.

As I said, I could reprint parts of "On Thinkable Forms, with notes towards a Logical Imaging Technique" here, but if I know you – as naturally I don't – you're a practical person. You have no interest in sitting through twenty pages on the Entscheidungs Problem, Gödel's Theorem, and Berryman's own unnerving theoretical extensions. Instead, there's a little indoctrination chat I know by heart and trot out for visiting dignitaries and purse-string holders. It's as practical as an Armalite rifle. It goes like this:

Kurt Gödel showed that all formal logical systems have flaws: true theorems that can't be proved, shattering paradoxes that won't go away. Alan Turing translated this into practical terms with his proof that some problems aren't computable: an ideal computer set to solve them would grind on forever. Vernon Berryman noted that the human mind can be thought of as a computer, assumed that Turing's "computability" has a parallel in human "thinkability", and set out to find the logical input which clouds the minds of men. His new insight: while the mind can always refuse to accept a problem, the pattern-handling systems of the visual cortex can instantly and willy-nilly accept huge blocks of data from the eye....

In other words, I'd say at this point as I poured out the restorative dose of single-malt, Dr Berryman thinks that with a neural computer system the size of the Supernode Plus in our basement, plus present-day knowledge of how the brain works, we have the key to "uncomputable" patterns that take advantage of the flaws which mathematics says the mind must have. A pattern which compels attention, perhaps, a pattern from which you couldn't easily look away. And depending on rather careful judgement of my audience (male? reasonably bright? sense of humour? like me or not?), I'd then produce a big card-mounted *Penthouse* nude and watch the sequence. Attention momentarily caught in quicklime; an artificial blink; a studied glance away, with excessive unconcern.... We're all so predictable. If I was lucky, they'd finish the sequence with a smile.

There, I'm not as old and stuffy as you'd expect of a Deputy Director. I feel I do need to wear a dark suit and waistcoat, but I draw the line at Whitehall's pinstripes. If I hadn't decided otherwise, there'd be years to go before retirement or even the big 6. Not past it at all.

Berryman was thirty-four. They say mathematicians do their best work relatively young. Turing cracked the Entscheidungs Problem in his twenties. I would never have made a fool of myself over Berryman, but ...

I did, though. I made an infernal machine.

The latest round of government cuts was threatening the Supernode Plus itself: if we fired two more operators, the shift system would break down and the wretched machine wouldn't be able to handle Berryman's all-night runs.

That was the week after I knew what was wrong with me, wrong or gloriously right. Absurd to tell of it: I passed Berryman in the corridor as he padded off to the toilet in his shirt-sleeves, and something turned over inside me. Narrow-faced and intense, very white skin and very black hair, and the dark shadow of his nipples through the thin shirt. I was married for eight tolerably pleasant years, until May went down with cancer. Nothing in those years ever hit with a lightning-flash like *that*.

One picks at these details, the turn of a head, the curl of a thin finger, and tries to pin down blame. The details explain nothing. It's the sum total that kills.

If Cambridge IV had to shut down, its director would be retired or just possibly transferred, while its mathematical genius carried his hat round half a dozen universities that would love to have him if only they could justify the project grants. Perhaps the Turner woman would follow him too: I felt sure she was making eyes at him. Never to pass in a corridor again.

I was very circumspect, very discreet. But I built an infernal machine. (Did a little shock of interest go through you then? Perhaps you're my man.) Nothing intricate or mechanical – I have the remnants of a science degree, but my fingers are too sausage-clumsy for work like that. No, I travelled first-class into the vast anonymity of London and bought two gadgets from a photographic outfit in the Tottenham Court Road. A cosmopolitan little shop in Soho supplied the newspaper, and I spent five pounds more on a piece of cheap plastic trash from an open suitcase on the pavement. I was insane, of course.

You might as well know the details. The "Sonic Shutter" is supposed to be for self- and group portraits: whistle or snap your fingers, and the shutter clicks, the flashgun fires. It had stuck in my mind for its sheer stupidity. Who wants to be photographed for posterity with pursed lips or cocked fingers? The electronic flashgun was the cheapest available, and the point about the trashy digital watch was its alarm. Wearing lab gloves, I taped and wired them all together, to give me a timed flash: but first I took pliers and wrenched off the flashgun's battery compartment cover. Now, as anyone could see, the battery would stay put only if wedged. A wad of paper did the trick nicely, folded from the imported Russian-language edition of *Pravda*.

There's no great level of internal security. Cambridge IV doesn't exist, so prowlers are not expected. Often you can pace alone through the dead light and air, listening to that feeble roar of ventilation which always makes me think "corridors of power". I paid one of my occasional visits to the computer hall, where in an unreal universe of silicon and optoelectronics a ghostly simulation of the human brain was under attack – assaulted by Berryman's image programs, and so far resisting every one. The brain's electrochemical immune system has fended off most of the conceptual viruses evolution can throw at it ... though intangible things can go wrong, can't they? And do.

As always, activity stopped while I looked officiously around. Ceri Turner lay with eyes closed on the interface couch, meditating or some such nonsense while the EEG fed the simulation with her brain rhythms. Her red-stockinged legs were stretched out vulgarly: the idea of *her* as a standard brainwave reference! The operators stared in resentment at their keyboards, unwilling to catch my eye in case I commented on paperbacks and playing cards. My package of junk went on to a high, blue bank of power conditioners. I blew my nose loudly into the handkerchief I'd wrapped round my fingers. That was all. The cleaners would be suspected, but you can't make an omelette, etc.

I *was* insane, of course. The miserly forces of Whitehall had made me insane. I wanted to turn their own murderous, paranoid logic against them, to jolt them into the notion that an establishment worth sabotaging must be an establishment worth preserving. But perhaps I'm being too clever for you? My infernal machine doesn't sound very deadly? Trust me. It was far deadlier than I thought.

In a vague spirit of self-improvement I always used to skim the computer newspapers sent free throughout the trade (officially we are Amber Data Systems, to account for our purchasing pattern). One can pick up some interesting information: specifically, the reason why flash photography tends to be forbidden in major computer installations.

Next morning floppy-jowled Symond, our security chief, explained it all to me pompously, with vast technical detail about the intricate electronics that had been used. He'd become important for a day, and was savouring it *ad nauseam*.

The misguided saboteur, he said, must have assumed the computer hall had an old-fashioned fire protection system. Electrical fires often start with a brilliant flash. (I nodded my wise nod of total incomprehension.) Had the sensors been connected to an old-style array of sprinklers, the entire computer system could have been soaked and ruined. Luckily, the saboteur didn't know one important fact. (I managed another blank nod.) Modern defences, like ours, stop fires in their tracks by sealing all doors and driving out every trace of oxygen with a flood of fire-retardant gas.

"So no damage was done?" I said. The operators, of course, are trained to run like hell when the siren sounds.

"There'll be a manslaughter charge when we catch the bastard."

For too long I stared blankly at the fossil lightning on my desk.

Afterwards I worked out that there was no trap: Symond failed to eye me critically while tossing his thunderbolt, failed to note the whirliness and shock that drove the sense from me in a flood of inert horror. Through the churning, I dimly caught the word "Doctor". Symond bored remorselessly on about unauthorized late-night sessions (Berryman had been driving himself hard), and the picture filled itself in automatically. A visit to collect print-out or whatever; sirens, panic, a slip and fall in belated haste, a moment's dizzy confusion, and the doors are sealed....

Then Symond dropped a new word into my numbness, and curdled it into something else. The word was "she"; a doctor can be a Ph.D as well as a D.Phil. Ceri Turner had been running late that night, on into the night with one of Berryman's runs, and the idiot woman had tested a private theory that I couldn't have predicted. She died through her own fecklessness. I refuse to accept any blame. I had nothing against her, nothing serious. I hoped she and Berryman hadn't had anything between them, because if so I wouldn't be able to be sorry.

Symond departed with hints that there were international ramifications and that he had a Clue. It would have been a terrible thing, on that morning, to laugh.

What an idea, though! More sympathetic magic than science. It was in her notebook – I have it here now – a pastel thing with flowers on its cover and the austerely scientific heading THINKS. "#136. Input reference-level brainwave patterns assoc. with forced loss of consciousness. Quaaludes?" And with the crazed open-mindedness of Darwin experi-

mentally playing the trombone to his tulips, she'd fed herself a safe dose
of barbiturates on the couch; only, that night, nothing that blocked out
sirens was safe. They found her convulsed and ugly, still linked to the
systems. I cannot accept –

Enough.

So I'd bought us time by the logic of Whitehall, at the cost of a
sacrifice. The investigation pottered on for a while, the only result being
a revised and slightly shorter List U. They might have found and deported
some suspicious immigrants, or cleared others from all shadow of doubt:
who knows? Funding was discreetly increased. What I'd done didn't
deserve to work, but it had.

Berryman worked on furiously. He said he was sniffing on the track
of something new. "Rich uncharted seas," he said. "Ceri ... I'm sorry. I
need time." There was a trace of guilt when he mentioned her name, as
though he and I were accomplices. I didn't understand that until later.

I had to ration my contacts with Berryman, for fear of being caught
staring at the fine silky hairs on the backs of his hands. Nor could I avoid
him: this was no time to distort the pattern of our days at Cambridge IV,
and perhaps attract attention. For almost the first time in my life I
regretted my middle-class education: at a public school, I'd gathered,
certain overtures are learned. Could I have picked up a body-language
familiar to Dr Vernon Berryman of Winchester and (like Turing himself)
King's?

Time passed. The project reports grew ever more optimistic. The
mathematical brain-model took some hard knocks: but in spite of Berryman's frantic, doomed intensity, we seemed no nearer to a real-world
version of the simulated success. One of the failed images is still pinned
to my dingy office wall: a horrid black thing like half a Rorschach blot, a
fractal shape whose outline vaguely suggested a bird. I remember the
weekly Project Working Party meeting at which we solemnly discussed
what safeguards should be taken against an "active" image, one that
really did stab into the visual cortex with stunning or paralysing force.
The Psychiatric Liaison woman suggested the scrambler glasses used in
some perception test: the things were specially made at a frightful price,
and we couldn't justify the purchase at that time.

(In the early days of the Manhattan Project, did they ponder on better
bullet-proof vests and stouter plate-glass to withstand the new weapon?
I wonder.)

Gradually the money supply began to fall off again, not overtly cut
but gently eroded by inflation. Three times a day I sighted Berryman and
felt the impossible gulf widen between us. Other times, I sat at the wide
mahogany desk appropriate to my rank and made wild plans. I would put

forward the theory of a broad spectrum of response to the image technique. Volunteers would be called for. I would steal equipment from the optics lab that we never used. Trial viewings of test images would take place under laboratory conditions. Somehow I'd manipulate the volunteer selection process. My weak-eyed, epileptic subject would come in for test on a sunny day, wearing polaroid glasses. Unknown to anyone else, the window opening on the harmless image would conceal a polaroid sheet which a hidden motor could rotate. Gazing through glasses and window on Berryman's latest effort, my victim's field of vision would flicker on and off as the planes of polarization crossed and recrossed. The blink rate would be five times a second. *Petit mal.* Berryman vindicated. Roars of applause.

That was one of my more sensible schemes. I had gone so far as to check that the optics lab had stocks of polaroid plastic. It was, of course, a mere fantasy. The real end of Cambridge IV has outdone any of my fantasies.

Each man kills ...

It happened between three and four hours ago. I can only write the postscript and obituary. Why did we think that when the human computer tried to tackle a visual program it could not run, the only result would be disorientation?

The nastiest of the ironies is that I, put out to grass as a mere administrator, laid the fuses of catastrophic success all by myself. Ceri Turner had a wild theory that brainwave feedback from drugged sleep would lower the Supernode simulation's defences ... later, when Berryman analysed the session records, he found something better than a digitized pattern of sleep. It could be the making of his career at her expense (and *did* he love the woman? Did he?). The electromagnetic signature of death.

The frozen lightning bolt sits on my desk, a souvenir from the gigavolt facility at – never mind. Most people think it's some sort of feathery white seaweed or coral, preserved in perspex. The plastic is charged to a whopping voltage throughout, and an earthed spike driven into the base. When the smoke clears, the forking, fractal paths of the discharge are captured forever. The final lightning-stroke in Turner's mind was caught like that, in silicon and optoelectronics, for Berryman to discover. Show a scientist a pattern, and he can usually work out how to reproduce it.

Oh God.

There is a grim scene I remember from Mark Twain's *A Connecticut Yankee in King Arthur's Court*, where knight after armoured knight is felled by an electric fence. A growing heap of death as each hapless knight touches the conductive armour of the last. This, brought up to date, is the picture I saw in Vernon Berryman's workroom ... the first fruit of our collaboration. His work is a brilliant success.

The desk faces his door. The graphics display is thus not visible until, one by one, the passing project technicians go to find why Berryman is slumped in his chair, and look over his shoulder into the terminal. Only I, on my own regular tormented visit, had the faith to believe in his triumph. Instead of peeping at once, I went away and thought.

It was with closed eyes that I snapped my way through roll after roll of the Polaroid (capital P this time) film they use to record EEG displays. This is the other reason why you should not have opened the sealed envelope. It also contains a standard-format computer diskette holding the last few days' notes and programs, downloaded from a dead man's terminal. You must know a bright computer enthusiast with your own political leanings, one who can make use of Berryman's graphics algorithms. Tell him to be very careful.

Why? Why all this? Indirectly, I killed Berryman myself. Whitehall killed him too, both through miserable funding (he *might* have viewed his latest, ungrateful pet through the scrambler optics we couldn't afford) and by starting a project which one might say was morally appalling. Before you sneer: these are all quibbles. I don't care about people any more. When I began to care specially, for you know who, the relationship was killed by intolerant, paranoid policies before it could ever be born. You are my revenge. Afraid of AIDS, are they? Now there's a psychic AIDS that's no respecter of rubbery protectives.

Open the envelope with great caution. Remember, politicians don't like to fiddle round with details; they want an overview of the big picture. Send a letter to your MP for me.

Myself ... A last glass of the pale Glenlivet, for VIP visitors only. A last walk outside Cambridge IV, briefcase bulging with Her Majesty's prepaid envelopes, to the nearby pillar-box in a crowded, sunlit High Street. And finally I'll join the sacrificial victims heaped behind my love like Egyptian servants in a noble's tomb, and before I look into the screen and over the edge I'll touch his hand at last.

• Published 1990, after a rare argument about the title: I wanted to keep the link to a Cambridge IV reference in "Blit", while David V. Barrett, editor of the *Digital Dreams* anthology, fancied a change to "Crashing the System". In the end I got my own way. Meanwhile Terry Pratchett – whose name, to the embarrassment of all, appeared in much larger print than David's on the front cover – perpetrated the title: "# ifdefDEBUG + 'world/enough' + 'time'".

I saw that paperweight many times in, ahem, a classified location, and wrote it into and out of several stories before finding a place where it seemed to fit.

comp.basilisk FAQ

Frequently Asked Questions
Revised 27 June 2006

1. What is the purpose of this newsgroup?

   To provide a forum for discussion of basilisk (BLIT) images. Newsnet readers who prefer low traffic should read comp.basilisk.moderated, which carries only high-priority warnings and identifications of new forms.

2. Can I post binary files here?

   If you are capable of asking this question you MUST immediately read news.announce.newusers, where regular postings warn that binary and especially image files may emphatically not be posted to any newsgroup. Many countries impose a mandatory death penalty for such action.

3. Where does the acronym BLIT come from?

   The late unlamented Dr Vernon Berryman's system of math-to-visual algorithms is known as the Berryman Logical Imaging Technique. This reflected the original paper's title: "On Thinkable Forms, with notes towards a Logical Imaging Technique" (Berryman and Turner, Nature, 2001). Inevitably, the paper has since been suppressed and classified to a high level.

4. Is it true that science fiction authors predicted basilisks?

   Yes and no. The idea of unthinkable information that cracks the mind has a long SF pedigree, but no one got it quite right. William Gibson's Neuromancer (1984), the novel that popularized cyberspace, is often cited for its concept of "black ice" software which strikes back at the minds of hackers – but this assumes direct neural connection to the net. Basilisks are far more deadly because they require no physical contact.

Much earlier, Fred Hoyle's The Black Cloud (1957)
suggested that a download of knowledge provided by a
would-be-helpful alien (who has superhuman mental
capacity) could overload and burn out human minds.

A remarkable near-miss features in The Shapes of
Sleep (1962) by J.B. Priestley, which imagines archetypal
shapes that compulsively evoke particular emotions,
intended for use in advertising.

Piers Anthony's Macroscope (1969) described the
"Destroyer sequence", a purposeful sequence of images used
to safeguard the privacy of galactic communications by
erasing the minds of eavesdroppers.

The comp.basilisk community does not want ever again
to see another posting about the hoary coincidence that
Macroscope appeared in the same year and month as the
first episode of the British TV program Monty Python's
Flying Circus, with its famous sketch about the World's
Funniest Joke that causes all hearers to laugh themselves
to death.

5. How does a basilisk operate?

The short answer is: we mustn't say. Detailed
information is classified beyond Top Secret.

The longer answer is based on a popular-science
article by Berryman (New Scientist, 2001), which outlines
his thinking. He imagined the human mind as a formal,
deterministic computational system – a system that, as
predicted by a variant of Gödel's Theorem in mathematics,
can be crashed by thoughts which the mind is physically or
logically incapable of thinking. The Logical Imaging
Technique presents such a thought in purely visual form as
a basilisk image which our optic nerves can't help but
accept. The result is disastrous, like a software stealth-
virus smuggled into the brain.

6. Why "basilisk"?

It's the name of a mythical creature: a reptile whose
mere gaze can turn people to stone. According to ancient
myth, a basilisk can be safely viewed in a mirror. This is
not generally true of the modern version – although some
highly asymmetric basilisks like B-756 are lethal only in

unreflected or reflected form, depending on the dominant
hemisphere of the victim's brain.

7. Is it just an urban legend that the first basilisk
destroyed its creator?

Almost everything about the incident at the Cambridge
IV supercomputer facility where Berryman conducted his
last experiments has been suppressed and classified as
highly undesirable knowledge. It's generally believed that
Berryman and most of the facility staff died.
Subsequently, copies of basilisk B-1 leaked out. This
image is famously known as the Parrot for its shape when
blurred enough to allow safe viewing. B-1 remains the
favorite choice of urban terrorists who use aerosols and
stencils to spray basilisk images on walls by night.

But others were at work on Berryman's speculations.
B-2 was soon generated at the Lawrence Livermore
Laboratory and, disastrously, B-3 at MIT.

8. Are there basilisks in the Mandelbrot Set fractal?

Yes. There are two known families, at symmetrical
positions, visible under extreme magnification. No, we're
not telling you where.

9. How can I get permission to display images on my
website?

This is a news.announce.newusers question, but keeps
cropping up here. In brief: you can't, without a rarely
granted government licence. Using anything other than
plain ASCII text on websites or in e-mail is a guaranteed
way of terminating your net account. We're all nostalgic
about the old, colourful web, and about television, but
today's risks are simply too great.

10. Is it true that Microsoft uses basilisk booby-traps to
protect Windows Ultra from disassembly and pirating?

We could not possibly comment.

• Published 1999, fulfilling a dream that had seemed impossible since I ceased to
work as a scientist in 1980. Thanks to the short-lived "Futures" column to which
numerous sf authors were invited to contribute, I finally appeared in *Nature*.

Different Kinds of Darkness

It was always dark outside the windows. Parents and teachers sometimes said vaguely that this was all because of Deep Green terrorists, but Jonathan thought there was more to the story. The other members of the Shudder Club agreed.

The dark beyond the window-glass at home, at school and on the school bus was the second kind of darkness. You could often see a little bit in the first kind, the ordinary kind, and of course you could slice through it with a torch. The second sort of darkness was utter black, and not even the brightest electric torch showed a visible beam or lit anything up. Whenever Jonathan watched his friends walk out through the school door ahead of him, it was as though they stepped into a solid black wall. But when he followed them and felt blindly along the handrail to where the homeward bus would be waiting, there was nothing around him but empty air. Black air.

Sometimes you found these super-dark places indoors. Right now Jonathan was edging his way down a black corridor, one of the school's no-go areas. Officially he was supposed to be outside, mucking around for a break period in the high-walled playground where (oddly enough) it wasn't dark at all and you could see the sky overhead. Of course, outdoors was no place for the dread secret initiations of the Shudder Club.

Jonathan stepped out on the far side of the corridor's inky-dark section, and quietly opened the door of the little storeroom they'd found two terms ago. Inside, the air was warm, dusty and stale. A bare light-bulb hung from the ceiling. The others were already there, sitting on boxes of paper and stacks of battered textbooks.

"You're late," chorused Gary, Julie and Khalid. The new candidate Heather just pushed back long blonde hair and smiled, a slightly strained smile.

"Someone has to be last," said Jonathan. The words had become part of the ritual, like a secret password that proved that the last one to arrive wasn't an outsider or a spy. Of course they all knew each other, but imagine a spy who was a master of disguise....

Khalid solemnly held up an innocent-looking ring-binder. That was his privilege. The Club had been his idea, after he'd found the bogey picture that someone had left behind in the school photocopier. Maybe he'd read too many stories about ordeals and secret initiations. When you'd stumbled on such a splendid ordeal, you simply had to invent a secret society to use it.

"We are the Shudder Club," Khalid intoned. "We are the ones who can take it. Twenty seconds."

Jonathan's eyebrows went up. Twenty seconds was *serious*. Gary, the fat boy of the gang, just nodded and concentrated on his watch. Khalid opened the binder and stared at the thing inside. "One ... two ... three ..."

He almost made it. It was past the seventeen-second mark when Khalid's hands started to twitch and shudder, and then his arms. He dropped the book, and Gary gave him a final count of eighteen. There was a pause while Khalid overcame the shakes and pulled himself together, and then they congratulated him on a new record.

Julie and Gary weren't feeling so ambitious, and opted for ten-second ordeals. They both got through, though by the count of ten she was terribly white in the face and he was sweating great drops. So Jonathan felt he had to say ten as well.

"You sure, Jon?" said Gary. "Last time you were on eight. No need to push it today."

Jonathan quoted the ritual words, "We are the ones who can take it," and took the ring-binder from Gary. "Ten."

In between times, you always forgot exactly what the bogey picture looked like. It always seemed new. It was an abstract black-and-white pattern, swirly and flickery like one of those old Op Art designs. The shape was almost pretty until the whole thing got into your head with a shock of connection like touching a high-voltage wire. It messed with your eyesight. It messed with your brain. Jonathan felt violent static behind his eyes ... an electrical storm raging somewhere in there ... instant fever singing through the blood ... muscles locking and unlocking ... and oh dear God had Gary only counted four?

He held on somehow, forcing himself to keep still when every part of him wanted to twitch in different directions. The dazzle of the bogey picture was fading behind a new kind of darkness, a shadow inside his eyes, and he knew with dreadful certainty that he was going to faint or be sick or both. He gave in and shut his eyes just as, unbelievably and after what had seemed like years, the count reached ten.

Jonathan felt too limp and drained to pay much attention as Heather came close – but not close enough – to the five seconds you needed to be a full member of the Club. She blotted her eyes with a violently trembling hand. She was sure she'd make it next time. And then Khalid closed the meeting with the quotation he'd found somewhere: "That which does not kill us, makes us stronger."

School was a place where mostly they taught you stuff that had nothing to do with the real world. Jonathan secretly reckoned that quadratic equations just didn't ever happen outside the classroom. So it came as a surprise to the Club when things started getting interesting in, of all places, a maths class.

Mr Whitcutt was quite old, somewhere between grandfather and retirement age, and didn't mind straying away from the official maths course once in a while. You had to lure him with the right kind of question. Little Harry Steen – the chess and wargames fanatic of the class, and under consideration for the Club – scored a brilliant success by asking about a news item he'd heard at home. It was something to do with "mathwar", and terrorists using things called blits.

"I actually knew Vernon Berryman slightly," said Mr Whitcutt, which didn't seem at all promising. But it got better. "He's the B in blit, you know: B-L-I-T, the Berryman Logical Imaging Technique, as he called it. Very advanced mathematics. Over your heads, probably. Back in the first half of the twentieth century, two great mathematicians called Gödel and Turing proved theorems which ... um. Well, one way of looking at it is that mathematics is booby-trapped. For any computer at all, there are certain problems that will crash it and stop it dead."

Half the class nodded knowingly. Their home-made computer programs so often did exactly that.

"Berryman was another brilliant man, and an incredible idiot. Right at the end of the twentieth century, he said to himself, "What if there are problems that crash the human brain?" And he went out and found one, and came up with his wretched "imaging technique" that makes it a problem you can't ignore. Just *looking* at a BLIT pattern, letting in through your optic nerves, can stop your brain." A click of old, knotty fingers. "Like that."

Jonathan and the Club looked sidelong at each other. They knew something about staring at strange images. It was Harry, delighted to have stolen all this time from boring old trig., who stuck his hand up first. "Er, did this Berryman look at his own pattern, then?"

Mr Whitcutt gave a gloomy nod. "The story is that he did. By accident, and it killed him stone dead. It's ironic. For centuries, people had been writing ghost stories about things so awful that just looking at them makes you die of fright. And then a mathematician, working in the purest and most abstract of all the sciences, goes and brings the stories to life...."

He grumbled on about BLIT terrorists like the Deep Greens, who didn't need guns and explosives – just a photocopier, or a stencil that let them spray deadly graffiti on walls. According to Whitcutt, TV broadcasts used to go out "live", not taped, until the notorious activist Tee Zero broke into a BBC studio and showed the cameras a BLIT known as the Parrot. Millions had died. It wasn't safe to look at anything these days.

Jonathan had to ask. "So the, um, the special kind of dark outdoors is to stop people seeing stuff like that?"

"Well ... yes, in effect that's quite right." The old teacher rubbed his chin for a moment. "They brief you about all that when you're a little older. It's a bit of a complicated issue.... Ah, another question?"

It was Khalid who had his hand up. With an elaborate lack of interest that struck Jonathan as desperately unconvincing, he said, "Are all these BLIT things, er, really dangerous, or are there ones that just jolt you a bit?"

Mr Whitcutt looked at him hard for very nearly the length of a beginner's ordeal. Then he turned to the whiteboard with its scrawled triangles. "Quite. *As* I was saying, the cosine of an angle is defined ..."

The four members of the inner circle had drifted casually together in their special corner of the outdoor play area, by the dirty climbing frame that no one ever used. "So we're terrorists," said Julie cheerfully. "We should give ourselves up to the police."

"No, our picture's different," Gary said. "It doesn't kill people, it ..."

A chorus of four voices: "... makes us stronger."

Jonathan said, "What do Deep Greens terrorize about? I mean, what don't they like?"

"I think it's biochips," Khalid said uncertainly. "Tiny computers for building into people's heads. They say it's unnatural, or something. There was a bit about it in one of those old issues of *New Scientist* in the lab."

"Be good for exams," Jonathan suggested. "But you can't take calculators into the exam room. "Everyone with a biochip, please leave your head at the door.""

They all laughed, but Jonathan felt a tiny shiver of uncertainty, as though he'd stepped on a stair that wasn't there. "Biochip" sounded very like something he'd overheard in one of his parents' rare shouting matches. And he was pretty sure he'd heard "unnatural" too. *Please don't let Mum and Dad be tangled up with terrorists*, he thought suddenly. But it was too silly. They weren't like that....

"There was something about control systems too," said Khalid. "You wouldn't want to be controlled, now."

As usual, the chatter soon went off in a new direction, or rather an old one: the walls of type-two darkness that the school used to mark off-limits areas like the corridor leading to the old storeroom. The Club were curious about how it worked, and had done some experiments. Some of the things they knew about the dark and had written down were:

Khalid's Visibility Theory, which had been proved by painful experiment. Dark zones were brilliant hiding places when it came to hiding from other kids, but teachers could spot you even through the blackness and tick you off something rotten for being where you shouldn't be. Probably they had some kind of special detector, but no one had ever seen one.

Jonathan's Bus Footnote to Khalid's discovery was simply that the driver of the school bus certainly *looked* as if he was seeing something through the black windscreen. Of course (this was Gary's idea) the bus might be computer-guided, with the steering wheel turning all by itself and the driver just pretending – but why should he bother?

Julie's Mirror was the weirdest thing of all. Even Julie hadn't believed it could work, but if you stood outside a type-two dark place and held a mirror just inside (so it looked as though your arm was cut off by the black wall), you could shine a torch at the place where you couldn't see the mirror, and the beam would come bouncing back out of the blackness to make a bright spot on your clothes or the wall. As Jonathan pointed out, this was how you could have bright patches of sunlight on the floor of a classroom whose windows all looked out into protecting darkness. It was a kind of dark that light could travel through but eyesight couldn't. None of the Optics textbooks said a word about it.

By now, Harry had had his Club invitation and was counting the minutes to his first meeting on Thursday, two days away. Perhaps he would have some ideas for new experiments when he'd passed his ordeal and joined the Club. Harry was extra good at maths and physics.

"Which makes it sort of interesting," Gary said. "If our picture works by maths like those BLIT things ... will Harry be able to take it for longer because his brain's built that way? Or will it be harder because it's coming on his own wavelength? Sort of thing?"

The Shudder Club reckoned that, although of course you shouldn't do experiments on people, this was a neat idea that you could argue either side of. And they did.

Thursday came, and after an eternity of history and double physics there was a free period that you were supposed to spend reading or in computer studies. Nobody knew it would be the Shudderers' last initiation, although Julie – who read heaps of fantasy novels – insisted later that she'd felt all doom-laden and could sense a powerful reek of wrongness. Julie tended to say things like that.

The session in the musty storeroom began pretty well, with Khalid reaching his twenty seconds at last, Jonathan sailing beyond the count of ten which only a few weeks ago had felt like an impossible Everest, and (to carefully muted clapping) Heather finally becoming a full member of the Club. Then the trouble began, as Harry the first-timer adjusted his little round glasses, set his shoulders, opened the tatty ritual ring-binder, and went rigid. Not twitchy or shuddery, but stiff. He made horrible grunts and pig-squeals, and fell sideways. Blood trickled from his mouth.

"He's bitten his tongue," said Heather. "Oh lord, what's first aid for biting your tongue?"

At this point the storeroom door opened and Mr Whitcutt came in. He looked older and sadder. "I might have known it would be like this." Suddenly he turned his eyes sideways and shaded them with one hand, as though blinded by strong light. "Cover it up. Shut your eyes, Patel, don't look at it, and just cover that damned thing up."

Khalid did as he was told. They helped Harry to his feet: he kept saying "Sorry, sorry," in a thick voice, and dribbling like a vampire with awful table manners. The long march through the uncarpeted, echoey corridors to the school's little sickroom, and then onward to the Principal's office, seemed to go on for endless grim hours.

Ms Fortmayne the Principal was an iron-grey woman who according to school rumours was kind to animals but could reduce any pupil to ashes with a few sharp sentences – a kind of human BLIT. She looked across her desk at the Shudder Club for one eternity of a moment, and said sharply: "Whose idea was it?"

Khalid slowly put up a brown hand, but no higher than his shoulder. Jonathan remembered the Three Musketeers's motto, *One for all and all for one*, and said, "It was all of us really." So Julie added, "That's right."

"I really don't know," said the Principal, tapping the closed ring-binder that lay in front of her. "The single most insidious weapon on Earth – the information-war equivalent of a neutron bomb – and you were *playing* with it. I don't often say that words fail me ..."

"Someone left it in the photocopier. Here. Downstairs," Khalid pointed out.

"Yes. Mistakes do happen." Her face softened a little. "And I'm getting carried away, because we do actually use that BLIT image as part of a little talk I have with older children when they're about to leave school. They're exposed to it for just two seconds, with proper medical super-vision. Its nickname is the Trembler, and some countries use big posters of it for riot control – but not Britain or America, naturally. Of course you couldn't have known that Harry Steen is a borderline epileptic or that the Trembler would give him a fit...."

"I should have guessed sooner," said Mr Whitcutt's voice from behind the Club. "Young Patel blew the gaff by asking what was either a very intelligent question or a very incriminating one. But I'm an old fool who never got used to the idea of a school being a terrorist target."

The Principal gave him a sharp look. Jonathan felt suddenly dizzy, with thoughts clicking through his head like one of those workings in algebra where everything goes just right and you can almost see the answer waiting in the white space at the bottom of the page. What don't Deep Green terrorists like? Why are we a target?

Control systems. You wouldn't want to be controlled.

He blurted: "Biochips. We've got biochip control systems in our heads. All us kids. They make the darkness somehow. The special dark where grown-ups can still see."

There was a moment's frozen silence.

"Go to the top of the class," murmured old Whitcutt.

The Principal sighed and seemed to sag in her chair a little. "There had to be a first time," she said quietly. "This is what my little lecture to school-leavers is all about. How you're specially privileged children, how you've been protected all your lives by biochips in your optic nerves that edit what you can see. So it always seems dark in the streets and outside the windows, wherever there might be a BLIT image waiting to kill you. But that kind of darkness isn't real – except to you. Remember, your parents had a choice, and they agreed to this protection."

Mine didn't both agree, thought Jonathan, remembering an overheard quarrel.

"It's not fair," said Gary uncertainly. "It's doing experiments on people."

Khalid said, "And it's not just protection. There are corridors here indoors that are blacked out, just to keep us out of places. To control us."

Ms Fortmayne chose not to hear them. Maybe she had a biochip of her own that stopped rebellious remarks from getting through. "When you leave school you are given full control over your biochips. You can choose whether to take risks ... once you're old enough."

Jonathan could almost bet that all five Club members were thinking the same thing: *What the hell, we took our risks with the Trembler and we got away with it.*

Apparently they had indeed got away with it, since when the Principal said "You can go now," she'd still mentioned nothing about punishment. As slowly as they dared, the Club headed back to the classroom. Whenever they passed side-turnings which were filled with solid darkness, Jonathan cringed to think that a chip behind his eyes was stealing the light and with different programming could make him blind to everything, everywhere.

The seriously nasty thing happened at going-home time, when the caretaker unlocked the school's side door as usual while a crowd of pupils jostled behind him. Jonathan and the Club had pushed their way almost to the front of the mob. The heavy wooden door swung inward. As usual it opened on the second kind of darkness, but something bad from the dark came in with it, a large sheet of paper fixed with a drawing-pin to the door's outer surface and hanging slightly askew. The caretaker glanced at it, and toppled like a man struck by lightning.

Jonathan didn't stop to think. He shoved past some smaller kid and grabbed the paper, crumpling it up frantically. It was already too late. He'd seen the image there, completely unlike the Trembler yet very clearly from the same terrible family, a slanted dark shape like the profile of a perched bird, but with complications, twirly bits, patterns like fractals, and it hung there blazing in his mind's eye and wouldn't go away –

– something hard and horrible smashing like a runaway express into his brain –

– burning falling burning falling –

– BLIT.

After long and evil dreams of bird-shapes that stalked him in darkness, Jonathan found himself lying on a couch, no, a bed in the school sick-room. It was a surprise to be anywhere at all, after feeling his whole life crashing into that enormous full stop. He was still limp all over, too tired to do more than stare at the white ceiling.

Mr Whitcutt's face came slowly into his field of vision. "Hello? Hello? Anyone in there?" He sounded worried.

"Yes ... I'm fine," said Jonathan, not quite truthfully.

"Thank heaven for that. Nurse Baker was amazed you were alive. Alive and sane seemed like too much to hope for. Well, I'm here to warn you that you're a hero. Plucky Boy Saves Fellow-Pupils. You'll be surprised how quickly you can get sick of being called plucky."

"What was it, on the door?"

"One of the very bad ones. Called the Parrot, for some reason. Poor old George the caretaker was dead before he hit the ground. The anti-terrorist squad that came to dispose of that BLIT paper couldn't believe you'd survived. Neither could I."

Jonathan smiled. "I've had practice."

"Yes. It didn't take that long to realize Lucy – that is, Ms Fortmayne – failed to ask you young hooligans enough questions. So I had another word with your friend Khalid Patel. God in heaven, that boy can outstare the Trembler for twenty seconds! Adult crowds fall over in convulsions once they've properly, what d'you call it, registered the sight of the thing, let it lock in ..."

"My record's ten and a half. Nearly eleven really."

The old man shook his head wonderingly. "I wish I could say I didn't believe you. They'll be re-assessing the whole biochip protection programme. No one ever thought of training young, flexible minds to resist BLIT attack by a sort of vaccination process. If they'd thought of it, they still wouldn't have dared try it.... Anyway, Lucy and I had a talk, and we have a little present for you. They can reprogram those biochips by radio link in no time at all, and so –"

He pointed. Jonathan made an effort and turned his head. Through the window, where he'd expected to see only artificial darkness, there was a complication of rosy light and glory that at first his eyes couldn't take in. A little at a time, assembling itself like some kind of healing opposite to those deadly patterns, the abstract brilliance of heaven became a town roofscape glowing in a rose-red sunset. Even the chimney-pots and satellite dishes looked beautiful. He'd seen sunsets on video, of course, but it wasn't the same, it was the aching difference between live flame and an electric fire's dull glare: like so much of the adult world, the TV screen lied by what it didn't tell you.

"The other present is from your pals. They said they're sorry there wasn't time to get anything better."

It was a small, somewhat bent bar of chocolate (Gary always had a few tucked away), with a card written in Julie's careful left-sloping script and signed by all the Shudder Club. The inscription was, of course: *That which does not kill us, makes us stronger.*

• Published 2000, and reprinted by that nice Mr Hartwell in *Year's Best SF 6*. Gordon Van Gelder, who accepted this for *F&SF*, suggested that the eventual lifting of the artificial darkness deserved greater emphasis: I agreed and, as it were, turned up the gain a little in the antepenultimate paragraph. Originally written for a children's sf anthology that filled up long before the deadline (and may in fact never have appeared), "Different Kinds of Darkness" astonished me by winning the 2001 Hugo Award for Best Short Story. Tanya Brown brought me down to earth with her insistence on calling it "Harry Potter and the BLIT".

It's hardly necessary to generalize about the things we do to kids for their own good. Once I used to walk a couple of miles to and from school on most weekdays, with a short cut through a more or less deserted cemetery – which today might cause social workers to have a stern little talk with the "negligent" parents. Why is the level of paranoia so much greater now than when the Moors Murders trial (alluded to in "The Motivation") was a fresh and ghastly memory? Discuss.

That's all. I really must try to write some more short stories....

Original Appearances

"3.47 AM": *The Gruesome Book* ed. Ramsey Campbell, 1983

"Accretion": *Andromeda 2* ed. Peter Weston, 1977

"Answering Machine": *Practical Computing*, February 1982, as "Friendly Reflections"

"The Arts of the Enemy": *Villains!* ed. Mary Gentle and Roz Kaveney, 1992

"As Strange a Maze as E'er Men Trod": *Shakespearean Detectives* ed. Mike Ashley, 1998

"Blit": *Interzone 25*, September/October 1988

"Blood and Silence": *100 Vicious Little Vampire Stories* ed. Stefan Dziemianowicz, Robert Weinberg and Martin H.Greenberg, 1995

"Blossoms that Coil and Decay": *Interzone 57*, March 1992

"Cold Spell": *13th Fontana Book of Great Horror Stories* ed. Mary Danby, 1980

"comp.basilisk FAQ": *Nature*, 2 December 1999

"Connections": *Andromeda 3* ed. Peter Weston, 1978

"Cube Root": *Interzone 11*, Spring 1985

"Deepnet": *Irrational Numbers* by David Langford, 1994, and *Shadows over Innsmouth* ed. Stephen Jones, 1994

"Different Kinds of Darkness": *The Magazine of Fantasy and Science Fiction*, January 2000

"Ellipses": *More Tales from the Forbidden Planet* ed. Roz Kaveney, 1990

"Encounter of Another Kind": *Interzone 54*, December 1991

"The Facts in the Case of Micky Valdon": *Dark Fantasies* ed. Chris Morgan, 1989

"The Final Days": *Destinies 3:1*, April 1981

"A Game of Consequences": *Starlight 2* ed. Patrick Nielsen Hayden, 1998

"Hearing Aid": *Practical Computing*, October 1982

"Heatwave": *New Writings in SF 27* ed. Kenneth Bulmer, 1975

"In a Land of Sand and Ruin and Gold": *Other Edens* ed. Christopher Evans and Robert Holdstock, 1987

"In the Place of Power": *Beyond Lands of Never* ed. Maxim Jakubowski, 1984

"Leaks": *Temps* ed. Neil Gaiman and Alex Stewart, 1991

"The Lions in the Desert": *The Weerde II: The Book of the Ancients* ed. Neil Gaiman and Roz Kaveney, April 1993

"Logrolling Ephesus": *The Thackery T. Lambshead Pocket Guide to Eccentric and Discredited Diseases* ed. Jeff VanderMeer and Mark Roberts, 2003

"The Motivation": *Arrows of Eros* ed. Alex Stewart, 1989

"Notes for a Newer Testament": *Afterwar* ed. Janet Morris, 1985

"Serpent Eggs": *Irrational Numbers* by David Langford, 1994; revised for *The Third Alternative 14*, 1997

"A Snapshot Album": *Interzone 43*, January 1991

"A Surprisingly Common Omission": *Drabble II: Double Century* ed. Rob Meades and David B.Wake, 1990

"Too Good to Be": *Imagine 3*, June 1983

"Training": *The Future at War I: Thor's Hammer* ed. Reginald Bretnor, 1979

"Waiting for the Iron Age": *Tales of the Wandering Jew* ed. Brian Stableford, 1991

"Wetware": *What Micro?*, November 1984

"What Happened at Cambridge IV": *Digital Dreams* ed. David V.Barrett, 1990

CPSIA information can be obtained
at www.ICGtesting.com
Printed in the USA
LVOW12*1932310518

579127LV00007B/55/P

9 781592 241217